Dido's Prize

By
Eugenia O'Neal

Other Titles
Just an Affair

Non-Fiction
From the Field to the Legislature: A History of Women in the Virgin Islands

Parker Publishing LLC

ZORA is an imprint of Parker Publishing LLC.

Copyright © 2008 by Eugenia O'Neal
Published by Parker Publishing LLC
12523 Limonite Ave., Ste. #440-438
Mira Loma, California 91752
www.parker-publishing.com

ISBN: 978-1-60043-039-8
First Edition

Manufactured in the United States of America

Cover Design by Jaxadora Design

Dedication

To Maris Hodge-Wright and Ana "America" Benders for the gift of time, and to my father, Eugene O'Neal, for gifting me with a love of history.

Dido's Prize

By
Eugenia O'Neal

Chapter 1

Dido hurried into the cool, shadowy alley leading off King's Street, glad to escape the heat of the day if only for a few minutes. She had taken the shortcut before, so she didn't think twice about it until she heard the footsteps behind her.

"Oy, me darling! Give me a kiss, one sweet kiss to quench my thirst," a man called, his voice sounding strangled as if he spoke through a mouthful of tamarind seeds.

Dido shuddered but didn't turn to look. Her mind raced. Should she run or just continue walking normally showing she had no concern? She thought she heard more than one set of feet but her heart was beating so hard she could be mistaken. Dido tried not to worry. Port Royal teemed with women who sold themselves for coin. Perhaps the stranger mistook her for one of them and would leave her alone once he realized the truth. She wished she'd kept to the main road as she usually did. Every vendor knew the stories about a small gang of men who waited until the women had sold their market goods and then waylaid them, stealing whatever profit they'd made. She'd heard the other vendors say that the Governor had promised to do something about it but promises were just words. Who really cared when the only victims were slave women?

"She ignores you, Daniel."

She was right. There was more than one man behind her. The second voice was deeper, harsher, but she was near the second entrance to the alley now. Holding her tray up before her like a shield Dido picked up her pace. It did not help.

"Hoy, *querida*. It is your own beautiful self I'm talking to, don't you know?"

Footsteps pounded the bricked ground. Before she could run, a hand grasped her shoulder and spun her so roughly she almost lost her footing.

There were three of them. Two whites and a black. She shot the latter a look but his eyes were narrow slits, she would find no help there. A chill chigger of fear erupted in the pit of her stomach and slithered upwards to lodge itself at the base of her throat. For a minute, the world closed in around her and she was again a little girl, too scared to even scream. Was it the gang? But why did the man want a kiss? She'd not heard that the gang violated the women they robbed.

"Why don't you answer me?" asked the one gripping her shoulder. A blue bandanna only partially covered his greasy blond hair. He'd been the first to call out to her. The one named Daniel.

"I am..." She coughed, clearing her throat, but when she spoke again her voice still shook. "S...sorry, Sir. I was heading home and thinking only of my journey," she lied. She had certainly been thinking but not about anything related to Beeston's Estate, the plantation on which she lived. Oh no. For months now, ever since Missus Sarah had given her promise, all that had been on her mind was a waking dream, a dream of the time she would have enough money to buy her freedom and that of her family. Nothing was sweeter to her than the thought of the little house she and her family would share as they made a life for themselves far away from the plantations, in the island's interior.

"As beautiful as you are, nothing should occupy your mind but thoughts of love," the man said, pulling her closer to him. His breath stank of rum and spoiled food.

"Please, Sir, I just want to go home." Dido pushed away from him, using the tray.

"You're a market-woman, are you not? Hand over your money." It was the other white man, his voice too deep for his runty size.

Oshun, grant me courage, Dido whispered, hoping the goddess could hear her. Her eyes scanned the road for something, anything with which to fight. A stick not too far away looked perfect but how could she get to it? The one thing she was clear about was that she had no intention of meekly handing over her money. She needed it. Badly.

"Hand over your money or do you want us to look about your person for it? God's truth I'd rather we do that." Daniel licked his lips, his eyes roving over her body.

"You may try." Dido's fingers tightened on the tray. If they thought she would just give up her earnings without a fight, well, she would show them different. This wasn't Nevis and she was no defenseless child. How she wished she'd never left the main road.

"The wench challenges us." Daniel reached for her but she stepped nimbly back and swung up the tray, hitting him on the chin. He grabbed at her and without thinking, she released her two-handed grip on her shield, to swipe at his arm. Seizing his chance, the black man snatched the tray away and sent it spinning back down the alley behind him. Dido wailed in fury and frustration.

"I likes a woman with some fight in her," he said, speaking for the first time.

"After me, Edmund. I saw her first."

The three men lunged at her. Feigning a stumble, Dido fell to the ground and quickly rolled for the stick she had seen earlier. Grabbing it in both hands, she rose to her feet in one quick motion and swung at Edmund's knees, the black man being the closest. Yelling in pain and clutching his wounded leg, he fell. Red-hot energy surged through her. Surely, the Lady Oshun fought beside her. She swung next at the smallest of them, the deep-voiced one. He tried to jump out of her way and fell, backward, over his friend. If she hadn't been in such danger, Dido might have laughed but there was still Daniel. An agile man despite his size, he ducked her slashing stick, dancing out of her reach before closing in again, feinting left then right, to get under her swing. Before Dido could stop him, he had her flat on her back, her arms pinned to the ground. She tried to twist away but he held her fast. The deep-voiced man wasted no time scrambling over to paw at her, searching for her money. His hands went up her dress. She clamped her legs together but he pried them apart.

"It's in my bosom," she cried out, her stomach queasy at the unwanted touch. "Take it. Take it and leave me alone."

"Too late," Daniel said. As the other man's hand finally reached her private parts, Daniel lowered himself to bury his face in her neck, his tongue rasping over the skin at her throat.

"No," Dido screamed. She wrenched herself around to bite Daniel on the shoulder but he gripped her chin in his hand, immobilizing her head as he ripped open her dress. Beyond him she could see the other man opening his breeches. Their black friend watched avidly from the side.

"No," she screamed again. "Help me. Please, somebody help me. Help me!"

"If you calm yourself, you'll enjoy it. I'll frig you better than any man ever has before," boasted the man between her legs.

Dido's only answer was to buck her body wildly, kicking and twisting to free herself. *No, please, Sweet Mother.* Her memories of pain and fear were like a screaming flock of night-witches, beating their spreading wings over her head, turning her world to night. *Please do not let them do this to me.*

"Lady, may I be of some assistance?"

The way Daniel held her chin she could not see who had spoken.

"Please, yes. Help me." She could barely grit the words out.

"This is no business of yours, stranger. You had best be moving on if you know what's good for you." Daniel had not even looked up at the newcomer.

"I think it is you who should move on. Clearly, the lady is not interested in your attentions. I'll count to three to give you both time to remove yourselves from her person."

The man between her legs thrust himself at her, not quite making the object of his desire while Daniel's hand remained on her breast, just as if the newcomer had not spoken. Behind them, Dido saw Edmund rise unsteadily to his feet, his expression a mix of surprise and fear.

"Three." A split second later there was a loud bang. The dirt behind Daniel's back swirled.

"Christ's bloody crown!" Daniel sprang off of Dido while the other man propelled himself backward so fast that he sprawled on the ground, his mouth opening and closing like a fish as his prick shriveled.

"A gentleman does not expose himself in the presence of a lady," the voice above her said.

The man who had been about to assault her quickly covered himself back up.

"El Negro, we didn't know it was you." He ducked his head. "Truly we didn't."

Dido rolled away to the side and jumped to her feet, clutching the torn bodice of her dress with one hand while she held on to her drawstring purse with the other. The newcomer was well-named. Tall and slim, he was also as black as coal but what caught her attention more than anything else was his clothes. Though it was now getting on for midday, El Negro wore a long-sleeved shirt of fine thin cotton with long frilly cuffs at the wrist. Over the shirt he sported a vest of scarlet velvet on the front of which two dragons embroidered in gold spat flames at each other. His breeches were no less elegant being also of velvet hemmed with a generous length of white lace in a style she had never seen before.

"Now that you know it is me, perhaps you'll do me the favor of going about your business." He waved an intricately carved pistol in the direction of the alley down which the men's black companion was hobbling as fast as his damaged leg would allow.

"We meant her no harm," the man called Daniel said. "Truly. We were only having fun."

"And truly, whoreson, if I ever catch you trying to have this type of fun again, you'll not live long enough to regret it. Is my meaning clear?"

"Yes. Yes, El Negro."

Lazily, without seeming to mean to, El Negro raised the pistol and the dust danced around Daniel's feet once more.

Without another word, the two men turned tail and ran down the alley.

"They run like the cowards they are," El Negro murmured, more to himself than Dido.

"They came on me asudden or they would never have beaten me down." Dido trembled but whether out of fear or anger she couldn't tell. Had she the strength of a man she would have followed the three vagabonds and laid about them with the stick until she could raise her hand no more but she was not a man. Dido took a deep breath to calm herself. She glanced at her rescuer. El Negro was watching her.

"You fought with courage even though the odds were against you," he said. "Next time they meet a lone woman, because of you they will think twice about attacking her."

"It's wrong. It's wrong to take what belongs to others. They should be hung or thrown in a dungeon to rot."

"They'll meet a bad end on their own account, you need have no fear of that. Men who live like rats must die like rats."

Dido sniffed, not sure she believed it.

"Do you live in the town? May I have the honor of escorting you home?"

"I belong...I live at Beeston's Estate on the Liguanea Plain."

"You have far to walk then." He looked her over and Dido clutched her torn dress tighter about her breasts. "Perhaps we should attend to that before you begin your journey."

He stepped closer to her.

"You are wounded," he said, frowning.

"No, I...."

He touched her elbow and Dido took a deep breath. He was different from the others. He meant her no harm so why should she suddenly feel so unsteady?

"Look," he said, showing her.

She had a long scrape along the back of her arm from her elbow almost to her wrist.

"And your cheek." He tilted her head gently, his fingers under her chin. "You're bleeding."

Dido could hardly breathe. His closeness unnerved her.

"It's nothing," she said, stepping away from him. She raised a hand to her face and felt the area, trying not to wince. "It's just a cut."

"Nevertheless, you should have your wounds attended to. Allow me to see to that, at least."

"There will not be many on the road and I prefer to be moving on or it will be nightfall ere I arrive. I have healing herbs where I live and can doctor myself."

"I'll not argue with you, but I know a seamstress, a woman quick with her needle. She can fix your dress in less time than they say it takes Preacher Green to deliver his sermon and get back to his rum bottle. I could take you to her. She'll be able to tend to your cuts as well."

Dido considered this. "I'd not inconvenience you?" The cuts were one thing but her dress needed mending.

"I assure you, you would not."

Dido thought some more. If she didn't accept the man's offer she would have to walk all the way to Beeston's clutching her dress with both hands lest a stray breeze reveal her nakedness.

"Let us go then," she said, coming to a quick decision.

"Follow me."

"Why do you dress so fancy? Who are you?"

"I am called El Negro though that was not the name my mother had in mind for me and I dress this way because it pleases me. ¿No le gustas?"

Dido shrugged. "You look well enough."

He laughed.

"Only that?"

"I'm not the one to judge. How can I say?" She looked away, not wanting him to see how nervous he made her. He looked much more than 'well enough.' In his fine clothes and with his good looks, he was like no other man she had ever seen, but she saw no good reason to tell him so.

Chapter 2

The seamstress Dido's rescuer led her to was a well-dressed, gray-haired woman with three rows of small diamond-shaped tribal marks across her forehead and both cheeks. She stared at Dido, expressionless, as El Negro explained the situation. Without speaking, the woman fetched a basin of cool water into which she dipped a rag she then offered to Dido. Wincing, Dido dabbed away the blood on her arm and her cheek. She was about to hand the rag back when El Negro took it from her. He rinsed it in the water then wrung it tight, before turning back to Dido. With one finger he gently lifted her chin and wiped her throat.

"His nails must have dug into your skin here," he said, his voice low.

Dido nodded. She tried not to look at him but he was so close. The sea-smell of him filled her nose and she wondered who he was that the men should have accorded him such respect.

When he stepped away from her, she felt that the ground itself had shifted but she looked away, determined not to betray the effect he had on her. He rinsed the rag and laid it on the side of the basin, shrugging away her thanks.

The seamstress removed a phial of a copper-colored liniment from a small cupboard and applied this to Dido's cuts in light strokes. The liniment smelled earthy and stung her skin. Dido thought she remembered the scent from somewhere but she couldn't place it. It was unlike anything she herself used.

Still silent, the woman rummaged among a jumble of clothes off to the side. She finally pulled out a simple white linen dress with three-quarter length sleeves and embroidery at the neck.

"She can have this," she said, speaking for the first time, her voice low and musical. "It should fit her."

"It…it's too pretty," Dido stammered. Slaves did not wear such dresses.

"It was for a French lady's maid but she and her lady left for Bermuda before I could finish it. It will do very well for you." The seamstress sat back down to her table.

"Don't you like it?" El Negro asked.

"Of course I do, but…" Didn't he understand that she worked in the fields, cutting cane, and hoeing the ground?

"I only wanted for this dress to be mended. It suits me well and is mine. I thank you for the offer," she added, looking at the seamstress.

The woman shrugged.

"Put it on while I fix yours, then. Quick now."

"Yes." But Dido made no move. She glanced at El Negro.

"Ah, you'd like me to turn around?"

"If it pleases you."

"It does not." He grinned at her and Dido's stomach tightened.

"I cannot change while you watch." She looked everywhere but at him.

"Go, man." The seamstress made a shooing motion with her hands. "Walk around to the harbor and back. She'll be ready by the time you return."

"There is nothing I'd like to see in the harbor but I'll do as you say, Anna." El Negro bowed in their direction before stepping through the door of the small room back into the heat and simmering danger of Port Royal's streets. The tension in Dido's stomach loosened.

"You've never known a man?" asked the seamstress, her eyes bright as a macaw's as she looked at Dido.

"No." Then glancing away. "Yyy…yes. I have."

"He was not good to you?"

"It was a long time ago. I prefer not to think of it."

"Ah, then I understand everything."

"What do you understand, Mother?"

"This man took you against your will, perhaps when you were no more than a child, perhaps many times but you escaped him."

Dido swallowed hard, her mouth dry.

"Now," the seamstress continued, "you are closed to men and to all desire for the pleasure their bodies can bring."

Dido touched her fingers to her cheeks. How cold she was. "I…how…"

"How do I know this?" The older woman asked for her. "It is in the way you hold yourself, daughter, like a finely-cracked vessel afraid of breaking. It is also in the way you look at El Negro, like a bird fascinated by a snake. Him you need not fear."

"I was no more than eight when it started," Dido whispered. It was not a thing of which she often spoke but the attack had brought her memories close to the surface. "Then he sold me and my family away when I was twelve and too old for his taste. I was free of him."

"Yes." The older woman nodded. "You escaped him, yes. But you are not free of him."

It was true. Even now, as a grown woman, she sometimes still woke in the night, the perspiration coursing down her back, her skin clammy, his face over hers until she blinked and it disintegrated in the darkness. Numbed by her memories, Dido allowed the older woman to remove her dress and to slip the pretty shift she'd been offered over her head.

"See it fits almost perfectly though it is a bit loose about the bust. You are smaller there than she was."

Dido looked down at herself. The material contrasted well with her dark skin but she had no need for such a dress. "It is too beautiful for me," she said.

"Daughter, have you never seen yourself? The truth is you are too beautiful for the dress. You would look like a queen in silk and velvets."

Dido laughed. "Anyone would look like a queen in silk and velvet."

"Would I?"

Dido's laughter died away. "Well, but Mother, if you had your youth."

The seamstress smiled. "You are kind, child. I was young once but never queenly. You have the fine smooth skin of the Yoruba and your eyes are big like a child's while your shape is definitely that of a woman's. See those hips, they were made for love and for babies."

"No, Mother." Dido shook her head. "Those things are not for me."

"So you say now." The seamstress's hands flew over Dido's torn dress. "Maybe El Negro will change your mind. Now there's a man makes me wish for youth and good looks. He is Yoruba too, like you, though he calls himself a man reborn."

"Reborn?"

"He was once a slave and owned nothing. Now he is a pirate and wealthy."

A pirate! So he was one of the men Hercules talked about. No wonder he wore velvet and carried himself as she imagined a prince of Guinea would. Hercules, who knew everything because he'd often accompanied the master on his trips away from Beeston's Estate, had said pirates answered to no one. He had also said they were little more than sea-robbers.

"His wealth is ill-gained." Did not all the gods, those of her people and that of the whites, frown on stealing? Her rescuer was no better than the men he'd rescued her from.

"Eh, eh. Can you say so when they are only taking what was already stolen? El Negro and his brothers steal only from the Spanish. It was they who enslaved him, you understand. When the English attacked Jamaica and the Spanish fled to Cuba, he took his chance and escaped to a free life on the sea. There was so much confusion, many did the same, running either to the sea or to the mountains."

"Massa Richard and his brother William were with the invaders." Dido was already seeing her woman's blood when she and her mother and her younger siblings were sold by Simon Becket, taken from his plantation in Golden Rock, Nevis, and put on the ship that brought them to Jamaica. Jamaica's new settlers were desperate for slaves, lots of slaves, to work the estates the Spanish had abandoned in the face of England's superior forces. She supposed Massa Becket had gotten a very good price for them. At San Jago de la Vega, the former Spanish capital, Dido's mother and her siblings were handed over to Neville Sedgewick who owned a plantation in Santa Cruz. A cross-looking man, he hadn't wanted Dido, saying young, fine-figured females were more trouble than they were worth. Since her sister was still a child of seven he'd allowed her sister to stay with their mother. Dido was sold to Richard Beeston and his wife, Sarah. She had cried all the way to the Liguanea Plains.

"The Governor gave them estates as their reward," Dido said, bringing herself back to the present with a deep breath.

The old woman nodded. "I know of them. Colonel William is an important man and a close friend of the Governor's it is said."

Dido shrugged. She had never seen the Governor in her life but the Colonel visited Beeston's at least twice a year and his wife had stayed with her sister-in-law for a couple of weeks when Master died.

"The Spaniards steal the gold and the jewels from the Indians of the Americas," the old woman said, returning to the topic. "You see, the Indians do not value their shiny things as the Europeans do and have not the guns or the weapons to secure their belongings."

This was not the kind of talk that occupied them in the quarters. "You are the first I've heard speak of such things," Dido said.

"How did you think the Spanish fill their galleons with the treasure they take home every six months?"

"I never thought on it." Ships? Treasure? She was a mere field slave. These things were no concern of hers.

The seamstress snorted. "And even if it's tobacco or cotton that the pirates steal, you can be sure it was already stolen. Either the land on which it was grown was stolen, or the labor with which it was grown was slave labor and thus a theft of time and strength and life itself."

"Well said, Anna. You're becoming a philosopher in your old age."

El Negro clapped from the door and Anna snorted again. Dido could not tell from the old woman's expression if the compliment pleased her.

"Are you almost finished?" he asked the seamstress, handing Dido the tray she'd forgotten about until that very minute. It had not even been on her mind as she'd followed him out of that alley.

"Yes, but you walked too quickly. She still has to put it on."

"No. You can wear what you have on until you are home, surely? It suits you." His eyes beamed with frank admiration.

"I cannot," she said, answering him but looking at Anna. What if Missus Sarah saw her?

"But you'll keep it?" He turned quickly to the seamstress without giving Dido time to answer. "How much will you charge me for it?"

"Nothing. Here." She handed Dido's mended dress to her and Dido looked at El Negro.

"I know, I know. I'll step outside."

After he had gone, Dido quickly stripped out of the new dress and put back on her old one.

"Thank you." The seamstress had also mended a couple of tears around the hem and at the back. "It's almost like new."

Anna didn't answer. Her expression was skeptical.

"El Negro, she's ready," she called.

The pirate stepped back into the room, looking disappointed at Dido's attire. "You'll, at least, take the dress with you?" he asked.

"It makes no sense."

But Anna folded it, wrapped it in coarse linen and thrust it at her.

"Maybe one day, who knows? It can be the dress you marry in."

"I will nev—" Dido started to say.

"Who knows?" the seamstress repeated, interrupting her. "Who can say where life will take them? It is yours." Anna pushed it at her so hard Dido stumbled, her arms rising involuntarily around the package.

"Thank you, mother. How much…"

"No charge, no charge. Come and see me the next time you are in Port Royal. Bring her, you good-for-nothing," she said to El Negro.

He smiled and winked at Dido. "If I see her, we will come. How could we pass up such a gracious invitation?"

Minutes later they were back on the road that led out of Port Royal and past Beeston's Estate.

"There is no need for you to inconvenience yourself further," Dido said when she saw he had no intention of leaving her.

"I can think of no inconvenience I've suffered this day and, as for my needs, I think I know them better than you," the pirate replied.

Dido frowned. He'd been very kind to her, saving her from the ruffians, helping her to get her dress mended and even going back to find her tray but his company made her uneasy. What would Old Philippa and the others say if they saw her in the presence of such a man?

"I prefer parting company here," Dido said, stopping and crossing her arms before her.

"I should like to assure myself that you are returned safely to your people." El Negro turned to face her. Dido stepped back from him. Now that all danger was far behind her and they were alone on the road, she was completely conscious of him. Hercules had not said that pirates were a handsome breed of men but if they were all like El Negro she could well see why women, even white ones, would throw themselves at them and carry on as scandalously as she'd heard.

"I can keep a better pace if I am by myself and besides the walk gives me time to think my own thoughts." She could have added, *and be my own person* but she thought it would be hard to explain to him the sense of freedom she got being alone on the road.

"What if you are again assaulted?"

"I'll defend myself."

He nodded. "No-one can doubt your courage. Were you a man any captain would be honored to fight alongside you."

"A pirate captain?"

"I make no distinction. Every captain of a fighting ship has need of good men with stout hearts but allow me to fashion a stick for your defense." So saying he walked into the bushes along the roadside and emerged, seconds later, with a stick the thickness of her arm. As she watched, he withdrew the knife from below his belt and used it to whittle one end into a sharp point.

"The seamstress called you a pirate."

"That I am."

"What pleases you about that life?"

"What do you know of it?"

Dido frowned, wondering if she should repeat Hercules's tales but her curiosity was aroused. "That their ships are often lost at sea, that there are powerful men who would as soon string up a pirate on the gallows as look at him." She lowered her voice. "That murder is as common among you as rum."

El Negro laughed. "All of that, eh? No wonder you look on me as many do a madman. Some of what you say is true but that is only the half. Pirates are equal among each other. No man thinks himself superior to another or rules the life of another as is true on the plantations. If my men wish to go to Cartagena and I wish to sail to Hispaniola, the matter is put to a vote and the wishes of the majority govern the choice."

"You said, 'my men'. Do you own them?"

El Negro laughed even more heartily than before. "I meant only that I am the captain and they serve on my ship so in that sense they are mine," he explained when he sobered.

"White men, too?" She could scarcely believe it.

"Primarily white men for there are few of our color among the Brethren of the Coast."

Dido considered this in silence.

"None among you owns another?" She wanted to be very clear on this point. It was not something Hercules had mentioned but she supposed he viewed pirates from the perspective of Massa Richard and not his own.

"None. I am free in a way I could never be if I did not live this life. On land, there are always people to trouble a black man and question his right to liberty."

"Do you pay these men, the ones on your ship?"

"That is not our way. They sign up to serve on my ship then, when we've taken a prize, a galleon or a merchant ship for instance, they get a share of whatever we take from her. That is how we earn our daily bread."

Dido was not entirely convinced it wasn't little more than thieving, whatever Anna said, but she left the point alone.

"Do you earn much?"

"Enough to get by." His lips twitched. With a few quick shaves he turned the opposite end of the stick into a rounded mallet.

"Will this serve?" he asked.

Dido hefted it in her hand. Neither too light nor too heavy, the stick was perfect. "I am well-armed now." She smiled her thanks.

"And if you will take this from me you'll be even better-armed." He held out the knife to her but Dido shook her head.

"That can be twisted away and used against me. It is for close-fighting but this will keep them away, perhaps even frighten them off." She twirled the stick in one hand while holding the tray up with the other like a shield.

"See you even think like a warrior. Had you been any less beautiful and had I not seen your breasts for myself I would suspect that you were, instead, a very pretty boy."

"You saw my…my…." Dido could not bring herself to finish the sentence. Suddenly she felt cold again. She clutched the tray and the stick to her chest as if, with his words, he'd ripped her dress open again.

"Only for a minute and the sight was pleasing. Has no one ever said so to you before? Why are you frightened? Where has my warrior gone?"

"I must be on my way," Dido said, not answering him. "It grows late." It was true. The sun had already begun to make its slow descent into the Blue Mountains. Giving him a wide berth, Dido walked around the pirate.

"Thank you for all you have done for me today. May Oshun grant you a long life and much happiness," she said, backing away from him down the road.

"You've not told me your name. May I not know your name at least?"

"Dido. I am called Dido." She turned her back on him and on Port Royal, walking so quickly she was almost running.

"Farewell, Dido. I'll look for you next Sunday if we do not sail. I will come to the market."

"If you wish it," Dido shouted over her shoulder. She kept walking. Her heart hammered in her chest as she strained to hear if he was following her but she heard nothing and when she finally turned around to look there was no sign of him.

Frowning because she had expected him to be there, Dido soon left Port Royal far behind. What a story she had to tell the others! Old Philippa and Delia and the others would hardly believe her. They would make clucking noises when she told them about the three thieves and they would laugh and clap at El Negro's dramatic rescue. Dido rehearsed her story, practicing for when all the slaves gathered around in the middle of the quarters. Only on Sunday nights could they get together and entertain themselves. They used the time to tell stories and sing the songs the old ones remembered from Guinea. On special occasions, like at the end of the cane harvest or on Christmas Eve, they danced.

"Oy, Dido. Missus Sarah wants to see all of you who went to town today," Old Philippa called out as she entered the quarters and neared her hut. The scrawny, wrinkled woman was sitting under a tree, shelling some of the peas she grew on her grounds.

"Why?"

"She does not say. Nobody knows but Delia and Rosannah and Leonora and the others are there already. You had best hurry."

"Yes. I'll go now." Stopping only to deposit the tray and her stick in her hut, Dido hurried off. Since Massa Beeton's death six months ago, Missus Sarah rarely came out of the house. Cubina who worked in the kitchen said she spent most of her time in her room praying and hardly ate the turtle meat and other delicacies she had once loved. Calculating the days, Dido realized she had not seen the Missus for more than two months. Not since the rains that had swollen the canes and made the ground soggy underfoot for days after. Missus Sarah had come to the fields to look at the crop and wring her hands as her only son, Massa Henry, and the overseer, Massa Charles, talked to her in low voices. Dido could not see the woman's face because of the heavy black veil she wore but she'd known that the men must have been telling her their fears. Heavy rains close to harvest could swell the canes with water, diluting the sugar content and erasing any chance of making a profit that year. Hercules and a few of the others had predicted that would happen but they had also said that Massa Richard had been so clever with money that the estate would not suffer, regardless of the rains. And, truly, in the days and weeks after the rains, nothing changed in the rhythm of life on the estate and any who had been worried about what the failure of the crop might mean for them ceased to voice their fears. They had all settled back into their duties and their small affairs but now this summons had come. Dido did not know what to make of it.

"You're late," Cubina said as Dido ran past her and up the steps at the back of the house. The light-skinned woman was shoving loaves of bread into the brick oven, her face, neck and arms glistening with evidence of the heat from the coals.

"Why has she called for us?" Dido stopped and turned around. "Do you know?" she demanded.

"I do not but it was the first thing she said when she came down this morning, that she wanted to see all of you when you returned. She's in the living room, go."

Dido had only been in the house a few times and she made a wrong turn that led her to Missus Sarah's unused sewing room before finding her way back. The living room had high ceilings and contained a lot of furniture, chairs with high backs carved in the shape of pineapples and flowers and dark, heavy, mahogany tables. Against one wall there was a big armoire that Cubina said contained Massa Richard's old army uniforms, though why they should be kept there and not in his former room she didn't know.

"Ah, Dido. You are the last. I've been waiting for you for some time," Missus Sarah said as Dido entered the room in a rush. Her face was unveiled. Massa Charles stood behind her and off to the side, his arms crossed, his face impassive but watchful.

"I'm sorry. I was attacked by robbers as I was leaving the town and was thus delayed."

Next to her, Leonora made a sympathetic sound and Dido heard a murmur among the other women. Most of them sold their produce in the market at San Jago de la Vega's, disdaining the long walk to Port Royal.

"Attacked? Did they rob you of your earnings?" Missus Sarah leaned forward, her eyes hard and bright.

"They would have robbed me of more, if they could." Dido shivered, remembering.

"But did they take your money?"

Dido was taken aback by the urgency in Missus Sarah's voice. Something was wrong here but she did not know what it was. Why was the Missus so concerned about the money? It did not belong to her.

"Yes, Missus." The lie slipped out without thought. Dido frowned. She would have corrected herself and told the truth but some instinct made her keep quiet.

"That is a pity. I am told you always do good business." Missus Sarah pushed herself back against her chair.

"Yes, Missus."

"I know you are all wondering why I have asked you here today. It is very simple. Massa Charles tells me that the rains have destroyed this year's sugar crop. Beeston's Estate faces bankruptcy unless strict measures are taken to save the estate from falling into the hands of our debtors." There was another murmuring among the women, louder this time.

"Massa Richard had many debts," his widow continued. "Here on the island and back in England, as well. If the crop had come in we would not be in financial trouble but that is life. I must ask you all to turn over your earnings to me."

The women shifted on their feet, their anger like a heat rising off them. Massa Charles moved to stand at Missus Sarah's back.

"You are the property of the estate," Missus Sarah's voice rose. "Anything you have, you have by my grace and not as a right."

"But we earned it," Dido said. She was furious but she knew better than to show it.

"Yes," the other women agreed. "We are the ones who grow the food and walk the countryside to sell it. Our hands till the soil and our heads carry the weight. Even the money we pay the town to use the market comes from us."

"And who owns the ground on which you grow the food?" Missus Sarah's voice was gentle but there was a brittle quality to her words as if she were having a hard time keeping her temper and speaking reasonably. Dido remembered that this was the woman who, years ago, when Massa Richard went away to St. Kitts on business, had wreaked her revenge on Yolanda, his favorite mulatto who was then with child. She'd had the slave tied up and had bade Massa Charles place a cloth bag filled with wasps over the woman's head and pull it tight. Yolanda had thrown herself from side to side, pitching this way and that on the ground, her cries like those of an animal at slaughter. But Missus Sarah turned and walked away leaving her son and Massa Charles to stand over the screaming woman with their guns.

Hours later, when the other slaves had at last been allowed to go to her and remove the bag, Yolanda's face was unrecognizable, black and bloated and running with pus. Delia and the other women took the body and buried it under the flame tree just beyond the boundary of the estate. When Massa Richard returned and found out what had happened he slapped his wife around and locked her in her room for a week but, afterwards, it was like nothing happened and Yolanda had never existed. If he ever looked at the earth mound where Yolanda and his unborn child rested none of the slaves saw him do it.

"In a few months, I will review the situation and it could be I may decide to allow you to retain some portion of your earnings. I can make no promises concerning this, however." She gestured at them and, one by one, the women around Dido stepped forward and emptied their purses on the table before her.

"Thank you. Dido, I understand that you've nothing to contribute this week, though it would seem that, but for the scar on your cheek, you escaped unscathed." Wordless, Dido raised the sleeve of her dress to show her the scrape that ran from her wrist to her elbow and inclined her neck so she could see the bruises the man Daniel had left on her throat. "Well, be that as it may, you and a few others..." Her eyes did not meet any of the women's. "...have been saving to buy your freedom. Massa Charles will accompany each off you to your houses and you will give him that money as well."

"But, Missus, that is not fair," Dido protested.

"Is it fair that I have been saddled with an estate so in debt? Is it fair that after a life of debauchery my husband should precede me into death leaving me with these responsibilities?"

Dido suddenly understood that what she and the others had taken as a sign of Missus Sarah's deep grief about the death of her husband was nothing more than a flood of self-pity.

"You first, Dido. The rest of you will stay here until Massa Charles signals his readiness for you to come."

Dido did not move. "I have twelve dollars. Will you not take it and grant me my freedom? If you allow it, I will come to you every month and pay off what I can on the price of my freedom. I will not fail in this." The last words came out in a rush. She was desperate for Missus Sarah to accept this plan.

"I told you I would not sell you for less than ninety dollars and, in any case, you are a valuable worker so I may not sell you at all."

Dido stared at her. "Not sell me? But you said if I raised the money I could buy my freedom. You said so, Missus." She took a step toward the woman but Massa Charles placed himself between them.

"Go get your money and be glad this is all I am asking of you." Beyond the man's shoulder, Missus Sarah passed a weary hand across her forehead. "My son tells me there are many planters who send their female slaves into Port Royal to whore. He assures me that they make a pretty penny from the trade."

Dido's blood ran cold and the other women muttered, horrified. Missus Sarah raised her hand.

"Do not worry. We are not sunk so low in depravity that I would send you into that den of vice for such an immoral purpose. Go with her." She nodded to Massa Charles.

Without another word, Dido spun on her heel and stalked out of the room.

Back in her hut, she retrieved her savings from under the grass mat she had woven as a covering for the floor and handed it over to Massa Charles without a word.

Later that night, around the fire in the middle of the quarter Dido listened to the other women as they talked bitterly about the money taken from them. She had already decided not to say anything about El Negro. It would be hard to talk about the pirate without revealing that she had lied to Missus Sarah and Dido did not trust everyone around the fire. She glanced over at Simon, Delia's eldest son, who always had something to run whispering to Massa Charles about every morning. Rosa, his young woman, sat next to him, her sharp eyes darting here and there among the crowd. Dido wondered if the women had so forgotten themselves they did not remember that it was this same young woman who first raised the alarm about Pablito. If Rosa had not reported his disappearance to the overseer that Sunday morning, he might have gotten away instead of being recaptured. Dido was sure that Pablito had not forgotten. Every now and then she caught him watching Rosa, a faraway look in his eyes. The young woman was aware of his regard, too. Dido noticed she avoided the one-eyed man.

On and on the talk went but Dido, tired and troubled, soon bid the others goodnight before making for her hut. If Missus Sarah was going to take her money every Sunday, buying her freedom would be impossible. The shock of the woman's betrayal was like a hammer sounding in her head. They had had an agreement. She had told Missus Sarah her intent and the Missus had named her price but now she was going back on her word.

Despite all her pretty prattle about letting them have half of their earnings in the future, Dido doubted this would ever happen. She lay down on the rush-filled canvass matting that was her bed and stared into the darkness. In her mind's eyes, she saw again the three-room house she had planned to build with her mother's help beyond the Blue Mountains. She saw the property so clearly, saw the rows of yam and cassavas planted in the grounds, saw her mother weaving baskets in the doorway, saw her brothers and her sister running with the wind, her sister's braids bouncing with each step. Dido blinked hard to stave off tears. There had to be a way and she would find it.

Chapter 3

The next day, Dido was up before cockcrow. She retrieved a piece of flatbread from a basket by her bedside and ate it quickly so she would have time to go by the well for a drink of water before Nico, the driver, blew his conch shell calling them to work. Delia and two house slaves, Cubina and Martha, were already there when Dido arrived.

"Did you hear they are sending Old Philippa away and Dora and Duchess's two little boys?" Delia asked Dido without wasting time on a greeting.

"Where did you hear that? Is it true?" Dido's gaze flew among the women.

"After you all left yesterday evening, I did hear Missus Sarah talking about it with Massa Henry," Cubina said. "It did seem like they had been thinking on it for a while but they kept it close to their chests so we never knew a thing. That is why we are come early to meet you."

"We do not know when." Martha spoke up. "Perhaps today, perhaps a week from now."

"But who will look after the young children while the mothers are in the field?" Dido asked. "They need Old Philippa. She is the best doctoress for miles."

"They say you know as much as she does about healing and that she costs more than she is worth," Cubina answered.

"I do not. It is not true. And she feeds herself. She grows her own food. What she doesn't have, we give her, don't we, Delia?"

Delia nodded.

"There's more." The two house slaves exchanged rueful glances. "If they can find no buyer for her, they mean to just let her fend for herself in the streets of Port Royal or maybe in San Jago de la Vega."

"No." Dido glared at them. "No. How can they even think to do such a thing? How will her God let them?"

The house slaves shrugged and grimaced at each other.

"We must be getting back before we're missed," Martha said. "Old Philippa did help raise me. That is why I did come bring the news. Give her this for me." She shoved an old pewter cup into Dido's hand. "It is all I have." Coins rattled in the bottom. "Is what I pick up here and there. Missus Sarah don't know nothing."

Dido seethed with fury but took the cup. *Why, Oshun, why*, she asked as she and Delia watched the two women hurry away. In the distance, the conch shell sounded.

"Old Philipa is like a second mother to me," she said to Delia as they made their way back to the quarter for the counting.

"I know. It is that way for many of us. It will be a sad day when she leaves."

From Delia's voice, Dido could tell the other woman had already prepared herself for Old Philippa's departure. Dido took the pewter mug with her into the field, tying it around her waist by the handle. She couldn't face seeing Old Philippa before she had more time to absorb the news. She should have hurried back to the quarters at the mid-morning break and delivered the mug and the news the house servants had brought but still she procrastinated. The sun was high in the sky and the other field slaves were on their lunch break when Dido made her way back to the quarters. By then, the mug seemed to weigh as much as a field of cut cane, being full of resentment, fury, regret and a thousand other emotions Dido could scarcely name.

But, except for the children too young to weed the fields or to look after the plantation's livestock, there was no one in the quarters. Old Philippa was not in her hut.

"Where Granny?" Dido asked a nearby child, pointing to the open doorway.

"Where Granny?" The little girl repeated, smiling up at her, thinking it was a game they were playing. "Granny gone. Where Granny?" She spread her hands before her like she must have seen an adult do.

Dido stared at the child. Gone, Old Philippa gone. It couldn't be true. Could they have moved so fast? She darted into the old woman's hut, her eyes taking in everything at once. The pitiful mattress on the floor, the one wooden chair Pablito had made when he was still a young boy, the cracked calabash gourd on the table, a couple straw baskets in a corner. Where were the other gourds and the wooden spoon Old Philippa ate with? The iron pot in which she cooked all her meals? They were gone. Massa Henry had come for the old woman and she had taken with her such things as she could comfortably carry. Dido's legs threatened to give way. She grabbed the chair and sat down. She would never see the old woman again. Tears streamed down her face. In a sudden fit of anger she tore the mug from her waist and threw it as hard as she could against the opposite wall. It made a dull clunking sound as it bounced off and came to rest on the wooden floor. The coins flew out, scattering all over the ground.

She was too late. If she had not been so selfish, thinking only of her own grief, she would have seen the old woman and would have been able to give her the mug and its contents. Maybe she could have added some of her own coins to it but no, she had delayed until she was too late. From far away she heard the conch shell blowing. The lunch rest was up. She had best get back to the field or Nico would be obliged to whip her. Dido scooped up the coins and flung them back in the mug. She retied it at her waist and ran out the door. She stopped only to check that the children were not hungry. Rosa's youngest sister had taken charge and was feeding the baby born to Daisy five or six moons ago. Dido made sure the others were all right and had not gotten into mischief then hurried back to the cane-piece.

"Old Philippa's gone. They're going to sell her in Port Royal. I think Duchess's two youngest have gone too. Pass it on," she said to Leonora, on her left and William on her right. The driver had not noticed her late return to the field being occupied in conversation with Massa Charles.

For the next couple of hours as the sun descended in the west, Dido occupied herself with her task. Massa Charles had decreed they would waste no time on the mature cane that, but for the rains, they would have been cutting down to send to the mill. Instead, they were to get a head start on hoeing the new cane. Despite the sun's decline, Dido's face, arms and shoulders, like those of the others was bathed in perspiration. Flecks of mud were spattered all over her clothes but she barely noticed. The slaves spread the word and she could see how it was received in the tightening of Leonora's jaw, the sharp thwack of William's machete. The air itself seemed to hum with tension and distress. Old Philippa was well loved.

Nico stared at them, warned by a sixth sense that something had changed. He muttered something to Massa Charlas, who turned to squint at them. Dido noticed that the white man put his hands on the pistol hanging from his belt to reassure himself that it was there and available should he have need. Her lips curled. He mistook the emotion of the people. 'His' people Massa Richard had often called them, but he had never really known them and neither did the men who now watched them so carefully. The slaves were angry, yes, but only because Old Philippa was taken so suddenly. Sales and removals were a fact of life they were accustomed to. Had not Dido herself been sold off from the plantation on which she was born? The slaves did not know, not yet, not unless Delia had told them, of the plan to simply leave Old Philippa in Port Royal to live off the streets if they could get no price for her. That news might have incited some, like Pablito, to unexpected action, to violence even, but she had not passed that on, she kept that to herself.

Unbidden, an image of El Negro's face came to mind and something warm unfurled itself in Dido's stomach. "Brave" he'd called her but she was so full of secrets, unable to stop the sale of an old woman who was like family to her, and powerless to prevent the theft of her own money by Missus Sarah. What would he think of her, if he knew? Shame pursed her lips and she dug her hoe into the ground, striking at the earth as if at an enemy.

That night, Duchess's wailing over her lost children prevented everyone except the very young from sleeping and it was a tired Dido who woke the next morning to the sound of the conch shell. Realizing she had gotten up too late to go to the pens to help Delia with feeding the chickens, Dido yawned widely and stretched to banish the tiredness from her bones. Old Philippa should have wakened her.

The old woman must have overslept herself, Dido thought, smiling. As she stepped outside into the chilly morning air she glanced over at her neighbor's hut and it came back to her. Old Philippa was gone. Averting her eyes from the empty and silent hut, Dido hurried off to where the overseer was waiting to count them all. *It is wrong, it is wrong*, she wanted to shout out. *Old Philippa belongs here among those who love her*. The words trembled on her lips, bubbled up from her heart but she willed her tongue to stillness and kept her eyes to the ground so the overseer would not see the fury she knew shone in them.

What would El Negro have done, if it was his mother or his grandmother who was carted off like that to an uncertain future, she asked herself. Though they had spoken only briefly she thought she knew the answer to that question. He would have gone looking for them. *He is free and you are not*, an inner voice whispered. He was not always free, Dido argued back. *Aaah*. The inner voice was like wind rustling the canes. *What, what*…Dido sputtered, but she already knew. A seed was planted. Over the next few days she tended it carefully, nurturing it like she had nurtured her carrots, tending to them every chance she got until they were full grown and ready for harvest. Her plans took shape and grew. She would leave Beeston's and run to the sea like El Negro. Anna, the seamstress, was right. Dido could see that now. What Missus Sarah had done when she took the women's money was nothing less than theft. Slavery itself was theft. The Missus had taken what she needed of Old Philippa's life and then discarded her like a broken clay pot for which she had no more use.

Dido could not allow this to happen to her or her family. She had to free them. And she had a plan. She would disguise herself as a man and go to Port Royal to find work on a ship, a pirate ship that would take her away from Jamaica and Beeston's. *Away also from your family*, the inner voice protested, changing sides. No, she would come back. When she had enough money she would come back and buy her family's freedom. They would build their home, the one she saw in her dreams, they would built it far away from the sound of the whip and the cries of bereft mothers. *You are a slave and a woman*, the voice scoffed. "I will be free," Dido said aloud. She murmured the words with every swing of her hoe, carving them into the island's black soil with wood and iron.

"I know what you're planning to do." The words were so low that, at first, Dido had the strange feeling her inner thoughts had somehow given themselves voice, a man's voice at that. "You'll get caught unless you heed my words."

Dido sprang bolt upright from her makeshift bed. "Who…who…"

"It is me, Pablito."

The moonlight shining in through the open door framed his silhouette. Dido made a face. Some pirate she was going to be if she could not even hear when somebody entered her hut.

"What do you want?" Dido cleared her throat so she wouldn't sound as woolly-headed as she felt. "What are you talking about? Why didn't you knock?"

"I do not want anyone to know I'm visiting you."

Dido pushed herself back against the wall, ready to jump up if he tried to touch her.

"May I close the door?" Pablito asked.

If he did, she would not be able to see him, the hut was blacker than the dungeon where repeat runaways were jailed. Dido's heart became overloud in her chest. She was surprised that the entire quarters did not wake up, startled by the strange booming.

"Yes. Close it." Her voice quavered. Massa Simon had come to her in darkness like this.

Darkness swallowed the moonlight. Dido strained to hear if he had come closer. It was hard to tell with the rushing in her ears.

"I know you're planning to run away," Pablito said.

From the sound of his voice, Dido could tell he had not moved from the doorway but she still didn't relax.

"How could you know that? It is not true." The tumult in her ears was like the sound of a huge waterfall. She had not said a word to anyone.

"I can see it in your eyes and the way you move, as if you are already gone."

"It's not true." Dido was so startled by the man, she could think of nothing else to say. "No."

"Never mind. I've spoken to no one of it but you must listen to me. If you plan to go to Port Royal to look for the old woman, you must not do so directly. Go into the hills first, straight as the night-witch flies, and wait a month or more. Keep to the streams and the waterways." She heard him shift on his feet, the soft crackling of his stiff osnaburg trousers. "Listen to me. Are you listening to me?" he asked, impatient.

"Yes. Keep to the streams, you said."

"That's right." He sounded relieved. "The dogs will lose your scent in the water. Speak to no one. Sometimes there are others hiding but keep to yourself for the color of one's skin is no predictor of friendship. That was my mistake. When do you go?"

She saw no need to dissemble further. "Tomorrow night, as soon as the quarter is quiet."

"Yes. Saturday night is a good time for there is no count on Sunday and it should be well into the day before you are missed. Keep to the shadows for they will shelter you from sight."

"Pablito, why don't you come with me?" she asked, feeling a sudden rush of affection for the strange man. It would be good to have someone she knew with her.

"No, your time has come. I will leave when my time comes again. Who knows? It may be sooner than anyone thinks." He opened the door a slit. "When you are come to Port Royal, disguise yourself so that none who know you will recognize you. They will put up notices in the public spaces describing you so you must hide your true image. May the ancestors keep you safe from harm." Like a shadow he was gone.

Dido sank down on her pallet as her heartbeat slowly returned to normal. Her mind was a jumble of thoughts. It was several minutes before she could focus on any one thing. Pablito had known, had seen right through her for all that he had only one eye. What about those with no such handicap? Rosa and Nico, for instance. Had they noticed anything different about her? She cast her mind back over the previous days, sifting through the images to see if she could remember anyone looking at her askance. Nothing came to mind. She could not even remember having noticed Pablito during the week though, of course, he had to have been around. She had paid him no particular mind but clearly he had been watching her. Who else watched her, Dido wondered. Who else? She rifled feverishly through her recent memories but found nothing out of the ordinary, no word or look that should have tipped her off that her intentions were as clear as white rum to anyone observing her.

Too nervous to fall asleep again, Dido spent the rest of the night staring into the darkness of the hut, alert to every sound around her. The rustlings of a mouse or some other small creature in the thrash roof, the sibilant whine of the mosquitoes, the gentle whoo-whoo of an owl somewhere close to the quarters, she heard it all but nothing caught her attention. Tomorrow would be her last day at Beeston's and nothing could be allowed to go wrong. Pablito had somehow, with the gift of the wounded, been able to divine her secret but no one else could know, not even Delía who was like a sister to her.

Outside a cock crowed and Dido turned on her side. Soon. It would soon be time to get up and start the day but not yet, not yet. Dido closed her eyes and was asleep almost instantly.

Saturday came and went like any other. Her last day at Beeston's – a day both terrifying and glorious. Dido could hardly wait for it to end. When the sky overhead was a silvery-blue and the clouds were tinged with the pale gold rays of the setting sun, she climbed the slope to the small plot of land where she grew the things she sold in Port Royal. Behind her, she could hear the sound of the other market women's voices as they too made their way to their plots but she ignored them, not wanting anyone to engage her in conversation.

In the gathering gloom, she dug up some carrots, and picked herself a hand of bananas and a small basketful of okra.

Returning down the hill, Dido almost broke into song. She was leaving Beeston's, leaving the friends she had made here, making her own way into freedom. If she never heard another conch shell blown again, she would be happy. Back in her hut, Dido placed the produce into a basket she had taken from Old Philippa's hut and ate her supper sitting at the doorway, staring out at the quarters. The chickens that ran around the place during the day were asleep in the trees and here and there a cook fire glowed in the darkness. From somewhere nearby came the dull sound of somebody pounding cassava or making foo-foo. The rhythmic pounding seemed to have a language all of its own. *Walk well, Dido*, she fancied it saying. *Walk well.*

Chapter 4

Dido kept to the hills, pushing through the forest in a straight line. She had spent slightly more than two turns of the moon scuttling from one dark cave to another and seeking shelter deep in the bush when there was no cave to be found. She hoped the weeks she'd spent in hiding would be enough for the slave hunters to have called off their search.

By nightfall, she was within sight of Port Royal and could see the faint glow of the oil lamps and candles with which people lit their houses. Picking her way carefully down to the road with the aid of the pirate's stick, Dido tried to ignore the complaints of her stomach. She was tired and hungry but the real test of her freedom would soon come. She had torn a strip from her old dress, folded it and tied it around her forehead like the bandanna her attacker, the man Daniel, had worn. Another strip of cloth was wound around her chest, flattening her breasts, but she had no way of knowing how she looked. Could she really pass herself off as a man or at least a young boy? Dido prayed to Oshun and Oludumare and all the gods of the Yoruba pantheon that her disguise would work but she was far from confident about it.

The smell of roasting pork was the first thing that assailed Dido's nostrils as she entered the outskirts of Port Royal. Her mouth watered and her stomach grumbled. The smell came from a nearby tavern. Dido peered in through the window. The rough tables and benches of the tavern were crowded with men drinking and shouting to each other, black jacks of beer or ale in their hands. Here and there she saw women at the tables too, loose women. Some of the men openly fondled them, their hands exposing a breast to the sight of anyone who cared to look. As she looked closer she saw that a few men were making even more lewd explorations, their hands disappearing between the women's thighs.

Dido's knees shook. She turned away from the window and pressed her back against the wall while she caught her breath. How could women allow men to do that to them? More, they seemed to enjoy the attentions, leaning into the men, burying their heads in the men's chests, their hands roaming over the men's bodies as freely as those that probed theirs.

It was not as though Dido was a complete stranger to what could go on between a man and a woman, she had seen men and women coupling out in the open, behind the tamarind tree at the edge of the quarters and even among the

cane. But it was an activity she wanted no part of. She had made that clear to
the men who approached her as she grew into womanhood. Eventually, any
pursuers she might have had gave up and none bothered to come near her. Not
even Hercules who declared his love for her to all who would listen. She didn't
care that Massa Charles often grumbled in her hearing about the uselessness of
barren slave women. At least once a month, he threatened to marry her off
against her will but she ignored him and he let her alone because when all was
said and done, she was a good worker who gave no trouble.

The rumbling in her stomach grew louder. Dido patted her belly to quiet it
lest the sound alerted the whole town to her presence. She needed to look for
somewhere else to eat. There must be a bakery or pastry shop where she could
buy a meat-filled turnover or a loaf of bread. She hurried away from the tavern
and was soon in luck. Down the street and around a corner, a brown-skinned
woman was calling out "Journey-cakes for sale! Get your fresh journey-cakes!"

"I'll have one," Dido said, stepping up to the woman. "Do you have
anything else?"

"Like what you looking?"

"Maybe something with minced beef or saltfish?"

"You in luck, boy. Here be two saltfish patties. Them be the last."

Dido eyed them hungrily, weighing her options.

"How much?"

"Three pennies for the journey-cake and five for the patties."

Thirteen pennies in all if she bought a journey cake too. Could she afford it?
She wasn't sure but she handed over the money, she was sure it was best to be
well-fed when trying to find work. If she looked too hungry and desperate, a
captain might not want to take her on.

It was only as she walked away, half a patty already in her mouth, that Dido
remembered. The woman had called her 'boy.' Yes, she had definitely called
her boy but Dido could have given herself a good round kick in the pants. She
had forgotten all about deepening her voice. If the woman had not gone by
Dido's attire alone, she would have known the sex of her customer instantly.
Dido had been lucky but she knew she couldn't expect anyone else to be as
easily fooled as the pastry vendor. She was a man now and she had to look,
speak and act like one or she might find herself back at Beeston's Estate quicker
than she could say Oshun.

Dido licked at some crumbs she could feel at the corner of her mouth and
started in on the journeycake. There were lots of people on the streets, more
than she'd ever seen on a Sunday morning. Most had the same rough look of
the people she'd seen in the tavern but now and then she caught a glimpse of a
silk coat and a well-groomed wig or satin skirts and jeweled buckles. No one
paid her any mind but she paid attention to everything.

It must have been almost midnight, a time when everyone in the quarters
slept but, in Port Royal, night appeared to have no meaning. The residents met
it with as much energy as the day. But what people! In the middle of one street
two white men sprawled on the ground, passing a tankard between them. Every
now and then, the fatter of the two leaned forward and refilled the tankard from
a barrel in front of him. Though they seemed like old friends, laughing and

talking, the fat one held a wavering pistol to the other's head and there was a challenging air about him. Dido shot them a curious glance and hurried on. There was something wild and desperate in the face of the bearded man holding the pistol. It didn't bode well for his companion who nervously tipped the tankard to his mouth, his gaze sliding from side to side as if in hope of rescue.

Around another corner she heard loud music and wild barking over the shouts of men. Dido stopped to look in through the open door. People had gathered around an area in the middle of the tavern's dirt floor, their eyes intent on whatever spectacle they were observing. Dido considered going in, curious to see what all the noise was about but, just as she stepped forward, she heard a low, rumbling growl that raised the hairs on the back of her neck. She marveled that the people in the tavern did not immediately stampede through the door. Instead, they clapped and shouted all the louder.

Dido turned away. If Oshun willed it she would return another day to see what strange thing happened there but this Port Royal of drunken carousing and bawdy behavior was new to her. She should digest it in bits before it overwhelmed her. In any case her tiredness was beginning to tell. She had hoped to find a quiet alleyway where she could sleep or maybe a street bench but the benches she'd seen were all taken and the alleyways reeked of urine and waste. Dido stumbled on, relying heavily on her stick for support. Her legs felt stiff and her feet ached. Now she had eaten, all she wanted was to find a quiet place where she could curl up and close her eyes. But quiet places not occupied by others with the same plan were hard to find. Dido felt she could not take another step but still she walked, hardly knowing where she was going until finally, the market appeared. Her feet had brought her to a familiar spot. Mumbles here and a rustle there indicated the presence of other sleepers.

Almost teary with relief, Dido made her way to a corner stall and curled up beneath the counter, an arm around her basket. She gripped the stick with both hands holding it over her knees so she could come up swinging if she needed to but any thoughts of fighting or worries over her situation faded as she closed her eyes. Overcome with tiredness, Dido was soon fast asleep.

The sound of splashing water woke her up the next day. For a minute, Dido expected to see the familiar woods around her but it was a black man pissing against a post not too far from where she crouched that she'd heard. The man nodded to her as she straightened up.

"Morning," he said, scratching his chin.

"Morning," she replied, remembering to deepen her voice, glad sleep had roughened it further. Her hand rose to the bandana to make sure it was still in place.

He nodded again, finished what he was doing and was about to walk off when he turned to her.

"You a runaway?" he asked.

Oshun. Why such a question? Her fingers turned as cold as mountain dew.

"No. Why?"

"Just wondering is all. You looking for work?"

"Maybe."

"I know a cooper by the name of Marlowe on High Street. His apprentice just run off to go on one of Morgan's ships." Dido gave the man all her attention. "He's looking for someone to replace him. Tell him, George send you."

"But…Morgan's ships. Who is Morgan?"

The man shot her a puzzled frown then shrugged.

"Some say he fights for the king, others that he's nothing but a pirate."

A pirate. Dido's heart sang.

"But surely it cannot be so easy to find work on a ship?"

The man frowned. "No, it ain't easy but they say he's getting ready to go someplace so he's looking for men. You better not think on it, though. You don't look nothing but a boy. They don't take on boys. Cause too much trouble," he muttered, more to himself than Dido. "Anyway, you go on along to Marlowe. He don't beat none too much and you'll get three meals a day. Looks like you could use it." The man walked away whistling a tune Dido didn't recognize.

Morgan. A pirate looking for men. Dido dug into her basket and pulled out the now hard and greasy patty. Taking a bite, she mulled over what the stranger had said to her. She didn't allow the part about pirates not wanting boys on their ships to bother her. As far as anyone watching her was concerned, she was a young man, not a boy.

She had to find this Morgan and the best way was to go where the ships were, by the docks not too far from the market. In fact, if she got to her feet she could see the masts of the ships lying at anchor in the harbor. Dido jumped up and almost fell down again as her legs, unprepared for the sudden move and having spent hours in a cramped position, collapsed under her. Dido grabbed the edge of the counter and pulled herself up until she was half-lying on the wooden surface. She straightened one leg behind her and then the other one, shaking each one to help the blood along. Off to her left, the heaping mound of filthy rags she'd heard snuffling the night before, unwrapped itself to reveal a woman with skin so dirty that Dido could only tell she was white from the long, thin gray hair that hung down in greasy locks to her shoulders. Despite her age and despite the dirt settled into the wrinkles about her nose and mouth, her eyes were those of a pig's, small and suspicious. She looked up, saw Dido watching her, and immediately covered herself again.

"Have no fear. I won't hurt you," Dido called, taken aback by the woman's behavior. The mound remained still.

"That is how she be. Don't worry none about it," a voice said below her. This time it was Dido's turn to be startled. She peered over the counter and saw a young white boy, he could not have been more than about half her age, watching her.

"That is Rosmun. She dursn't like strangers but she will offer you no harm," the boy continued, smiling at her to reveal stumps of blackened teeth like sugar-apple seeds in his mouth. "Who you be? I never seen you around afore now."

"I am new to the town," Dido answered.

"Run away and come to be a pirate, have ye?" he asked, getting to his feet.

"N…n…no," Dido stuttered. Curses! Was it written across her forehead or did all of Port Royal's residents have the gift of second sight? "I do want to be a pirate but I have not run away from anywhere."

The boy lifted his thin shoulders and let them fall. "It dursn't matter to me but if you are a runaway, they'll catch you."

"They who?"

"Slave hunters. There is money to be made in that, men say."

"And what do you say?" asked Dido, amused by his grown-up ways.

"The owl is born in freedom and the pelican, so why not the black man? I can understand a person's wanting to be free, though I'm nowt but a boy." He frowned at her as if her smile annoyed him and Dido pressed her lips together. "I dursn't hold with neivver slavery or insureship."

"Insureship?"

"That be like slavery for whites. My favver did always talk about it. He was insured for seven years to a Bajan and he used to say he hated every minute of it. When Cromwell offered land to everyone who would come here to Jamaica, my favver jumped on a ship and came on over. Cromwell gave him thirty acres near Porras."

She understood less than half his words but land she knew about. "So why are you not there, helping him to work them?"

"He died a year ago from the bloody runs and our neighbors did take the place over."

"I am sorry." Her mother had always said she did not know who Dido's father was and that it was a subject best left alone. None of Dido's siblings looked alike though all had their mother's full, curving lips.

"His dying din't bother me none." The boy let his shoulders rise and fall again. "Favver used to raise his hand to us for the least thing and since I din't too truck with farm work he had plenty excuses for it. Patience warn't none of his virtues." He grinned. "I'm Ian. What are you called?"

"D…" Dido caught herself. "Domingo," she said, taking the name of a Beeston's slave who had been sold off a year ago.

The boy nodded. "Means you was born on a Sunday, yes?"

"Yes," Dido answered, relieved her answer was so readily accepted. In truth, she could have been born on a Friday for all she knew but she liked the name Domingo and she liked Sundays.

"So are you ready to go?"

"Go where?"

"To sign up with a ship. Ain't that what you're aiming to do? You sure din't sound none too happy about being a cooper's apprentice."

"Being a cooper had never entered my mind, no." Dido shot the boy a look as he vaulted over the counter to stand by her. How far could she trust him? "I hear there's a lot of money to be made from pirating," she said. "I need to make me some."

The boy nodded. "'Tis what I'm aiming to do myself, once I'm of age. If I've not gotten myself killed off from something by then." He grinned cheekily and Dido tried not to notice his teeth. Her mother had always said that chewing cane was good for children's teeth and she must have been right because Dido had all of hers and none had ever caused her any pain.

"Come on." The boy set off down the street.

"Where are we going?"

"To The Sugar Loaf. They was signing men up there yesterday so maybe they are still at it. I did hear Morgan aims to sail on Monday."

Monday. But Dido had no idea how many days away that was. If she asked Ian outright he would think her soft in the head but she needed to know.

"That is only two days away, is it not?"

"Three if you count today," Ian replied over his shoulder as he weaved in and out of the people making their way through the streets.

So it was Friday. She had arrived near the end of the week. She still had no way of knowing how long she had been in the mountains but it didn't really matter. She was accepted as a youth, Domingo, and she was being led to where she could sign up on a pirate voyage. Dido followed Ian as closely as she could, ignoring the passing people and the drunks passed out here and there along the way.

The tavern Ian led her to was not very different from the one she'd seen the night before, being just as big but much less crowded. Ian took a seat at one of the empty tables and clapped his hand on it to attract the attention of the two women standing behind the counter.

"Breakfast for me and me friend here," he called out to them.

"Well, if it isn't Hizzoner." The brown-haired one winked at the other who rolled her eyes at the sally. "And what will you be wanting for breakfast, m'lud? Some rashers of bacon with your eggs? Or pumpkin soup with dumplings and pork?"

Dido's stomach growled and her mouth watered, the patty she'd eaten forgotten. "Whatever you got will be fine, Blanche. You know I ain't fussy."

"And what about you, young Ian's friend? Are you fussy?"

"No, Ma'am." Dido shook her head. "I ain't. I'll have some of whatever you give him."

Blanche gave her a friendly smile but the older, blonde woman sniffed and turned away, disappearing up the stairs to the right of the counter.

"I'll be with the two of you in a second, Ian," Blanche said, coming round from behind the counter with a tray of black jacks for the men sitting at the next table.

Beside Ian and herself, the men were the only other customers in the place. Dido let her gaze wander over them. If their dress was anything to go by, a few had to be pirates for they were clothed as flamboyantly as El Negro though none of them carried it off with his flair.

"Those are the quartermasters," Ian murmured. "They sign on the new men. The one with the long black hair is Thomas Cobb. He's Morgan's quartermaster. The loud one as does most of the talking, he's Trevor Jackman of the *Dragon's Adventure*. The quiet one is Michel Le Basket, or something like that. He's a Frenchie." He frowned as he craned his head. "The furthest one over, the one with the hat, that's Diego Grillo, they say he sails with Delander but he ain't the quartermaster unless there've been some changes I dursn't know of. The other men around them are signing on."

"So I'd have to go over there?"

"Yes. See they've got the papers on the table." Every now and then when the men shifted Dido caught a glimpse of a sheaf of papers in front of the black haired man. "Them be the articles."

"Articles?"

"Like an agreement, see. You gotta agree to certain rules or they won't let you on. They'll tell you about them."

"I never signed nothing before. How do I do that?"

"Can you write?"

Dido shook her head. Writing was what Hercules called the marks he sometimes made in the dust of the quarter. It had interested her but, though he offered to teach her, she never made the time.

"I can't neither but if you could, you would just put down your name. That be your signature, see. People who can't write their name just sign with exes."

"Don't know an ex either."

"Don't they teach you nothing on these plantations?" Ian pursed his lips at her and Dido shrugged.

"They do," she said. "They teach you how to work from sunup to sundown, they teach you how to hoe a ratoon and slice through a line of cane in a day. They teach you how to listen and not disobey." She tried not to sound too bitter. "I learned a lot of things at B…working sugar." Not anything that could be useful *off* the plantation but then that was how life was, life for slaves and for the insures Ian had talked about.

"This is how you make an ex." The boy dug his thumbnail into the rough wooden table, already scored with stains and marks. "See?" He did it again.

Dido copied her teacher, slowly at first and then with more confidence until she had made a row of exes in front of her.

"Pleased to have the services of an artist, I'm sure but can't you draw nothing else?" The brown-haired woman's voice bubbled with laughter.

Dido started guiltily. "I'm sorry. I meant no harm." She rubbed her palm over the table.

"It's alright, boy. I'm only joshing you. If it had been Libby now, who'd caught you, you'd be out on your ear but the table's seen worse and will no doubt see worserer." She deposited a plate full of eggs, bacon and beans between Ian and Dido. "You boys said you'd share. I can't be wasting my clean plates on you. Here's spoons. Eat and be merry." She ruffled Ian's red hair and walked off.

Dido held the spoon up to her face. She'd never eaten with a metal spoon before. In the quarters, the only utensils the slaves had were those they made of wood. Even their plates and bowls were wooden while the plate in front of her was of the same metal as the spoon.

"Eat," Ian commanded, his mouth full, bean sauce dribbling down his chin. Dido ate.

At the other table, the men talked in low voices but every now and then she heard snippets. "Whether it is Havana or Cartagena, we will give the Spanish a drowsing they won't forget."

"Attack the cities and the booty is all ours, attack ships and the Crown must have its share." To Dido, the men may as well have been speaking Fulani, for all she could understand them.

"Havana is Cuba's capital and Cartagena is in New Spain. Morgan means to take a city," Ian said, his eyes bright with excitement. "If only I could go…what fun it would be." He looked as if he were seeing it all in his mind's eye, the fleet rolling over the sea, the rush into the rich cities, the search for booty, and then the triumphant return to Port Royal. "I would go straight to Muvver and tell her she can buy whatever she likes and when she says she canna afford it I would show her me doubloons. Her eyes will get really big like they do when we've done something very good or very bad and then she'll take me into her arms and tell me she loves me and that I am her own best son." His eyes shone and his lips quivered.

"All done here?" Blanche was back.

"Yes, ma'am," Dido answered. "Thank you very much."

"That'll be a piece of eight or thirty pennies, if you've got it."

Dido was shocked. "A piece of eight?" That was almost half of all the money she had with her.

"He dursn't have no money," Ian piped up, pushing out his chest. "But he's going to sign up with Morgan. If you let us have credit, he'll come back and pay you ten pieces of eight. How's that for a bargain? You give the mister one and keep the rest for yourself."

Dido almost fainted at this extravagant offer made on her behalf but Blanche, clearly accustomed to such deals and accustomed also to Ian, laughed.

"Ten pieces of eight, hmm?" She arched an eyebrow at Dido. "What if you're killed and don't come back? Or worse, what if you're a rogue who does not repay his debts?"

"I repay my debts, Ma'am." Dido straightened up on the bench. "If I'm not dead," but she hated to think of that possibility, "I'll be back and you'll get what is owed." She glanced at Ian. They were going to have to have a little talk. She had plans for her earnings that did not include turning them over to a tavern owner.

"Ten pieces of eight," Blanche said, sensing reluctance and wanting to clarify the deal on the table.

"Ten. Yes. I know." It was more than Massa Charles had taken from under her pallet.

"Don't worry, Blanche. He's a good man, you will not regret it." Ian almost danced away from their table, pulling Dido with him.

"Here's a sailor as wants to sign up," he said, clearing a way for Dido through the small crowd around the pirates.

The men made way but they were silent, all their attention focused on the black-haired man who was reading from a document in front of him. The man glared at Ian, angry at the interruption and continued.

"No person is to game at cards or dice for money. Lights and candles must be out by eight o'clock at night. No boy or woman to be brought on board." Here the man looked Dido up and down. She squared her shoulders and stood up straighter, unsure which of the two he suspected her of being.

"Any man deserting during battle shall be punished by death or marooning. Any man disobeying captain's orders shall receive such punishment as the Captain and a major part of the company shall deem fit. These are the articles of the *Satisfaction*, the *Dragon's Adventure*, the *Wind Dancer* and the *Fortune's Gift* and all the other ships of this expedition. If you agree to them, you must sign your names to this." He pointed to the papers in front of him. One by one, the men around Dido pushed up to the table and grabbed a quill to affix their signatures as indicated.

"Go on," Ian said behind her, nudging Dido in the small of her back. "Go on."

"Don't push," she whispered back. The black-haired man took no notice of her but Dido was almost faint with excitement. Had he seen through her disguise? Did he know she was a woman?

"Are you signing up, boy?" a kind-faced man asked her.

"Yes. I want to."

Ian gave her another push.

"Come on, then." The man beckoned her forward. "It's easy. If you cannot write your name just tell me what it is and I'll write it down for you. Then you can make your mark against it.

"I am called D...Domingo."

"Domingo what? Do you have a surname?"

"N...Yes." She was hit by sudden inspiration. "Freeman, sir. Domingo Freeman."

The man smiled into his goatee. "Freeman, eh? Well, that's as good as any other." He bent over and made what looked like snaky wiggles below other snaky wiggles before handing her the quill. "Make your mark there. Your initials or whatever." A stubby finger pointed to the place and Dido confidently made the x she'd practiced on the table just minutes before.

She was the last to sign up and after she did so the black-haired man pulled the paper to him and started calling out names. "Bill Farthingate, *Satisfaction*. Edward Gilby, *Dragon's Adventure*, Piet Ahlgren, *Wind Dancer*." Dido listened hard, her heart pounding as he went on and on until finally... "Domingo Freeman, *Fortune's Gift*."

He rolled up the paper. "Alright, men. Report to your captains. We sail in three days."

The men peeled away from the table and Dido and Ian followed them out of the tavern door.

"*Fortune's Gift*, that's a great ship." Ian's tone was frankly envious. "El Negro's one of the best captains there is." Dido stood stock-still at the name but Ian continued on oblivious. "He got his ship off a Spanish merchant on the coast of New Spain. It is small and fast like the wind, people say. Hey, come on Domingo," he said, at last noticing that she had stalled.

"El Negro." Dido repeated the name, speaking the words in wonderment. Her heart set up a loud beat in her ears, as deafening as the *gombay* drums Hector played on special occasions at Beeston's Estate

"Yes, El Negro. He's a fair captain, better than Rock Brasiliano, him you don't want to be around, especially if he's drunk." Ian made a face.

"El Negro is the captain of my ship, the...the..." In her confusion, she couldn't even remember its name. Her grip tightened on the stick in her hand.

"The *Fortune's Gift*." Ian frowned at her. "Are you unwell? You're looking poorly-like."

"I am...I feel...It must be the heat." But she knew very well, it was not. Her mind raced. She would have to get rid of the staff. The pirate captain would certainly recognize it. Dido looked around her in a daze. She would have liked to keep it but now she couldn't, she'd have to discard it somewhere. It was more than half Ian's size and would be no use to him. Dido wiped a finger across her forehead below the edge of her bandanna and tried to think clearly.

By now all the other new recruits had disappeared but the streets around Dido and Ian bustled with people going about their business.

"We could go back and ask Blanche for some water, if you want it." Ian looked anxious, as if afraid he had invested his hopes for piratical glory, even if by proxy, on the wrong would-be pirate.

"No. No, the spell is passing. Pay me no mind. Let us go on." She suited action to word, setting off down the street.

"This way," he said, pointing in the direction of the harbor.

"No, there is someone I must look for. A woman." She had meant to search for Old Philippa as soon as she'd arrived but it had not been practical last night and now the morning was almost gone.

"You had best go make yourself known to El Negro, see. You're his man now."

"I'm no-one's man," she bristled. She was free and she had no desire to be ruled by anyone ever again. That was why she was staking everything on becoming a pirate. Had not El Negro said all were equal on a pirate ship?

"Do not eat me up. I mean, you are one of his sailors. You are with him, you should go and introduce yourself-like."

She should. Dido knew it made sense but what she didn't know was if she was up to it. Why of all the pirate ships in the harbor of Port Royal on the blessed island of Jamaica did it have to be El Negro's to which she was sent? *Oshun*, she whispered, *why, why have you done this to me?* If she heard, the lady did not answer.

"I need to look for this old woman. She is frail and may be ill for aught I know." And the longer she could postpone coming under the regard of those piercing, mocking eyes the better. Would he recognize her? Surely, he would. Yes, better to postpone their meeting until perhaps the evening hours when the sun had already begun to travel to its nightly home.

"Shall I come with you?"

"She is my business. Not yours." She had not meant to speak harshly but if Ian came with her, he would discover her secret. She did not know him well enough to risk that happening. Ian looked relieved, however. Going in search of some old woman he did not even know had not appealed to him.

"I'll see you tonight, by the harbor then." He waved and walked off.

Dido took a deep breath and turned away. She had done it. She had signed on to a pirate ship. She would sail in three days. *Not if El Negro recognizes you*, a little voice said. *If he recognizes you, that is the end of your little plan and what will you do then?* It was a good question and, like all good questions, it was one to which she had no answer.

Chapter 5

For the rest of her first day in Port Royal as a free black, Dido walked up and down the town's streets and alleyways looking for Old Philippa but the woman was nowhere to be seen. Dido even tried to ask for her at the workhouse and at the poor house, but the guard at the former would not let her in and a guard at the latter told her there was no-one there fitting Old Philippa's description. She searched without rest, worried the old woman was just around the next corner or down a nearby lane and she would miss her if she interrupted her search. But it was no use. If Old Philippa was still alive, she was not on the streets of Port Royal. Tired and hungry, Dido finally gave up and made her way to the docks that evening. At first she looked around for Ian, sure the boy would be able to lead her to the right ship. There were eight or ten tied at the wharves and several more in the harbor though most were of a size that could not be described as 'small.' But Ian couldn't be found either so she asked a passing man who pointed out a ship at the end of a pier. As she approached, Dido saw that the boat, like the others around it, was a hive of activity. Men moved to and fro between the deck and the dock, lugging barrels and what more besides. What Dido took for chaos resolved itself into order when she came closer. Men boarding the ship went up the ramp on one side while those departing took the other. A line had formed on deck so that men handed off things to each other in an efficient relay.

"Pardon me," Dido said, stepping up to a brawny white man who was engaged in coiling a length of rope.

"Yes, boy. What do you want?"

"I…" Dido suddenly lost her nerve.

"Go on, boy. Spit it out."

"I…" Dido had no more success than the last time.

"If the cat has got your tongue, you'll need to buy it back again, eh?" The man laughed.

"I've signed up. My name is Domingo Freeman."

"You?" He looked her over from head to foot. "We do not sign little weasels like you. It is the Navy as takes grommets, not us."

"I am not a grommet." She didn't even know what the word meant. "I signed up I tell you." Her belly grumbled and she glared at the man. She hadn't found

Old Philippa, she was hungry, and now this. Dido switched her basket to her other arm.

"This here's El Negro's ship."

"Yes, I know. I signed up and they assigned me here. *Fortune's Gift*, the man said."

"Damn that Cobb. It was he who sent you, wasn't it? Trying to foist all the rejects off on us. Why did *he* not take you? Damn and triple damn him."

"Calm yourself, Richard. Why do you curse so?"

Dido stood as still as a pillar of salt.

"Do you not see it, captain?" The sailor turned around to face the man who had joined them. "Cobb sends us these greenhorns so we will fall behind and not earn our rightful share of the loot. He seeks to undermine you."

"No matter, it will take more than one greenhorn or even ten to keep us back." El Negro smiled at her.

Dido would have liked to return that smile with careless confidence but she could barely raise her eyes to meet his, much less manage to move her lips. She tugged at the edge of her bandanna, pulling it down almost to her eyebrows.

"Are you Domingo Freeman, boy?"

"Y...yes," Dido stuttered.

El Negro took a step toward her. It was only with a supreme effort of will that Dido stopped herself from taking a corresponding step backward.

"You've never been on the sea before, have you, boy?" The pirate captain dipped his head to try to look her in the face. His voice was not unkind.

"Only once, sir. When I was brought here from my home in Nevis."

"See! That's the fourth one he's palmed off on us." The man, Richard, fingered the dagger stuck in the belt around his waist. "The damned son of a misbegotten drab."

"I'm not scared of the sea. I will be a good sailor. Please." Dido risked a glance at the shirtless El Negro. His body betrayed no spare ounce of flesh. Hard muscles rippled under his midnight-black skin. Did she imagine it or could she feel the heat of him from where she stood? Dido swallowed and brought her mind back to the issue at hand. He had to let her on his ship. Her money was running out and if word got around that one captain rejected her, might not the rest do likewise?

"No need to worry. I'll not turn you away."

Relief coursed through her like hot molasses.

"And you will pay for it later," Richard grumbled.

"If anybody will pay, it is the Spanish." El Negro winked at Dido who began to relax now she knew she was staying. "Take your things on board. You can sleep below deck or on deck, as it pleases you."

"This is all I carry with me." Dido held up the arm with the basket.

"I may be able to find you a hammock in my cabin but have you no weapons? Nothing with which to fight?"

Dido thought of the stick she'd discarded behind a heap of old barrels before heading to the ship. "No, sir. Sorry, sir."

"No matter, boy. No matter." El Negro patted her kindly on the arm and Dido almost jumped at the unexpected contact. He was so close she could smell the sea and his own man-smell on him. A scar, a thin, raised line of flesh, curved below his left nipple to his navel, a fleshy button protruding from his hard, flat stomach. Dido wondered how he'd been wounded.

"First one as spies the sail of a prize gets the pick of any weapons on board," Richard growled at her. "You'll have to look sharp, though. You will not be the only one wanting a fine weapon."

"A hawk will look no sharper. I can hardly wait, sir." Dido's eagerness was like a second heartbeat in her chest.

"We'll see, boy. We'll see. Pirating is no child's game. It is for men stout of heart and strong of limb." El Negro turned away. "You there, be careful man. That's our food." He was talking about a cage full of chickens a sailor was about to toss onto the ship.

"Best go on board and help," Richard told her, more conciliatory now that his captain had spoken.

"I am hungry, sir. Will there be anything to eat on board?"

The man started to laugh but there must have been something on her face that moved his pity because he choked the laughter off and pointed to a tavern, one street over from the dock. There, he said, if sailors had no money, the owner would give them credit, payable upon their return. Until they set sail, the captain would provide no food to the men he explained. Dido thanked him and left, promising to return as soon as she had eaten.

An hour later, after a dinner of stewed mutton and cornbread, Dido was back at the docks. The men were still loading barrels on board but both El Negro and Richard had disappeared. Ian had not surfaced, either. Dido missed his company but she was too tired to go looking for him by the market. In any case, she'd told Richard she would be back. She was not sure where her help would be most appreciated but she was a pirate now, she had to assist her shipmates. Dido ducked her way past the men hurrying between the dock and the ship and scurried up the gangway to the deck. She had never been on a ship before but night had closed in on the island. All she could see were the puddles of light thrown by the lanterns hanging along the ship's rails and around the two masts. Dido steadied herself, feeling the gentle tug and sway of the waves lapping against the side of the boat. The motion dizzied her but she took a series of deep breaths and the sensation passed. Had she felt this way on the ship from Nevis? It was so long ago she couldn't remember.

"Hey you, take these below." A man pushed another cage of squawking chickens into her arms.

"Where... I..." But the man had already gone. Dido's eyes roved up and down the ship looking for the hatch she dimly remembered from the Nevis ship. She adjusted the basket on her arm and, holding the cage in front of her with both hands, walked slowly to the back of the ship to see if she could find it. She was lucky. Not too far from where she stood she discovered the opening in the deck but now another concern gripped her. Somebody had lit a lantern down there. She would have to turn and take the steps backward or she would stumble headfirst into she knew not what. In her hands, the chickens squawked and rocked their twig cage. They were creatures that went abed early, before nightfall, and Dido fancied they were protesting their ill-treatment.

She took her time descending. When she came to what looked like a second deck below the first, she stepped on to it. From what she could see in the dim light thrown by the smoky lantern, the area was used to store all kinds of things–rolls of canvas were packed against a nearby wall, coils of thick rope lay in a pile, and about forty or fifty small round clay jars sat in long, neat rows. Behind her, the steps descended into a darkness as black as a nightwitch's wing. Dido stashed the cage beside the canvas and climbed back up on deck.

She made her way to where the men were still loading barrels. The ship had a lot more room than she'd expected looking at it from the dock. It was, she thought, bigger than the ship that had brought her to Jamaica. Maybe it was on a ship such as this that her mother was carried away from Guinea as a girl. Her mother had described the darkness of the hold where she and the other captives were kept as the darkness of death and despair. She had said the smell was something from another world, an odor of mingled waste, decay and disease as thick and heavy as smoke, poisonous. Guinea slaves said their noses were still full of it, months, even years after their arrival in massa's new world. Dido remembered her mother telling her one night before they landed that the trip from Nevis to Jamaica was nothing like the crossing from Guinea. But Dido doubted the *Fortune's Gift* had ever been a slaver. The air below deck was not redolent of death and waste, only musty, like the storeroom at Beeston's Estate which was rarely opened to the sun and the clean fresh winds that blew down off the hills.

"Here, boy," a man called out to Dido. "Join the line."

Dido put her basket down out of the way. For the next two hours she worked next to the men, loading the barrels of beer and water on board. Finally, when they were done, she retrieved her basket, crawled to an unoccupied corner of the deck and was soon fast asleep despite the strangeness of her surroundings and the motion of the ship.

She woke the next day to a sharp oath. Her heart raced. She sat up straight. For a minute, everything around her was unfamiliar and she didn't know where she was. Then the fog of sleep lifted. She was a crewman on the *Fortune's Gift*, a pirate ship that would soon sail out of the harbor, away from Jamaica. A man swore again and she looked across the deck just in time to see one of her shipmates bring a piece of wood down hard on a sleek, brown rat in front of him. The man missed, swore, and tried again. Unhurt, the rat disappeared behind a pile of sail cloths.

"Bloody creature," the man mumbled, settling himself back down on the canvas sheets that served as his bed. He closed his eyes and was soon asleep again.

Dido got cautiously to her feet. A few lucky men had strung hammocks where they could but most were lying all about on the deck. Behind her, she heard a muffled laugh. She spun around, her hands going instantly to her bandana. The kerchief had become untied. It sat on her head more like a veil than a pirate's head-tie but that was not what had inspired the laughter. In fact, she doubted whether the man and woman swinging in the canvas hammock a few feet away had even noticed her. It was the woman who laughed, tickled by the man's groping hands moving under the loose dress she wore. From what

Dido could see from where she stood, the woman's hands were just as busy inside the man's pants. Not wanting to see more, Dido backed away, bumping into someone right behind her.

"Watch it, young fellow."

El Negro. Dido turned around so quickly she almost fell. Her hands were about to rise to her bandanna to check it once again, but she caught herself and pretended to wipe sleep from her eyes, instead.

"I...did not hear you," she stammered, remembering to deepen her voice just in time. The man walked like a cat.

"I am just come from Morgan's ship. The commodore has decided to leave one day earlier so we must finish our preparations today. We sail at dawn tomorrow."

"Dawn," Dido repeated, saying the word with as much reverence as she would use in calling out Oludumare's name.

El Negro smiled, his teeth gleaming in his dark face.

"You wish very hard for departure, don't you?"

Dido nodded. If he only knew *how* hard.

"Do you not have family, friends that you will be sorry to leave behind?"

"I do." Last night, she had dreamed of her mother and Old Philippa but she could not remember what they had said to her or she to them. The would-be rat killer had driven the dream from her thoughts with as much efficiency as he'd driven the rat, itself, away.

El Negro looked at her curiously as if waiting to hear more but she had nothing else to say. He had been kind to her when they first met, he had perhaps even saved her life, but he was still a stranger to her. Pablito's words about trusting no one rang in her ears.

The pirate captain looked at his sleeping men.

"They worked hard yesterday. I will give them a half-hour more of their dreams. Then we must begin again."

"Is there still more to load?" Her arms and her back ached.

"There's the gunpowder still to come on and the foodstuffs."

"Foods?" Dido's mouth watered.

"The flour, the salt-beef, salt-fish and other things. When you sail with Morgan you can never be sure where you will end up–Saint Marten or Mexico. And this time, he is even more close-mouthed than usual."

"You mean no-one knows where we are going except him?"

"We know we're going to fight the Spanish and I believe that it is in Cuba we shall attack them but Morgan has said nothing of his exact plans."

"That's not right. You are a captain," Dido protested, thinking him insulted.

El Negro shrugged. "In Cuba or on the coast of New Spain, it matters not to me where we take booty. What does matter is that my men do not run out of food. Starving men make neither good sailors nor good fighters." He winked, clapped her on the arm and walked past to climb a ladder leading to the front of the ship.

Her arm still tingling from the pressure of his hand, Dido left the ship to buy herself some bread and cheese and a bottle of cider for her breakfast. She was emerging from the tavern, with her purchases under her arm when she saw the patty vendor she had encountered on her first day in Port Royal.

"Buy some journey-cakes, boy," the woman called out, seeing her at the same time. "The best journey-cakes.

Dido crossed the street, arguing with herself. She had a couple guineas, a piece of eight, and about ten pennies left to her name. If she bought the journey cakes, she would have even less but what if the ship ran out of food? Or what if, because she was the youngest or the newest, she got less food? At Beeston's, drivers, coopers and other skilled slaves got three salted bonito fishes per week, pregnant or nursing women received two, everyone else got one. Maybe it was like that on the *Fortune's Gift*. I an might have known but the boy had disappeared like a puff of smoke on a windy day. Dido bought five of the journey cakes and a handful of fig bananas that were not completely ripe. This purchase left her with only the guineas and ten pennies. A good thing the secretive Morgan had changed his mind and decided to leave earlier. She could not have afforded too many more days of this.

Dido found a quiet corner of the dock to eat a hunk of bread and a small piece of cheese before wrapping them back up in the waxed paper in which she'd bought them. The two loaves of bread, the one piece of cheese, the journey cakes and the bananas were all she'd have to supplement whatever food she got on the ship. Dido wiped off the crumbs around her mouth. When she'd left the ship, most of the men were still sleeping, but, in the time it took her to buy a meal and eat, the ship had become a hive of activity just like its neighbors around it. Small livestock, dozens of barrels, demijohns of rum and many, many other goods were again arriving in groaning wagons at the wharves.

Dido picked up her purchases and hurried back to the *Fortune's Gift*. The last thing she needed was for anyone to accuse her of being a slacker. She threaded her way around the men until she found the hatch in the floor leading to the place where she had put the chickens. She climbed down quickly, and deposited her hoard behind some coils of rope, thick as her arm. Looking around to make sure there was no one around, she undid her shirt and unwrapped the cloth binding her chest. It had become loose over the course of the last couple of days and she re-wound it even tighter than before though her breasts hurt. She re-buttoned the shirt carefully and scampered back up the steps to the deck.

That morning, El Negro was everywhere, instructing the sailors on where to put what, making sure the men fixing the sails were doing a good job, checking the quality of the flour, the gunpowder and the other purchases. Once, Dido looked up from what she was doing and caught him watching her with a puzzled look on his face. In the next instant he turned away, and she thought no more about it. Her disguise had fooled everyone and soon, very soon, they would set sail and it would be too late for them to do anything even if they did discover her true identity. Dido smiled to herself as she helped to get the barrels into the hold. She had been worked like a man on the estate so why should anyone care if she chose to pretend she was a man in reality? Despite her exertions, Dido began to whistle, nothing she'd ever heard before, not even really a tune, it was more an expression of her happiness. Two or three months ago, she had been a slave, a woman who rose from sleep at the sound of a conch shell, who worked in the fields all day, rain or shine, to the crack of a whip. Now, as far as her shipmates knew, she was a man, Domingo Freeman, about to set sail on his first piratical voyage. And this, this life on a ship, was something she had chosen for herself, something she obtained on her own. Yes, Ian had helped her, but she'd been accepted on her own merit. Choice, it was all choice, her freedom to make a choice.

Dido worked with a will, anxious to prove herself the equal of the men, most, if not all of whom appeared to be seasoned sailors, accustomed to the ship and each other. Listening to them, she could tell many had sailed together before and that they looked forward to this new expedition. They spoke freely and easily. It was as El Negro said. All were equals, none considered himself better than the others though she and a young mulatto came in for a lot of jesting because they were landsmen, unaccustomed to ships.

"It is fine while we are in port but you'll have a hard time of it when we put to sea," one man warned her.

"He'll be wanting to join Davy at the bottom if we come upon a gale," another one said, laughing behind the hand covering a mouthful of rotten teeth.

Dido and the mulatto glanced at each other. Dido grinned to show she was taking it in good part but the young man's face tightened with worry. Dido herself had never heard of gales happening at sea. She suspected the men were making up stories to frighten her. Still, if storms could occur on land, what was to stop them from also happening at sea? The very idea of it made her queasy. Dido quickly turned her thoughts elsewhere, ignoring the men's sallies. Where could Old Philippa have gone, she wondered. And Ian. The boy had gone to ground with all the skill of the land crabs that made their home beneath the cool, soft earth. Sometime around the half-day when the men took a break from their work to eat and drink, Dido set off again to search through the town for the old woman and the boy. She had as much luck as the last time and returned to the ship downhearted.

"You look as gloomy as a man who has just learned of the death of all whom he loved." El Negro sat on a cask on the pier, smoking a clay pipe. Preoccupied with her thoughts, she had almost walked right past him, unaware.

"They might as well be," Dido said, and instantly regretted it. The gods sometimes took their devotees literally. *Oshun, I did not mean it, you know I did not.* "It's just time for leaving and…" She had not thought about it before but suddenly it occurred to her, when she left no one would know where she was. She was leaving everything she knew behind. If, Oshun forbid, she perished, no one would say the prayers for the dead over her body. Worse, if she fell into the sea, perhaps demons of the deep would snatch her spirit. Dido shivered.

"It's not too late to back out. Only the Navy presses men into service, the free men of the coast do not."

"I signed."

"We have many more than we need." He sucked on the pipe.

"Are you always so nonchalant with all matters?" Dido asked, recalling their first meeting.

El Negro frowned, blowing the smoke out through his nose.

"Always?" he quizzed.

She had made a mistake and he had caught it. "I mean, you take things so easily. Like this morning," she continued, suddenly inspired, "…when you said Morgan had changed his mind."

"Ah." His features relaxed. "It is simply this, boy, I don't mean to spend the precious hours of my life worrying over things that are of no moment to me now and that will be of no moment to anyone one hundred years from now."

"And whether I sail with your ship is one of those things?"

"Should it be otherwise?"

"Well, I'm coming," she snapped, nettled. "I put down my x and I'm coming. You'll just have to put up with this landlubber."

El Negro shrugged. "As you say. At least it will not now be a landlubber whose visage recalls that of mourners at a funeral."

She had forgotten all about Old Philippa and Ian during her exchange with the pirate captain but his comment brought her worries back.

"I've lost two friends of mine and have been unable to find them these past few days," she said. "I don't believe they are dead." Of the two, she would more quickly believe that of Old Philippa but she refused to entertain the idea.

"A man who hopes to make his life on the sea must not think he can continue to live the life of a landsman." He drew deeply on the pipe.

"Only landsmen have friends? Family? People who care about them?" Was there no woman who went to sleep with his name on her lips, whose bed felt empty without him beside her?

El Negro gave her an oblique look.

"Yes." The pipe clenched in his teeth, he straightened up from his perch, rising to stand. "You would do well to remember that. The sea is not for the faint-hearted or for those who treasure their family and friends. Now, if you're sure leaving this island is your desire, you'd best be getting back on deck. There is a lot more to do ere the sun sets." He waved his hand in a dismissive gesture and Dido did as she was told, glad to be away from his unnerving presence. He spoke as if he cared for no one and no one cared for him. She stole a look backward.

A tall, bearded, white man had come up to talk to him. Dido had noticed the man on the street earlier. Eddies of attention followed him and she'd heard his name whispered by the awestruck townspeople. It is Morgan, they said to each other, the commander of the fleet that will sail tomorrow against the Spaniards, the man who sacked Granada and sent its people scrambling through the forest for their lives. An air of power surrounded him but, as Dido watched, she compared his thick frame to El Negro's lean, lithe one and found it wanting. A heaviness surrounded the white man that was absent in her captain. She noted with pride how graceful and alert El Negro stood.

Dido spun away and walked back on board her ship.

By nighttime, the ship was noticeably lower in the water and Dido's whole body ached. Her hands which had begun to forget their roughness up in the hills were raw, the calluses already forming on her fingers and palms. She was becoming a real sailor. She listened attentively to the men around her, her ears alert for any snippet of information that would help her in her new life. By the time, she found her way to the hammock El Negro had given her, she knew that the front and back of ships had specific names and she knew what they were.

She knew too that the ship was guided by the whipstaff and that the anchor was raised by means of the capstan which the men turned like the donkeys did the crushers at the sugar mill on the days when no wind stirred. As she closed her eyes, Dido repeated these new words to herself, until, lulled by the rocking of the ship one word ran into another and she fell asleep, dreaming of treasure and of her family.

Chapter 6

A horn blew. The men on deck craned their necks to get a better look at whatever was happening on the dock. If El Negro was around, she could not see him. Dido squirmed her way to the side. A man in a long, flowing brown wig and a heavy coat with gold embroidery stood on the forecastle of Morgan's boat reading something. Although he held a speaking trumpet to his lips she could hear his words only indistinctly above the murmuring of the men around her and the cries of the seagulls wheeling overhead. Words and phrases floated over the sea. "Henry Morgan, Admiral and Commander in chief of all the ships, barques and other vessels."

"Further authorized and required to take prisoners of the Spanish nation."

"On the old pleasing account of no purchase no pay."

"Putting the men-slaves to the sword and the women-slaves prisoners to be brought hither." Dido grimaced at this. Would she have to fight slaves? The voice rolled on. "You are to endeavor by all means to make all sorts of people sensible of your moderation and your loathing to spill the blood of men." The man contradicted himself.

"Who is he?" she asked, nudging the sailor beside her.

"Don't you know your own Governor? That's Thomas Modyford, the king's representative as they say."

She had heard of an English king who ruled from a country far, far away but she'd never seen the Governor. Such personages did not, could not, concern slaves who were governed by their masters and Missuses.

"Does he rule over the planters?" she asked, wanting to make sure she understood his role and position in the island's society. She remembered his broken promise to do something about the cutthroats who stole the market vendors' money.

"Over everybody, except, maybe us. He answers only to the king, you see."

Dido mulled this over.

"When you say everybody except us…?"

"Because we're pirates, boy. We're free. No one rules us except as we lets him. Like El Negro, see?"

She thought she did but she wasn't sure and she had no more time for questions because the horns blared again. The men yelled. Somewhere, cannon roared, frightening Dido until she realized it was all part of the show. Governor Modyford descended from the forecastle to chat briefly with Morgan before being lowered into a small boat. Cannon fired again but the sound was fainter. Dido guessed it came from the fort on the headland, Fort Carlyle.

Morgan's ship began to make its stately way out of the harbor followed by the other two big ships of his fleet.

On the dock, sailors scrambled to release ships from bollards while others pulled at the rigging to raise the sails. A small boat carrying El Negro drew up alongside the *Fortune's Gift* and Dido realized he must have been on Morgan's ship with the other captains, listening to the Governor's words. Once on board, he issued orders to untie the ship and hoist the sails. Dido saw he was as excited as the men around her. His eyes glowed and there was a spring in his steps.

Port Royal was busy with the chaos of departure. Women shouted their goodbyes from the dock and men waved and blew kisses. A few made more lewd gestures aimed at showing the women what they could expect upon their return. Captains walked their decks issuing instructions and trying to impose order. Slowly, the smaller ships began to pull away from the dock, following in Morgan's wake like children behind their mother. Dido stood off to the side watching all the activity. Her eyes flew from face to face looking for Ian or even Old Philippa but among the strangers arrayed along the shore there was no one whom she knew.

In minutes, the ship was out in the open sea. Dido continued to stare at the receding island. Had she done the right thing? For one horrible minute, she wanted to shout "stop," to tell them she had changed her mind. The ship rolled on and Dido wanted to cry as the people seeing them off gradually blurred. In time, she couldn't see them anymore, just the blue hills and the fort looming over the town. Her mother, her sisters and brothers, were all there on the island she was leaving and none of them knew she was going, to them she could as well be dead. If she never saw them again they would not know what she had done, or that she had done it for them.

"Have you taken root there, boy?"

Dido's head snapped around. It was Richard, the man who had objected to her assignment to the *Fortune's Gift*. He sat on a chest with a torn sail on his lap watching her with a small grin on his lips and a strange look in his eyes.

"No, sir." She stood with her feet shoulder-width apart to steady herself and held on to the railing with both hands.

"Come over here, then. I want you to watch as I mend this sail so you will know how to do it."

"Yes, sir." Dido did not move. If only the sea were as calm as it had been in Port Royal but, now that the island was a blue haze in the distance, some of the waves rolling past the ship were as high as half-grown cane.

"Now, boy." His tone brooked no disobedience.

"Yes, sir, I am coming." She still didn't move.

"One foot in front of the other," said another sailor, encouragingly, his blue eyes kind but twinkling with merriment. "Don't worry about falling, the deck's as solid as a house."

Over on the starboard side, the mulatto retched, leaning over the sea to release his insides. Dido did her best to ignore him.

She took a step forward and paused. The dizziness made her weak. How had she ever managed the trip from Nevis? She took another step and released her hold on the railing. Another step and she almost fell as the deck rose and quickly gave away under her after a particularly high wave. Dido recovered her balance and bit her lips. She would not throw up. She would not throw up. She took another couple of steps. The ship pitched again and she fell, sprawling on the deck. The sailors laughed but Dido was up again in the next minute. She glared at her shipmates, willing to bet none of them was born with sea legs. They had had to learn just as she was learning. She took another couple steps and finally stood before Richard.

"Good," he said, his lips twitching. "Now see what I'm doing."

He showed her the stitches he had made and how he used the strap wrapped around his palm to drive the needle through the stiff cloth.

"Even and regular," he said, handing her the sail. Dido sat down, square-legged on the deck and followed his example. She was used to mending her own clothes ever since she was a child so it was no great challenge for her. The man soon left her to it after nodding his approval.

Around her, some of the sailors played cards while others occupied themselves cleaning their guns. After the previous days of hard work, the men seemed glad to relax as the ship ploughed on. From where she sat, Dido could see El Negro's back as he stood at the whipstaff, guiding the ship through the waves. Every now and then she looked up from her task, her gaze wandering over the deck to him though she took care that it should not linger on him too long. Her queasiness eased as she grew accustomed to the thrust and roll of the ship.

Dido worked away at the sails, her attention divided between the banter of her shipmates and her task. It should not have surprised her that she felt so happy but it did. Her mind was free and at ease, as if she had no worries, no cares, despite the fact that she was a woman masquerading as a man on a ship among thieves and murderers. Dido hummed to herself as she threaded needle through canvas and pulled, threaded and pulled. If she could have trapped that moment in time and stayed like that for all eternity she would have. The sun beamed down on her like an old friend and a steady breeze filled the ship's sails, caressing her face like a teasing child. If her mother could only see her now. The thought of her family brought a temporary gloom until she banished it away. She would make a fortune and come back and free those she loved, her mother and her brothers and her sister, maybe even Delia, if she could. Oshun would keep them safe until her return. She would not allow herself to think otherwise.

"Grub time."

A hand pushed a big pot of steaming food through the hatch followed quickly by a stack of tin bowls. Before Dido could even rise to her feet, most of the men had already snatched up the bowls and began ladling the food into them. There were no more bowls left.

"I…I need a bowl," she said, bending over to yell into the hatchway. She jumped back as a bowl tumbled up out of the dark depths toward her. Clutching it gratefully, she ladled some of the dark stew into it and was looking around for a spoon when another pot, this one filled with biscuits emerged from the hatch. Quicker off the mark this time, Dido grabbed two and retreated. She could go down to the hold where she'd stowed her things and get a spoon or she could mop up the beef and bean stew as best she could with the biscuits. It was not even close. Dido sank down on her haunches like she saw many of the other men do. She dipped the bread in the stew, using it as scoop, and took a big bite. She had not expected much but it was better than passable. The cook, whoever it was, had made an effort to use spices and the dish was quite savory. Dido took another bite and another until she had eaten the last crumb and wiped up the last drop of sauce. Following the lead of her shipmates she put the bowl back by the now-empty pot. In a few minutes, the same hairy arms emerged to retrieve everything.

Dido folded up the sails she had repaired and looked around for Richard. He was talking with some of the sailors and did not seem to notice that she had finished the work he'd assigned her. Dido wanted to find a quiet corner and sit down, her body still ached from all the lifting and carrying she'd done in the last couple of days but the ingrained habits of years on the plantation would not let her.

"Uh, excuse me," she said, going over to Richard.

"Yes?"

"I've finished."

He looked behind her at the stack of sails she'd laid across a barrel.

"So you have." He walked over to inspect them, turning the sails this way and that.

"Not bad," he said. "I think I'll make you our official sail mender." He smiled at her and returned to his conversation. Dido was nonplussed.

"Don't you have any other work for me?" At Beeston's Estate she'd had something to do every minute of the livelong day. The driver and the overseer made sure of that.

"There's nothing else as needs doing right now." Richard waved his hand at her in dismissal. Dido backed away, frowning at him suspiciously. Was this some sort of strange jest? Or perhaps a trick? Did he mean for her to become idle just so he could complain again about landlubbers to the captain? But no, he was completely wrapped up in his discussion with the other men. Dido shrugged, turned around and almost tripped over her own feet. El Negro was watching her from the forecastle.

"Come, boy," he called.

Dido's heart skipped a beat. Could he be summoning someone else? She glanced around but the other sailors were all involved in what they were doing. No one pushed past her to go to the captain. It was her he wanted, or rather, the man he thought she was, Domingo Freeman.

"Yes, sir." Dido hastened to obey. She tried not to feel put upon because the captain had singled her out for attention just when she was getting used to the idea that she would sometimes have free time on her hands.

"You are new to the sea and should seize every chance to learn the ways of it," El Negro said when she came up to him. "Come here."

Dido followed her captain to the side.

"Look, do you know what those are?" He pointed to some kind of fish darting through the waves. There were at least a dozen or more of them, their skins gray and gleaming.

"It is the first I've seen them. They're so fast."

"Porpoises, that's what they're called. Sailors are glad to see them when they're low on provisions for their meat is good, tender and tasty both."

"Are they fish?"

"Some consider them so but they have no scales and there are tales of them rescuing those who are shipwrecked. Where there is smoke there is often fire even if one cannot see it from where one stands. All I can say is, they make fine eating."

"A gift from the gods," Dido whispered, more to herself than to him.

"As you say."

"What country is that?" Dido asked, her attention drawn by the distant hazy blue silhouette of land she could see in glimpses though the gaps between the ships to their right.

"Jamaica, still. We'll round the western tip and then turn north by northwest to reach the South Cays. Morgan has decreed that we will rendezvous there before attacking Havana." But Dido no longer listened. She concentrated all of her being on keeping and holding sight of Jamaica. Without thinking, she stretched her arms over the side of the ship, opening and closing her hands as if she was trying to draw the island to her.

"It will be many weeks before you see the place again. Domingo!" Startled, Dido clutched her hands to her chest before dropping them quickly to her sides, fearing the gesture too womanly. She had not heard him. What had he said? "Why do you already seem to miss it so?"

"What? Jamaica?"

He nodded, frowning.

"It's my home. My family is there."

"Your family may indeed be there but it's not your home. You are from Guinea. All of our skin are from Guinea. This is not our land. Nor is it the white man's."

Dido looked around to see if any of the men had heard their captain. If they had they gave no sign of it or maybe they were accustomed to his views.

"Whose land is it?" she asked, dropping her voice, genuinely puzzled.

"Such as him. Look." He turned back to the ship and indicated a short, brown-skinned man on the lower deck. Dido had seen him before, noting with interest his flat brow and wide, dark eyes, as black as nightfall in the hills.

"Tainos," she said, suddenly remembering the word her mother had used. A few of them were slaves on Massa Simon's plantation but there were none at Beeston's.

"Yes, Tainos. They were here before us, before the white man even. Now they are as few as the barnacles on a newly-careened ship."

"Why?" she asked.

"Why what?"

"Why are they so few in number?"

"The diseases of the white man, and his greed also, have killed them off."

He must have read the puzzlement on her face because he went on to explain.

"Hundreds, perhaps thousands of them were killed by overwork on the white man's plantations. Previously they'd lived a life of ease. Many others died from diseases like smallpox which were unknown to them. They succumbed like babes in arms."

"You pity them." She could hear it in his voice, see it in his face.

"Pity? I would not call it so." He spread his hands in front of him, shrugged. "I feel regret, awe, a number of things when I look at Yacahüey. But mostly I feel angry at the gods for the world they have made."

"Oludumare did not will this." She could not say how she knew this was so but she was convinced of it, nevertheless.

"No? Then they are powerless, too? So what's the use of them?"

Dido was scandalized.

"Use? Gods are not for use. They…they…" She groped for words. "They help us…they protect us from those who would do us harm. They answer our prayers."

"Are you saying the Taino did not pray well enough?"

Dido looked at the man he'd called Yacahüey and grimaced. "Mayhap their gods are different and were weaker than the god of the white man who is indeed very powerful."

"Bah!" El Negro rubbed his hands together as if washing them. "Man is alone. The gods, if they exist, care nothing for our well-being."

"So why is it that the white man is so powerful, almost like a god himself, with the power of life or death over us?"

El Negro's eyes closed to slits. "The white man has only the power you grant him." His nostrils flared. "Remember that. Remember also that he has no power over me and none over you now unless you give it to him."

"It is Morgan, a white man, who is commander of these ships," Dido objected.

"Morgan commands me only for as long as I let him," El Negro said. He lowered his voice. "And when I have had my use of him and of his battles then I'll take my leave."

"Where will you go?" Dido asked, alarmed. He spoke like someone thinking of vanishing under the cover of night, leaving ship and crew behind.

"Who knows?" His expression turned mischievous. "The world is a big place. Bigger I think than even we know. Who knows where a man with a good ship and a good crew may not end up?" He winked at her.

So he was not thinking of leaving them behind. Sure that her relief must show on her face, Dido attempted to distract him with a question and he spent the next few minutes explaining what sails were used when, and why.

"It's a lot to learn," Dido said, when he was finished. She was not sure she'd understood everything he'd said but she had not wanted to interrupt or to seem like a numbskull.

"Do not worry, boy. I've the feeling you'll take to the sea like a true sailor. Give it time." He patted her on the back.

Not twenty feet away from where they were, a man clambered over a board sticking out from the bow, his pants pushed down to just above his knee and his bottom bared to all and sundry behind him.

"What…?" Dido could scarcely get the question out. Was the man mad?

"That is the head. Where you go to relieve yourself." As soon as El Negro said it, Dido realized she needed to go. She had not relieved herself since the previous day when she was on shore and had taken advantage of the public toilets in Bird's Alley.

"There is nowhere else?" Dido looked around wildly. If she went there in full view of everyone her secret would be out. How would El Negro react to discovering she had falsely declared herself a man in order to sign up? The articles were very clear that no women were allowed on board once the ship was under sail.

In front of her, the man concluded his business, backed down the board and, once on the deck, hauled up his pants and walked away buttoning them.

"Go on, boy. You've nothing to fear. Just hold on tight and you'll be fine." El Negro's lips twitched. Did she imagine the speculative look in his eyes? Why did he watch her so closely?

"Uhh, yes." She had not even thought about the danger of finding herself perched on a plank over the tossing sea. Was this how her adventure ended?

"If you wait much longer we'll be in a passage where the sea will be rougher. Best to get it over with now."

"Captain." Richard came up on the forecastle. "I'd like a word."

El Negro motioned him forward and turned away from Dido who took the opportunity to sidle across to where the board jutted from the ship. It was a solid plank of wood, as thick as her little finger, into which a hole had been carved two-thirds of the way along its length. Below her the waves rolled against the ship, blue and indifferent to the cares of a young woman masquerading as a man. Prodded by the sensations of her stomach, Dido mounted it as she had seen the man do, hitching one leg up and then the other so she straddled the board. The ship pitched. Dido suppressed a small scream. "Oshun. Oshun." Whispering the goddess's name over and over, she carefully inched her way down the board until she was almost directly over the hole. Not daring to look back, she gripped the plank tightly between her thighs and released one hand to unbutton her breeches. With a quick movement she lifted her hindquarters in the air and pulled the breeches down while launching herself forward so that when she landed her bottom was squarely over the hole. Holding on for dear life, she released the contents of her bowels and her bladder, hardly daring to look around her at the other ships, much less to look down at the sea below her dangling legs. When she was finished, she backed away down the board, stopping to draw up her pants and re-button them before pushing herself backward onto the deck. She had done it. She had climbed up on that perilous mount and done what she had to do and made it back on deck.

Dido glanced around to see if anyone was watching her but El Negro was deep in his conversation with Richard. The two men appeared almost to be arguing. Nobody looked in her direction. She had mounted the head as a man and come off it as a man with none the wiser. Dido breathed a sigh of relief.

Chapter 7

L and. They were within sight of land. The news raced through the crew of the *Fortune's Gift* who crowded the deck, craning their necks to see. But it was late evening. The islands were only dark shapes in front of them. The *Fortune's Gift* had made good time and left the faint lights of the other, bigger, ships behind.

On the forecastle, El Negro stood behind the man at the whipstaff, helping him navigate among the islets until they reached a wide harbor where he gave orders to drop anchor.

"Are these the South Cays?" Dido asked Yacahüey who stood beside her. She had to raise her voice to be heard over the squeaky groans of the capstan and the excited talk of her shipmates.

"Among my people they were just called *bieke*, small places." His heavy accent lent his words a throaty burr. "But now, yes, they are known as the South Cays."

"What are they like? Have you been there?"

Yacahüey shrugged. "Full of iguanas and yuccas and not much else." He waved out to sea. "The Isle of Pines is much better with many streams and good soil for planting."

"Do people live there?"

"My people did once but the Spanish removed us to work on their mines in Cuba and the *yucayeque* is empty. The water vessels lie broken and the fishing nets are heavy with seaweeds."

"The yuca...yuca...?"

"*Yucayeque*. It means village."

Dido nodded, not knowing what to say. Yacahüey looked neither sad nor angry as El Negro had, yet there was something bleak and hollow in his voice, as if the years of hurt his people had suffered tore at his heart. Dido shivered. Remembering her conversation with El Negro, she looked over at the forecastle. The captain and some other men were looking back the way they had come, waiting for the other ships to join them in the harbor.

"Domingo! Hey, boy. Domingo!" A man clapped his hands at her.

"Why do you shout? I'm not deaf."

"Might as well be," the man grumbled. "I've been calling you ever since.

Cap't wants you to bring him a tankard of beer."

Dido frowned. She'd seen the captain issue no order.

"Me?"

"It's you as named Domingo, ain't it? Best hurry up about it. He's not one should be kept waiting."

Dido hurried off, clambering down the hatchway that led to the lower deck where the cook stirred a big iron pot on a brick stove.

"What do you want?"

"The captain asked for a tankard of beer."

"So why are you here?"

"I…I thought I'd get it from you. Don't you have any?"

"Of course I have, but the captain's got his own supply. His own barrels of beer and his own tankards. If he wants something to drink, it's from his cabin you'll get it."

"Oh." Dido turned to go back up on deck.

"You can tell him, supper will be ready in two shakes of a duck's tails," he called out after her.

Dido hurried to the captain's Great Cabin under the forecastle, muttering under her breath. Why hadn't the man who delivered the message told her where to go? Now the captain would be irritated with her. She opened the door and slipped in.

The Great Cabin was aptly named, being about three times the size of her hut at Beeston's. The room contained a proper hardwood bed such as she'd seen in the Great House, a number of chairs of various designs, and two long tables. Rolls of paper sprouted from a stand by the door while an open armoire by the bed revealed where the captain kept his fancy clothes when he was on the sea. There were three casks on her right. Dido grabbed up one of the pewter tankards she found on a small table. She had just dipped it in a barrel when the door opened behind her.

"Why are you taking so long?" El Negro snapped.

"I'm sorry. I went below deck. I did not know you had beer in your cabin."

"Give it me." He held out his hand for it, sank into one of the chairs and took a long draft.

"Have one," he said, motioning with the tankard and spilling a couple drops of the beer.

Dido considered refusing but she was thirsty.

"Do you have water?"

He pointed to a half-barrel that sat on the table beside her.

Dido helped herself to a tankard full but she almost spat it out. The tankard had not been properly washed and the water tasted strongly of beer.

"It'll taste even worse when we have been weeks on the sea. You'd better drink it while you can," El Negro said, his dark eyes amused. He took another long swallow and held the tankard out to her to be refilled.

"You know," he said, when she handed it back to him. "You may speak as yourself around me."

Dido's throat constricted as if she'd drank an obi man's poison and could not breathe.

"I don't understand," she said, keeping her voice neutral.

"I know who you are, Missy-boy. Have known it almost from the first though you've disguised yourself well."

Dido shook her head, not trusting herself to speak. She clutched the tankard to stop her hands from shaking.

"Your words puzzle me."

"You're the girl, Dido, from Beeston's Estate, who I met two months gone and took to Anna, the seamstress."

"You're wrong," she managed to say, her tongue thick and heavy, barely able to form the words. What magic was this? He had but seen her, seen the woman she was, once. She shook her head again. "No," she said. "I'm a man. A man. I have not heard of this place you mention. I come from the area between Esquivel and San Jago de la Vega. My family is there." That much at least was true.

"If you wish it so, Missy-boy, we will speak no more of it." He smiled. "Know this, Dido…Domingo, I'll not reveal your secret. You had no thought of turning pirate when we talked on the road and I do not know why you're here. I don't believe you chose this lightly but I consider that, perhaps, my words influenced you." He leaned forward, his expression grave. "If that's so, then I bear the responsibility for your safety."

"I, alone, am responsible for myself," Dido burst out. "I am free."

He held up a hand to quiet her. "You're a woman on my ship. I should have you put ashore on one of the nearby cays but there is a good chance you'd die there or be picked up and used most sorely by whoever found you."

He wouldn't leave her anywhere. He couldn't. He mustn't. If he tried to force her off the ship, she would fight him off. She had to stay on the *Fortune's Gift*.

"It is because of me you're here. Do you deny you would have remained on your plantation if we'd not spoken?"

"I do deny it. I'd never have stayed there." But neither would she have thought of turning pirate. Missus Sarah's treachery would have driven her to run away but she would probably have gone up into the hills or fled to the *marronas*.

"Would you have come here to my ship?"

Ah. He thought she'd signed up with him on purpose. How like a man to believe all a woman did was for his benefit or designed for his notice. She kept silent. He could think what he wanted.

He nodded slowly, confirming his suspicions to himself.

"I'll see you returned safely to Port Royal. After that, do not think to do this again. Some men believe a woman aboard a ship under sail assures the ship's doom, others will want their way with her. Our articles were not written for spite but out of common sense which you have shown little of in devising this adventure."

Dido glared at him. It was on the tip of her tongue to tell him why she was on his ship but she restrained herself.

"I do not like this 'Missy-boy' you're calling me."

"No?" He grinned. "I, on the other hand, find it a charming moniker for a charming rarity." He leaned back in his chair and looked her up and down. "Charming," he said again.

"One of your crew might overhear you," she protested.

"No-one will learn your secret from me. I promise you this. You will not be discovered."

A promise was a comfort to a fool but she'd have to place her faith in him. She had no choice. "If that is all…"

"It is not. I've been thinking you should serve as my cabin boy. It will keep you out of the way of the men though none seem to suspect. Richard would like to send you down to the bilge but you cannot do such heavy work."

Impelled by curiosity and glad his thoughts had turned elsewhere, Dido asked something that had been on her mind ever since Richard put her to mending the sails.

"Is he the overseer? I do not understand his position. He behaves as if he is as much captain as you."

"Richard? Richard is my bo'sun. He's next in charge after the quartermaster. Even ahead of the quartermaster, in some ways. He has not worked you ill or troubled you, has he? I've been preoccupied with our departure and then with the plans for this expedition."

"No. He treats me in a passable manner."

El Negro tipped his head back to drain the dregs from the tankard.

"So you'll be my cabin boy, Missy-boy?" His eyes flashed with amusement. He was clearly much pleased with the nickname he'd given her. She suspected her dislike of it added to his pleasure.

"I do not really understand what it means."

"You'll fetch and carry for me and generally do my bidding. Richard says you sew an excellent line so I think we'll make you our official sail mender. Of course, you'll do anything else that needs to be done and is within your capability."

"But I'll mainly be working at your direction."

"Mainly. It will be best if we are to continue with this deception."

Dido thought about it. She did not see how she could refuse.

"Suppose I…I mean, suppose I'd rather not be your…er…cabin boy." She darted a glance at him to see how he took this.

His lips twitched.

"I was not asking you, but worry not. Your duties will not be overly onerous. I am not crippled. I can dress myself and require only minimal assistance on rising. I do not sleep well and expect that you will turn in long before I am ready to do the same."

"Wait…you mean, I'll have to help…to help you with your toilet?" The thought sucked the air from her throat.

"I'll require you to bring me water in the mornings and to bring me my meals and suchlike, nothing more. The boy who did these things for me left the ship in Tortuga and since then I've had no-one."

Dido shrugged. The tasks he'd outlined were nothing compared to hoeing the ground for the ratoons, cutting the mature canes, picking cotton in season, or any of the dozens of things she'd done throughout her life.

"Since you have no objections, Missy-boy." His lips twitched again and Dido frowned. He was having fun at her expense. "Perhaps you'll be so kind as to fetch dinner. Richard and a few others usually join me in the cabin so bring a tureen full of whatever slop Cook is dishing out tonight. I have bowls in there." He indicated a small cupboard to the right of the door.

By the time Dido returned, the captain, Richard and three other men, were sitting around the table, drinking and talking. Dido placed the tureen on the table, took some bowls out of the cupboard and began to ladle out the chicken and crab stew Cook had prepared.

"...as big a force as possible," El Negro said as she handed him his bowl. He nodded his thanks at her and continued speaking. "I know Havana's strength."

"The Spanish do be more wary now but Morgan knows what he's doing," Richard responded. "He was with Davis in New Spain and knows the ways of the devils."

"I don't say he does not, my friend, but Havana is not a little town." El Negro paused to chew his food, swallowed and continued. "For more than a hundred years it has been the place where the ships of the fleet meet before heading back to Spain. Its fortifications are continually strengthened. They are not to be underestimated."

"You sound as if your mind has turned from this expedition," broke in a gruff-voiced white man who spoke with an accent that reminded Dido of Ian. "If that's so, let us not dawdle. We can be on our way by dawn."

"Not without Morgan seeing us," objected the sharp-eyed one who wore a kerchief on his head as Dido did. "We'd be fools to think to outrun him. We'll have to wait until we are on the open sea again to try slipping away."

Dido watched them wolf down the food. A wave of nausea hit her but she shook her head when El Negro motioned for her to take a seat. He cocked an eyebrow. "Not hungry," she mouthed. He turned back to the conversation and seemed to forget she was there but she took the opportunity to study him and watch his interactions with the other men. It was obvious they deferred to him though they had their own strong opinions and were ever ready to voice them.

"This fight is not that of my people," said the man with the accent. "We have our own struggles with the English and I would rather be out hunting a rich prize than following some fool in their service."

"You talk so of your country-mate?" El Negro's tone was mocking.

"By my faith, the man is as Welsh, why, as you yourself," the man grunted. Laughter rose around him. "He may have been born a Welshman but the man is so taken up with his English friends he's only Welsh in name now. Were the Mari Llwyd to knock at the door of his Great House in North Clarendon, the revelers would have to exact some merry punishment for he'd not know enough to give them mead, or even rum punch."

"Be that as it may, I've pledged this ship and its men to his service for as long as he may have need of us," El Negro said, pushing away his bowl. He took a swallow of beer. "I'll not go back on my word. Do any of you challenge this?"

Dido's gaze flew around the table. One by one the men shook their heads.

"Good. Now I want to hear no more of deserting this mission. I'll join the other captains on the *Satisfaction* tomorrow and we will make our plans. I'll reveal them to you and the men on my return."

"You will tell him of your own misgivings about the strength of the fleet?" asked Richard.

"I've done so before but I will again." El Negro's expression was grim. "He has promised that Davis, Smith, L'Ollonais and the others will join us with big ships of thirty guns and more but nothing has been heard of Francois since he sailed for Nicaragua and who knows where the others are."

"Up along the Carolinas or around the Bahamas islands getting rich off plunder, as like as not," the Welshman said, gloomily.

"Maybe hanging from a gallows in Boston or run ashore on some cay somewhere," the sharp-eyed man countered, motioning to Dido to refill his tankard.

The smell of food commingled with the odor of sweat and the heat in the cabin made Dido wish she'd been firmer about not wanting to be cabin boy. As fascinating as the talk around the table was, she would have much preferred being outside where at least the cold night air could have washed over her face, freshening her spirits.

El Negro must have seen her distress because he called her over to tell her she could leave.

"Return early in the morning to clear away these dishes," he instructed her.

"Yes, captain." Would she always have to follow the orders of others? Dido pushed open the door and took a deep breath of the fresh air that instantly blew against her cheeks.

That night she dreamed of ships made of gold that glimmered in the sun and saw herself and her family walking about the streets of an unfamiliar town dressed in silks and other fine clothes. A man walked on her right, their arms interlinked. When she looked, it was El Negro beside her. She was so happy she thought she'd burst.

Something prodded her foot.

"I am busy now, can't you see?" Dido mumbled. She squeezed El Negro's arm, delighting in the feel of the muscle beneath his silks.

"Busy now, are ye? You'll be even busier in a minute. Get up this instant or I'll upend you, I will."

Who dared to speak to her that way? Did they not know she was a lady? El Negro looked puzzled. She smiled to reassure him and patted his hand. How good it felt to touch him so freely.

Suddenly, something swung her up and then down. Dido fell to the ground. Her eyes flew open but the curse on her tongue died instantly.

She was no lady but a sailor, cabin boy to El Negro and it was morning. She'd been dreaming. The gruff voice speaking to her belonged to Cook who loomed over her, grinning at her disorientation.

"What?"

"Time for you to take the captain some hot water for his toilet."

Dido scrambled to her feet. "Where is it?"

"Below deck, boy. Do you think I'm going to heat it and do your work as well?"

Dido followed him to the hold without answering. She picked up the big black kettle from which the steam was still rising. Gritting her teeth, she climbed slowly back up and walked carefully to the cabin. She knocked. When there was no answer, she pushed open the door. El Negro lay on his back, sleeping. She noticed that he still wore the pants of the day before and wondered if washing his clothes was among her duties. He had not said but she rather thought it might be. When he took them off she would do what she could to spruce them up.

Dido put the kettle down on the big table where the men had eaten. She gathered up the bowls and tankards, trying to keep them from clinking against each other. She had just tiptoed back to the door and was about to open it when El Negro spoke.

"These pants need mending," he said. "Will you do that for me today, Missy-boy?"

Dido clutched the things in her hands to her chest and spun around, startled.

"I did not know you were awake. Good morning."

"I expect to be gone for most of the day," he said, ignoring her greeting. "You must occupy yourself as best you can learning the ways of the ship in my absence."

"Why are you so insistent on that? You've remarked on it more than once."

"About learning the ways of the ship?"

Dido nodded.

"When you look around you how many black faces do you see?"

"Three," Dido answered after a pause while she thought about it.

"You are counting yourself and me?'

Again, Dido nodded.

"And the mulatto?"

"He's black too, isn't he?" It had always confused her that someone born of parents of different races should be considered to belong only to one.

"Yes and no."

"Don't you trust him?"

"He is half-white and it is that part I don't trust for I do not know how well the humors of the different races can mix in one body."

"But you've not really explained why you want me to learn the ways of the ship. You don't even think I should be on board."

"That's true but you are like me, Missy-boy. See." He got up off the bed and put his arm against hers. "We are the exact same shade." It was true. Dido looked down at their arms. All she had to do was turn hers in a certain way and they would be interlinked as they had been in her dream. Of course, she had not been holding any dishes then. Her mind wandered away to the dream. It had been a foolish one. She was no lady and she certainly wasn't El Negro's wife. Nor did she want to be. Did pirates even marry?

"We must learn as much as we can from the whites–all of us, men and women, too. Who knows when we will have need of that knowledge?" El Negro crossed his arms and stepped away from her. "Surely we who have been stolen from our homes and brought to this new world have more right to seek its riches than those of any other nation? But to do that we men must become sailors, good sailors, so that even when they would as sooner spit on us than on a dog yet they will hold back their water knowing that they need us. Knowledge is the treasure women also should seek."

Dido frowned.

"On land?"

"Wherever they find themselves, Missy-boy. Go." He waved her away. "The water is becoming cold while I talk. Return later for my pants and have them fixed by this afternoon. I have only two pairs I wear on board."

"Yes, captain. As you wish, captain." If he recognized her sarcasm, he gave no sign. Dido stalked through the cabin door.

Later that morning, she clambered down to the hold and begged some warm water off Cook to wash the mended but stained and soiled trousers. She draped the wet pants over one of the cannons to dry and ate her breakfast with her shipmates around mid-day.

El Negro returned as the sun was setting. He had put on some of his pirate finery to go talk to his commander and wore a long, silk waistjacket of a deep red color over a white linen shirt, blue velvet breeches, and a pair of shiny black boots. As he came closer, Dido saw that the black sash across his chest held two pistols.

She wondered if he brought news of their departure from the Cays but El Negro stopped only to talk to the sharp-eyed man before striding to the door of his cabin. Dido wondered if she should go to him or leave him alone, his lowering expression was forbidding, but, with his hand on the handle he looked around and motioned her to him with a curt nod. Dido slid down from the chest on which she had been sitting and hurried behind him.

"Did you mend my pants as I asked?"

Dido pointed to the bed where she'd placed the dry calico trousers. He picked them up, turning them this way and that.

"A good job, Missy-boy. Richard did not lie about your skills."

She could control herself no longer. "Will we sail for Cuba on the morrow? Have the other ships arrived?" She'd seen nothing of them but the crew was full of talk about the absentee captains. Some speculated that maybe they were moored in another harbor waiting for Morgan as the commander himself waited. Others of a more dire turn of mind claimed Francois L'Ollonais and the missing pirates sought greater prizes off New Spain and had no intention of joining the expedition.

"They've not arrived and our commander has decreed that we wait." He sat down on the bed and stretched his leg out to her. It took Dido a minute to realize she was supposed to help him remove his boots.

"I and others have persuaded him of the foolhardiness of attacking Havana without a greater force, both in men and guns, but he is an unpredictable man. The Spanish have held the city for more than a hundred years and fortified it well, too well." His voice dropped and Dido realized he was continuing the argument begun on Morgan's ship. "Does he think the forts of El Morro and San Salvador are made of nought but straw?" He passed his hand over his eyes, looking weary. Dido's heart went out to him. Being a pirate captain was a more complex thing than she'd thought.

"Would you like your dinner?" she asked, wanting to offer him whatever ease she could. "I can go tell Cook."

"I ate on Morgan's ship. Thank you. Now I think I'd appreciate some time alone. I've need of my own counsel. Attend me in the morning."

"Yes, captain." Dido let herself out of the cabin, surprised that she felt both disappointed and glad.

Outside, a man jostled her and Dido suddenly became aware that something was going on. The men stood together in a large knot, the mood among them raw and tense.

"...free men." Dido caught the last words of a speech of which many approved if the shouts were anything to go by.

The sharp-eyed man stood on the forecastle watching everything. Even in the encroaching darkness, Dido could see he was angry. His eyes were narrowed almost to slits and his arms banded his chest as if he hoped they could thus contain his rage. Beside him, Richard clapped his hands for silence.

"We'll do as the captain says," Richard said. "He wishes us to wait until Morgan is ready to sail so we'll wait."

"We signed on for booty," shouted the man beside her whose elbow had dug into her ribs without him even noticing, he was that intent on the five men standing on the forecastle. Four had dined with El Negro the night before but the fifth was Yacahüey. Dido was surprised to see him there. The Taino stood with his arms hanging loosely at his sides, somehow managing to look both alert and thoughtful at the same time.

"Booty," the other men cried, though she could see some among them were silent.

"And you'll get booty," the sharp-eyed one retorted. "All of you know the reputation of El Negro. You know he took this ship from a Spanish merchant, he and six others, only three of whom are here with us on this mission. Each of those six men received three thousand pieces of eight and gold and precious gems besides. He gave each man his proper share and was generous withal, giving the one who was wounded more than was his due."

"It's true." The men around her murmured, nodding. "He does not lie."

The man who had shouted "booty" scowled, not liking the way things were turning.

"I trust El Negro and El Negro trusts Morgan so we'll wait," the sharp-eyed one said.

"Havana has not been sacked in many years, it will also wait," Richard interjected. "And while it waits it will grow fat, like a pig being readied for a feast. Is it not better to roast a pig when it is good and ready than to kill it before it has grown fat and stupid with its increased girth?"

The men laughed.

"Go now and sleep. Dream well of the doubloons you will take and of the wenches who wait for your return."

The men laughed again, shouting and clapping. Their mood had changed in a flash from what it was when she had joined them but a glance at the face of the man beside her told Dido they were not all happy. There could be trouble if they didn't make a move on Cuba soon.

Chapter 8

El Negro was already up and poring over a document spread out on the table before him when Dido entered the Great Cabin the following morning. He greeted her absently and, after she'd poured out the water into his wash-basin, she retreated to the door.

"Is there anything else you wish me to do?" she asked. He was wearing the trousers she'd mended and it pleased her to see how well they looked after her attentions.

"Do you know what this is?" He motioned to the paper in front of him.

Dido had glanced at it when she passed but had not been able to make head nor tail of the strange drawing that depicted neither man nor beast. She drew closer to take another look but the drawing remained a mystery to her. She shook her head.

"It is a map of the Spanish Main. See," he pointed. "This is Jamaica from where we have come." Dido looked but was unable to find what she knew of Jamaica, the cane, the mountains, the trees, and the rivers, on the paper.

"It doesn't look like Jamaica," she said.

"It's a representation. That's what maps are, a representation of the real world. This is the shape of Jamaica." His finger traced an outline. "And, over here, see how much bigger it is…this is Cuba. We're here." He pointed to some small dots like a scattering of black pepper.

"Where is Guinea?"

"Guinea is not on this map. I've seen Guinea on a map that also showed the England of Modyford's king and the countries of Spain and Portugal also. Guinea is very much bigger than these countries." He fell silent, staring at the map once more, his expression somber. Dido would have liked to smooth his brow and rub those hunched shoulders but instead she quietly opened the door and let herself out.

El Negro did not emerge from his cabin that day nor the next but his officers, Richard, the sharp-eyed man whom she'd learned bore the title of quartermaster and was named William, Yachüey, who was the carpenter, the Welshman, James, who was the navigator, and Drummond, the master gunner—these she saw go in and out throughout the day. She herself took him his meals but he was not in a talkative mood and hardly spoke to her.

On the third day, when she was beginning to wonder if something ailed him, he came out wearing a dark blue waistcoat over a shirt of a lighter hue, loose red pants that reached just below his knees and the black boots she'd seen before. This time, only one pistol was tucked into the red sash he'd tied around his waist. A red kerchief at his neck gave him an air of distinction.

It was time for another meeting with Morgan. Two more ships had sailed within hailing distance of the fleet. They rested at anchor beyond the sand spit at the mouth of the small harbor, their masts visible over the tops of the mangroves that grew there. They were not the big ships Morgan had expected. Neither carried more than eighteen guns according to the discussions she'd heard among El Negro's grim-faced crew. More than a few of them had cast angry glances, not only in the direction of Morgan's ship, but also at the closed door of their captain's cabin. Dido had fretted over it, wondering if she should tell him but she knew William was aware of the men's mounting dissatisfaction by the way his eyes tightened as he watched them.

When El Negro came out on deck, the men crowded around him.

"When do we leave?" they clamored. "We've had enough of this lying about."

El Negro's expression grew thunderous.

He looked about him fiercely and the men quieted.

"We leave when Morgan says we leave." His voice was dry and hard, flinty. "Any one who harbors second thoughts about his desire to be part of this expedition or about being a member of my crew, may tell me so now. I need not remind you of the penalty for mutiny in the articles you signed."

"This ain't mutiny," a man muttered.

"We ain't mutinying," another man said. "We just want to know that be all. We been here three days now. Morgan said we'd leave in three days and the time is up now."

"You do not decide when the time is up. When you own a ship, as I do this one, then you'll decide but until then…" His words hung in the air. His smile did not quite reach his eyes. He was reminding them that he'd taken the ship with only six men. He had not needed a big crew to gain a prize. How many other pirate captains could say the same thing?

The men muttered but they dispersed.

The way before him cleared, El Negro strode past Dido.

"Come," he said.

Dido looked around to see if he was talking to someone else but no, it had to have been her he'd spoken to, there was no-one else close enough. She hurried after him, dodging ropes and crewmen. By the time she reached the side of the ship where the launch had already been lowered, he was halfway down the rope ladder.

"Go," Yacahüey said. The Taino was among the small knot of men around her.

"Go where?" she asked. She was having trouble understanding these terse orders. What was it these men expected of her now?

"Down."

Dido stepped backward. He could not possibly be serious. Into that small boat that was barely bigger than the captain's bed? She definitely did not think so.

"The captain wants some of us to go with him today and he has chosen you," Yacahüey explained, his tone impassive. "It is a great honor he does you." His tone suggested he thought, *too* great.

Dido looked back down at the boat bobbing in the water. The Taino was right. It *was* an honor but one she could have done very well without. El Negro looked up at her, his face split in a wide, mischievous smile. The man had probably only invited her so he could enjoy her discomfiture. Gritting her teeth, she swung over the side and lowered herself carefully down. The boat pitched and rocked as she stepped onto it and Dido pitched with it, collapsing across her captain's lap. His arms rose to catch her but she pushed him away only to fall at his feet a split second later. Above her, she could hear laughter and ribald comments. Dido scrambled backward. Gripping the sides of the boat with each hand, she hung on for dear life. What did it matter that her crewmates thought her a pitiful landlubber? To them she, at least, remained a pitiful *male* landlubber and that was the most important thing.

"It is more comfortable in the seat," El Negro said, grinning at her.

"I am well enough here."

He shrugged.

They were joined in short order by Yacahüey, Richard and William all of whom she now noticed were almost as well-dressed as El Negro in their waistcoats and breeches. The launch pulled away from their ship. It must have reached the *Satisfaction* in minutes but to Dido, still sitting on the bottom of the boat, it felt like an entire day. Four rope ladders dangled from Morgan's ship for the convenience of the arriving captains. El Negro boarded first, followed by William, then Richard, then Yacahüey and finally it was her turn. Dido contemplated staying put but the oarsman scowled at her as if he resented the fact that such a lily-livered specimen should have been granted the chance to sit in on a meeting with the famed Morgan. Dido quickly climbed the ladder not wanting to be left behind with the surly man.

The deck of the *Satisfaction* was crowded with pirates, most of whom, she was relieved to see were dressed no better than she was. Dido turned her head in time to see Yacahüey disappearing through a door at the stern. She pushed through Morgan's sailors but was blocked by a burly man, with arms as thick as small barrels, who stepped in front of her.

"Where do you think you be going?"

"In there. I'm with El Negro."

"Who says? I didn't see you come on board just now."

Just then the door opened from inside. El Negro beckoned to her. The man stepped aside and Dido scuttled past.

"Stay close to me," El Negro murmured in her ear.

"I would have if I'd seen where you went," she hissed. If he hadn't come for her at that moment, the beefy man might have just tossed her into the sea as some sort of impostor. Which, in a manner of speaking, she was but not in the way he thought.

"Follow me and try to keep your wool-gathering for when you are back on land," El Negro murmured again, his breath tickling her ear.

Dido decided to let that one pass. The room she had entered was about two or three times the size of El Negro's on the *Fortune's Gift* and was even more comfortably appointed. Wall hangings covered the sides and several armchairs were ranged against the bed. Morgan had done his best to enhance the room's ability to hold as many men as possible. Two tables were pushed together end to end across almost the whole width of the room. Every place was taken or so it seemed to Dido but, as El Negro approached, room was made for him reminding her of the esteem in which he was held. Once seated, he looked back at her and, with a slight motion of his head, indicated that she was to approach and stand with Richard and the others behind him. Her crewmates didn't look her way as she joined them but Dido was undisturbed by this as, to a man, they appeared to be sizing up both their surroundings and their companions. Though there were probably around thirty men squeezed into the room, they made no large commotion, speaking quietly to each other.

The commander, himself, sat where the tables joined together, in the middle, not far from El Negro's own position. Watching him, Dido thought he looked every inch a leader of men but though he seemed as lively as everyone else, the dry, wrinkled skin around his eyes and mouth told a different story. The man was tired and his skin had a grayish tinge, as if he was troubled by some disorder of the blood or the organs. He looked around, appearing to take a count of who was present. Satisfying himself that all the captains were now accounted for, he slapped his hands on the table and called for silence.

"I told you we'd sail in three days and that time has now come," he rasped. "Yet only two more ships have joined us." He nodded at a couple of men to his right and Dido supposed them to be the recently arrived captains. "We have discussed the disadvantages of an attack on such a city as Havana without a large force. I wish to know whether those of you who felt then that our numbers were insufficient, feel any differently now that the captains of the *Laughing Dragon and the Wildcat* are with us."

El Negro was the first to speak. "No," he said, firmly but without raising his voice. "The addition of these ships leaves my opinion unchanged. As I said three days ago, we'll need at least five more of greater size for any attack on Havana to succeed."

"Even with the likes of Abraham on our side?" asked Morgan, frowning.

El Negro inclined his head in the direction of a tall man with shoulder-length hair the color of a sugar loaf. "Had we one hundred more marksmen as expert as he, I'd say we might have a chance. In the event…" He spread his hands leaving the rest unspoken.

"I do not agree," said a man with a thick, bull-like neck who sat at Morgan's left. "We can take Havana. The Spanish are nothing but sniveling cowards. Sores burnt it to the ground with only 200 men and we have at least twice that."

Men nodded around the table.

"Jean, you Frenchmen persist in thinking nothing has changed in the last hundred years," El Negro said, leaning forward to speak directly to the man. "From everything I've heard, Havana was little more than a village when Sores set it on fire. Isn't it true that there was then only one small fort and less than a thousand residents? Now it's a small city with more than eight thousand citizens as well as hundreds of slaves. Now it has three large castles for its defense. El Morro alone is formidable enough but do you discount San Salvador and the other?"

"We can attack under cover of darkness," Jean broke in, his accent thickened by emotion.

"Yes," agreed another. "If we surprise the city, the deed will be done before the forts can ready their defense."

What?" asked a red-haired man, at the lower right end of the table. "And fight our way through the streets? I do not understand your meaning."

"Of course not, Thomas," answered the man who had spoken before. "That would invite near-certain death. I propose we land some ways distant and make our way into the city by night as Thomas suggested, find the houses of their priests and take them prisoner to guarantee our safety. The papists will never fire at us while we hold their precious *padres* captive."

Morgan rubbed his chin.

"El Negro, what do you say to this?" he asked.

"It is a nonsensical proposal."

The men who backed it tried to shout him down but Morgan raised his hand and they subsided into silence. The commander nodded to El Negro to continue.

"There are too many things that could go wrong with such a scheme. Suppose we are discovered and the alarm given while we're searching out the ecclesiastics? Suppose the Governor has no great love for the priests around him and is pleased to use them as cannon fodder?"

"I must support El Negro in this," the red-haired man said. "I and my men have been prisoners in that city and it is well-defended by able fighting men. I'd not like to be held captive there again. We barely escaped with our lives. If you adopt this plan, Morgan, my men and I must withdraw."

"Let us forget Cuba altogether," El Negro suggested. "Let us, instead, range along the coast of New Spain where many of the rich towns are not as well-defended and the pickings are easier."

"No," Jean said. "We are here now. Cuba is but a day's sail away. If Havana is out of our league." Here he sneered at El Negro as if he really meant it was out of *his* league. El Negro merely shrugged. "What then of Puerto del Principe?"

El Negro burst out laughing.

"Why do you laugh, whoreson?" The man glared at El Negro who kept laughing. "You, yourself, have not made one sensible suggestion." Suddenly, he jumped up and reached over to hit the laughing man. El Negro was too quick for him. In an instant, he had caught the Frenchman in a lock-hold around his neck, his pistol against the man's head. Dido tensed. Beside her, she felt rather than saw Yacahüey and the others reach for their weapons.

"That is enough, my friend," Morgan said, shaking his head, the weariness creeping into his voice. "Let him go. We must not fight against each other when we have the Spaniards to face."

"He must learn respect for me." El Negro stroked the man's face with the mouth of his pistol. "He speaks to me as if I were not his equal when I am his better."

Morgan's eyes flashed with amusement but he controlled himself. "Even so, let him go," he commanded again.

El Negro pushed the man away from him. He returned his pistol to his sash and dropped back into his seat but Dido could tell from the set of his shoulders and the way he held his head that his guard remained up. Yacahüey murmured something to Richard and William and the men laughed. Around the table the other captains remained watchful and suspicious.

"Tell me more of Puerto del Principe, Jean," Morgan said to the bull-necked man. "Is this a place to which you have been?"

"On more than one occasion for the wenching is good. You'd enjoy it, Morgan."

"The wenching is good in many a place but I do not attack cities for that."

"Puerto del Principe is second only to Havana in wealth for it is the chief place from which the Hides of Havana are obtained. The Hides themselves are famous throughout Europe and highly valued."

Morgan's eyes gleamed. Dido looked around the room. The other pirates were similarly rapt.

"The hills around the town are green with the leaves of the tobacco, another source of the town's wealth. But there's one special thing about this town that I think will commend it to you, Morgan. It has never been attacked."

The commander frowned.

"Why not if it presents such rich booty as you've described?"

"It's too far from the sea. None have cared to make the journey, contenting themselves with raids on the port towns."

Morgan nodded. It was a reasonable explanation.

For the next two hours, the pirate captains and their officers debated whether to take Puerto del Principe or move on to New Spain as El Negro had suggested. El Negro remained convinced that Puerto del Principe could not possibly offer the riches of even the smallest town on the coast of New Spain but those who sided with him were in the minority. The majority, Morgan included, voted to attack Puerto del Principe.

"It's because he likes the element of surprise, that's why he cannot think straight and see we are on a fool's errand, dreamed up by a witless imbecile," El Negro said to Dido later, when they were back in his cabin.

"You said nothing of your doubts to your men," Dido replied, putting his boots away. All he had told them was that they would sail at dawn.

"No." He removed his pistol and slipped his sash over his head. Dido watched him warily, wondering how far his stripping would go but after he'd pulled off the waistcoat and untied his shirt laces he appeared content to begin eating the turtle stew she'd brought him minutes earlier.

"Had I done so, it would only have renewed their fervor to have done with this whole expedition." He spooned some stew in his mouth. His eyebrows soared. "This is excellent. Cook has outdone himself."

"I think Yacahüey might have had something to do with it. I saw them down there bent over the pot together after we got back."

"The Taino is a useful man to have on board in many ways." He looked her over as he took another spoonful. "Have you eaten? We were on Morgan's ship overlong."

"Thank you, yes." She saw no need to add that she had only managed to swallow two mouthfuls of the stew before Cook had pushed her out the hatch with the captain's tureen in her hands.

"Have some more, Missy-boy. You look like you could use it." He reached across and picked up one of the pewter bowls on the small table along the wall and shoved it along the table in her direction.

"No. I…" She would have preferred to find some quiet place on deck to curl up with her bowl and with a couple of the increasingly harder biscuits and have her dinner in silence. Or as close as one could get to silence on a ship with sixty or so men on board.

El Negro pushed the tureen to her and Dido sat down. She ladled some of the stew into the pewter bowl, making sure she got good pieces of turtle meat as well as dumplings and carrots. For an instant, when she saw them in front of her, the carrots reminded her of Beeston's Estate and her provision ground. She couldn't think of her old home without thinking of Delia and the others, couldn't think of Delia who was like family to her, without thinking of her mother and her brothers and sisters. She'd left the ship's stern while Jamaica was still a misty blue stain on the horizon, not wanting to see when it disappeared completely from view like the abrupt ending of a story-teller's well-loved tale.

"Are you thinking of your family?" El Negro's voice broke in on her thoughts, startling her back into an awareness of her surroundings.

"Yes," she said. She blinked quickly, hoping he hadn't noticed her eyes were teary.

"You'll see them again and, when you do, you will be a rich young woman. Are they free?"

"Yes," she said. If she told him the truth he would know immediately why she was on his ship. People who thought they knew you inside out also thought they owned you. "They are free."

El Negro gave her an unbelieving look.

"They're free but you're a slave?"

"Not a slave. I'm free."

"You're a runaway. If you're caught, you will be returned to Beeston's. They'll not let you buy your freedom then. If they did, all the enslaved would run away to the Brethren. If such is your intention, you should rethink it."

"It is not." She planned never to see Beeston's again. Gaining her family's freedom was her intention and they were not on Beeston's estate. It was for them she was now a pirate. She would buy their freedom fair and square so they would never have to fear the slave hunter or his dogs.

"God's tears, you are a secretive woman and no mistake. What do you hope to gain then?"

"My mother's navel string is buried in Guinea but I was born in Nevis. I wanted to travel on the sea and learn more about…about the New World." *Oshun, forgive me,* Dido prayed, hoping the goddess would understand the need for deception. El Negro was a good man, he had not touched her and he kept the secret of her identity. But it was in his interest to do so. His men would certainly take it amiss if they uncovered her and realized their captain had violated his own rules.

"And are you? Learning, I mean?" he added, when she looked at him, puzzled.

Dido lowered her eyes quickly. "Yes," she said. "Much more than I sometimes think my head can hold."

"Do they know you've sailed with me?" He was like a dog with a hambone. "That you've sailed at all?"

"My family? No." In this at least, she could tell the truth. "They don't know."

"They believe you to be in Port Royal?"

"Yes." More lies again. *Oshun, forgive the necessity.* She did not embroider, hoping he would finally leave the subject alone.

He did not. "What do they think you're doing in Port Royal? Surely they'll have some concern that you do not fall in bad company."

"There are many opportunities for a young woman in such a big place." Dido shrugged and risked a glance at him. El Negro folded his arms across his chest. He watched her in astonishment. "I could have found employment in the home or store of some merchant, or maybe as a barmaid," she continued, defensive.

"Or you could have turned whore."

Dido shook her head violently. "Never that."

"Hmm, no," he agreed. "Instead, brave Missy-boy, you are on a pirate ship, serving under the command of a privateer commissioned by the governor."

"Yes." Even now, she could hardly believe it.

"I'm sure your people must be worried," El Negro persisted. "You are…" He stopped, started over. "You seem so slight, delicate almost."

Dido held her breath.

"I can see how a mother might worry for such a daughter's well-being."

"A mother need not," she responded, more sharply than she'd intended. "You see that I was sick only on the first day and have been well ever since and capable of carrying out my duties."

"I'll offer no argument there." He smiled. "But battle will be another thing." His mood turned sober. "I cannot keep you from the fight or the men would question it. In any case, to leave you behind risks your exposure. Yet, in battle, you'll see things to trouble your very soul."

"Is your soul troubled?" She had not seen anything about him to think that.

"No day goes by I do not see again the faces of those I've sent from this world. I'll remember them until the end of my days."

"Surely you had no choice. It was either you or they."

"Of course. That's true but their screams, their death rattles, are no less real for that. They were men, like me. They had dreams, desires, like me. Yet I live and they are dead." He lapsed into silence, staring at the table in front of him.

Dido didn't know what to say.

"Each time I sail away after a battle, I am troubled by doubts." His voice was so low she had to lean forward to hear. "Is it really me on the deck, feeling the wind against my face and smelling the sharp salt air, or do I lie dead back there and it is my soul that moves on, unaware that its time on earth has ended. It is days, weeks even, before I feel comfortable again in my own skin."

"You think grim thoughts."

"Yes. I believe all who hunt booty have these worries. I suspect this is what the days and weeks of whoring and drinking are all about, an attempt to silence our fears."

"Do they help you?"

"Whoring and drinking?" He shrugged. "To no greater or lesser degree than any other man, I suppose."

Dido was disappointed. She'd hoped to hear him say he did not behave as his friends did but it was a hard life he led. Given what he'd just told her, she supposed he was within his rights to seek solace where he could find it.

"And you, Missy-boy?"

"What?"

"In what do you find pleasure?"

Dido thought about it. No one had ever asked her such a question before. Slaves who dwelt on thoughts of pleasure were doomed to bitterness. "In the colors of the sun at daybreak, in the taste of sweetsops just before they are about to spoil." She glanced at him from under her lashes to see if he laughed at her. His face was grave, his expression attentive. "I like also the feel of the earth under my hands and to see things grow. The smile of friends when they greet me. I believe there are more things but I cannot think on them now."

"Perhaps when this is over you can add the sound of doubloons chinking in your purse and the knowledge that you can buy as many fine stockings and silk dresses as you desire."

"I have another purpose for whatever I earn," Dido said, rising to gather up the bowls and the empty tureen.

"I'm sure you do, I'm sure you do." He looked at her shrewdly, leaning his elbows on the table.

She could have asked him what he meant as she made her way to the door but, by now, she was almost sleepwalking. It was all she could do to wish him 'goodnight' and stumble out.

Chapter 9

Guns barked and the smell of sulfur rose into the air. Dido saw the water near the man spray in response but he kept churning through the waves until he finally reached the rocky shoreline. Keeping low to the ground, he darted into the brush ringing the bay known as El Puerto de Santa Maria. The pirates had arrived there only minutes before. The man who had swum to shore was a Spaniard, a captive from one of the other ships, who jumped overboard as soon as they were close enough to land. Dido thought his escape was an omen but when she consulted Oshun on its meaning, the goddess was silent.

"So much for the element of surprise," Richard said bitterly and turned away from the side of the ship. "Even if he speaks no English, he must know what we intend. In hours, he will reach El Puerto del Principe and we will find ourselves fighting a force that has had time to prepare themselves for our arrival, not a people going contentedly about their business with no awareness of what is about to befall them."

"Have faith, Richard." El Negro's voice was warm. Now that it seemed his enemy's plans were on the verge of disaster, he appeared willing to be generous, indulgent even. Richard gave a strangled laugh.

"Even if they have half a day, it will still only be half a day," El Negro continued.

Despite his confidence, however, it was actually several hours before all the necessary preparations were concluded by the different captains of the small fleet.

The crew of the *Fortune's Gift* was one of the first to lower their row-boat over the side and make ready for departure. The small boat made three trips back and forth before most of the men and their weapons were unloaded. El Negro chose William and Yacahüey to stay behind and watch the ship along with three others. William took his assignment with the stoicism Dido had come to associate with him but a frown of annoyance crossed the Taino's face. He looked about to protest but El Negro's expression brooked no arguments.

"You stay close to me," he commanded Dido.

Dido nodded. She had been in more than one fight in her life but, except, for the men who assaulted her in Port Royal, it had always been with her friends, boys and young men who loved to stick-fight and taught her how. The men she would soon encounter would offer her no quarter, nor would they expect any. She remembered what El Negro had said about seeing the faces of the people he had killed in his dreams and shivered. *This is what you came for*, her inner voice reminded her. No, not for killing, not for that. *Did you think they would just hand their valuables over to you because you asked*, the inner voice scoffed. Dido didn't respond. She climbed down into the launch behind El Negro and followed on his heels when he went to consult with the other captains gathered around Morgan in a small clearing a little distance from the shore.

The commander's instructions were terse. "We march in rank and file, each captain being responsible for the conduct of his men. Drummers to the front and standard-bearers before each ship's detachment. I want the men in tight formation. No stragglers."

The captains dispersed. When the order came to march, El Negro motioned Dido beside him.

"I'll need you to take messages back and forth between me and Morgan or between me and the other captains as the need arises so stay where I can find you," he said.

"Yes, Captain." If she had to go into battle, she preferred it to be at his side.

The men moved through the countryside in near silence. Dido caught glimpses of rainbow-feathered birds fluttering in the trees. An agouti, an animal like a rat but bigger, watched them with anxious eyes from a big rock they passed. Overhead, the early afternoon sky was blue and bright, innocent, Dido thought, of their design on the city and its inhabitants. For a minute she entertained regrets about what they were going to do but then she remembered the stories her mother told her about the white men who swept down on her village with their Dahomey friends. They had bound her and the other women, shackling them for the long march to the coast where the captives were warehoused until the next slaver arrived. The slave catchers had no pity or heart. She must be like them, like El Negro, hard and unyielding though it poisoned her dreams.

The pirates marched grimly on. The forest quieted around them until Dido could no longer hear the calls of birds or the snuffling sounds of wild pigs. They were not cutting their way through virgin forest but walking over a road, one that the residents of Puerto del Principe probably used often for it was not overgrown but fairly smooth and even. Dido looked uneasily at her captain. If this was the road to Puerto del Principe then it stood to reason that whoever was in charge of the city would expect them to use it. Perhaps they should have done like the *marronas* of the Blue Mountains who did not use well-known walkways but melted through the trees like spirits of the forests. From the way El Negro looked about him, she could see he was aware of the danger and on the alert for anything out of the ordinary. It had taken them hours to set off after the escapee, precious time during which the city would have readied its defenses.

Dido was just about to offer up another prayer to Oshun when, up ahead, shots rang out. Steel clanged with steel over men's shouts. El Negro and his crew raced forward. As they rounded a bend they saw that logs had been strewn across the road to delay their approach. Morgan's men and those of the *Laughing Dragon's* were engaged in hand-to-hand combat with some of the town's defenders. When the Spaniards saw the pirates from the other ships, they turned and fled.

"How many injured?" El Negro asked, pushing his way to Morgan's side, Dido at his heels.

"None, I thank God. They were too few but this fellow here." He indicated a surly-looking man, ringed by pirates. "He says there are more ambuscades set up along the way. Our escapee made quick time and the Governor has been busy."

"We must go through the woods to bypass them."

Morgan nodded soberly and gave the order to divert from the road and take a more roundabout route. It would take them hours out of their way, El Negro said, passing the order along to his men, but at least they would not lose any lives by it. The men fanned through the forest, picking their way past thorny bushes and flowering plants alike until they reached a large open plain.

"La Savana," El Negro breathed beside Dido.

"Look." Dido pointed. Across the plain, scores of men had assembled on horseback.

A pirate ran up to El Negro.

"Morgan says that at the signal of his drum you must fan out to the left but remain tight. We'll meet them in a half-surround," the man told them, panting. He ran on to deliver the message to the other captains.

"Is it a good plan?" Dido asked.

"Very good. We'll trap them like how a crab gathers food." He made a pinching movement with the thumb and forefinger of his right hand.

The two forces eyed each other in the fading light then Morgan's drummers began to pound out a martial rhythm. The pirates moved forward, silent again, their faces hard and grim. Dido gripped the axe in her hand, wondering if she would dare use it. In the distance a horn blew. The Spaniards galloped toward them, the weak sunlight glinting on their spears and their helmets. From where she was behind the frontlines, Dido could not see the horses bearing down on them but the thunder of their hooves shook the earth beneath her feet.

The fighting began. The smell of blood rose into the air with the death cries of men and the unearthly screams of fallen animals.

"Strike at the horse's legs. Unseat their riders," El Negro shouted at her as he himself dug his axe into the neck of a horse and pulled down the horseman. He drew his knife across the man's neck and pushed the suddenly slack body away from him without waiting to see the red stain that spread over the man's shirt and seeped into the ground. Dido ran behind her captain, covering her mouth to hold back the sick threatening to rise from her stomach.

"Fight with all your strength," El Negro urged. "Fight."

And she did, swinging her axe at every man she could identify as a Spaniard, whether by his clothes or by the language he spoke as he called to his god. She avoided injuring the horses. She had no quarrel with the innocent animals who did only as their masters bid them and were not to blame for having the wrong owners.

The Spaniards came upon them in waves. Dido had already felled three when she, herself, was thrown to the ground by a soldier who had apparently lost his weapons. His hands closed around her neck. She could not pry them loose. Her axe was useless. He was too close. Heat filled her face. Her eyes dimmed.

"Die ill-born dog!" El Negro shouted and buried his cutlass in the Spaniard's back. The man fell on her, squeezing the air from her lungs. She pushed him off and El Negro helped her stand. It was the second time he had saved her.

"Thank you. I…"

But he was not paying any attention to her. "It is finished," he said, wiping his face and looking around.

It was true. The few horses alive on the battlefield were rider-less and the men still standing were Morgan's. Vultures, big, brooding birds Dido had rarely seen in Jamaica, watched from the trees. One or two of the more courageous made darting attacks on nearby bodies and flew away again.

"Their Governor is dead," Richard said, walking up to them. He had a cut on the left side of his face and walked with a slight limp but looked otherwise unharmed. "He was among the first to die and it seems they have no more soldiers to send out to us."

"How many have we lost?"

"From the *Fortune's Gift*, only two, I believe. But overall thirty or so with a few more wounded."

El Negro whistled. "The prize had better be worth the pay."

Richard nodded and was about to say something when a man came up to them.

"Morgan says we are to move into the city now. He wants to make sure it is in our hands by nightfall."

The men started walking again in under an hour. They entered El Puerto del Principe while the roosters still flapped in the trees.

Kapow! Kapow!

"Damn the hell-spawn. They're shooting at us," El Negro said, ducking.

It was true. The townspeople had barricaded themselves inside their houses and were taking potshots at the pirates from behind their shuttered windows. Confusion reigned as the invaders tried to find cover in the unfamiliar city.

"God's blood. I've been shot." Dido whirled to look. "My leg." El Negro pressed his hand to the wound, grimacing in pain.

Dido bent down and saw the blood running down from just above his knee. It was just his leg, he was all right. She breathed a sigh of relief. But if they stayed out in the open as they were, who knew where the next bullet would strike.

"Come!" Forgetting herself, she grabbed El Negro by the arm and pulled him behind a tree where they hunkered down.

"The bullet did not enter," she said, peering at the wound. "It is a deep cut, however." She slipped the calabash with her needle and medicinal herbs off her shoulder, glad she had thought to bring it with her. Using the dim light from a nearby street lantern, she gently sopped up the blood around the wound with the edge of her shirt.

"Wait! What are you proposing to do?" he asked, seeing her attempting to thread the needle.

"If I don't sew you up, you will take twice as long to heal and there's the chance of corruption setting in." She squinted and tried again with the needle. "Ah. Got it."

"Have you done this afore now?" he demanded.

Dido glanced at him and almost laughed at the look of apprehension on his face.

"Many times. My mother is a doctoress as was…is a dear friend who was…is a second mother to me." She refused to think of Old Philippa in the past tense. "Do not worry. You'll not need many stitches. It is not a wide gash."

He nodded, gritting his teeth.

"It will hurt," she warned.

"I'm well aware, Missy-boy."

Dido's cheeks warmed at the nickname. She glanced around thankful there was no-one around to hear.

The operation was over in minutes for it needed only three stitches to close the flesh.

Dido pulled out a few leaves of the fresh-cut plant from her calabash.

"I need your sash."

He handed it to her, his face drawn.

Dido laid the leaves along the cut and then bound it tightly with the sash.

"You should get the *Satisfaction's* surgeon to attend you." She had learned that Morgan's ship carried a surgeon though many smaller ships such as the *Fortune's Gift* did not.

"Why? You've done a good enough job." His voice was a low rumble in his chest. Dido glanced at him then looked quickly away. The way he watched her! His eyes were like dark mountain pools full of pain. She found herself leaning into him. Bullets flew all around them but she felt safe there with him, safer than she'd felt even in the peace of her own hut during the whispering nights at Beeston's Estate.

"Return fire," someone nearby yelled into the darkness. Startled, Dido threw herself back and away from her captain. His teeth flashed in a sardonic smile and he shifted around to sit beside her. Their shoulders touched. Dido stiffened, all of her awareness concentrated on where her flesh touched his, separated only by the thin material of their shirts. The contact burned her skin. She couldn't stand it. Slowly, slowly, the movement so gradual it might almost not be movement at all but blurred thought, she inched away from him. Had he noticed? She couldn't tell. El Negro pushed his head back against the rough trunk of the tree. His cheeks were drawn tight. He squeezed his lips together as if to stop himself from giving voice to his pain. Dido reached out to touch his face but was stopped by another round of gunfire.

From where they hid Dido and El Negro saw the flash of musketry and heard a pirate scream. The shooters behind their doors were firing blind but they still managed to hit their targets.

"Quiet!" El Negro roared. "Quiet! They're shooting at the sound of your voices."

In confirmation, a bullet whistled past his head, landing with a dull thwack in the stone wall behind them. Dido found she was suddenly breathing in short panting gasps and made an effort to slow her breathing. The men quieted and the guns went silent.

"They could just stay inside and pick us off tomorrow morning," Dido said. "There's nothing to stop them. They're in a perfect position, in their homes with food and water." She fought against the rising tide of hysteria tightening her throat and turning her voice squeaky and high, like a woman's.

"Morgan has to use the fireballs or at least threaten their use." El Negro looked up and down the darkened street. "He must be up ahead. I'm going to find him."

"No, let me go. You're injured."

"It's nothing. Only my leg."

"Your injury will slow you down. I will go." She slipped from behind the tree before he could try to physically restrain her, making for a stone bench behind which she'd seen three pirates dive. The men were from the *Satisfaction* but they didn't know where Morgan was. Dido scurried over to another bench and got the surprise of her life.

"Ian!" she exclaimed, hardly able to believe it was really the boy who crouched there.

"Domingo! Oh, it's good to see you." The boy threw himself at her and they hugged, before springing apart self-consciously, sure that such behavior was not becoming to pirates at war.

"But how…? I thought…When…?" Dido stumbled over the questions she wanted to ask.

"I hid away on the *Satisfaction*," Ian said, grinning from ear to ear. "That last night I saw you I just snuck on board and hid in the hold until they sailed. I want to be a pirate, too. Why should you have all the fun?"

"But wasn't Morgan angry?"

"He said he was but he said, too, that he remembered when he himself was a lad and did the same thing. He was a stowaway more than once he said."

Dido ruffled the boy's hair. "I looked all over Port Royal for you. I thought you'd think me a right gint for not telling you 'goodbye.'"

"You wouldn't be the first to leave town without my knowing it till after they were gone." He smiled cheekily at her.

Just then another volley of gunfire reminded Dido of her mission.

"Where's Morgan?" she asked.

"There." Ian pointed and Dido saw several dark shapes crowded under the thick stone arches of an imposing building not far from where she and Ian crouched.

"I've got to get a message to him."

"Want me to come?"

"No. You're safer here. Stay till I get back."

Dido ran over and the men made room for her.

"El Negro says we should use our fireballs," she said, breathless from the quick run and from nervousness. Morgan glared at her.

"Did he say how many he brought with him through the bush?" he grated. "Or did he pick some up in the Savanna? Perhaps he thinks we should ask the merchants hereabouts if they have any for sale?"

Dido bridled at his tone.

"He said he'd send me back to the ships for some," she improvised. "But that you must, you should," she corrected herself, "let the Spaniards know of your willingness to use them."

"You?" One of the other men broke in. "He's going to send you back alone? You'll get lost."

"No, I won't."

"When daybreak comes they will pick us off like ripe mangoes from a tree. The fireballs are a good idea," said a third man.

"So we trust our safety to a boy?"

"He's quick and slight. He has a better chance of dodging their bullets."

"The boy can take the road," Morgan broke in, making up his mind quickly. "It should be safe now but you must hurry for, as Samuel said, we cannot stay long at such an impasse. If any escaped into the woods they will have gone for help. I do not want to be trapped in this town when it comes."

"I understand."

Dido was off like the wind, stopping only to tell Ian where she was going. She regretted it instantly when the boy rose to join her. Dido didn't dare risk going back to El Negro. He would argue against her mission though the idea of the fireballs was his.

With Ian right behind her, Dido raced down the dirt road back to the ships. Morgan was right, they didn't encounter the enemy along the way and reached their destination quickly enough. The crew members left behind had been keeping an anxious eye out for their brethren. They were quick to launch the boat and come to shore when they heard Dido hallooing them from the rocks. They took Dido and Ian back to the *Fortune's Gift* where it was agreed that Yacahüey would return with them, carrying as many of the clay containers as he could while Ian and Dido would be responsible for the tar and the rags. By the time they had assembled the items, some of the skeleton crews from the other ships had rowed over to hear news of what was happening in the town. Seven volunteered to help. When they headed back to town, Dido was at the head of a small procession of men who carried at least fifty of the clay grenades between them.

Warning the men of the need for quiet, Dido led them up a back street that she was gambling passed right behind where Morgan and his men were holed up. They cut across an alley behind a church and emerged on the street to the sound of sporadic gunfire.

"Ah, excellent. You have done well." The commander said, drawing her into the shadow of the doorway. "And brought reinforcements, too, eh?" He chuckled. "Now we will show the Spaniards we mean business with this town of theirs."

Before anyone knew what he was about, he strode out into the middle of the street.

"*Silencio!*" he shouted. In surprise, the guns stopped spitting and barking. "Surrender now, people of El Puerto del Principe, and no harm will come to you or your town. Continue your resistance and I'll set fire to your homes, to your houses of worship and to your stockhouses. I'll tear your women and children to pieces and make you choke on their bones."

In response, a musket whined and a bullet spat up dust in front of him. Without shifting or even turning around, Morgan gestured with his hand. Yacahüey fumbled with a grenade, poured in the tar, dipped in the rag, then set the whole thing alight. For a minute he stood there wondering if to give it to Morgan but when the commander gestured again, the Taino threw the fireball onto the wooden verandah of one of the houses in front of him. Dido heard the clay shatter. She didn't see any flames and thought he would have to try again but then the flames rose. A man and a woman emerged, frantically trying to put out the fire before it spread.

Morgan walked further down the street and gestured again. This time the Taino was ready and there was no waiting before the fireball was thrown at the house.

"Surrender, people of Puerto del Principe," Morgan shouted. "Or your houses will become your fiery graves. God's truth, I'll not warn you again."

His listeners took him at his word and crept out in small frightened knots to stand in front of the pirates. When Dido saw it was over, really and truly over, she ran to find El Negro. The pirate captain was leaning against a wall when she found him. His expression darkened at the sight of her.

"Where were you? Where did you go?"

"I did as you asked." She had been so happy to see him and now he was angry with her. "I went to talk to Morgan."

"Morgan? You had time to talk to ten Morgans!"

"I went back to the ship, to fetch the fireballs. See, the people are surrendering now." The Spaniards were exiting their homes all around them but it was as if El Negro could not have cared less.

"You went back to the ship all by yourself?"

"No...I..." She looked around for Ian but the boy had an aversion to trouble. He was nowhere to be seen.

"Why did you not tell me you were going back to the ship?"

Dido folded her arms about her chest. "Because if I'd told you, you might not have let me go. The fireballs were needed."

"So you deliberately lied?"

"I didn't lie," Dido protested. "I just didn't tell you."

"Did you ever think I might have worried you'd been shot? That I'd think you were lying dead somewhere in the street?"

"Oh." Dido looked down at her feet. No, lying dead on the street had definitely not occurred to her. Neither had she imagined he would worry about her.

"Morgan is having the townspeople rounded up," said Yacahüey, running up to them and saving Dido from withering under her captain's glare. "He wants them locked up in the churches."

"I thought I told you to stay on the ship." The glare focused on the Taino.

The Taino shrugged. "Domingo and the boy needed help carrying the fireballs. I helped them." His nostrils flared as if he were daring his captain to send him back but El Negro only gave Dido another frowning glance before setting off down the street.

After the pirates hauled all the townspeople out of their homes and marched them into a church, the looting of El Puerto del Principe began. All day and the next, the men ransacked the houses, the churches, and the government buildings looking for valuables. These were all gathered on sheets of canvas in the main square and guarded by men from Morgan's ship.

"I do not understand why we can't just take what we want," Dido groused to Ian, on the second night.

They were in one of the taverns that the pirates had taken over and had just eaten a meal of roasted oxtails, potatoes and yams. Despite the fullness in her belly, Dido was unsatisfied. What was the use of spending all your energy looking for valuables if they had to be turned over to Morgan?

"There'll be less for us all if some just took what they wanted, I've told you," Ian said, through a mouth full of oxtail.

"It should be finder's keepers."

He gave her an amused look.

"Suppose you only found dross?"

"Then I'd look harder."

He shrugged. "Well, that be the way of it, anyway. The commander will get the most, then the captains, then the quartermasters."

"I know," Dido broke in. "Then finally us. When there's hardly nothing left." She looked around for El Negro. She had not seen him since around mid-day when the surgeon from the *Satisfaction* had come to take a look at his leg. The surgeon, one of the best according to all who spoke of him, had inspected Dido's work closely. Just when she felt about to faint from the anxiety, he pronounced it good.

"I could not have done it better myself," he had said and Dido beamed with pride.

El Negro had given her a sour look, still angry with her, and hobbled off using the cane Yacahüey had made for him that morning.

"You know, I dursn't think Morgan's best pleased with what we've got so far," Ian said, bringing her back to the present.

"*I'm* not," she said, grimacing.

"No, really. I heard him talking to his men and says he 'this was not worth thirty lives.' Heard him with my own ears." He tipped his plate to gather up as much of the sauce and rice as he could then opened his mouth wide to take in the overflowing spoon.

"He's right. It ain't."

But if Morgan had a problem with the results of the pillaging he was not a man to do nothing about it. The next day, when Dido woke up, she found that several of the captives who'd been held in the church had been brought outside. Dido joined the captain and crew of the *Fortune's Gift* under a large saman tree in the square.

"What is happening?" she asked.

"Morgan intends to make them tell where their fortune is," Richard answered.

"There's no fortune," said El Negro, biting down hard on the clay pipe between his lips. "These are farmers, rural people. This was all wrong from the beginning."

Dido looked out at the men and women in the square and shivered. It was hard for her to remember her hatred of Spaniards when she looked at the miserable people. She realized that this was the first time that they were breathing fresh air and seeing the sun since they were locked away.

"Was food given to them? Are the captives being fed?" she asked, not sure she really wanted to hear the answer.

"They are our prisoners, Domingo. We owe them nothing," El Negro snapped.

"But they must eat," she protested. "It's not right that they not be fed. Why, at Be..." She corrected herself in time. "Even on the sugar plantations the animals are fed and they are only dumb beasts."

"Very right. Dumb beasts who have never done you harm. Can you say that of a Spaniard?"

Dido remembered Massa Simon's thick body over hers, the painful thrusting, the curses when she could not suppress her whimpers of fear and loathing. Those curses had been in English.

"I can," she said.

"Here comes Morgan," a man whispered. The pirates watched in silence as he strode through the men and up to the captives.

"Where have you hidden your money?" he asked, stopping in front of a small, bearded man.

"*Señor*, we have no more money than what you've already found," the man said, drawing a hand across his lined forehead. He glanced at Morgan and looked away again as if afraid of meeting the commander's eyes.

"You are lying." Morgan spoke quietly, without inflection.

"No. No. You must believe me, *señor*. We are not rich people."

"I was told that you are."

"Whoever said such a thing, lied."

"We'll see." Morgan gestured to one of his men. "Shoot him in the leg."

"No." The man scrambled backward trying to get away but Morgan's men held him tight. The pirate to whom Morgan had gestured pulled back his flintlock and fired but the bullet hit the paving stones and ricocheted. His crewmates ducked.

"God's wounds." Morgan drew his own pistol and fired. The shot caught the Spaniard in the knee. He tumbled to the ground, screaming in agony, clutching his injured leg. A woman in a pale blue dress threw herself, weeping, beside him but the man pushed her away, turning himself from her.

"Will you tell me now where you have hid your money?" Morgan asked, bending over him.

"*No dinero. Yo no tengo dinero*," the man yelled, his pain making him revert completely to Spanish.

"Is this your wife?" Morgan grabbed the woman in the blue dress.

"*No. No es mi esposa. No. No.*" He almost wept with the effort of convincing Morgan.

"You should not mind then if I do this."

Dido flinched as, with sudden motion, Morgan ripped the woman's bodice open, pulling aside the torn flaps to expose full, heavy breasts the color of arrowroot pap. The woman tried to hide herself as the pirates laughed.

"She is not my wife...*por favor*...*por favor* let her be," the man on the ground sobbed. He tried to push himself between Morgan and the woman.

"I am glad she's not your woman because she seems a fine specimen, if a little worn. Do you think she'd be averse to lying with me?"

Dido bit her lip. She would have liked to have gone to the woman and covered her up and told her nothing more would happen to her but she felt powerless even to move.

"No. No, *señor*." The man grabbed Morgan's boots. "Yes. Yes, she is my wife. *Por favor* let her go, *por favor*."

"Only if you tell me what I want to know. Where are the riches of this town buried?"

"In a cave, *señor*," the man, answered, speaking in gulps. "Above the town. He can show you. He knows." He pointed to a young, frightened looking boy who blanched at being singled out.

"Is he your son?" Morgan asked.

"No," the man grunted. From where Dido stood she could see the perspiration beading his forehead, smell the metallic scent of his blood. Morgan kicked him in his injured leg.

"I have no son," the man screamed as his wife struggled to pull herself free and go to him.

"You'd best be telling the truth, for if I find nothing in the hills worth my while, it will go ill with you." Morgan turned away and began calling out the men who would go to the caves. "You, boy, of the fireballs," he said, motioning to Dido. "Do you want to go?"

"I...I..." Dido stuttered.

"The boy stays with me, Morgan," El Negro broke in.

The commander grinned and shrugged.

"How did you know I did not want to go?" Dido asked her captain as they walked away.

"You would have been at Morgan's side even before he opened his mouth. In any case, danger may wait in the hills. The Governor died on the plain, defending his town but he may have sent other men to guard the people's valuables, if they exist."

Dido turned to look back at the square. The captives were being led back to the church, their prison. From where she was, she couldn't see the woman in the blue dress but Dido did not think she would ever forget her face or the expression on it when Morgan uncovered her.

"I didn't think he could be so cruel," she said, more to herself than to El Negro who had dropped down onto a stone bench.

"Morgan? Don't fool yourself. There is darkness in every man."

Dido seated herself beside him and digested this in silence.

"In you?" she asked, not sure she really wanted to know.

"In every one," he repeated.

"Not in me. I could never do as he did today, shooting a man in cold blood."

"Do you see these men?" El Negro pointed to the pirates who were wandering, aimless about the town now, all the buildings and people having been robbed of anything remotely valuable. "Morgan is responsible for them. The Governor wants Jamaica protected from the Spaniards so Morgan launches an attack to cripple them before they can strike but these men care nothing for that. They've followed Morgan because Lady Fortune smiles on him. When Lady Fortune ceases to smile they will leave Morgan high and dry and he knows it."

"That does not excuse what he did," Dido argued. "You haven't done such a thing, have you?"

El Negro turned to face her and smiled. "Do not play the innocent. I know you have seen the scars our people bear on their backs from the lash of the whip. If you've been in Port Royal any long time I know you'll have seen the sale of slaves, seen how the buyers rushed forward like hyenas falling on bewildered prey. You'll have known women raped and raped again by those who own them. Cruelty is as natural to man as breath."

"No." She had seen or heard all he'd described and experienced some of it herself but she'd seen acts of kindness too. In her mind's eye she saw again how gentle Miguel was with his brother after his recapture, heard Delia humming a wordless lullaby to her soon after her own arrival at Beeston's, felt Old Philippa's hands behind her head, encouraging her to eat when she was struck with cholera and food was the last thing she wanted to see. "You are wrong." She could have reminded him about how he came to her rescue in Port Royal but she didn't continue the argument. Her belly rumbled. She'd had nothing to eat since she woke up. In truth, food was becoming scarce in the town, unaccustomed as it was to feeding an extra seven hundred or so men.

"We'd better hope Morgan finds food in the hills," El Negro said, as if reading her thoughts.

Dido nodded, despondent. She did not know exactly what she'd expected when she'd signed up in that tavern but it was not that she would be hungry and more impoverished than when she left Beeston's. If Ian had been around she would have told him she felt let down. As it was, something of what she was feeling must have shown on her face.

"Go find something to eat," El Negro said, giving her a little push. "You'll feel better about things when your belly is full."

She did not think she would ever feel better about seeing Morgan shoot a begging man in the knee and half-strip his wife, revealing her to the lustful gaze of hundreds of men, but she did not say so. El Negro was accustomed to this life. She glanced back at him as she walked down the street and almost stumbled. He was watching her, an expression she couldn't quite fathom on his face, his eyes unreadable. She raised her hand in a tentative half-wave but he turned away without responding.

Chapter 10

There were no guards in the hills keeping watch over the townspeople's belongings but neither were there the great riches Morgan hoped for. When the pirates trudged back to the town later that evening, it was with sacks and sacks of grains, bales of hides tightly packed together, and rolls and rolls of tobacco; goods that would fetch a high price in Havana's markets or even at Port Royal but which were not the gold and jewels the pirates desired.

"We've stripped this place clean, Morgan. There is nothing more for us," El Negro said.

The pirates were again gathered in the square. Jean, the bull-necked pirate captain who'd advocated the raid on the town, skulked on the outskirts of the crowd keeping a low profile. Some pirates from another ship had attacked him the day before but his crew had fought them off. Apparently, never popular, he was now actively disliked. Even a few of his own men spoke disparagingly of him.

"He is right. We were wrong to come," agreed the red-headed man who had spoken against it before.

"Go bring the leading townsmen before me," Morgan instructed his quartermaster.

Dido squirmed beside her captain. Would they bring the man Morgan had shot that morning? She'd heard he'd developed a fever and was very weak. The doctor among them had done his best to relieve the man's pain but without his instruments and his liniments there was little he could do. Morgan refused to give him leave to fetch them.

When the pirates returned, the wounded man was not among the captives.

"We have retrieved the things you hid away from us in the hills," Morgan said. "And now we are ready to depart but before we do we wish to claim a ransom of you. If this ransom is not paid, we'll burn your town to the ground."

The Spaniards' faces registered their horror and shock.

"We have no more money," a man said, his face dark with anger. "You brigands have taken everything we own. How are we to pay any ransom?"

"That is a question to which you must find the answer," Morgan said. "I'll give you thirty minutes to devise a plan."

"And if we do not?"

"Then many of you will die."

"¡*Mierda*! You cannot do this. We have done you nothing." The man made to spring forward but his friends held him back.

Morgan withdrew his pistol from his sash and cocked it.

"*Señor*, he did not mean what he said," an older man pleaded, shielding his friend with his body. "He apologizes. We apologize for any offense."

The commander raised the pistol and pointed it, cocking it this way and now that, squinting as if making up his mind on the best position from which to fire. Dido held her breath.

"Morgan," El Negro called. He did not raise his voice but the commander lowered his weapon and smiled at the captain.

"Thirty minutes," he said, his eyes sliding to the captives. He wheeled away to confer with his quartermaster.

"So you abhor cruelty as much as I do," Dido whispered to El Negro.

"When it is without purpose, I probably hate it more. Shooting that man would have served no purpose whereas the one this morning was lying. He deserved to be shot. This one shows courage."

"You admire that."

"Yes," he said.

Dido looked around the square. Most of the pirates were either lounging nearby or were engaged in the process of bundling up the loot and loading it on the backs of the few horses and donkeys still alive in the town.

"I have to go somewhere," she said.

"Do not get into any trouble with that young friend of yours," he called after her.

"I promise," she said over her shoulder. She ran down an alley, down a cobblestone street and then cut across another alley. The church was right in front of her. Though tall and imposing, it was not the biggest of the three holy buildings in the town but it was probably one of the prettiest with its towers and huge, elaborately carved doors. Dido wasn't on a sightseeing visit, however.

"What do you want?" the guard Morgan had set to watch the prisoners asked as she approached him.

"Morgan said I was to spell you," she said, betting he was too lowly a member of the commander's crew to question the great man about the truth of her claim.

"He did?" The man glared suspiciously at her.

"Yes, he said something about you joining the fun at the whorehouse." She tried not to let her mouth turn up in distaste at the word.

"Whorehouse? I didn't hear nothing about that." His whole face brightened at the prospect.

"It's close to the plaza with the statue of the mounted man." She couldn't think of any other landmark furthest from the church. "That way."

The pirate hurried off.

After he was out of sight she looked both ways and, assured none of the brethren was around to see her, she picked the heavy lock on the doors. They swung open with a loud groan of their hinges. The smell hit her like a fist. The people had been cooped up inside for days with nowhere to wash their skins or perform their business. Dido staggered under the stench as the people gathered around her, touching her arms, plucking at her clothes.

"*El hombre*?" she asked in her halting Spanish, holding up her hand and curving it into the shape of a gun. Pablito and Miguel, Spanish slaves who'd been left behind when their owners fled to Cuba, had taught her a little of the language but she didn't know the word for 'shot'.

She brought her hand down on her leg, stabbing with her index finger. Wordlessly, the captives pointed to a third-row pew.

Dido hurried over. He looked in a very bad way. His wife cradled his head in her lap and looked at Dido with tears in her eyes. "He is dying," she whispered.

"I want to help," Dido said, putting a hand on the woman's arm. She saw a movement out of the corner of her eye, one of the young men had edged toward the church door. He was about to make a run for it.

"No!" Dido drew her pistol. *Oshun*! She did not want to fire it but she would if she had to. She had not come to free the Spaniards, only to help the husband of this woman who looked at her now with drowned eyes.

"Get back," she called, motioning with her gun. The young man merely stared at her.

"What can *este pirate* do? He is only one and *un joven* at that," a thick-bodied man said, rising from where he sat to look around at his fellow Spaniards. "If we rush him..."

"You'll rush no one," a voice said in Spanish from the doorway. Dido inhaled sharply. "Now do as the boy said and get back." El Negro held a pistol in each hand.

The would-be escapee's eyes turned to slits but he did as he was bid, joining the others halfway down the aisle.

"Carry on," El Negro said, reverting to English as he dropped into the pew on the opposite side of the aisle.

"How did you...?"

"How did I know to find you here? I had a feeling and followed you. I would hurry up. That poor bastard won't be too happy when he finds out there isn't a bevy of Spanish beauties waiting for his whipstaff to bring them unbearable pleasure."

Dido bent over the wounded man, her cheeks hot. He was right, she had bought only a little time with her ruse. If Morgan discovered her there with her captain she did not think even El Negro's friendship with the man would help them.

She asked for a lantern and one was quickly brought to her. The doctor had already cut away the man's trousers and bound the injury. She quickly undid the wrapping, peering at the torn flesh in the dim light. The man groaned. Dido placed her hand across his forehead. It was not hot to the touch but he shivered as with ague. Dido used a sharp knife to cut away the seared flesh and was surprised to find the doctor had left the bullet lodged in the man's flesh. He had given him up for dead and not even made an effort. Grimacing, Dido dug it out with the knife and then cleaned the wound with the aloe solution she had brought with her. Using the waxed thread and a clean needle she stitched the man carefully up, taking her time with it though she could feel the impatience rising off of El Negro like the vapors from boiling sugar. When she was finished she took the leaves of the fresh cut plant which she had pounded in lamp oil and left to steep that morning and bound the poultice to the man's leg with the clean cloth she'd brought with her.

"You must re-apply this to the wound each night and every morning and give him a little of this to drink," she said to the wife, handing over a jar full of the fresh cut and oil as well as a bottle of the tea she'd made with river bitters. She reinforced her advice with hand gestures to make sure she was understood.

"How? He does not drink, he does not eat. Only sleeps," the woman said, putting the things carefully down on the floor beside her.

"A sip every couple of hours will bring down his fever."

El Negro rose to his feet.

"Just give him a spoonful. Bring it to his mouth, wet his lips. Like this." Dido showed her.

El Negro strode to the door.

"Do as I've said and he will be well." *Please, Oshun, let it be so.*

The woman grabbed her hand. "*Gracias,*" she whispered. Bending over quickly, she fumbled with a bag beneath the pew and drew out a beautiful wooden carving. "*Jesu Cristo,*" she murmured, offering it to Dido. About a foot tall, the Christ figure bore a cross over its shoulders. "For bless you, for bless you," she said, smiling and nodding.

"No." Dido tried to give it back. Surely it would offend Oshun if she took the image of the white man's God but the woman wouldn't let her return it. Dido rested it on the pew beside the unconscious man but the woman picked it up and pressed it into her hands again as if she thought Dido didn't understand it was a gift. Dido pushed it into her bag of herbs. She could always dispose of the small statue later she supposed

The woman wasn't finished yet. She slid a hand under the waist of her dress and removed a small, red silk pouch. "Take this," she said extracting something and pushing it into Dido's hand without even looking at it. Dido glanced down. A man's chunky gold ring. A big yellow stone surrounded by smaller red ones glinted moodily in the light of the lantern. Now *this* was valuable. Dido could tell by its weight in her hand. But suppose the man died? Dido tried to hand it back too. With a quick shake of her head, the woman indicated she would not receive it. "*Vaya con Dios,*" she said, glancing at her husband, her blue eyes alight with hope.

"*Oshun bless you and yours,*" Dido responded, unsure of the etiquette of invoking the goddess in the house of the white man's god. She hurried to the doorway and slipped out past El Negro who quickly closed and locked the door behind them.

"We must go look for the guard," El Negro said, taking her arm and walking her down the street in the direction the duped guard had taken.

"Why?"

Morgan had ordered the gas-lights on in some areas. The darkness of the warm night pushed against the weak illumination. Dido was exhausted and wanted to sleep. She really did not think it was a good idea to go traipsing through the town looking for a man who could be anywhere.

"If he finds others and asks them where this brothel is and they scoff at him then he'll know you lied to him and will wonder as to your purpose. Do you want Morgan to find out you've given succor to a man he, himself, shot?"

When he put it that way, she could see the advantage. He loosed her arm and she almost stumbled at the sudden loss of contact. She glanced at him to see if he had noticed but he'd walked ahead, his eyes darting here and there as he searched the darkness. As it was, they didn't have long to search. The sailor had apparently found a barrel of rum, drunk himself into a stupor and passed out in the middle of the street. Dido grabbed his feet and El Negro his shoulders to cart him back to the church steps.

"He's not going to want anyone to know he left his post, so I think you'll be safe," El Negro said, wiping his hands on his breeches.

"*I* will be safe? You were right there with me."

"Yes but I did not sew anyone up and nobody gave me anything which I've not passed on to Morgan."

"I…I tried to give them back. She wouldn't…"

"Have no fear, Missy-boy," El Negro said, interrupting her excuses. "I'll not report you and I'll not take them from you either. Whatever the woman gave you, if her husband lives or even if he dies, your effort on his behalf earned it."

Back at the square they learned that the captives had promised to pay the ransom. Four of them had been allowed to go into the surrounding countryside and to other towns and villages to beg for whatever goods their inhabitants could afford to give. Yacahüey told El Negro that many of the pirates doubted they'd be successful. All the townspeople who had fled to the woods had already been captured and, with the retrieval of the items in the caves, it was doubtful anything else of value remained in the area. As for the nearby farmhouses, had their owners the kind of wealth Morgan demanded, they would already have attracted attention. Their anonymity, like El Puerto del Principe's before this ill-conceived invasion, was a clear result of their poverty.

El Negro agreed with the Taino's assessment. Neither man was surprised when, three days later, the four men stumbled back into town, haggard and begrimed, to report their failure.

"If you give us fifteen days more, we will go and return again with all you desire," they said, dropping to their knees to talk to Morgan who sat in a tall, iron-studded leather chair under one of the square's great saman trees.

"No," the commander replied. "I've given you all the time I intend to. My men and I are ready to depart."

The Spaniards' facial expressions did not change, but the joy they were afraid to voice brightened their eyes.

"I require that you bring five hundred heads of cattle to El Puerto de Santa Maria and enough salt with which to salt their meat."

"Five hundred!" the Spaniards cried. "We have not so many."

"Five hundred," Morgan repeated. "I'll take six of you with me to the ships and give the rest of you until tomorrow morning to arrive there with the cows. Should you fail in this, I will kill the six and come back to turn your town to rubble."

The pirates left El Puerto del Principe quicker than they had arrived, flowing out of the city in wave after wave. Many wore fancy clothes looted from the homes of the town's leading citizens. Dido left with nothing new but the pistol and the heavy gold ring she had tied on a string around her neck and hidden beneath her clothes. She'd had no time to return to check on the condition of the man in the church but she had heard he was still alive and had woken from the daze into which he'd fallen.

Dido had never thought she'd be glad to be back on the *Fortune's Gift* but she was. In El Puerto del Principe she'd felt rootless, resting in a different place every night. Some of the pirate crews had taken over whole houses, sleeping in the beds and eating out of the household's dishes. Morgan, himself, had taken a big stone house overlooking the Plaza de Armas, the largest of the town's squares. Wanting his captains around him, he'd turned a nearby row of houses over to El Negro and the other captains. For her part, Dido preferred to sleep outdoors, curled up among the roots of a fig tree or stretched out on a wooden bench. It had comforted her to know that the same stars she could see above her shone over the huts of her family and friends far away in Jamaica.

The Spanish arrived in the bay before daybreak herding the cattle before them. They demanded the release of the six hostages but Morgan refused to hand them over until all the cows were slaughtered and their beef salted. The lowing of the frightened, maddened cows, the heat of the day, and the buzzing of hundreds of flies attracted by the fresh meat, gave Dido a headache but she worked as hard as anyone. By the end of the first day the smell of blood was everywhere–in the pirates' clothes, their hair, their skin. The pieces of salted meat were put on racks in the sun to dry while the discarded bones were thrown to one side. It took them three days to finish.

The salted meat was shared out among the twelve ships. The prisoners were freed and the pirates made ready to depart the bay. Morgan had decided that they would meet at a small island to the south to make a proper division of their booty.

El Negro called for his crew to weigh anchor and let out the sails. The men jumped to his bidding but nothing happened. Wind filled the sails of the other ships and sent them scudding out the harbor but the sails of the *Fortune's Gift* betrayed no hint of even a breeze.

"There's no wind, captain," William said, looking up at the masts.

"There *is* wind!" El Negro snapped. "The other ships are not having this problem." It was true. William frowned. The other men scratched their heads and looked from their own sails to the other ships. Soon the *Fortune's Gift* would be the only ship in the harbor.

"It's witchcraft," a man near to Dido murmured.

"It's Davy as doing it," said another. "He don't want us to leave."

"All the others have. Why would he keep us back?" someone scoffed.

"I don't know. I don't…but there's something devilish here." The man looked fearfully up at the masts.

"We've been cursed," a man cried out. The sailors huddled together looking less like fierce sea robbers than frightened children.

El Negro ordered a change of sails and tried different combinations of them but, in more than an hour of frantic activity, nothing worked. The *Fortune's Gift* was stuck in a pocket of dead calm. There was nothing they could do. The men watched the last of the other pirate ships disappear around a bend at the mouth of the harbor.

"Pray," William commanded. "Pray for wind." He suited action to words and dropped to his knees, eyes closed. One by one the men followed his example, all except for El Negro who strode, hard-faced, to this cabin. Around Dido, voices rose in a confused babel. Only Yacahüey was silent though he knelt like the rest. Dido's prayer was simple. "Please, Oshun, give us wind. Give us wind, Oshun." But still the *Fortune's Gift* sat, becalmed.

Dido's knees were aching when William finally jumped to his feet. "Our prayers are either not being heard or are being ignored," he said. "We'll wait it out. It cannot last."

Another hour went by and the wind showed no sign of picking up. Were the gods ignoring them, Dido wondered. Had Oshun turned her back on her? Dido looked over the ship's side and saw the waves rolling past the ship. There was wind but it just wasn't reaching the sails. Perhaps the gods were angry with the pirates of the *Fortune's Gift*. If so, she didn't understand why they hadn't extended their anger to all the other ships of the pirate fleet. El Negro's men had acted no worse than those of any other captain's. That was when she remembered the Christ image the Spanish woman had given her. Could it be that it did not want to leave the island? Or was Oshun angry that she'd kept it?

Dido ran to where she'd stowed her medicine bag and drew the Christ out. Was it the cause of their problem? Quickly, without giving herself a chance to think about it or question herself into knots, she tossed the carving overboard. The effect was almost instantaneous. The sails billowed in the wind. The ship began to move. The sailors clapped their hands and did a quick dance as El Negro burst out of his cabin. Below the jubilant men, the carving bobbed on the waves, unnoticed.

"We've got wind, captain," William yelled. "Wind."

El Negro did a little celebratory hop and skip and almost ran to the whipstaff. In minutes, they were sailing out of the harbor.

Dido looked back at Cuba, full of questions she couldn't ask anyone. Was it Oshun or the white man's God that had stopped the wind? She supposed that was something she'd never know.

With the wind behind them, the *Fortune's Gift* reached the rendezvous point in the mid-afternoon. El Negro immediately had himself and Dido rowed over to the *Satisfaction* with his officers.

"I've counted out the booty," Morgan said, when all the captains and their officers were gathered in his cabin.

"And?" asked Jean. The bull-necked man looked even more tense than he had at the last meeting.

"And the take is forty-eight thousand, four hundred and fifty pieces of eight," Morgan replied, crossing his arms over his chest. He glared at the bull-necked man who turned red and seemed suddenly to cave in upon himself.

"Only that?" Dido heard him whisper.

"You're sure, Morgan?" asked another of the captains as the rest muttered to each other.

"As sure as I am that my name is Henry."

The muttering became louder but the commander said nothing, merely watching the men. When he thought the complaints had gone on long enough, he clapped his hands and called for silence.

"This is outrageous," the man Jean said.

El Negro laughed. "What is outrageous is that this was your idea," he said.

"No, El Negro," Morgan broke in. "We made a decision that was agreed to by the majority. We cannot fault Jean who was only mistaken in his calculations."

From the looks the other men threw at the bull-necked man, Dido could see that her captain wasn't the only one ready to lay the blame at his feet.

"Cobb has divided up the money according to the spoils due each ship and will hand them to you as you depart. Many of you, I know, are disappointed. The division will mean some of your men will earn less than twenty pieces of eight." Twenty pieces of eight! Dido drew a horrified breath and glanced at El Negro who shrugged. Twenty pieces of eight was nothing, not even a quarter of what she needed to buy her family's freedom. Her mind reeling, it was with a struggle that she pulled her attention back to what Morgan was saying. "I am of a mind to sail to the coast of New Spain to seek there what fortune I may find. And, of course, to carry out our mission. I urge you, all of you, to come with me." He looked around at the men, some of whom avoided his eyes.

"The *Fortune's Gift* will come," El Negro said, almost before the commander had finished speaking.

"The *Wind Dancer* also."

"And the *Laughing Dragon*."

One by one, the captains called out the names of their ships. None of the voices had a French accent.

Morgan looked at the Frenchmen. "And what of you, my friends? You've said nothing."

"We will go our own way," Jean said.

"Do you mean you and your crew or you and your countrymen?" Morgan asked.

"He means us as well, Morgan," said a tall, thin man. His accent was not as thick as Jean's but he seemed somehow more exotic than the bull-necked pirate. Dido had heard of this country France but had seen none of its people before that first meeting on Morgan's ship. "We lost men here," the pirate continued. "And gained nothing. We think we will do better on our own than as members of such a large fleet."

"You mean that if you find a good prize you do not wish to have to share it with four hundred others," Morgan said, his expression amused.

"*Exactément*," the pirate replied with a small smile.

Jean nodded morosely.

"And what if I promise you the booty will be worth the effort?" Morgan cocked a brow at the Frenchman who had spoken.

"We expected that at el Puerto del Principe."

"That wasn't Morgan's fault," El Negro bristled.

"Was it not he who led us?" the Frenchman responded.

"At whose urging?" El Negro asked.

"Enough," Morgan said. "If you have made up your minds, then let it be so. You are courageous fighters. It was my honor to have your service. I hope I can count on it again when I have need in the face of our common enemy."

"You have only to send for us," the thin Frenchman replied.

The pirates clapped each other on the back and began emptying out the cabin.

"Domingo."

"Ian!" Dido allowed herself to be pulled aside. He had obviously been waiting for her. Besides, El Negro was talking to another of the captains and did not look immediately ready to leave the *Satisfaction*. "Did you hear? We're going to New Spain."

"You might be going," the boy said, looking downcast. "I am not."

"You're not? But Morgan said…"

"I know what he said but I don't want to go. I…" He glanced at her as if trying to gauge how she would react to what he was about to say. "I miss me muvver and you know, the farther I go…well, I might never see her again."

Dido nodded, understanding everything.

"You do not think me a Missy Kate, do you?" It was what sailors called an effeminate man.

"No, Ian. Of course not." He was a boy, still a child, but Dido knew he would appreciate her pointing that out no more than being called a Missy Kate.

"You know, I dreamed of going to her, giving her a handful of gold coins and telling her she could buy anything she wanted." Dido's heart went out to him. His dream was not so different from hers. "Maybe she could have gotten herself some new clothes, even a house. Nothing fancy, just something that did nah leak at the smallest drop of rain, with a proper floor and proper beds. But now I'm going back no richer than when I left."

"So come with us."

"No…I cannot. Every week I go to see them. I did not send to tell them nuffing. They will be wondering where I am. My muvver will be worrying. I…I cannot." He looked about to cry.

"How will you get back?"

"I don't know. It is not me alone as wants to go back. There are a couple others, too. They say Lady Fortune has deserted Morgan."

"The French captains said as much, in there." Dido nodded at the commander's cabin. "But El Negro believes in him still."

"They were in Cartagena together and took fine prizes. El Negro dursn't be a man to desert an old friend. You do nah think I'm deserting you, do you, Domingo?" The boy's eyes searched her face anxiously.

"No, Ian. I understand. Believe me, I understand." *Better than I can tell you.* She saw El Negro begin to make his way to the side of the ship. He was ready to go. "Come." Grabbing the boy's hand, she dragged him beside a cannon and dug beneath her shirt. The ring felt warm and heavy in her hand.

"Here," she said, pushing it into his hand as the woman had pushed it into hers.

"A ring! It's beautiful," the boy breathed, twisting it this way and that. "How did you get it?"

"A Spanish woman gave it to me. Take it."

"I cannot, Domingo. It's yours." He tried to return it to her.

"I'm giving it to you," she thrust his hand away, already beginning to retreat. "I've got to go."

"Why would you do this? You dursn't hardly know me."

She knew his heart and, thus, knew him almost as well as anyone else.

"Walk well, Ian. I will look for you when I return. Walk well." She would have hugged him but she felt it would be taken amiss, by others if not by the boy.

"You are a good person, Domingo." His eyes shone. "Thank you. You do not know what this means."

Dido winked and turned to scurry over to the ship's side. Ian was wrong. She knew exactly what it meant but she would have another chance at winning the riches the boy wished for. He would not. She had done the right thing. The ring might not be enough to buy his family a new house but perhaps it could buy them something just as necessary. And she would get it back, Oshun willing, she would get back the value of the ring and more in New Spain.

Chapter 11

"**L**ower the sails! Faster, men, faster! Do you sleep?!"

The men flew to obey El Negro's commands. A high wind had come up. Dark clouds boiled on the horizon foretelling the coming storm. Dido did her part, stowing away everything in the hold that could not be lashed down on deck. Below, three men pumped the bilges as fast and furiously as they could, the water rising up to slosh about the deck. Dido forced herself not to think about how high the waves had gotten or how alarmingly the ship rocked from side to side. The sea was as gray and ominous as the sky while the waves billowed like sheets in a tempest, blown this way and now that.

The other ships of the fleet no longer maintained any semblance of order. The crew of one small ship was having difficulty lowering its sails. It spun jerkily as its captain tried to prevent it from smashing into any of its neighbors.

Oshun. Shango. Oludumare. Dido called on the gods of Guinea and fought her doubts about their ability to intervene so far from the source of their power, the continent from which her mother was torn. She thought she saw fear in the eyes of her crewmates as their lips thinned and they hurried to obey the orders of the captain and the quartermaster.

The storm lasted the afternoon and continued well into the night. When it had passed and morning came, the men of the *Fortune's Gift* could see none of the other ships of the fleet. They had disappeared. The *Fortune's Gift* was on its own.

Dido mended the torn sails as El Negro huddled in his cabin with his top officers. From where she sat on deck, whenever the door opened and closed Dido could catch a glimpse of the frowning men bent over a chart on the table.

The *Fortune's Gift* drifted as the sun climbed higher in the sky, bringing a light sheen of perspiration to Dido's forehead. Not that she was complaining. The heat of the sun was a welcome blessing after the wind and rain of the night before.

At last, El Negro emerged and ordered the spare sails mounted. Dido heaved a sigh of relief. They would be on the move again soon but were El Negro and the rest sure of their direction? Dido crouched over the sails, praying with every stitch she made that they were not lost and that the foretop man would soon see the sails of the fleet through the lens of the bring-'em-near he held to his eye. Nobody played cards or sang.

Four days came and went before the pirates heard the cry they longed for.

"Sail to labboard, captain. Sail to labboard."

Captain and crew rushed to the side and Dido put down her mending to follow them. The sail, if indeed it was a sail, was little more than a small blot on the endless horizon. Dido intensified the fervor of her soundless prayers to Oshun. She did not like the lonely sea, was uncomfortable in the absence of any sign of land, and hoped with all her heart that it was a ship of the fleet they were seeing and not some illusion born of despair.

El Negro ordered more sail. The *Fortune's Gift* picked up speed, the sailors bending to their work with a will. As they drew closer they realized that the other ship was unfamiliar. More than that, its crew was aware that the *Fortune's Gift* had given chase. They too laid on more sail. To Dido's bewilderment, excitement ran through the watching pirates.

"Why are we following it?" she asked Yacahüey. She would not criticize El Negro behind his back but were they not losing time by going after this unknown ship, time that could be better spent trying to find Morgan.

"Because it doesn't want us to." The Taino grinned from ear to ear. "It must be a Spanish ship or it would have slowed down to hear our news."

Dido understood a little more now. If Morgan's commission was to attack the Spanish then El Negro was obeying his commander's mandate. Not that she thought the chase wise. They were losing valuable time they could have spent searching for Morgan's fleet. Nobody sought her opinion, however.

All through that day and the night, the *Fortune's Gift* plunged through the waves after the bigger ship. In the early morning, the ship ran up a French flag but this gave the pirates no pause. El Negro strung up his Jolly Roger in response, three skulls over a pair of crossed swords. It was the first time Dido had seen the huge red flag with its grim emblem. Quivers of anticipation raked her spine.

"We take it, whatever nation issued its letter of passage," El Negro said grimly, beside the helmsman.

The pirate captain strode to the bow of his ship and raised his speaking trumpet to hail the ship but its crew ignored him. The ship plowed on though the *Fortune's Gift* was now almost right beside it. El Negro ordered a shot fired across its bow and the pirates gathered along the side, raising their cutlasses and pistols, hooting and hollering. The mystery ship tacked to starboard and fired off a broadside but the balls fell harmlessly into the water as the *Fortune's Gift* danced out of the way.

El Negro's eyes narrowed. The mood on the pirate ship darkened. Their prey was clearly not from any navy so the pirates had not expected it to put up a fight. The men were affronted by the other captain's gall. They wanted a quick surrender.

"Boy." El Negro called Dido over. "Go to my cabin and bring me my musket."

"Your musket?" The ship was shooting cannon balls the size of grapefruits and he wanted his musket. Was he mad? "Why do we not return cannon fire?

Cannon fire…" But she never got to finish.

"Fetch me my musket now or, by God's teeth, you'll ask your questions of Davy Jones in a minute," El Negro shouted, the veins standing out on his forehead. Without another word, Dido spun around and flew to his cabin. She wrenched open the doors and ran to the cupboard where he kept his guns. He had two muskets but when she grabbed the darkest one she noticed the cock was broken so she picked up the other one of lighter-colored wood. She was almost out the door when she had a second thought and ran back to the cupboard.

"Good," El Negro said, nodding in approval when she returned on deck and gave him the musket. She handed over the five musket balls and the patch box he must have forgotten to clip to his belt that morning and his smile broadened. The knot in her belly disappeared.

El Negro steadied himself on the deck of the forecastle. He extracted a patch and wrapped it around the ball he quickly loaded into the musket, his actions quick and economical. He brought the musket to his shoulder as Dido peered at the other ship. What on earth was he up to? The *Fortune's Gift* drew up alongside its quarry, passing it before tacking slightly so that another broadside from the ship's guns would be impossible.

"Steady," El Negro called to William who had taken over the helm. "Steady." He drew back the cock and pulled the trigger. The effect on the other ship was almost instantaneous. The ship slewed around crazily. Dido saw several of the crew stumble and fall. El Negro had aimed at the helmsman and struck true. The ship was out of control.

"Fire," Richard shouted to a man on the deck below.

The cannon spoke but the ball landed in the sea some distance from the ship. Richard swore.

"At their sails, you pock-marked loons," he shouted. "Their sails."

The men quickly reloaded and fired again. This time the cannon ball hit its target and tore the mainsail to shreds. Dido heard the screams as the ball hit the deck and shot a spray of splinters into the tender skin of those unlucky enough to be nearby.

The pirates had just reloaded their cannon and were about to fire once more when the men of the other ship displayed a white flag over the side. In minutes, the pirates' launch had crossed to the other boat. El Negro was one of the first to climb aboard. By the time Dido reached the deck he, Richard and William, were deep in conversation with a man who she took to be the captain. The man produced his letters which apparently showed he was actually Dutch though he spoke English as well as any Englishman Dido had ever heard.

"We are on our way to Mexico," the captain explained. He was a stout, balding man who appeared unable to meet El Negro's eyes, speaking instead to the pirate captain's chest, his forehead creased with worry.

"What do you carry?" El Negro asked.

"*De Tweede Kans* is a slaver. We carry nothing such as you would want," the man permitted himself a small, ingratiating smile.

Dido's eyes widened. She was on a ship like the one that took her mother to Nevis. She looked at El Negro to see what effect the news would have on him but he merely frowned.

"Do not presume to know my wants," he snapped. There was something in his voice that made the other captain look him in the face for the first time. What he saw there made him step back in alarm.

"I did not mean to offend, sir. If I have offended…"

El Negro raised his hand to silence him.

"Stay with him, Richard," El Negro commanded. "Is that the hatch to the slave hold?" he asked the captain, pointing.

"Yes, but there is no need for you…I am telling you the truth. We have no hidden treasure aboard, only the slaves."

El Negro ordered the hatch open. Dido staggered at the stench that rose, as thick as smoke, into the air around them. Could it be possible that people were alive down there? El Negro and Yacahüey descended down the hatch as unconcerned as if their noses were stoppered with cork. Dido hesitated for a minute before following them. The darkness of the hold was the darkness of evil. All around her Dido sensed rather than saw figures huddling, moving. Their breaths stirred the air and she felt the hairs rise on the back of her head. *Oshun, oh, Oshun*, she whispered, holding her hand over her nose and mouth. *Oshun*. She repeated the name of the goddess she revered and it was like the wind rushing through the forest of her thoughts, cleansing her of fear. El Negro lit a lamp and the people took on shapes and faces. She saw the platforms built to allow the ship to accommodate twice as many people, saw the iron fetters around the legs of the men, women and children who watched the newcomers wild-eyed, unable to determine how their arrival would affect them.

"It's a good number," Richard said.

"A couple hundred or more, I'd estimate," William agreed.

El Negro said nothing. He traversed the length of the hold and then made his way back, pushing past Dido and the others.

"How many?" he asked the Dutch captain when they were back on deck.

"Two-hundred and forty. I have had only eleven deaths."

Dido's hand opened and closed on the handle of her cutlass. *Eleven*! He spoke of them as one would speak of cattle or some other mute beast.

El Negro and his officers withdrew out of the man's hearing.

"If we sold each for at least seventy, no man among us would make less than two hundred pieces of eight," William said, his voice urgent.

"And if we left the captain and his crew somewhere, we could sell the ship itself for a few thousand pesos, doubling our prize," Richard added.

Dido could not believe her ears. She glanced at El Negro confident he would correct his officers' mistake.

"They are probably waiting for slaves in Mexico, it would be the best port and the closest," El Negro said, finally breaking his silence. "Then we could sail south and fall in with Morgan."

"Nothing simpler," William agreed.

"Wait." Dido could hold herself back no longer. "You mean, you're proposing to sell the people into slavery yourself?"

"They've already been sold, Domingo," El Negro responded, matter-of-factly. "The Dutch have the *asiento* to sell slaves to the Spanish colonies. In each year, scores of their ships go to Guinea to purchase men and women and bring them to the New World. I would merely take my profit from an event that has already occurred."

"They've not been sold to the plantation owners," Dido protested. "They are waiting to be sold."

"They have been sold. Someone sold them to a Dutch merchant in Guinea very cheap and now they are on their way to be sold again in New Spain very dear." El Negro frowned at her as if she were stupid for not understanding how trade was conducted. "That is how the wealth of slave dealers is made, boy. Why should some of that wealth not belong to me?"

"Because you shared the same fate." Why did he not understand? "Remember, you said we all share the same skin." Richard and the others stared at her but she did not care. "We are all one people. My mother…" Her breath caught. "She was one like them. How can you think to sell them? It is horrible." She thought again of what she had seen in the hold. He could not sell them. He could not. She thought of her mother's kind, beautiful face and almost wept

"They deserve to be free," she said. "Like me and you. Like how they were in Guinea."

"I've heard that African kings like those at Whydah and Jakin have hundreds of slaves," Richard interrupted. "There be nothing wrong with making a man work for you as long as you feed him and see to his basic wants and needs. Slavery has been around since the days of Abraham."

"I do not care," Dido said, rounding on him. "I do not care about your Abraham. How do you know those people were not free? That they didn't have lives of their own, families, farms, they cared for."

"You do not know that they did," the bo'sun countered. "They may have been captured in war or mayhap they committed some crime and were sold away as punishment."

"Before the white man came, my people knew nothing of this thing." Yacahüey spoke for the first time. "In war, our enemies, the Kalina, killed our men and took our women for their wives but they never claimed to own us as they did their dogs."

"Domingo appears to feel we should set these people free. Is that your thinking too, my friend?" El Negro asked the Taino.

Yacahüey shrugged. "The Brethren speak highly of liberty and of the equality among us. Why should this not extend to others as well?"

"If we'd not happened along, these people would be on their way to the slave market," Richard said, hotly.

"But we did happen along," Dido cried. "Maybe we are the answer to their prayers."

"Pshaw," William scoffed. "And how do you know what they pray for?"

"If I were chained as they were in that place, I would pray for liberty," Dido replied, seeing the hold again. "Of one kind or another."

El Negro looked at her sharply.

"You realize that if we do not sell this ship and if we set the captives free you give up more than a thousand pieces of eight as your share of the prize?"

So much! Enough to buy her whole family's freedom, land, and much more besides. But she pushed the thought away.

"I know," she said, her chin rising. "I could never accept any money at such a price."

"You cannot listen to the boy, captain," Richard argued, leaning in toward El Negro. "The men are dissatisfied with their share from El Puerto del Principe. They'll not thank you for letting this prize slip through their hands."

"We must put it to a vote," El Negro responded.

"A vote!"

"What tomfoolery!"

"I will speak to the men." El Negro raised his voice to be heard. "And lay the case before them."

"That's not fair. You're not impartial," Dido objected.

"That is why I will give you a chance to speak as well." El Negro smiled. "If you move them with your honeyed words, I'll concede." He raised his hand as Richard opened his mouth to interrupt. "I'll abide by the decision of the majority."

Dido took a deep shuddery breath. The fate of two-hundred and forty men, women and children rested in her hands. She didn't know if she was up to the challenge El Negro had laid before her but, for them, she had to try her best.

Oshun, help me, she prayed as they returned to the *Fortune's Gift. Inspire me with grace and power so the pirates might understand how we will wrong these people if we fail to set them free*. She closed her eyes, concentrating with all her heart. *Oshun, I need you now, stand by me.*

Chapter 12

"Since I've been on this ship, I have often heard you men talk with pride of the free life of a pirate who is his own master and serves no-one except as his own heart wills." Dido's gaze roamed over the faces of the men gathered in front of her. They stared back, impassive, giving nothing away. They had clapped heartily when El Negro was finished. This duel between her and El Negro was an unequal one but she persevered, the fate of those people on the other ship depended on her ability to bring these toughened sailors around to her way of thinking. El Negro stood to one side, watching her with a faintly derisive expression on his face.

"This is a blessed thing, to live your life for yourself, to direct your energies to your own ends. These are things slaves can only dream of though they are no different from me or you."

"Maybe no different from you," one of the men called out, the others laughed.

"They are…they are…" More of the men were jeering now. Her words stuck in her throat. Tears pricked her eyes and she took a deep convulsive breath. No, she wasn't going to break down in front of these men, in front of El Negro. *Oshun.* And the goddess answered her prayer, sending white-hot anger surging through her, giving her strength.

"You know nothing of it," she shouted. "How dare you?" Surprise widened their eyes. They had thought she was about to break down and snivel like a child. "How dare you take the liberty of men and women for a jest? Look at him." Whirling she pointed to El Negro. "Is he not a man equal to any of you? Is he not an excellent marksman? Is he not a man you are proud to call your captain? You've put your life in his hands but he is as black as the people in yonder hold." El Negro rocked forward on the balls of his feet. There was a look of sudden admiration in his eyes…but no, it could not be. She was mistaking his expression. She wrenched her gaze away, disconcerted. "And what of me? I have fought alongside you like a brother yet I am of the same race as those still shackled over on that ship. Only the gods know why I am free and they are not because there's no difference between us. And there's no difference between you and I whatever the color of our skins. My blood runs as red as yours. I have the same fears, the same dreams." Had her mother heard she'd run away?

Would she guess the reason why? Dido prayed they would remain safe until she could come for them. "You know nothing of those people in the hold, you do not know where they came from, if they are fathers, mothers. You do not know if this man was a good person who helped his neighbor thatch his house or if that woman attended the birth of her friend's children. You know nothing of them but you would consign them to a life of misery with no more compunction than you'd step on an ant. Is not a human life worth more than the pieces of eight with which you can buy that life in the slave market?"

There, she was done. Dido stepped back and folded her arms. While she spoke it was as if Oshun and all the ancient gods of Guinea used her for a speaking trumpet. Mortals could not bear such usage over long. She felt spent and tired.

"A vote, men," El Negro called. "Yea, to sell. Nay, to set them free."

Dido closed her eyes. They would vote to sell. She knew it as well as she knew the fine lines in the palm of her right hand. She had failed. Her eyes blurred and she made her way over to the bow so she would not have to see *De Tweede Kans*.

"Yea. Yea."

The men's voices rose behind her. It was going the way she expected.

"Yea."

"Nay."

"Nay."

A small flame of hope flickered but she did not turn around, did not go back to watch. She stared at the waves without seeing them, her mind completely bent on the vote unfolding behind her. She held her breath at every Yea, expelled it with every Nay.

"Thirty Yeas, thirty-seven Nays," the man who took the count said when all had spoken. An uproar ensued and he raised his voice. "The Nays have it."

She had won. Dido couldn't believe it. The people on the slaver would go free. She sent out wordless thanks to the gods and finally allowed herself to face the crew. Several grinned at her, nodding.

"You did well," El Negro said, coming up to her. "There is a point on the coast of New Spain that is uninhabited but is not hard to find. We will sail thence and put them ashore."

Dido was confused. "What about Guinea? Can they not go back there?"

"Use your head. They've no navigation skills. How will they find their way across an ocean hundreds of times as big again as Jamaica? It will be best to set them safely on land as soon as we can and let them create their own settlement far from the Europeans. A settlement of free men and women, isn't that what you wanted?"

Not exactly, Dido wanted to say, but he had a point. Left to themselves, the Africans would probably run aground somewhere or be captured by another set of pirates less tender-hearted than those of the *Fortune's Gift*.

El Negro was as good as his word. He put twenty of the men who had voted for the captives' freedom on *De Tweede Kans* to teach seamanship to the Africans and to sail the ship behind the *Fortune's Gift*. In two days, they reached their destination, an enclosed harbor where white, sugar-soft sand, ringed a wide beach. His men begged to be allowed on-shore to re-stock their water supply and hunt for whatever game was available but El Negro refused. They had lost too much time and needed to make it up if they were to reach Morgan's rendezvous point before the commander launched his attack. They would stay in the harbor only long enough to see all the Africans safely off the ship with whatever they would need from it in the way of food, linens and such like. There were fresh-water streams aplenty in the area so they would not lack for water and could use the wood of *De Tweede Kans* to fashion their new homes. The captain of the slaver and his officers were held prisoner on the *Fortune's Gift* but any of the crew that wanted could stay with their former captives or join the pirate crew. More than half of the Dutch sailors opted to turn pirate.

From the side of the *Fortune's Gift*, Dido watched as the liberated people began to row themselves ashore.

"If they keep out of the white man's way and order their society well, they'll have a good life," El Negro said, joining her. "Perhaps it will be better than what they had in Guinea."

"At least they'll be free," Dido responded.

"Yes, they will."

Dido looked at him sharply. There was something in the way he'd spoken.

"You…you wanted them free all along," she accused in surprise. It was there in his voice, on his face.

"If I'd said such a thing, the men may well have mutinied." He sent her a sideways smile. "I had to tread carefully."

"But you could not have known they'd be persuaded by me," Dido cried.

"I knew you would speak from your heart and, sometimes, that is all that's needed to sway men to good."

"If you'd been wrong…You had no right to gamble in that manner." She could still hardly believe it.

"If I'd lost, the people would have been no worse off than they were before."

"You're the captain. You could have made the others do as you wanted without all this pretense."

"No." He shook his head. "You overestimate my power. This ship is mine because I captured it but the men know I need them as much, if not more, than they need me. Fail or disappoint them once too often and they will jump ship or, worse, mutiny."

"Take over your ship? They would not dare."

"No? Others have done it. Killing their captains or marooning them on some small cay or uninhabited island. I've worked too hard to achieve my present standing to risk that."

Dido nodded, understanding him a bit better though she still was not sure she cared for his argument.

"I am sorry for yelling at you earlier," he lowered his voice. "I cannot be seen to go easier on you than I would on another, Missy-boy."

"It is I who should apologize." Dido twisted her fingers, remembering. "I should not have tried to argue with you. We were in the midst of battle."

"Very right but even so…Forgive me my harshness."

"It is already forgotten."

On shore, some of the Africans did a small dance, stamping their feet while the women's voices rose in ululation. Dido smiled, enjoying their excitement from afar. They had what she wanted for herself and her family. She glanced at El Negro. He watched the dancing people of Guinea with a small smile on his face. It pleased her to see him happy. She would have liked to place her hand over his, to let him know something of what she felt for him though it confused her, this strange emotion she'd never experienced before. She wasn't sure if it was love or merely desire.

El Negro turned to her. Dido swayed forwards, the heat in her belly propelling her, her breasts pushing against their restraint. His arm slid around her waist. Dido felt her blood become liquid lust. She raised her mouth to his. He could make her forget what had happened to her. He had the power. Then it all changed. His face grew rock-hard. With a strangled oath, he pushed past her and strode to the stairs. Dido heard the slam of his cabin doors even above the suddenly over-loud beating of her heart. She glanced around to see if anyone had noticed and, satisfied that they had not, she stole to the deck and down the hatch to the hold. Digging around in the ropes, she found her small basket and extracted a hard journey-cake. Sinking down, with the coils of rope at her back, she nibbled on the oily bread and tried not to think about her captain or what had just happened between them on the forecastle.

Dido would have dozed off, she was that tired, but from the muffled shouts of the sailors above her and the rocking of the ship, she realized they were putting back out to sea. She scrambled to her feet and ran up on deck. The main sails were unfurled. The ship was plowing through the waves on its way to the open sea. Dido hurried to the stern for a last look at the freed Africans who lined the beach, watching the departing ship. Seeing them raised her spirits. She raised both arms and waved. Slowly, tentatively, a woman waved back and then another until the whole line was shouting and waving and jumping. Dido smiled to see their joy. *Oshun, guide and protect them*, she whispered, *let them find happiness in this place you have chosen for them*.

The freed Africans and the two white figures among them dwindled in the distance and Dido turned back to the ship. In addition to the main sail and the jib, the top sails had also been unfurled. El Negro wanted to catch every possible breath of wind to speed them on their way to the rendezvous with Morgan.

Should she go to him and apologize? But for what? She had done nothing to apologize for but why then did she feel so miserable? Unable to sleep that night, she climbed up the ratlines to the crosstrees of the main mast and stared out over the inky sea. At first, she paid no attention to what she was seeing, but the beauty of the stars winking in the darkness and the implacable majesty of the ocean worked their magic on her. In time, the rhythm of the ship, the cool night air blowing against her face, and the wash of the waves, lulled her into a state of dreamy contentment.

"Boy! Domingo!"

She almost fell off her perch.

"What are you doing up there? Get down." It was El Negro.

Dido rubbed her eyes. Why was he on deck now? Once he retired for the night, he rarely emerged until the next morning.

"Yes, sir."

She scrambled down as fast as she could. Maybe she was still half-asleep or maybe it was his speed but she never saw his hand coming. The slap spun her head and she staggered to the side.

"No one takes the foretop except at my command," he shouted at her. "What did you think you were doing? You could have been killed!"

Dido cupped her hand over her stinging cheek. She had never seen him so angry before. Was this the same man who had apologized to her for his harshness hours before? She glared at him, rigid with rage and hurt.

"Damn you for a half-wit!" He spun around and marched back into his cabin.

For a minute or two there was complete silence on deck. Dido looked around at the other men on the watch but they all avoided her gaze, embarrassed for her. Only Yacahüey looked her in the eyes.

"Why...? What...?" She could not even frame the question. El Negro's behavior had completely stunned her.

"Men have fallen asleep on the foretop and crashed down to their deaths," Yacahüey said. "That is why it is done only at the captain's command on the *Fortune's Gift*."

"I was not asleep," she objected.

"Sure looked it from where I am," a sailor said from his hammock.

"I wasn't...I'd just closed my eyes for a little bit but I was awake."

Yacahüey shrugged. "As you say, but even so it is best that you close your eyes down here rather than up there." He permitted himself one of his small, rare smiles.

Dido glared in the direction of the captain's cabin. She had half a mind to follow him in there and slap him right back. See how he liked being on the receiving end. But she knew it was not the best idea she'd ever had. In fact, she was beginning to doubt the value of all her ideas. If she had not decided to run away and become a pirate she would be safely in her bed at Beeston's all now. Of course, she would still be a slave. Yet what did it profit her to be free if some mystifying man was going to raise his hand to her for a little paltry thing?

Chapter 13

For the next three days, the *Fortune's Gift* raced before the wind, taking advantage of every breeze, to catch up to Morgan.

Finally, arriving at the rendezvous point, an island off Costa Rica, El Negro immediately ordered his launch lowered and crossed over to the *Satisfaction*, leaving Dido behind. Dido told herself she didn't mind but she did. The man had either completely ignored her or been as cold and distant as a stranger since his assault. She didn't understand his behavior. If anything, she was the one supposed to be acting haughty and disdainful. He had wronged her, not the other way around. Still, she had to hand it to the man, he had a rare talent for making her feel like she was the one to blame for the discord. She was polite to him but inwardly she fumed, wanting to demand the apology that was her due but afraid of the consequences. If there was one thing she had learned from the old talk of the pirate crew it was that the displeasure of a captain could sometimes land one on a desert isle with nothing to keep one's company but a pistol and a jug of water. Dido watched the launch being rowed away and seethed.

The sailors sang songs and told tall tales to while away the time until the captain returned. They did not have long to wait. El Negro came back just as the watchman was turning the hourglass over for the third time.

"Where are we going?"

"When do we leave?"

The men crowded around him with their questions. The air of barely-suppressed excitement about him was infectious. William put two fingers to his mouth and whistled the men to silence.

"We sail at once for Puerto Bello," El Negro said, raising his voice so as to be heard by all the men. His eyes gleamed. "Morgan has conceived a bold plan to take the city."

The men objected at once.

"Captain, if our force was not strong enough to attack Havana when the French were with us how can we think to attack such a city as Puerto Bello?" asked the master gunner.

"He's lost his mind," a pirate exclaimed.

"Puerto Bello is too well-defended," said another.

"Morgan says that even if our number is small, our hearts are great." El

Negro raised his voice to be heard. "He asks also that you remember that the fewer we are, the better our shares in the spoil."

"Yet the castles that defend the city are the strongest in New Spain," the master gunner protested. "No ship can enter the harbor except with permission and that I do not think they will grant."

"That's true, captain," another man called from where he swung on the rigging. "I have been there and the castles are bigger than those at Cartagena and as well armored. Nothing can pass below those guns unless the governor allows it."

Worried murmurs rose from the men but El Negro smiled.

"That is the beauty of Morgan's plan," he said. "We will not invade the city from the sea but from the land. They'll be unaware of our attack until it's too late and the castles will be of no use. Men." El Negro rocked on the balls of his feet, his voice fairly vibrating with enthusiasm. "This is a chance to be part of an adventure of which songs will be sung. They'll talk of the time Morgan took Puerto Bello for years to come. When age has dimmed your eyes and your bones creak, when you but raise your hand for your bowl of pap." The men chuckled at this image of themselves. "You'll remember the sack of Puerto Bello and it will put a spring in your step and iron in your whipstaff. You'll tell the young men in the tavern about it and they will be silent and listen to you with respect because they know that no battle since the sack of Puerto Bello in 1668 can compare to that great and glorious action. Nothing you've done before and nothing you'll do after will demand half the valor or offer half the treasure. For glory!" He raised both hands above his head.

"For glory!" the men shouted in response, their objections forgotten.

"And for spoil!"

"And for spoil!" they cried, even louder than before.

Dido shouted and shook her fists above her head with the rest. Another chance to make the money she needed! If only El Negro would look at her, smile even, but he did not, striding instead to the forecastle to oversee the crew's preparations for their immediate departure. Some men scurried up the ratlines to unfurl the sails while others sang a shanty as they pushed on the capstan to raise the heavy anchor. All felt a renewed energy and enthusiasm. They exchanged jokes and sallies with each other. Dido heard El Negro's laughter floating away from the forecastle.

The wind was with them. By evening, they arrived at the mouth of a huge and placid river into which the ships turned, one by one. As the moon rose above the masts, they came to a harbor Dido heard called Puerto Pontin. Richard took a sounding and the *Fortune's Gift* dropped anchor.

Having made sure their captives from *De Tweede Kans* were tied in such a way they could not free themselves El Negro wasted no time getting into his launch. Five of his men, including William, would sail the ship around to Puerto Bello the next morning. When the city was taken, the pirates would fire the castles' cannons three times. That was the signal for William and the others to sail the ships of the fleet into the unguarded harbor.

Scouts sent up the coast brought back additional small boats for the pirates. In the hubbub, Dido lost sight of El Negro and found herself sitting among men she didn't know. They rowed in silence, the only sound that of the oars dipping in and out of the moon-silvered river water.

On shore, the moon threw huge, hulking shadows beneath overhanging trees. Every now and then, branches shook and they heard the cries of unfamiliar animals. The air was still and close, smelling of earth and decaying plants. The pirates rowed up-river for a couple hours before Morgan signaled them to draw their boats up on the rocks. The men jumped into the shallows and did as they were bid. Dido weaved in and out of them until she found El Negro and Yacahüey near Morgan. Yacahüey nodded at her but El Negro ignored her arrival. Dido shrugged. She was becoming accustomed to his bad mood where she was concerned. As long as he did not raise his hand to her again, he could glare into the distance whenever she was around as much as he liked. And if he did raise his hand again, well, either Oshun would hold her back or she would give as good as she got and the devil damn the consequences. She had not left Beeston's Estate to be treated so.

Morgan sent two of his crew members to creep up on a sentry post on the outskirts of the city and capture the watchman on duty, warning them not to kill him. Morgan wanted the Spaniard alive so he could question him about the town's defenses.

Dido shifted the cutlass in her sash and sank down to rest among the roots of a great ficus tree near where the pirates milled silently about. The mosquitoes in the area were not as fierce as those on Beeston's Estate but she curled her arms under her knees to make it harder for them to get at her skin. Yacahüey sat cross-legged beside her, seeming not to notice the tiny pests at all.

Soon after they'd departed, Morgan's men returned with the guard, his hands bound behind him. The terrified Spaniard told them that the castles were ill-equipped, he'd heard rumors they were short on cannon. Morgan drew the point of a short dagger across the man's throat, digging deep enough to draw blood. "I do not believe you tell the truth," he said, gripping the man's long hair in his other hand and pulling his head back to expose his throat.

"*Es la verdad, señor*," the man said, almost weeping. "I swear to you."

"On the holy cross? Do you swear on the holy cross?" Morgan asked, shaking the man's head from side to side.

"Yes. On the holy cross, I swear it."

Satisfied, Morgan ordered the pirates to march on the city, prodding the hapless sentry before them. The sky was lightening in the east when they emerged from the woods. They had come out behind a castle whose high, thick walls rose out of the ground as if it was a thing as natural and solid a rock or a tree. Dido had never seen anything even half as big. Port Royal's forts were tiny in comparison.

"The Spaniards built it more than fifty years ago," Yacahüey whispered in her ear. "Its walls were constructed on the backs of our people, yours and mine, their blood mortared the walls."

Dido rubbed her cold hands. The castle suddenly seemed an evil place.

Up ahead, Morgan prodded their captive to call to his brothers and tell them to give up or they'd receive no quarter. Almost as soon as the man finished speaking, the soldiers within the castle began to fire on the pirates. The defenders' first volley missed the men but curses filled the air. The pirates would have preferred a rapid surrender but the soldiers clearly had no such intention. Morgan ordered his men to surround the castle, throw up their grappling hooks and fight their way inside any way they could.

The sentry had spoken the truth. By mid-day, the pirates had overcome the poorly armed soldiers. They poured over the city walls like angry red ants, engaging those Spaniards still willing to fight in hand-to-hand combat. Men from the city came to the assistance of the soldiers and Dido found she could not always tell pirate from Spaniard.

"Speak," she commanded one shirtless man who emerged from the thick of a melee before her.

Instead, he took aim at her chest but the shot missed. He did not get a chance to reload his pistol before she swung her cutlass into him.

The pirates quickly overwhelmed the thirty or so men still on their feet and herded them to the powder room in one corner of the castle.

"What does Morgan mean to do with them?" Dido asked her captain. El Negro had fought beside her for most of the battle though she was unable to pinpoint exactly when he'd first appeared.

"Blow them up," he answered. He had sustained a long scrape on his arm and another, smaller one, on his cheek. Dido reached out to wipe the blood away with her fingers but he flinched away from her.

"I am fine, boy," he growled, emphasizing the last word.

His reaction hurt but she tried not to let it show. He had allowed her to sew him up back at El Puerto del Principe so why the sudden squeamishness?

"Run," a pirate said, pounding toward them.

Without a word, El Negro spun on his heel, pulling Dido after him.

"Why…are…we…running?" she asked, panting.

"They have lit the fuse," El Negro replied.

Dido contemplated this in silence. All the Spaniards in the castle would die. Killing them in battle was one thing, locking them up and blowing them to smithereens was something else altogether. But it was too late to do anything about it. She was almost at the city gates. To turn back was suicide. Even if she somehow managed to free them, she would probably never make it back to the gates in time.

Boom! A small explosion shook the ground, quickly followed by another. Boom! Dido felt her chest would burst. The pirates erupted out of the castle doors running at full tilt. And not a moment too soon. KABOOM! To Dido it sounded as if Olodumare, himself, had stomped on the ground. The earth shook. She staggered and would have fallen but for El Negro who pulled her along. Only when they were near the houses on the outskirts of the city did Dido turn around to see that parts of the castle had collapsed on itself, leaving huge, jagged holes where stone and mortar had been.

She had little time to contemplate the destruction, however. The fighting had now moved street to street. Several of the residents had taken up arms to repel the pirates. A black man slashed at Dido with his sword though she yelled that she was with Morgan. She countered with the cutlass, holding it in a two-handed grip. The man feinted to her right and slashed again. Dido responded by bringing the cutlass up and out then swiftly swinging it back to slice into the man's arm. He dropped the sword, his face contorting in pain as he held his other hand to his arm, screaming. She had cut him to the bone. His screams were in Spanish and she belatedly realized that he was probably a slave sent out to defend his master's belongings or maybe, even a free black. Grabbing him by the back of his shirt, she half-pulled, half-dragged him off to the side of the street. She had no time to do anything more for him.

"Where have you been?" El Negro asked, grabbing her by the arm as she came out of the alleyway. "I was on my way to help you and then you disappeared."

"I dragged an injured man out of the fighting." She did not mention he was a Spaniard.

"I should have known. Look, the people are trying to dump their valuables into their wells and cisterns or to bury them in their gardens. I have assigned Yacahüey to intercept as many as he can. Find him and help him."

"I'm needed here," Dido objected over the clash of metal upon metal.

"Don't argue. Do as you are told." He pushed her away. "Find Yacahüey. We came to Puerto Bello for its booty. Not to die like dogs in its streets. Go."

Dido went. By the time she reached the end of the street, El Negro was obscured by the men around him. She debated returning to the fight. If she could not see him, chances were he couldn't see her but she decided against it. His face had looked downright thunderous when he'd pushed her. He would not take kindly to her disobeying his orders.

Away from the fighting, the city's residents raced through the streets in hopes of finding refuge, the women crying and the children screaming as their mothers dragged them along. On one street, Dido met a young girl struggling to push an elderly man in a wheelbarrow. The man's hands, thin and tremulous with age, patted the air in front of him as if seeking the outlines of a familiar face. From the poor quality of their clothes and the girl's unkempt hair, Dido could tell they were not rich people. The sight of them tugged at her heart but she ran on, skipping over crazed chickens, pigs and dogs, running in every direction.

When she found Yacahüey, the Taino man was holding a sobbing woman around the waist with one arm while with the other he ripped her dress.

"No," Dido shouted. She ran up to them, prepared to fight her shipmate if necessary but when she came nearer she gasped in wonder.

The woman's neck was draped with necklaces of precious stones that glinted and winked in the afternoon sun. Under her dress, she wore an undergarment to which she'd pinned bracelets and brooches as big as the palm of Dido's own hand.

"You were saying?" the Taino asked, dryly.

"Umm…oh, oh, nothing," she stammered.

"Nothing like the sight of pretty baubles to make a sea robber forget speech." Yacahüey laughed and began to yank the necklaces, one by one, from the woman's throat. He winked at Dido and dropped the first into a pouch inside his shirt. With a quick downward movement and a flick of his wrist he threw something to Dido. It glinted and glimmered in the pale light of the afternoon sun as it tumbled toward her. Dido caught it overhand, her breath catching at the beauty of the brooch. It was intricately made, with alternating clear and green stones radiating outward from a milky-white stone the size of her thumbnail. Yacahüey winked at her again and threw the other pieces of the woman's jewelry onto a square of cloth almost as big as the Spanish flag that had flown over the castle the pirates destroyed. The cloth was already piled high with coins and confiscated jewelry that had been meant for the stone well just a couple yards away. Dido pinned the brooch to the inside waistband of her trousers with a mental note to move it to the bind around her chest when she was alone.

When he was finished, the pirate shoved the woman away and began to tie up his cache. Whimpering, the woman picked up her skirts and ran down a cobbled street.

"No need to stay here," the Taino said to Dido. "She's been the only one to come in the last half hour. Word must have gotten around or there's nobody more to come."

They rejoined the other pirates to find out that many of the city dwellers, including the Governor, had fled to the second castle. Morgan had, at first, tried to storm that one as he had the other but it was better defended than its twin. Many pirates were dead. "Scores," El Negro told Dido, his face grim. A lot of Spaniards died too for Morgan used his marksmen to great effect but still he suffered great losses and ordered a retreat.

El Negro began to push through the pirates milling about in the field to the side of the castle. Dido followed in his wake, having nothing better to do. Part of her was glad that he appeared to have thawed toward her but another part was mystified by his behavior. One minute he ignored her, the next he stuck to her side like cornmeal pap to a spoon. Dido frowned at him but the back of his head held no answers for her.

El Negro came to a stop before Morgan.

"They've taken all their money into the castle," he snapped at his commander.

Morgan's eyes narrowed. "I know, captain. What would you have me do? Send more of our men to their deaths? I fear, my old friend, that we may have overestimated our strength. The Governor is a stubborn man. He does not surrender however much I entreat him."

"I see this but we have to take action," El Negro responded, his tone more conciliatory. "We must make shields for ourselves and storm the castle if we are to go away from this with the booty we imagined." He forbore to mention that if anyone had overestimated their ability to take Puerto Bello it was Morgan. "If we attempt to wait them out, we may find a Spanish man-of-war or two at our backs and we'll be unable to escape."

"This, too, I realize. But we have no breastplates, nothing which we may use as shields."

"Begging your pardon, commander," another captain interrupted, joining the conversation. "My men have rounded up the ecclesiastics and religious women of the city. Look them yonder." He pointed through a gap in the men around them to a huddled group of more than a hundred men and women. "Surely the people of God should be better shields than any armor."

Dido grimaced at the man's brutal logic. The suggestion was a more murderous variation of the hostage-taking idea proposed by the Frenchman in Morgan's cabin weeks before.

"Use them before us...." Morgan rubbed his chin, his brow furrowed.

"It is an evil plan," El Negro said.

Dido could hold back no longer. "What about throwing fireballs into the castle?" She ignored El Negro's warning glance. "It worked in El Puerto del Principe."

"Ah, the fire carrier." Morgan smiled into his beard, not seeming the least put out by her temerity in addressing the commander before his captains. "Cuba was different—then the people were in their houses which could readily burn. The high walls of La Gloria will not admit of defeat so easily. They were built to withstand such attacks."

Looking back at the fort, Dido had to concede he was right but the alternative proposed by the dark-haired captain was too grisly for her to contemplate.

"Is there not something else we can do? Some other way?" she asked.

El Negro smiled ruefully at his commander. "This is the... ah...boy's first voyage. His heart is not yet hardened by battle."

Morgan nodded but it was clear his thoughts were elsewhere. "Thomas," he said, calling his quartermaster to his side. "See to the construction of twelve stout ladders able to carry four men abreast. They must be tall enough to scale the castle. Waste no time in this."

Thomas hurried off. He and the carpenters of the pirate ships worked furiously, cutting down the nearby trees, sawing and hammering. The ladders were ready the next morning.

"Surrender now and save your religious people," Morgan called up to the castle, using his speaking trumpet.

The sun rose over the hills to the east, bathing everything in pink-gold light. It was a beautiful day, Dido thought to herself as she stood at El Negro's side. Not a day for dying. She started to murmur a prayer to Oshun but stopped halfway. What would the Goddess do if warriors back in Guinea used her priests and priestesses in the way the pirates proposed to use those of the Catholic God? The answer was obvious. She would rush to the aid of her people and slay their enemies. Dido expected nothing less of the Spaniards' God.

The defiant Governor refused to give up. He shouted threats at Morgan and the sea-robbers, telling them they could expect no quarter when reinforcements came from Panama and Cartagena. Morgan's expression grew foul. As each ladder was finished he ordered the priests and nuns to set it against the wall. The holy people cried out to the Governor to hold his fire as, weeping, they came beneath the range of the castle's marksmen but Morgan was right about the man's stubbornness. Time and again, the Governor ordered his men to shoot the ladder carriers until more than sixty ecclesiastics lay dead or wounded at the foot of the castle walls, their robes stiffening with blood. Their groans filled the air like the sound of heavy, beating wings. Dido fancied she could almost see the angels in whom Missus Sarah had believed hovering over the broken and contorted bodies. She expected the Spanish God to hurl a thunderbolt at Morgan and his men at any minute but the sky remained cloudless and unbroken. Dido wondered if perhaps he slept or if he simply did not care.

The Governor's stubbornness met its match in Morgan who sent in more and more of his human shields until all the ladders were arrayed around the castle's walls. At the commander's order, the pirates charged up, dodging bullets and bearing fireballs and smoke grenades which they threw over the walls among the castle's defenders. Several pirates plummeted to the ground before they reached their target but others swarmed to take their place, overwhelming the castle's defenders.

By the time Dido climbed the wall much of the fighting was over. Outnumbered, the Spaniards had given up. Only the Governor fought on, refusing all offers of mercy extended by a half-admiring, half-frustrated Morgan who finally killed him with a sword thrust through the man's valiant heart.

The wounded men and women of the castle were put in one part of the castle and the others were locked up in another with twelve well-armed sentries put to guard them. Then the pirates went wild. They fell upon La Gloria's stores of beer, salted fish, ham and grains like hungry boars, ripping into sacks and barrels and scooping up great mouthfuls with hands still bloody. After their hunger was satisfied they started in on the wine and rum, competing with each other to see who could drink the most in the shortest time.

Dido wandered around searching for El Negro, unable to bring herself to look among the dead bodies piled against a wall awaiting either burial or flame. By evening, tired and hungry, she stumbled into a small, darkened room the pirates must have overlooked since the furnishings were neither broken nor torn to pieces. Dido thought it must have been the sleeping quarters of one of the officers because the bed was not only well-made but the linens were clean and soft. She ferreted about and discovered a loaf of bread and a chunk of headcheese which she ate ravenously, washing it down with the water she found in a pitcher on the nightstand. She unpinned the brooch at her waistband and re-pinned it between her breasts. Too exhausted to resume her search for her captain, she crawled into the bed and was instantly asleep.

Chapter 14

The next day, Dido screwed up her courage and went to the one place she had not yet searched for her captain, the place where the dead still lay piled. She saw him as she rounded the corner. El Negro was crouched down, digging among the bodies.

"What are you doing?" she asked, appalled. He whirled to face her almost unbalancing himself. If she could only read him better she might have thought she saw relief and joy mixed with the shock registered on his face.

"Have you no respect for the dead?"

"The dead?" he asked, perhaps stupid with drink.

"That you would rob them," she said, wrinkling her nose and stepping backward. The bodies were beginning to smell. Dido gave an inward sigh. His greed must indeed be great for him to have been willing to get so close to decaying corpses.

El Negro's jaw line hardened. His eyes became chips of flint.

"They have no further use for their belongings," he snapped.

Sickened, Dido turned on her heel and walked away. At least she now knew he was alive.

Dido kept herself to herself for most of that day, staying far from the packs of pirates roaming through Puerto Bello, looting and raping. They tortured the rich men and women whose silk and satin clothing revealed their wealthy status to make them reveal where they'd hidden their coins and jewelry. One frantic woman, dipped repeatedly into a cistern to make her confess, died without speaking. Later, a Spanish whore who had taken up with Morgan, told him the drowned woman was a mute who communicated only by means of notes. If he expressed regret about the manner of her death, Dido didn't hear. Eleven English prisoners were freed from La Gloria's dungeon where the Spanish had kept them for more than a year for crimes against Spain. Maybe Morgan thought the Spanish had paid but a small price for their rescue.

Most of Puerto Bello's wealthy residents lived close to the cathedral and that was where the pirates concentrated their looting, there and the Royal Treasure House in La Gloria. From the houses they removed money-boxes, rich tapestries, heavy silver candelabras, everything moveable of value. From the Royal Treasure House they took silver bars, emeralds, rubies, and curiously shaped gold masks and figures that had not yet been melted into ingots. A pensive Yacahüey said the figurines were seized from the native peoples and represented their gods.

Slowly, slowly, the ships in the harbor filled with the goods pillaged from the city. Barrels and barrels of water, salted meats, flour and beer and other liquor were also loaded into the holds of the five ships. But Morgan had not finished with the city. He sent a message to the prisoners that he wanted one hundred thousand pieces of eight or he would raze the city to the ground and kill them all. He gave them two days to consider what he'd said and to devise how best to fulfill his demand. Morgan was generous with his time because he had other things on his mind. The President of Panama, had heard that Puerto Bello had fallen to an army of pirates, and had sent a force of five hundred men to take back the city.

Morgan dispatched a hundred of his best marksmen, under El Negro' command, to meet this army at a narrow passage only a few miles away from Puerto Bello. In a complete rout, the pirates killed more than eighty of the Spaniards and sent the others into flight without losing any of their number. Morgan had high words of praise for them when they returned. Dido glowed to hear El Negro lauded. That night the pirates celebrated their victory.

"Come all, you gallant seamen bold, All you that march, let's go and look for Captain Ward, Far out on the sea he roams, He is the biggest robber, That ever you did hear," they sang, with some substituting Morgan's name for Ward.

"Why do you not join in the revelry, boy?" Richard said, seeing her sitting on a wall, overlooking the dancing men and their whore companions.

Dido shrugged, her eyes on the bench were El Negro sat, his back to her, his arm draped around one of the prettiest of the olive-skinned women.

"I have no interest," she answered.

"No interest? No interest?" he laughed, leaning into her. He slurred his words and she could smell the wine on his breath. Dido inched away. "Mayhap your interest lies elsewhere."

"What do you mean?"

"Oh. Oh. Oh," he said. He tapped the side of his nose and winked at her.

"I do not take your meaning." Dido didn't want to leave where she was. She had the perfect vantage point for observing El Negro but if the bo'sun did not move soon, she would.

"Do not play the innocent with me, boy. I've been around the world. I've seen a thing or two. Do you know that in parts of Barbary, every man has at least ten boys to attend his whim?"

He was obviously too drunk to make sense and Dido came to the end of her patience.

"I think I will have me a drink, after all," she said, jumping down from the wall.

"Not so fast, boy." His hand shot out, gripping her arm in a vice-like hold. "Look, he's
not that way inclined but I know there's nothing sweeter than a man's tight love-hole, particularly when it belongs to one as young as you."

Dido wrenched her arm free and sprung away from him. "You speak of filth," she cried, panting with emotion. What in the name of all the gods did he take her for?

Richard looked taken aback by the vehemence of her reaction. "Why do you deny your nature? I have seen the way you look at our captain betimes."

"The way I look at the captain?"

"Do not worry, boy. No one else has noticed how you watch him when you believe yourself unnoticed. I am just saying he has no interest in his own kind. He is not like me, like us." Before she could spring away from him, he had grabbed her again, this time pinning both her arms to her side.

"No!" She struggled to get away from him.

"Let us find somewhere quiet," he said into her ear, propelling her in front of him along the side of the wall. "I will be good to you, boy. Ah, the games I will teach you."

Dido's response was to stomp on his bare feet but he only laughed and picked her up around her waist.

"Richard, do you leave the festivities so soon?"

The bo'sun froze at the sound of his captain's voice.

"I...I..."

"And you have my cabin boy with you." El Negro walked around to look at her. "Have you found better entertainment than we offer, Domingo?"

"N...n...no, sir." Dido widened her eyes in mute appeal. If she denounced Richard, the man would never forgive her. He could make life hard for her back on the ship.

"I thought I'd asked you to keep close by me in case I have need of you this night?" the captain said, raising his brow at her.

"I..." Dido did not remember any such request.

"I'm afraid I must spoil your fun, Richard." El Negro rocked forward and backward on the balls of his feet. "I have had much to drink and will have more. Without my boy around to keep an eye on me, these strumpets may manhandle me into a barrel of gunpowder as their sisters did to the Frenchman, Francois, in Cartagena. A bad end, that." He grimaced and gave a mock shudder.

Richard released her so suddenly Dido stumbled and would have fallen but for El Negro's steadying hand.

"Go now, Richard," he said, his tone gentle. "There are many young boys about the place who should serve just as well."

Richard walked away, half-shambling, half-trotting, without responding.

"I had no idea Richard fancied you," El Negro said as they walked back to where the other pirates still sang and danced.

"Neither did I," Dido answered sourly. She thanked Oshun that Richard had not managed to get her where he wanted, she did not like to think of what would have happened when he discovered that, instead of the boy he desired, a woman stood before him.

El Negro's lips twitched. "You have a worthy admirer, Missy-boy," he said.

"So do you," she said, nodding at the woman who stood up, smiling, at their approach.

"Whores admire any man with coins about him."

He led Dido to the wall and sat beside her, ignoring his former companion who gracefully re-seated herself on the bench.

"Still, I would not have thought that, with her on your mind, you'd have noticed what Richard was doing."

"I did. I notice everything." He allowed his shoulders to slump and his back to slouch, his features darkening until he looked like one of the grim creatures carved into the wall over the doors to the city's churches. Unable to imagine why his mood had suddenly turned black, Dido sat quietly beside him watching the revelers. Every now and then, the woman with whom he'd been consorting glanced their way but El Negro appeared to have entered his own little world. He was completely oblivious to the yearning looks the whore threw at him.

As much as it pleased Dido that he ignored the woman, she was still miffed that she, herself, got no greater attention.

"Do you think the Spaniards will have the money for us tomorrow?" she asked.

"What?"

"The ransom Morgan demanded, do you think we'll get it tomorrow?"

"I hope so with all my heart." He rubbed his chin, scratching at the small hairs there. "It is time to get out of this place. I don't like to stay so long in any one city."

"Any city or more particularly one you have robbed?"

"Any city. They make my skin itch."

"Pardon?"

"I do not know what it is, but in big cities my skin itches. I can find no salve to give me ease. It is not until I am back on my ship or away from large companies of people that it stops."

"Perhaps it's nothing but a fancy of your mind."

"Perhaps so but it is a fancy that feels real to my skin, nevertheless."

There was a brief silence that was again broken by Dido.

"I do not need too many people around me, just those I love," she said, thinking of her family.

"In that, then, we are alike though I do not have to love them so long as they are few."

"Do you hate people, then?"

"No. I just have no need of them. Too many have evil hearts and are happiest only when they do evil."

Dido thought back to when she'd seen him rifling among the dead.

"Isn't what we've done here evil?"

"This was war."

"Torturing that mute woman until she died?" Dido persisted.

He straightened up, scowling.

"In war, these things happen."

"But she wasn't a soldier. She was just a…a woman." Like herself.

"She was an innocent, I grant you that. But do you not understand yet that if the Spaniards landed in Jamaica the residents there would experience nothing different? This is how wars are fought, they are dirty and they are bloody and sometimes innocent people get killed through no fault of their own." He paused. "Dido, this is why you must never do this again. You have not the heart for it."

Dido looked at him in surprise. Where was this coming from? "When you get back to Port Royal, go look for your family and stay away from the coastal towns and from the brethren."

"Why do you say such things? Have I not served you well? I have as much courage as any man."

His face softened. "I do not dispute that, brave Missy-boy, but this." He waved his hand around the fort, taking in the revelers, and, beyond them, the captives in their cells. Morgan had ordered his men to throw the dead over the side and burn them. The fetid smell of burnt bodies hung in the air. "This is not for you."

"And yet I am here."

"Yes, and you've fought well but what would you have done if I hadn't stopped Richard just now?"

She had no answer to that.

"I will be able to stop his designs on you so long as you are on the *Fortune's Gift* but what if you sign up on another ship and meet such as he? Or what if your secret is discovered? Who will save you then?"

"I'll save myself," she growled, knowing he spoke the truth.

"May your Goddess grant you the power," he said. He reached up and touched her cheek before she could flinch away in surprise. "Your skin is so smooth."

Dido did not move, did not blink. His palm cupped her cheek and his thumb brushed her lips. In the flickering light of the nearby fire his eyes were as soft as fresh molasses. Dido groaned, a small sound, like that of a yawning kitten but it was enough to startle him. His eyes widened and she heard his swift intake of breath.

"I…" His hand dropped. "I…I must go." He sprang up from where they sat. Before Dido could recover, could say anything to stay him he had crossed the square, grabbed the delighted whore by her arm and pulled her down a dimly-lit street. Dido felt numb. Unable to move or think she continued sitting on the wall even as the music died down and the revelers melted into the shadows.

Yacahüey found her there the next morning, her knees hunched under her chin, her eyes red with sleeplessness.

"Today the Spaniards must pay the fine or suffer the consequences," he said by way of greeting. He lowered himself unto the wall next to her and offered her a piece of his bread.

"Not hungry," Dido said, not bothering to raise her head. Her thoughts were consumed with images of El Negro and the laughing woman she knew he'd taken to his bed. Long after he'd gone she had considered going to look for him but she had no idea where he slept. He could have been in any one of the dozen officer's quarters or he could just have taken the woman in the street or some alleyway, though she did not think that was quite his way.

"Among my people, a woman as thin as you is not desirable. You should eat more." The Taino took a big bite of the bread and chewed contentedly.

It said a lot for Dido's state of mind that it took a full minute for his words to sink in.

"What? What did you say?"

"You heard aright."

"What do you mean? For the love of Oshun, tell me what you mean."

"My meaning is clear."

"I'm not a woman."

The man shrugged. "That is what you would have people believe but I know your true nature."

"How?" she whispered. "How do you know?"

Yacahüey wiped his mouth and dusted his hands on his breeches.

"You are a woman. I know it like how I know water is wet or that fire burns." He pulled on the amulet around his neck. "It is of no moment to me."

"Does anyone else know?"

"Unless it glitters, these men cannot see it though it be right under their noses."

Dido sighed in relief.

"Why have you kept my secret?"

"As I said, it is of no moment to me if women not of my race decide to dress like men and to act as men do." He slid her a sidelong glance and smiled. "A lucky thing, too, for if you were found out it would go ill with you."

"What would happen?"

"Most likely they'd leave you alone on a small island somewhere with just enough food and water for a day. You need not fear that fate for I doubt your ruse will be discovered."

"El Negro…" Dido started to say.

"I know he knows. He considers you under his protection and wishes you to leave his ship with your innocence as intact as possible given what you've seen and done during this voyage."

"I've experienced worse on the plantations."

The Taino nodded. "That I do not doubt. He cares for you, you know. He was like a madman when he could not find you the day we took La Gloria."

"He was?"

"He looked everywhere. He was convinced you were dead but he did not want to look among the corpses for you."

"I caught him."

Yacahüey raised an eyebrow at her.

"I caught him stealing from the dead. The morning after. He was going through the bodies."

"His lust for treasure is indeed strong but not that strong. He was looking for you."

Dido pondered this in silence. She could have kicked herself for instantly assuming the worse. They were both looking for the other. She had done him a great wrong. But why had he not said anything when she'd accused him as she did? The Taino had given her a lot to think about but, around them, pirates were beginning to emerge from wherever they had spent the night. Dido reluctantly decided to let the conversation go. She would have to pick it up another time though she didn't know when. With the additional Dutch pirates, the *Fortune's Gift* was so crowded it did not allow for many private conversations outside of the captain's cabin. Her eyes searched the growing crowd for El Negro but he was nowhere to be seen.

"Did you know the Spanish call that island Isla de Draque?" Yacahüey pointed to the small island at the mouth of the bay, a little distance beyond the pirate fleet.

"Drake's Island?"

"Yes." Yacahüey stared at it morosely. "Many hundreds of moons ago, when the Spanish still controlled much of the New World there was an English pirate by the name of Sir Francis Drake who preyed on their ships and the cities they sought to build. The English were jealous of the riches the Spanish had found."

"You mean the riches the Spanish took from the native peoples."

Yacahüey nodded. "The gold flowed across the sea to the King of Spain as if pulled by a current but Drake did his best to seize as much of it as he could for England's Queen. He was a most successful pirate and did great harm to Spain. After he captured the city of Nombre De Dios, he set out to take Panama City but he became very ill and died. His crew buried him in the waters yonder. It is said that whenever England is at war with Spain, the people in Puerto Bello hear the sound of a distant drum. Those who pass the island claim to have seen a man in old-fashioned dress standing on the shoreline looking out to sea. Drake—waiting for his ship."

"Do you believe that?" Dido asked, remembering the statuette of Jesus.

The Taino shrugged.

"There are mysteries in this world that cannot be explained by human knowledge."

Dido accepted this in silence and squinted at the island trying to see if she could see anyone or anything.

Behind her, the roosters crowed in excitement and men's voices quieted. Dido and Yacahüey turned back to watch as Morgan strode out to speak with the assembled men.

"This morning I received a messenger from the President of Panama," Morgan shouted, standing on a ledge along the castle wall in order to be seen by all. "He asked to be shown a few of those arms with which we took this city and with which we overcame the force he sent against us." This was news to many who murmured to each other in surprise. "I've sent him a pistol, some small bullets and a bottle of wine along with the message that he may keep the pistol and bullets for twelve months at which time I'll return for them. The bottle he may keep." The pirates laughed and Morgan grinned under his moustache. "It is time to find out whether we will leave this beautiful city more or less as we found her or if we must burn it to the ground." He nodded to some men who hurried off, returning presently with two Spaniards.

The captives carried a heavy chest between them and the pirates carried an even larger one. These were placed on the ledge beside Morgan who pulled back their lids. A sigh of satisfaction went up from the pirates in the front of the crowd. Dido craned her neck to see. The chests were full of pieces of eight. The Spaniards had saved their city. The pirates cheered.

"We've got what we came for," Yacahüey said, beside Dido. "It's time to take our leave."

"Do we go back to Port Royal now?" she asked, her eyes once again scanning the swarming throng.

"No. Now we go to some isolated cay where Morgan can divide the spoils," Yacahüey grinned. "There'll be at least one thousand pieces of eight for every man," he winked at her, "and woman."

"One thousand," Dido breathed, her attention caught by the riches. It was about the same as they would have made had they sold the slaves. Doubtless, Oshun and the gods of Guinea had rewarded the pirates of the *Fortune's Gift* with victory for giving the Africans their liberty.

"Probably more," Yacahüey said, holding his amulet in his hand and massaging it with his fingers. "The jewelry and other coins obtained will be part of the final count and should raise the number we each collect."

Dido thought of the necklace Yacahüey had pocketed and of the brooch now pinned to her chest in the same way its original owner had worn it.

"How much is…" She looked around to see if anyone was within hearing distance or paying attention. "How much is it worth?"

"Your pretty bauble?" He grinned, keeping his voice low. "More than one hundred pieces of eight I'd be willing to bet. I've never seen a pearl as big as that."

"Pearl." Dido rolled the unfamiliar word around on her tongue.

"The one in the middle's the pearl. The shiny stones around it are diamonds and emeralds." Seeing her look of puzzlement, he explained. "The green ones are the emeralds, the clear, diamonds. In Port Royal, they'll think it a bargain at five hundred pesos. Go to the Jew, Joseph, on High Street. He gives honest prices. Though, if I were you, I'd save it against a time of deepest need." He nodded at the thinning crowd of pirates. "Most of these will squander all their earnings within a month of their return to Port Royal. They think not of tomorrow but spend their money as if they expect the world to end the next day and them with it."

"It is time to make for the ships." The voice of Thomas Cobb, Morgan's quartermaster, broke in on them. "We sail on the morrow."

Dido and the Taino jumped down from the wall.

Chapter 15

Three of the other pirate ships had already left the harbor the next morning and the *Satisfaction* was just beginning to make its way to the open sea when El Negro finally arrived at the shore. From where she stood at the side of the *Fortune's Gift*, Dido could see that he was still holding on to the Spanish whore as tightly as he had when he'd left the revelry two nights before. She'd heard the other men whispering that he'd locked himself up in a room with her, emerging only for meals and to do his business. Her heart turned to pap and swished around at the bottom of her belly as he pulled the woman to him and kissed her, appearing almost to devour her face. His crew cheered wildly but Dido turned away, trying not to be sick. He was just like Morgan and the rest, no different. How could she have thought so? She crossed over to starboard and pretended to be fascinated by the turtles swimming about in the clear sea but there was a crashing in her ears and her eyes were dry and itchy. She did not turn around when she heard the men greet him as he came aboard. She did not look his way once.

He ordered the Dutch captives set ashore for the Spanish to attend to and then commanded his men to get the ship under sail. Dido avoided him all day.

In the evening, when she was down in the hold with cook, he sent a sailor to call her to his cabin. On the way she passed Richard who stared at her intently, a lascivious smile on his lips and lust in his eyes. She gave him a wide berth and almost half-ran into El Negro's cabin.

"Your haste surprises me," the captain said when she hurried in. "I did not expect you'd be in such a hurry to heed my summons."

"I am not." She was also not in the mood for banter. The memory of him with his arm draped around the Spanish woman made her feel as raw as if someone had taken a caulking iron to her skin.

"Do you suffer from something? You have not looked yourself this past day."

And what did he know about it, Dido thought to herself.

"I am perfectly well," she said aloud. Had he not made his pleasure in the whore's flesh plain she might have told him how she longed for the feel of him and damn the consequences. Instead, all day she'd heard laughter from the forecastle as he made one ribald joke after another about the prowess of his whipstaff.

"Has Richard bothered you again? I swear I'll have him flogged and keel-hauled if he's harmed you."

"He's not been near me."

His eyes scanned her face and must have been satisfied by what they found there because he sat back down.

"By tomorrow we will be at the Isle of Pines where Morgan will split up the booty. By the end of the week, if all goes well and no storm hinders us, we should be back in Port Royal." He looked at her, his expression almost diffident. If she didn't know better she would have said that there was something almost unsure about him. "What will you do when we get back?"

"I have my plans."

He nodded, glancing at her then away again. *What was wrong with him*?

"My wound has healed almost completely."

"Oh. Good."

"I…look…" He took a deep breath. "I just wanted to say that if you think I've acted in any way inappropriately toward you, I am sorry."

This was unexpected. Dido frowned at him.

"Your behavior has been as it should be, I've found no fault with it." To the contrary she would have liked more of what she thought he was referring to; his hand caressing her cheek, his arm around her waist.

"Good." His face cleared. "I'm very glad to hear it. Well…" He looked around the room. "Bring me my dinner and then you may occupy yourself as you desire."

"Yes, captain." She left the cabin feeling even more dejected than she had that morning.

For the next day and a half, until they arrived at the Isle of Pines, Dido and her captain were scrupulously polite to each other.

"You see! He does not want you," Richard said, coming up behind her as she watched El Negro and his quartermaster being rowed over to the *Satisfaction*. "Why do you persist in this fancy like some kind of moonstruck girl?"

Dido ignored him, hoping he would go away.

"We could give each other such pleasure." He grabbed her behind. Instantly, the day became confused with night and her memories of another man's unwanted touch.

"Fool." Swift as thought she reached inside her shirt for the dagger she'd taken to carrying, spun around, and dug it into the palm of the offending hand with as much force as she could muster. "Damn you to hell," she screamed, pulling it out and digging it into his stomach before he could react.

He let go of her and clutched at his belly. A wine-red stain spread over his shirt-front. Blood dripped onto the salty deck.

"Cease," Yacahüey grabbed her arm as she was about to strike the quartermaster again.

The pirates of the *Fortune's Gift* crowded them, their voices raised in excitement.

"Silence," Yacahüey shouted. "Who saw what happened?" he asked.

At first no-one answered then the master gunner stepped forward.

"The sodomite grabbed the boy and the boy defended himself. I saw."

"Who else?" the Taino asked.

"I," said the mulatto. "I saw and the master gunner speaks the truth."

"It is the truth," called another man sitting in the rigging.

Richard groaned. "Help me, please, please, Yacahüey." He knelt in a widening pool of blood.

The Taino bent over him. "I can do nothing for you. When El Negro returns, we will vote on your fate. You were warned." He instructed one of the men to find some cloth with which to bind the quartermaster's hand and stomach and they left him where he was. When his groans became more than one of the men could bear, he threw a bucket of sea-water on him. Richard did not make any noise after that.

El Negro and William returned to the *Fortune's Gift* near evening when the sky had begun to darken.

Told about the incident as soon as he stepped on deck, the captain reminded his crew that they should be merciful for Richard had been a good bo'sun and could not help his nature. A vote was called and the pirates agreed to leave him behind on the Isle of Pines with a week's supply of beer, two loaves of bread, a pistol with five bullets and a small horn of gunpowder. The island had many fresh-water streams and was also populated by wild goats so if he recovered from his wounds and conducted himself wisely he would not starve. They also agreed to give him his share of the spoil as he had fought bravely and well so one thousand, two hundred pieces of eight were counted out, put in a cloth pouch and stashed among his other belongings. As the other ships began to make their way out of the small harbor, El Negro ordered two men to row Richard ashore. The divvying up of the other men's share of the spoils would wait until the men ferrying him ashore had returned.

Dido watched the small boat with a mixture of regret and relief. She was sorry he would be left alone there but she was glad she would no longer be made uncomfortable by his presence on the ship. The men returned in less than half an hour. El Negro had them searched to ensure they had not stolen Richard's share of the booty and then the share-out began. First, the captain put aside his share which included two thousand pieces of eight, twenty bolts of silk, an elaborate dagger with a mother-of-pearl hilt, five heavy gold rings with stones in all colors and a silver goblet studded with gems. William received one thousand five hundred pieces of eight. Finally, the share-out to each of the ordinary seamen began, the master gunner being counted among them since his services had not been used. Puerto Bello was taken by small arms and cutlasses not with cannon.

As the youngest of the seamen and the last to sign up, Dido received one thousand pieces of eight. She hefted a handful of the silver coins in her hand, taking pleasure in the feel of more money than she had ever touched in her life.

"Thanks be to Oshun and to Oludumare and all the gods of Guinea," she whispered to herself, scooping the coins into the small wooden box Yacahüey gave her. She could buy her mother, her sister and her two small brothers and still have enough to send Missus Sarah the rest of what she owed her for her own freedom. She'd give Delia some too and use the rest to buy the supplies she needed to build her family a house. She glanced at El Negro. If her dreams came true, she would never see him again.

"Are you still upset by what happened with Richard?" El Negro asked as she set his plate of stewed beef on the table in front of him later that evening.

"A little," she said. "I feel sorry for him."

"He should not have touched you." He bent to his food.

"No." She remembered the groping on the grass mat, the furious thrusting and the pain like a blood-red flower between her legs. But that man was still alive, still the owner of his plantation, still hurting other little girls for aught she knew. Richard had only touched her and now he was on an island all by himself. He might recover from his injuries as well as he might not, in which case he would die alone and be forgotten by all who had known him, except for her.

"Have you eaten?"

Dido shook her head.

"Come, Missy-boy." He indicated the seat next to him. "This is too much for me. Have some."

Dido sat down, accepting the spoon which he pushed her way, along with the plate. The stew tasted as good as it looked. Dido quickly took another spoonful and passed the spoon back to him. They ate like that, sharing the spoon between them until the plate was empty.

"Would you like more?" El Negro asked.

"My belly is full," Dido replied, yawning.

"You have a perfect mouth, do you know that?"

Heat suffused her cheeks.

"Your lips are perfectly formed, the lower being only slightly fuller than the top. The other women of Beeston's Estate must have been jealous of that perfection, wishing it for themselves."

"Jealous? Of me?"

He nodded.

"They are perfect, perfect." He had not raised his eyes from her mouth.

"For what? Eating?" she asked, to distract him because a knot was forming in her stomach. She felt lightheaded. The air in the cabin suddenly seemed warm and close.

"No, not for eating." He leaned forward in his chair. "For this."

Before she could move, before she could do anything at all, his lips were on hers and then his tongue was gently, oh, so gently, forcing her mouth open and his arms were around her waist pulling her to him. Desire snaked through Dido like a river of burning sulfur as he kissed her cheeks, her eyelids, her ears. Her hands floated up to rest on his shoulders and she arched her upper body against his, returning his kisses with equal fervor. The feel of his hard muscles under her hands, the sea-salt smell of his skin in her nose, it all worked on her until she thought she was dreaming and none of it was real. Not the kisses, not the hardness of his chest, not the bulge at the crotch of his breeches over which her fingers fluttered as delicately as moths' wings. Frightened by the feel of his manhood and by the sudden unbidden memory of Richard and that other man, she gasped. El Negro reared back as if bitten. Dido's eyes snapped open. His face was a mask of horror.

"Out." His voice was a guttural whisper. "Get out."

"I…"

"Get out," he repeated, not letting her speak. Suiting action to words, he shoved her to the door.

"I do not understand," she said, tears of frustration welling in her eyes.

"Out or my honor is lost." He shoved her again, his face remote, a scornful stranger's. "Leave now."

Dido fled.

Like a wounded animal seeking shelter, she dived down the hatchway into the hold and buried herself among the piles of canvas and the ropes. There, she finally allowed herself to cry, confident she could not be heard above the creaking of the ship and wash of the waves. Her gasp had broken whatever spell Oshun had cast over him and had reminded him of his vow to see her safely returned to Port Royal. She dug her fists into her eyes and cried until she had a headache and her hiccups threatened to give way to loud retches. She had lost whatever chance she'd had with him. He didn't want her.

She spent the night in the hold and emerged on deck the next day, her eyes swollen, her spirit empty.

As soon as he saw her, Yacahüey rushed over to lead her back to the hatchway.

"The captain says he does not want you above deck," he said, his voice low but concerned. "You are to stay in the hold until we reach Port Royal and then he'll give you back your box. He has piled on as much sail as the masts will take without breaking. The men are worried but he is determined to waste no time returning to port."

Dido listened to all this in silence, her head spinning.

"I will go now and bring you some food."

She was not hungry but it was as if she'd forgotten how to speak. By the time she opened her mouth to tell the Taino not to bother, the man was already halfway across the ship. He returned with two biscuits and a bowl with some leftover beef stew from the night before. He thrust the food into her hands and then pushed her gently toward the hatch.

"Don't be concerned. The time will go quickly."

He was wrong.

Every turn of the hourglass was like a hundred years to Dido as she replayed the scene in El Negro's cabin over and over again in her mind. By the morning of the second day, when Yacahüey came to tell her the hills of Jamaica were in sight, she had come to the conclusion that El Negro had treated her unjustly, whatever his reasoning. Her fury and grief grew and became a cold, hard gobbet in her chest. He had wronged her. She repeated this to herself with every creak of the ship, every roll of the waves. By the time Yacahüey came to give her the box of money and take her on deck so she could be among the first to leave the ship, she'd decided she would think no more on the pirate captain. She would devote all her energies, of mind as well as body, to her original dream of making a home for herself and her family. He would never be part of that particular dream now, she saw that clearly.

Sitting in the launch taking her to shore, she faced away from the *Fortune's*

Gift, her eyes glued on the storehouses and wooden piers lining Port Royal's harbor. In her mind she went over the list of things she had to do. She pushed away every thought of the captain as fast as it surfaced. He had abandoned her and she would think on him no more. But every pull on the oars was a stab in her heart and it was only with the greatest restraint that she stopped herself from jumping in the sea and swimming back to the ship, back to him. "Oshun, lend me strength," she whispered. "Heal my heart, Oshun. Restore my joy." Her prayers brought her a measure of peace but she knew it would take time for Oshun to truly cleanse her spirit of the feelings El Negro had wrought in her.

Yacahüey sat beside her, out of companionship and pity or because El Negro had instructed him to see her to shore she did not know but she was glad for the man's silent presence. His frequent visits to the hold had been a source of great comfort to her.

"Where will you go?" Yacahüey asked, nudging her from her reverie.

"To find my family and pay the cost of their freedom." He knew so much about her, there was no reason why he should not know that, too. "If the owner will agree to this." It was the first time that it had occurred to her he might not. Having the money with which to pay him had always been a distant and indistinct dream. Now it was a reality she was brought up short by the realization that Master Neville Sedgewick might have no interest in selling a woman who worked as hard as her mother, Unmi, did and whose skill with healing herbs was known far and wide.

"It is my belief that at the sight of silver and gold, most European men will agree to anything." The Taino laughed.

"And what of you?" She knew so little about him.

"I will stay in Port Royal for a time. If El Negro decides to sail again soon, I will sail with him, if not…" He shrugged. "I like to observe the ways of Europeans. Towns are the best places for this."

"Are you not afraid you'll be abducted and enslaved?"

Again, the expressive movement of his broad shoulders. "We have a saying, 'what the gods will, the gods will'."

They had reached one of the piers along the waterfront and Dido clambered out of the boat, clutching her box tightly to her chest.

"Do not let anyone see your treasure," Yacahüey said in a low voice, climbing out to stand beside her. "Take out a few coins and keep them separate from the rest. Use those for your expenses so people around you will believe you have only a little money." Dido nodded thinking of the three men who had attacked her. Her masculine garb might give such robbers pause but not stay them altogether. "Tell no-one you were on Morgan's expedition for word of the booty will get around and all will assume you are rich."

He leaned forward, searching her face.

"You are an honorable woman and you fought bravely. It has been my honor to know you."

"Thank you. It…it was my honor to fight with you, too," she said, shyly.

The Taino grinned. "Remember what I have said and I know you will fare well." He began to walk away down Cope's Alley and was just about to round a corner when he turned back.

"May I know your true-true name?"

"Dido," she shouted, not caring who heard. She was back on land now. Where could they maroon her? The Taino waved and disappeared.

Chapter 16

irst, Dido went to the nearby tavern where she'd run up a tab before her departure and paid her bill. Then she made her way to The Sugar Loaf.

Blanche was scraping bones into a bin at the back. Dido rapped on the rough wooden counter to draw her attention and called her over.

She placed ten pieces of eight in a line before the woman. "For Domingo Freeman's debt," she said to the astonished barmaid.

"I thank ye." The woman's smile lit her face.

Dido hurried off, making now for the High Street market. As she walked, she took out some more coins from her box, dropped them into her pouch and wrapped her sash around the box. The box was still recognizable as a box under the yellow cloth but she thought it would not draw the eye as much as leaving it uncovered. She placed it in her basket and covered it with her other belongings. In the absence of any other means of hiding her riches, it would have to do. The beautiful brooch Yacahüey had given her lay beneath the coins. She would try to hold on to it as long as she could. It would be her surety for the future when all the pieces of eight were spent.

Dido strode quickly through the crowds. The pirates from one of the other ships of the Puerto Bello expedition were already in the town but if any recognized her, they gave no sign. Men and women talked excitedly to each other on street corners, dazed with news of the sack of one of the greatest cities in the New World. They said that Morgan must now be richer than the king himself. People speculated on when he would return to Port Royal, some thought he'd go to Tortuga and spend his money there instead. Others said he was headed for Virginia or the Bahamas. Avid-faced men took wagers on exactly how much he'd seized. Dido heard all kinds of outlandish figures bandied about but she paid them no mind as she hurried to the marketplace.

The third thing on her list of things to do was find Old Philippa but, as it happened, the fourth item came before the first. Ian was standing by one of the stalls eating an orange, the thin yellow juice running down his chin. When she saw her, he let out a delighted yelp.

"Domingo," he shouted and dived toward her. He grabbed her by the hands and did an excited jig. "You made it back. I knew you would. Tell me everything." His words bubbled out of him like a mountain spring. "Did you kill a Spaniard? What did you get?"

"Shh, shh," she whispered, trying to quell the boy's excitement. He was attracting altogether too much attention.

"Yes, I unnerstand." he whispered back, immediately catching on. "It did go well, Domingo?" His eyes shone.

"Very well, Ian. What about you and your mother? I'm so glad you made it back safely"

He smiled from ear to ear.

"The captain of *The Flying Dragon* said he was going to Hispaniola so Morgan made him promise to stop here first. Listen." He dropped his voice. "I did get fifty pieces of eight for it, for the ring." Dido frowned. She was willing to bet it was worth far more. "And I did give me muvver forty. You should have seen her face, Domingo. I never seen her look so."

"Did she buy the new dress?"

"No, she's a washerwoman now and she also takes in sewing so she bought herself a bigger tub and some brushes and other things. It dursn't matter about the dress, she said." He pushed his forelock back. "I guess she's happy and that be all that counts."

Dido nodded. Ian's mother had made a wise decision. Better to spend an unexpected windfall on things that will bring you more money in the end than to spend it on fripperies that would soon decay, leaving you as impoverished as before.

"And all is well with you?" she asked, looking him over with relief.

"Oh, yes, Domingo." He looked around and dropped his voice. "And I still have six of the pieces of eight. I've been most frugal."

Despite herself, Dido laughed. He looked so proud of himself.

"Good for you, Ian. You've done well." She considered giving him ten more but decided against it. She had much to accomplish. If she did everything she set out to do and still had money left over she would give him what she could.

"I need your help," she said, sobering. "I am looking for the old woman I sought when we first met."

"Old Philippa." He nodded. "I remember her name. I found someone as might know her. Come."

Dido threaded her way through the vendors, following the bobbing cap of brown hair in front of her.

"That woman there says she saw her." He indicated a market woman who sat on the ground behind an array of straw goods.

"You went looking for my friend?"

"Figured it was the least I could do, in case you din't get back. I was planning to give her a couple of the coins. I thought that was what you'd want me to do."

"Ian!" Dido was touched to her core.

"It weren't nothing." He looked bashful. "I gets about so what the hell?"

She could have kissed him.

"She knows her?"

"So she says."

They walked over to the woman.

"This is Old Philippa's friend as I was telling you about," Ian said to the woman. She had a pleasant, round face and wore a scarf on her head, tied in the manner of some of the women newly come from Guinea.

"Your friend wanted to know if I knew the old one," she said. Her voice had no trace of the continent. "Why do you seek her?"

"I knew her from Beeston's. I did not get a chance to say good-bye or to give her something I had for her." The pewter mug was in her basket. She meant to fill it with pieces of eight when she gave it to Old Philippa.

The woman grimaced. "Then it is sorry I am to tell you she is with the ancestors."

"No."

"I am sorry, child. We did our best for her, me and a couple others, but…" She let her words hang in the air.

"How…from what did she die?"

"That I cannot tell you. We found her in the street a month ago, shivering and talking out of her head though she was able to give us her name. No-one nearby laid claim to her so we took her to the poorhouse. The next day when I went to see about her, she lay stiff on the pallet. She'd died during the night and none had moved her." The woman sucked her teeth in disgust and indignation.

Dido sank to the ground, burying her face in her hands. Tears streamed down her cheeks and through her fingers.

"Aiieee," she cried. If El Negro had stabbed her in her heart, this news was a stab in her belly. "Nooo."

Ian patted her back and made hushing noises but it was a long time before she could gather herself again.

"A man in the poorhouse told us she came from Beeston's Estate on the Liguanea Plain," the vendor said, continuing her narrative, "He did not know how she came to be in Port Royal."

"Missus Sarah had her brought here and dumped in the street," Dido said, reliving the day she'd gone to the quarters and found the old woman gone. "They said they could not afford to feed her but they were not feeding her. What they gave her was next to nothing. She fed herself."

"So it goes, my child." The woman grimaced again. "So it goes."

Dido clutched her basket to her chest, unable to push herself off her knees to her feet.

"And you," the woman said. "Are you a runaway too, like the market-woman Delia?"

"Delia has left Beeston's?"

"So I've heard. She ran with four others but I know only her."

"Where did she go? What were the names of the others?"

"The men were called, hmm, let me see. Miguel, I remember that name because I know another who is so called. They say one of the other men was his brother."

"Pablito."

"Yes." The woman nodded. "And the third was Nicholas. I cannot remember the name of the second woman. Betty or Daisy or something like that."

Daisy. Nicholas's woman.

"As to where they went, it is said that they followed another slave into the lush forests of the mountains in the center of the island."

"Another slave from Beeston's?"

"Her name was Dido."

Dido rocked back, surprised to hear her name.

"She was a market woman, too. You favor her."

"I do?" Dido glanced at Ian and rose to her feet. "Thank you, mother." She dropped a piece of eight in the woman's lap.

"I told you only what I know," the woman said. She picked up the coin and put it into a pouch at her waist.

"Where are we going to now?" Ian asked as Dido bought a couple loaves of bread, some salted fish and a clay jug of water from another vendor.

"I have a journey to make to a plantation near San Jago de la Vega." She was so nervous at the thought that she would soon see her family after so many years away from them, she overpaid the vendor but she did not care.

"That be more'n a day's walk," Ian protested.

"So the earlier I set out, the better."

"I'll come with you. Wait, let me buy my own bread."

He darted away before she could stop him.

Dido debated leaving without him but she could not do that to the boy. He'd been a good friend to her and did not deserve her sneaking off. She decided to be firm with him when he returned.

"You cannot come with me, Ian," she said, when he reappeared.

"I want to."

"But why? My mission has nothing to do with you. I am going to buy my family's freedom. They are slaves on the estate of Massa Neville Sedgewick."

"I am wanting to meet your family."

"It will be a long walk and I'll not be returning to Port Royal if I am successful." If! She didn't know what she would do if she wasn't.

"All the more reason for me to come then." He smiled broadly. "I want to hear all about Morgan and Puerto Bello and everything. You have to tell me. I'll make my own way back, do not worry about that."

And he would too. He was the bravest boy she knew.

Unable to think of a further argument, Dido led the way out of Port Royal. They walked quickly but, by nightfall, Ian was tired. Though Dido could have walked on, her yearning for her family like a wind at her back, she reasoned that it was best to stop so they could arrive rested. Massa Neville was a hard man. She would need to have all her wits about her. They stopped under a huge tamarind tree by the roadside and made themselves comfortable among its roots. The moon was almost full. The stars shone with twice the luster of the diamonds in the brooch she still wore pinned to the bindings around her chest. Dido cradled the box in one arm and rested her head in the palm of her other hand.

It was the first night of September. The air was not yet chilly. It seemed to Dido that the ground rocked gently under her but she knew this had more to do with the months she'd spent on the sea than with Shango shaking the earth. It would probably take her a while to become accustomed to land again. She was just about to doze off when Ian spoke.

"If their owner will not sell your family, will you go back on El Negro's ship?"

The mention of the pirate's name brought a chill to her heart.

"No, Ian, I do not think so." She paused but she'd have to tell him sooner or later. He had already proven himself a good friend and she was sure she could trust him. "There is something you don't know about me."

"That you are a girl, you mean?"

"Ian!" Her head snapped around. The boy never failed to surprise her. Was her nature an open secret? How many others had known and said nothing?

"I knowed all along. I just never saw fit to say nothing, figured you'd tell me when you was ready."

"From the time you met me in the market, you knew?"

"You din't have no hardness about you. I could see it straight away. When you lives on the street, you gotta be able to tell straight away about people."

"Well…" His revelation took her breath. "I guess I owe you my thanks."

"It ain't necessary. You been like a brother…a sister to me though I ain't known you but so long."

"You have my gratitude just the same. If you'd told, I would never have gotten what I needed to purchase my family's freedom."

"You'd have done it some other way." He turned to look at her. "There's something driven about you. You're Dido, ain't you? You're the one the woman talked about."

"Yes." She could barely keep her eyes open now. "I did not know the others would follow, though. They said nothing to me." She wondered where they were and if they were safe. Ian did not respond. She glanced at him. He was fast asleep. Dido turned on her side and closed her eyes.

Chapter 17

"Dido! Dido! Is it you?" The body of the woman running toward her was thicker than Dido remembered but the voice was the same.

"Mumma!" Dido tore off the bandana she still wore around her head and raced to meet her mother. "Mumma." Her mother's arms opened to receive her and Dido hurtled into them, almost knocking the older woman over.

"Child. My own child." Unmi reared back to look Dido in the face, not letting go of her daughter for one second. "I never thought I'd see you again or that these arms would hold you. How goes it with you? Are you well?"

"Mumma, yes," Dido said through her laughter and her tears. "I'm well but what of you? How goes it with you and the little ones?"

"We are all well. None have been taken in death, thanks be to the gods. Oh, my child." Unmi stepped back to look her daughter up and down. "You are so thin. Why are you dressed as a man?"

"It is a long story, Mumma. I can tell you when we leave."

"Leave? What do you mean, 'leave'?"

"I have come to pay for your freedom." She grabbed her mother's hands in hers. "I've come to pay Massa whatever he wants for you and the children."

"Child, what crazy talk is this? Look, your brothers have come to meet you." She pulled two round-faced young boys to her.

"Ah, Mumma." Dido's stomach twisted as she saw that the boys did not recognize her. They had been little more than babies when she was sold away. "George. Zacchariah. Do you not remember me at all? I used to make you dolls of straw."

The boys shook their heads and would not leave their mother's side.

"Where is Claribel?"

"I left her in the fields without telling her anything for I did not want Massa Taylor to ask questions. I thought the child you sent to call me must be mistaken. He said your son, Dido. Now I see why he spoke as confusingly as he did."

Dido grinned. "And this is my friend, Ian, who came with me all the way from Port Royal."

Ian touched his forelock. Unmi nodded to him, her expression puzzled but friendly.

"Mumma, I do not want to stay here long but I wanted to see you before I went up to look for Massa. I've come to pay for your freedom and take you away from here. I will pay for you all."

"What madness has seized your mind?" Unmi's eyes searched her face. "You do not seem to have any ill humor," she murmured, pulling Dido's eyelids gently down, pinching her arms.

"Mumma, stop. Look." Dido dropped to her knees in the dust, drew her box out from the basket, unwrapped the linen covering and opened it.

Her mother fell down beside her, speechless, her eyes round as she contemplated the silver coins. She put her hand out tentatively to touch them. Her fingers caressed the metal pieces as lightly as a woman stroking the cheek of her sleeping child.

"I got it for us, Mumma, so we may live free." Dido watched her mother closely. This was not going quite as she had expected. Her mother should have been ululating in joy by now. Instead, she clasped her hands to her chest in silence, her face glum.

"It's for us, Mumma," she said. "Aren't you glad?"

Her mother's shoulders shook. She was crying but whether in joy or grief, Dido could not tell. She glanced at Ian who hunched his shoulders. She guessed he had not expected this either.

"They will kill you for this," her mother said, her voice raspy and brittle like old leaves.

"Kill me?"

"We are flogged near to death for much less. The theft of such a sum…" Unmi was unable to complete the sentence, unable to face the thought of her daughter's execution.

"Mumma, this is mine. I earned it."

"She speaks the truth, Ma'am," Ian said, nodding vigorously. "She was a pirate."

"A pirate?"

"Yes, Mumma, but never mind. There will be time enough for me to tell you everything."

"You did not steal this?" Unmi's eyes moved backward and forward from the box to her daughter as if she feared one or the other would vanish like a dream.

"No, I mean, in a manner of speaking it was stolen but the captain of my ship gave it to me. It is ours, Mumma, you and me and the boys and Claribel. Ours." The word billowed up from her chest and out her mouth as if she herself had just made it up on the spur of the moment, and it had never been heard before.

"Is Massa Neville up at the Great House?"

"That is where he spends his days now, drinking his money away."

"Come, Mumma, take me to your hut."

Once there, Dido counted out three hundred pieces of eight and wrapped them back up in her sash. She was going to give the box to her mother to hide but a sudden premonition made her give it to Ian. Yacahüey's advice rang in her ears.

"Hide it off the plantation," she instructed him.

"By the river," he said, nodding. He'd seen the river that bordered the property on the east and become excited about the prospect of finding crayfish. "Maybe I can find a cave or something."

"That would be perfect." Dido threw her small bundle of coins over her shoulder. "This should be more than enough to purchase my family's freedom even if he charges me dear."

"Mumma." She sought her mother's embrace once more.

"I will come with you, daughter," Unmi said, her arm still around her daughter's waist.

Dido nodded, grateful.

"He will not refuse you," Ian said, giving her an encouraging smile before he turned away, heading back the way they had come.

The women walked slowly. Unmi sighed heavily several times and once clicked her tongue as if in conversation with herself.

"Is something wrong, Mumma?"

"Ah, child." Unmi hugged her daughter closer. "I never thought you would fill my eyes again. Were you well-treated by the new Massa?"

"Better than I was in Nevis." She shuddered. "I can never forget Massa Simon. The stink of him. The noises he made when he was inside me."

Unmi squeezed her arm.

"Daughter, I wanted to take your place. I...asked, I begged him..." Her voice cracked. "He did laugh and say I was too old. He liked your young flesh. I am so sorry. So sorry. I never had the chance to tell you that. I hated him. I wanted to kill him."

"Mumma." Dido turned to face her mother. They stood so close their noses almost touched. "It was not your fault. I know that. I know."

Fat tears rolled down Unmi's cheeks.

"I did make up my mind to kill him, you know," she whispered.

"Mumma." Her mother's admission shocked Dido.

"I was going sink my cane knife into his neck when he did come for you. I did pray about it and I was ready for him the next time he came but then he sold us off." Her mother sighed, making more of those strange clicks. "I did think then that it was the will of the gods so I could live long enough to see my children bear children in their turn."

"Maybe it was, Mumma, maybe it was." Dido no longer pretended that she could even guess Oshun's intentions. In fact, her conversation with El Negro and the killings she'd witnessed had shaken her faith. Though she loved the gods of Guinea no less, she now doubted their power.

"Freedom," Unmi whispered. "This word tastes funny on my tongue after so many years. What if he will not sell us?"

"He must," Dido cried, fiercely. "He cannot refuse. If he does...if he does...then you must run."

"With the children?" Unmi looked skeptical.

"They are not babies to hold you back. Others have run with younger children."

Her mother only shook her head. If Massa Neville refused to sell she would not run and risk her children's lives. Neither would she leave them behind, she would stay if she couldn't take them with her. Everything hinged on Massa Neville. Dido whispered a prayer to Oshun, wishing for success with all her heart.

In minutes, mother and daughter had passed through the citrus grove and made their way past the cook house.

"Tell Massa, Unmi and her daughter Dido are come speak to him," Unmi said to a young mulatto girl on the back steps of the Great House. The girl turned and ran inside the house.

As Dido waited, anxiety slowly squeezed the air out of her lungs. She pushed back her shoulders and stepped away from her mother. It would not do for Massa Neville to think her weak. Her breath came in small pants.

"Massa Neville, good afternoon, sir," she managed, when he came out the door.

"Unmi's girl. Well, bless my soul." He came down the steps, planting his feet down heavily and carefully as men in their cups are wont to do.

"Beeston dresses his girls like boys, now, does he?" He laughed.

"Massa Richard died this twelvemonth."

He hiccupped in surprise, bleary eyes peering at her.

"So what brings you here? Does his dam want to sell you? I am not buying."

"Sir, I want to buy my family's freedom, that of my mother and that of my brothers and my sister."

"I told you I'm not buying. I don't need any more women about the place. Wait. What?" He blinked. "What did you say? It comes to me like you said you wanted to buy Unmi."

"That is what I said, Unmi and her children." Dido glanced at her mother but Unmi was looking at the ground below her feet as if searching for chiggers in the soil.

"You…you…" He couldn't finish, he was laughing too hard. "That's a good one, girl. Ho, ho. I like that one." The laughter doubled him up. He slapped his knees in merriment.

"I make no jest."

"No jest!" A fresh gale of laughter shook him. Tears ran down his cheeks. "I haven't laughed so in years, girl."

"How much do you ask for them? Tell me and I will pay."

"Tell you…oh, this is rich, this is the best yet."

"Tell me."

"One hundred pieces of eight and not a whit less for Unmi. See how I humor you."

"And the boys and Claribel?"

"Fifty each for the boys and eighty for Claribel."

Dido sighed in relief. He had asked less than she'd expected for Unmi and the boys though his price for Claribel was at least thirty pieces of eight higher than she'd imagined it would be.

She repeated the prices he'd quoted to her and when he nodded impatiently in confirmation she undid the bundle at her shoulder. Under the planter's astonished eyes she counted out two hundred and eighty pieces of eight.

"Did you steal that money, girl?" he asked, suddenly sober. His eyes fastened on the money.

"It's mine and if you'll sign the papers freeing Mumma and the others, it will be yours."

Without taking his eyes off the silver coins, he told Unmi to go fetch Massa Taylor and Massa Johns.

"Why do you need them?" Dido asked, putting a restraining hand on her mother's arm, suspicious.

"We'll need witnesses, will we not? Won't be legal except as it is witnessed." He licked a fleck of spittle from the corner of his mouth and smiled at her. "Go on, now," he said, nodding at Unmi. Dido released her hold on her mother. It had been stupid of her to leave her weapons behind. She bit her lip, keeping a close eye on the man in front of her but he made no sudden moves, seemed almost to have forgotten she was there as he hummed some funny tune, his eyes trained on the direction Unmi had taken.

She was back very quickly with the overseer and the manager behind her.

"Good, Unmi, now we're going inside to get them papers ready." Massa Neville put his arms around his employees. "You go and pack up such of your belongings as you want to take and get the children ready. Dido will come back to you when we're done."

Unmi looked at Dido who nodded. She did not know exactly how it was done but she knew papers were always involved in the white man's world. When she first became a market woman Massa Richard had signed a paper giving her permission to sell things on her own account. Without it she could not have gotten a stall in the market and could have been arrested by the militia for selling her things illegally.

After her mother left, Massa Neville led her to an airy room with a desk and some chairs and not much else. The men dropped the pieces of eight unto the desk and turned to face her.

"So you've gone and gotten yourself some money, eh, Dido," said Massa Taylor, a tall man with a peeling nose.

"Just enough to free my family."

"You know, now." Massa Neville dropped into a chair. He watched her intently. "I do not believe this is all you have. I believe you've got some more hid away like."

Dido shook her head.

"I do not, Massa. Just what I brought."

"That is what you say, but I do not believe you." He rested his elbows on the armrests and steepled his fingers. "What about you, men, do you believe her? She's brought that there." He waved at the desk. "I says she's got more left back."

"Could be all," Massa Taylor said. "She's nought but a slave."

"It is all," Dido insisted, growing uneasy. "Where are the papers? You said you had to sign some papers."

"And I will," Massa Neville said, narrowing his eyes. "Soon as you tell us where the rest of your money is."

"There is no more," she cried. "That is all there is. I swear to you." *And may Oshun forgive me.*

"Tell us where you got it," said Massa Johns, crossing his arms. He didn't believe one word of what she'd said, she could see it on his face.

"Did you steal it from Beeston's widow?"

"No. No."

"Where then? If you did not steal it, was it some man who gave it you?"

"I…I just got it. It's mine." Telling them where she got it would be as bad as telling them where the rest was. She was caught between Davy Jones's Locker and the deep blue sea.

"I could have you brought to the town square in San Jago and flogged for a thief. Do you think anyone would stop me? Who would believe a slave came by such a sum honestly?"

"You are the dishonest one. You named your price and I've met it and now you threaten me because you want more." Shades of Missus Sarah all over again. Was it impossible to trust any slave owner?

"Or I could take you back to Beeston and ask the good widow if she knows how you came by such an amount." He continued right on as if she hadn't spoken. "I'm sure she'd be glad to have the money back and you too."

"It's not hers. I swear it. You cannot take me back there. I'm a free woman. As soon as she could she'd send Missus Sarah the rest of the money she owed her and then she'd be free in truth, whatever the law said.

"Tell, and I sell. Refuse and you will rue this day."

"But you promised. I met your price!" Dido wanted to strangle him, to put her hands around that fat, greasy neck and squeeze and keep squeezing until there was no more life left in him.

Massa Neville pushed himself back in his chair so that its front feet left the ground and grinned, saying nothing. He did not have to. Dido understood it all. He was not going to sell, had never meant to write up any papers. Sending Unmi away was just a sham to isolate Dido.

She spun on her heel and strode over to the desk. She laid out her sash, grabbed a handful of the coins and was just about to drop them on the cloth when Massa Johns grabbed her by the wrist.

"Stop!" she cried. She tried to hit him with her other hand but he deflected the blow. Dido raised her knee to catch him in the groin but he twisted her around savagely, bringing his arm around her neck and pulling her against him backward. The coins dropped to the floor and rolled in every direction. It seemed to Dido that everything else froze, all sound and all movement. The only thing she could hear was the money. Each coin hit the ground like a hammer striking an anvil, hammering hope out of her world.

"Where are the rest?" Massa Neville's voice was indistinct as if he spoke from a great distance or as if cotton stoppered her ears. Massa Johns held her so tightly she could scarcely breathe. "I know you have more. Tell me, you tarry whore."

Dido frowned, trying to clear her head. She pulled at Massa Johns' arm but he was much stronger than her. The world dimmed. The last thing she thought she heard was Massa Neville saying, "Christ, man, she will tell us nothing if she's dead." Night fell on her, swift as a curtain.

Chapter 18

Dido awoke to the beating of a drum inside her skull. She groaned and tried to sit up. Her head spun and she realized it was a better idea to stay as she was. She lay on dirt but she knew she was not outside, the air was too still and foul for that. Dido swallowed hard. Her throat ached. Massa Johns had almost killed her. It was clear they had locked her up somewhere. She closed her eyes and thought hard, trying to figure out where she was, her ears pricked for any sound. The silence surrounding her was as total as the lack of light.

Though it hurt to move, she reached out and was rewarded when her right hand encountered a stone wall. Instantly she knew. She was in the dungeon, the cell built to hold slaves who had talked back to their massas or run away or committed some other violation of plantation rules. All the estates had them.

"Pssst! Dido."

"Mumma?"

"It is me, child."

"Mumma." Dido would have given every piece of eight she had to have been able to rest her head on her mother's bosom, and have her mother stroke her forehead and say everything was going to be alright.

"Child, I been calling to you all night. I was beginning to fear they done killed you."

"No, Mumma, but...my head aches. It aches bad."

"Oh, daughter, daughter. If I could tear these stones apart with my hands, I would."

There was a silence on both sides of the wall as each contemplated their separation.

"They took the money, Mumma," Dido said, remembering.

"Yes, daughter. I know. That boy, your friend, he says he has gone for help."

This news brought a small smile to Dido's face.

"From who?" she asked, curious. The militia would not help such as her. They were composed almost exclusively of planters like Massa Neville and would side with their own kind.

"He said your captain would help you, that he is an honorable man and does not hesitate to look out for his sailors."

El Negro. The boy had gone for El Negro. The pirate would send him packing in no uncertain terms when he heard what the boy had to say to him. If he was even still in Port Royal.

"The Massa says we're not to bring you any food but I will bring some come morning, daughter. Hold on, you hear. Hold on."

"Yes, Mumma."

Massa Neville had taken her money. Everything she'd fought for and dreamed of had slipped through her fingers like water. Dido didn't think things could get any worse but they did. Her mother did not return, not that morning, nor that night, nor the next. Only Massa Neville came but, each time, she turned her back on him and he went away without the answer he sought.

Hungry and starving, Dido felt she was floating in the middle of the sea, far from land, far from even the memory of land. Once she thought she saw El Negro and heard his voice but when she reached out to touch him, he vanished. The kind, sorrowful face of her goddess floated above her in the darkness of the cell and Dido knew she was dying. Dying without even getting a chance to tell the only man she'd ever loved how she felt about him.

The shouted curses and the sound of gunshots came from far away. Her thoughts were taking her back to Puerto Bello. Or was she dreaming?

Kablam!

The door to the dungeon burst open. A man stood in the doorway, blinking as his eyes got accustomed to the dark. In two strides, he bent to scoop her up in his arms. Out in the sun, everything was noise and heat as people surged around, shouting. Dido turned her face away into his chest. The sunlight burned her eyes. She sniffed, inhaling his scent, her brow furrowing as she tried to understand what was happening. El Negro tried to put her down but her knees were like water. She would have fallen if he had not grabbed her up back up again. He lowered himself carefully to the ground, holding her in his lap. Gently, he moved her so she could face her mother.

"Dido," Unmi murmured. "My baby." She held a calabash of water to her daughter's mouth.

Dido sipped the cool water, slowly at first, her mouth and throat so dry they couldn't move, then in great gulps.

"Not so fast, daughter. You will choke." Unmi took the calabash away and replaced it with a spoonful of honey from a jar. "This will ease your throat. Sip. Sip."

Dido's stomach roiled. Her mother gave her a small piece of bread and she wolfed it down despite the pain.

"Just a little for now. To give you back your strength. A little more later." Unmi ran her hand over her daughter's head, her face. "I don't know what I would have done if you'd died, daughter. I don't know. I had such anger in me. They locked me up in the house cellar so I couldn't come to you. They knew nothing else would keep me away."

She gave Dido another spoonful of honey, followed by more bread.

"Massa Neville's dead. Massa Johns, too."

Dido couldn't take it all in. *El Negro here! To release her from her prison! And now this. This was important, this was very important.* The thought floated to her like something from a distant shore. She had trouble focusing on it.

"Dead?" Dido asked, the word bursting out of her with great effort.

"Yes, dead. He killed them, your captain."

Dido turned her head.

"You came."

"As soon as the boy found me."

Ian! Dido pushed herself up to look around for him.

"I'm here, Dido." Ian poked his head over El Negro's shoulder.

Dido smiled weakly.

"How can I thank you?"

"You dursn't have nothing to thank me for, twas him did all the work. You should have seen him." Ian's face shone with hero-worship. "He had a pistol in each hand. Bang, bang. They din't even have time to fire." He laughed.

"The money?"

He held up the box in his hands, grinning proudly.

"I said I would keep it safe, din't I?"

Dido nodded. He had done better than most adults.

"Where is he?" she whispered.

"Who?" El Negro bent to hear her.

"Massa Neville."

"He lies where he died. In his house."

"I want to see him."

He searched her face.

"Are you sure?"

"As sure as the thunder of Shango."

El Negro nodded, his face grim.

"Can you walk?"

"Yes."

Straightening her legs hurt so she leaned on his arm. The slow procession encountered Massa Johns first. His body lay in the doorway of the room where he had almost strangled her. Dido stepped over him and made a beeline for Massa Neville's obese corpse.

"He was trying to escape, Dido," Ian said, able to keep silent no longer. "But the shot caught him on the shoulder, see."

Dido looked the body over in silence. Massa Neville had stolen her money and locked her away to die. Now the part he'd played in her life was over. She crossed to the table and pulled out the drawer. The pieces of eight lay scattered inside. Dido gathered them up in handfuls and put them back in the box Ian held out to her. She pushed her way back through the press of bodies behind her. One, by one, the people followed her outside.

"Captain, Massa Taylor gone. He gone to San Jago I sure," a man shouted, running up to them.

"What?"

"Abraham and a group of us did tie him up like you told us but he did get his hands loose." Perspiration ran down the man's forehead. El Negro cursed and he shrank back as if fearing a blow. "I sorry, sir, we did do our best. He did treat us better than the rest. We did not want to hurt him too bad."

El Negro swore again. "Now we will have little time to escape," he snapped.

"Before we had know it, he were running for the stables. We could not catch him because he did too far in front and then he did come out on Renegade. He the best horse Massa Neville have, did have," he corrected himself. "He gone San Jago. What going happen to we, sir?" The man's fear showed on his face as he looked anxiously at El Negro.

El Negro took a deep breath. Dido thought he was going to let lose another string of curses but he held himself back.

"You were not the ones who killed these men. I do not think they'll hold you responsible."

"Do you mean to stay, then?" an older woman asked.

"No, of course not. The gallows will not have me for ending the life of curs."

The woman nodded. "As I thought. And do you think the whites will care overmuch who they hang as long as someone is hanged?"

"Or someones," muttered the man beside her.

They made a good point. El Negro rubbed his chin, thinking, his eyes searching the landscape as if it could present him with an answer to their dilemma.

"We've got to make for the hills," he said. "There is no other way." His voice rose. "We must hide out in the hills until the militia is tired of searching for us."

"They will never tire," Unmi whispered. "White men are dead at the hands of a black."

"We will make them tire," El Negro said, hearing her. "Where did the man keep his guns?"

"I know," said the young girl who was on the steps when Unmi and Dido had arrived at the house.

"Show me. The rest of you, get the things you think you cannot leave behind and run for the hills as quick as you can. You and you and you," he said, pointing to men. "Go to the grounds and get all the food you can. Food enough for all. You and you." This time he singled out two women. "Fill some sacks with whatever food is in the house, bread, cheese and so forth."

"But if we do this we will not be able to bring our things with us," one of the women objected.

"The others will share what is theirs with you."

"We should all leave together," a man said. The people nodded, their eyes wide and frightened. Dido saw that they were scared. They needed someone to lead them into their new lives of freedom where they could decide on things for themselves and make their own choices.

"Meet me then at the edge of the cane piece facing the hills. Quickly, now."

The people scattered, most running to the quarters while those at whom El Negro had pointed ran to do his bidding. Only Dido and Ian remained.

"Ian, you must go now," she said, going over to him. "Return to your family."

"What will happen to you?"

"I do not know. But now that El Negro is here and my family is with me, I will not fear whatever comes." She took out the pewter mug from her basket and filled it with pieces of eight. "Take this for your mother."

"It is so much. I cannot."

"You must. It is what I planned to give Old Philippa. It would gladden my heart for you to have it."

Ian threw his arms around her, his cheeks wet.

"Will I see you again?"

"I hope so, Ian. A better friend to me, I could not have asked for."

He pulled away from her and ran across the yard, heading for the road.

"Go with Oshun, Ian," she whispered.

In about two hours' time, the freed slaves were running for the hills in a slow, shambling trot. Some had wanted to move faster but El Negro did not allow it, pointing out that they would only tire themselves long before they had reached the high mountains to the north of them. Youngsters carried the belongings of the elderly but there was none among them so old they could not keep up. Though anxiety shadowed some people's eyes, many faces also shone with joy. Dido knew they were thinking Moses had appeared to lead them out of Egypt to the land of milk and honey. No one looked back.

Behind them, the house and the cane pieces burned.

The idea to set fire to the plantation had come from Unmi. El Negro had agreed to it quickly, pointing out that the blaze might slow down the militia who would probably stop to try to put it out.

By nightfall, the people had reached the bottom of the mountains. Some of the older ones needed help picking their way up through the bush and Dido was glad the moon was able to light their way. El Negro wanted to put as much distance as possible between the plantation and themselves and kept them going, though the children were weary and some had to be carried.

"We will stop now," he finally said, as dawn broke in the east. "Eat and get what rest you can for we must be on the move again when the sun has climbed into the sky.

People groaned but settled down among the roots of trees, on fallen logs and wherever they could find. Three of the women, including Unmi, set about distributing food. Dido wondered if what they had brought was enough to feed the ninety or so mouths. She expected that within the week they would have to live off the land.

El Negro settled himself beside Dido.

"I…I never thought I'd see you again," she said, staring at him, letting the sight of him fill her eyes.

"I was not sure you'd want to."

"You treated me terribly but it didn't stop me from…from…" She couldn't finish.

He looked at her, looked away again, suddenly diffident.

"Are you saying…is it…do you feel something for me?" he asked. Though she had to bend forward to hear him she caught the quaver in his voice. He did not know, she thought wonderingly, he truly did not understand.

"I love you," she whispered.

"How can you?" he growled, drawing his brows together. "I hit you and had you locked up in the hold for days."

"If you'd done those things before I knew I loved you, you'd certainly never have taken possession of my heart." At least, she didn't think so.

"Do you jest with me because you take me for a fool?"

"No fool." Realizing he would never take the first step and that she must do it, she put her arms around him and pulled him to her, crushing her lips to his. At last, at last, his arms held her tight. She closed her eyes. He smelled of earth and sweat and sea. She thought that no matter where they went or what happened to her she would always recognize his scent.

"You know, for days after I met you in Port Royal I would dream of you," he said, against her throat. "On board the ship, I thought I was going crazy not being able to touch you. I didn't want to risk the men finding out your secret. I knew what could happen to you, to us, for I'd have defended you onto death." He shook his head. "I locked you up for your own protection though it killed me to do it. I didn't think you could ever forgive me. How could I speak to you of love after that?" His breath warmed her neck. "So I refused to see you. I was ashamed. I had wronged you. I was twice a cur. Then the boy came…at first I didn't believe him, a little ragamuffin with some story about you in a dungeon. I almost sent him on his way with a clout." He paused, scowling. "If you knew how many sleepless nights you've put me through. You are so beautiful, my beloved."

Dido took his hands in hers. "No need for shame. Or guilt. I forgive you with all my heart. You've saved me many times over." She cupped his face in her hands. "I see a brave man, full of honor and integrity, who cares for his men and for his people. I see a man who loves justice and fears no-one. I see a man who, were we in Guinea, would be a king among men."

"I care for none of that so long as I have your heart. That above all is important to me." He took a deep breath. "My Missy-boy is gone but I never thought I'd find a woman such as you."

He kissed her again. With a boldness she didn't know she possessed, Dido allowed her hands to wander over his back, over his thighs. Desire snaked through her.

"I want you," he whispered. "Oh, woman, how I want you. But we have far to go, my very own sweetsop, if we are to reach our place of refuge by night." He rained kisses on her face, rubbed his nose against hers. "I cannot take you now."

Dido tried not to feel disappointed. He was right, of course, but that didn't make what he said any easier to bear. The fear that had paralyzed her around men had not gone from her completely. She could sense it like a smoke-gray thundercloud at the edges of her mind. Union with El Negro would drive it away, she thought. Around him she felt safe in a way she had never felt with another man. Their lovemaking would be like a cleansing cane-fire, red-hot and sweet scented as it burned away the trash.

"How do you know these mountains so well?" The question had been at the back of her mind since they'd started out.

"I fought with Juan de Bolas," he said, "but that is not something I generally tell people."

Juan de Bolas. The former slave freed by the Spanish. Every now and then, he and his people swept down from the mountains to harry the English soldiers and settlers in lightning raids.

"You must have been very young." Only one or two slaves from Beeston's had ever run away to join the *marronas* as Bolas's fighters were called. The plantation was never bothered by them.

"I was a boy."

"Why did you leave him?"

"Juan shot a friend of mine who no longer wanted to fight. Just shot him in the head where he stood. Another time he whipped a woman whom he suspected of spying for the militia. She died of her injuries and later we found out Juan was mistaken. The spy was somebody else. I could not stomach his cruelties any longer so, one night, I slipped away. I'd heard a man's fortune could be made in Port Royal and that's where I went." He nuzzled her cheek. "I signed on with a privateer by the name of Cavendish and found I liked life on the sea."

"Will you ever live on land?"

"Though I love sea-life well I am becoming too old for the vagaries of it. Two years ago, a storm took us into the Atlantic. We survived the waves and the rain, but we ran so low on food we took to boiling our leather satchels for soup, having already killed and eaten all the rats on board."

Dido made a face. "Rats!"

"If Roberts had not come upon us and given us some of his store, we would have starved before making it back to any port." He shook his head at the memory. "Scurvy had begun to set in among the men yet all survived, thanks to Roberts' gift of various foods."

"Dido," her mother broke through the trees around them. "I've been looking for you everywhere, daughter. Oh, you are with the captain." She started to turn around.

"You wanted me, mother?"

"I brought you bread and a piece of ham," Unmi said, stepping forward.

"Thank you."

Dido ate hungrily as her mother watched her, nodding in approval.

"You must build back up your strength. How do you feel?"

"Safe." She looked at the two people she loved most in the world. "Happy."

"Did they treat you well at Beeston's? Was Massa Richard a good Massa?"

Dido shrugged. "He left me alone so he was good enough."

Unmi nodded again. "I thought maybe you would have had children of your own by now. I used to wonder what they looked like, if I'd ever see them."

El Negro raised his brows at her. Dido shook her head. "No, Mumma. I couldn't let...not after Massa Simon."

"This man raped you, Dido?" El Negro asked.

"When I was a child. In Nevis."

"Nevis." El Negro repeated it softly to himself as if wanting to remember the name.

"It was a long time ago," Dido said, wanting to turn the topic away from that nightmare.

"And now you have a good man, one who will protect you. This one was worth the wait, eh, daughter?"

"Yes, Mumma."

Unmi chuckled to herself and left them.

"She likes me," El Negro said when he thought she was out of hearing.

"I think so too."

They kissed, holding tightly on to each other. Dido didn't want to let him go but El Negro needed to check on everyone and she wanted to sit with her family. In less than an hour, the pirate had them pushing their way through the forest again as the sun rose higher in the sky.

Chapter 19

As the people pushed further and further into the hills, El Negro sent a man to double back and see if the militia was after them. The sun had begun its descent when he returned. He reported that half the militiamen had stopped to fight the fire but it had already died down because of the lack of wind. The other half, about sixty men, came on into the hills, leaving their horses behind them. At the rate they were going, the man said, they would be on them by the next morning unless they stopped to sleep. The people hearing him shuddered and cried out in disbelief. They were going as quickly as they could, they said to El Negro, but there were the old people and the children to consider.

"The men and such women of you who are able will stay and fight," El Negro said, his voice breaking over them like thunder. "The rest will go on ahead. I will tell you what landmarks to look for. We will catch up with you when the fight is over."

"Suppose you are killed. We will be lost," a woman said.

"You will not be lost. Even now, eyes watch to observe what manner of people we are."

The people looked around them, uneasily.

"Unmi." El Negro called Dido's mother forward. "Come, you will lead them. Continue in this direction and you will come to a guinep tree. Turn north when you reach the tree. You will know you are going as you should if you see a rock formation like a hand on the mountain before you. You will be able to see it by moonlight. Head straight for that formation. Stop for nothing."

Unmi nodded, grimly.

"Will you stay and fight, my daughter?" she asked Dido.

"Yes."

Mother and daughter hugged fiercely, needing no words to speak their love.

After the older people and the children had moved off behind Unmi, El Negro ordered the people to take up their stations. This was a fight to the death, he said. If they feared to kill a man they should run to follow Unmi, battle was no place for the faint of heart. Each had already been given a gun from Massa Neville's small arsenal and most had come with their own cane knives. El Negro moved the people in an arc formation among the trees and rocks, ordering them to hide. They were to engage the troop when he fired his gun, not a minute before. He wanted the militia to be well-enmeshed in the trap he'd set for them before fighting began.

When El Negro was satisfied all was in accordance with his wishes, he crouched down behind the rock where Dido had already taken up her position.

"I suppose this is more than you bargained for when you first rescued me," she whispered.

"Just a little bit," he answered, grinning mischievously. "But I'd not change a thing. Yacahüey says our destinies depend on each small action we take. If I had not walked down High Street that day I would not have seen you in that alley and I would not now be beside you." He passed his hand lightly over her head in a tender caress.

"About to face armed men who wish to kill you." She felt she was to blame for all that had happened and all that was about to happen but she could not think of anything she would have done differently. Running away from Beeston's Estate, signing on with the *Fortune's Gift*, falling in love with El Negro. No, there was nothing she'd change about any of that, even if she could.

"Dido." El Negro turned her face to his, his fingers at her chin. "There is no other place I'd rather be than beside you, dear heart."

Unable to speak, she threw her arms around his neck and covered his face with silent, fluttery kisses.

The oooeek, oooeek of a nightwitch startled them apart. It was the signal El Negro was waiting on. Massa Neville's former slaves readied their gun and clutched their cane knives. The members of the militia were composed of a few of the island's leading citizens and a lot more of its poor whites. El Negro knew that Governor Modyford must have quickly mustered such men as were in San Jago de la Vega after Massa Taylor galloped into the town. The militia was thus an odd assortment of men. They were in no way a disciplined force. Their shouts and curses as they made their way through the forested hillsides could be heard from almost a mile away.

El Negro watched and waited as Dido peered through the trees for her first glimpse of their enemy. She did not have long to wait. The men began to straggle through the trees in twos and threes. Dido feared they would stumble upon the people hidden in the shadows but the former slaves were well-placed.

She looked questioningly at El Negro as the white men came on. Surely it was time but he shook his head. On and on they came. Dido was ready to burst out of her skin. Was he waiting until they stepped on him to give the signal? But at last he was raising his pistol, aiming it at the men, pulling the trigger. Whooping and hollering, Massa Neville's former slaves fired into the gaggle of startled whites. Many dropped to the ground, killed by that first salvo. The others attempted to dive behind a rock, a tree, any cover they could find, but found themselves, instead, facing an onslaught of blacks whose work on the sugar plantation had acquainted them well with the uses of a knife. Those whites who could, fled the way they had come. In under an hour the battle was over.

The wine-red blood of the wounded and the lifeless stained the leaves of the forest and turned black on the ground. Among the dead, Dido counted twenty-nine white men and three blacks, a man and two women. She was not surprised at the disparity in the numbers for her people had fought well. The gods of Guinea must be proud. But there was no time for self-congratulation. It was time to march again. Luckily, the whites had been too surprised to inflict much real damage. None among the living was so hurt they could not continue their flight deep into the heart of the mountains.

Dido said a quick prayer over the bodies of the three former slaves. Having no time for a proper burial, the people did the best they could and covered the corpses with leaves and dirt before leaving the area. They grieved for the dead but they were excited about this victory over the forces that had enslaved them for so long. They talked to each other in low animated tones, still disbelieving and awed that they were alive and no harm had come to them. In front of them, Dido hugged El Negro's arm to her side.

"I do not think they really believed they'd come out of it alive," she murmured to him.

"Did you?"

"I had no doubt," she replied.

"Why not?"

"Because you led us. Though, when you took so long to fire, I wanted to scream."

He chuckled. "I needed to make sure we caught all of them in our net. Fortune rewards the patient warrior with victory."

"Why do you never offer thanks to the gods? I have never even heard you call the name of Oshun, nor Shango or any of the others."

"The gods of Guinea abandoned me when they allowed me to be sold into this New World. Why should I make time for gods who make no time for me?"

"The gods have not abandoned you," Dido said, picking her words carefully. "They walk with you still even though you have closed your heart to them. Did you not quote Yacahüey to me? If you had not been sold, we would not have met and my life would have been dirt in my mouth."

"Ah, Dido." As if unable to stop himself, he sighed deeply and drew her close to him, kissing her on the mouth, his tongue probing hers. Behind them the people whooped but softly, still unsure if they were being watched from the trees. Dido returned his kiss with all the zest she possessed. He was the first to break it off.

"We have far to go still," he murmured, his lips against her cheek. "We cannot stop for love."

"I know," Dido said. She brushed her lips against his and stepped back, reaching for his hand. In this way, they continued their climb into the moon-lit mountains as around them the cicadas screeched and the tree frogs sang.

El Negro set a fast pace. By morning they had caught up to Unmi and her band of children and elders.

Dido squinted at the hand-shaped rock formation miles away on another hill. "Is that where we're going?" she asked. "Why there?"

"The hand is a sign," El Negro said, shading his eyes and staring at it.

"A sign?"

"It is there to guide us."

Above their heads, a brightly-hued parrot screamed and wheeled away.

"They know we're coming," El Negro said, grimly. For the first time since she had met him, he looked apprehensive.

"Who? The *marronas*? Is that who you're taking us to?"

El Negro nodded.

"We will be safe there."

"What of your quarrel with Juan de Bolas?"

"He is dead. I've no reason to believe we will not be welcomed."

But the farther in they went among the mountains, the tighter his face grew.

The air grew progressively cooler and crisper as they ascended into the mist. Dido was delighted by the landscape. El Negro led them into a valley between the mountains and everywhere she looked was lush vegetation. Swarms of brightly-colored butterflies flitted over the yellow and purple flowers bobbing their heads here and there, while birds darted busily among the treetops, singing and chattering to each other. By mid-day, they had passed two streams that bubbled up at their feet from underground springs.

"Oshun." Dido was convinced it was the goddess who had led them to what must surely be a place sacred to her as the deity of fresh, flowing water. "How can you not believe when you see a place such as this?" she asked El Negro.

"She is here," she insisted when he only raised an eyebrow and did not answer. "Do you not feel the Lady?" It seemed to her that the very wind carried the clean, fresh perfume of the goddess to their faces, cooling the weary travelers.

"I suppose you believe she meant for me to bring you here all along and everything that happened at the plantation happened for that reason?" he said, as they walked along at the head of the procession of former slaves. Unmi and Dido's siblings were right behind them.

"It's self-evident," she replied, swinging his hand joyfully. She would not allow his unbelief to dampen her enjoyment of the beauty Oshun had wrought.

"Your violation, that too, was Oshun's doing?" he asked, scowling. "If you believe this is her doing then you must accept that was her doing as well."

"I cannot understand the mind of Oshun or any of the other gods for that matter," she said, slowing down and clasping his hand tight. He had to understand her. Her worship of Oshun was part of who she was. It was how her mother had taught her. She glanced back at Unmi who carried George on her back.

"They are not like us." She struggled to find the right words. The last few months had shaken her faith but her belief in the gods of her ancestors remained alive. The trust she placed in them was the bedrock of her existence. She couldn't explain why Oshun had allowed Massa Simon to violate her or even why Shango had not sent a thunderbolt after the first slave trader who attempted to remove his people from Guinea. If she were a god, there would be no such thing as slavery but she was not a god. "They do not think as we do or behave as we do. I do not know why they sometimes allow bad things to happen to us but I know they must have their reasons. I thank Oshun for the good she does me and accept the rest as her desire for me even though I do not understand the why of it."

El Negro snorted. "I will never accept what I do not understand."

"Maybe not today but tomorrow you will and be the wiser for it," she said, her voice gentle.

He snorted again but Dido didn't attempt to persuade him further. He had spent most of his life in unbelief. She could hardly expect to change him in one day.

Though they stopped for lunch when the sun was directly overhead, El Negro would not allow the tired people to rest for more than a couple hours. They reached the rock formation they'd seen in the distance just as the sun slid down into the hills to the west.

Up close, Dido could see that while the orange-colored rocks that formed the fist looked as if they had been there from the beginning of time, the gray rocks of the finger pointing to the skies were clearly placed there by unknown hands.

"We stop here for the night," El Negro announced. "Tomorrow we will arrive at our destination."

The people were too weary to cheer this good news. Most dropped to the ground where they stood, using their belongings or the rocks as pillows on which to rest their heads. In minutes, all of the children and a few of the adults were asleep. His hands at her waist, El Negro propelled Dido around the rocks and down a small incline to the side where there was a small hollow, almost as if Oludumare had started to create a cave before changing his mind.

"Come," he said, clearing the depression of loose debris and pulling her down beside him. "Holding you feels even better than counting doubloons after boarding a rich prize."

Dido laughed. "Are you comparing me to metals?"

"I am saying that I value you above such things." He nibbled her ear. "You are worth far more than silver or gold to me."

"Why me and not another woman? You must have known many before meeting me."

"I did."

"Like the woman in Puerto Bello," Dido prompted, feeling a flash of jealousy at the memory.

He buried his face against her neck.

"I thought I was going crazy, wanting to frig you but knowing I had to keep your secret!"

"When you threw me out of your cabin, I felt sorry for Richard."

"You did?"

"He couldn't help himself and, in the end, he did not have the chance to do me real harm. I think he must have been very lonely, misunderstood and reviled by other men as he was."

"I did not revile him," El Negro protested. "I think he was the most capable quartermaster I ever had. It was his sexual habits that gave me pause."

"And he must have known it, sensed it in the way you interacted with him. Just as I sensed both your attraction to me and your refusal to surrender to it."

He twisted them around so she lay under him.

"Do you sense any refusal now?" he rasped.

Dido's arms rose to caress his face, his hair. "No, my love, I do not."

They kissed. Dido thought she was melting in a vat of hot molasses. She wrapped her legs around him, straining to feel and touch him with every possible part of her body. With a muffled groan, he twisted himself off her and pulled her shirt open.

"Damn!"

"What?"

"I forgot about your bindings."

So had she, they had become so much a part of her. She sat up and he quickly freed her of the rolls and rolls of cloth. When her breasts were finally free, he shifted so he could look at them in the pearly light of the moon. Her nipples puckered and hardened in the cold mountain air.

"Take your pants off too," he commanded.

When she had done as she was told and lain back down, he looked her up and down, his eyes traveling slowly from her head to her feet and back again like a starved man brought to a feast.

"You're so beautiful," he murmured, reaching out to cup first one breast then the other in his hand. His thumb flicked over her nipples and a flame of desire arched upward from her belly.

"I want you," she said, spreading her legs. A stab of shame shot through her and she quickly closed them again, crossing her legs at her knee.

She saw the puzzlement on his face and tried to explain. "I...I..." But how could she when she, herself, did not understand what she was feeling? Massa Simon had taken her against her will, again and again. Now she felt she had no right to offer herself to the man she loved, she was unworthy of him and his love, tainted by her evil experiences as a child. Tears leaked out of her eyes and trickled down her temples. Dido turned her face away and curled her knees up against her chest.

"No, Dido." He held her by the shoulders and turned her around. "Do not ever turn from me," he whispered, holding her tight and rocking her gently from side to side.

Dido began to cry in earnest. He was so strong, so good, and he loved her but he deserved somebody else, an unsullied woman without any shadows in her past, who could love him without reserve.

"You cannot love me," she said. "You do not know my sin."

"I know you," he answered, his voice calm, his face radiating kindness. "I know you and I love you. Do you really think anything in your past could cause me to deny my love?"

"I'm dirty. I'm no good." Dido buried her face in her hands but he pried them away and lifted her chin to look in her eyes.

"Why are you saying these things?"

"Massa Simon," she cried. "Do you not understand what he did to me?"

"But not because you were no good," he objected. "He was an evil man. His behavior had nothing to do with you. Do not believe you were the only one who suffered his vice. You must know, men such as he never stop at one child. There are a few like him among the Brethren—men who prefer little girls. Others are like Richard and prefer young boys. It is their dark nature. They are always looking, always hunting for fresh prey. None can lay the fault for this on their victims."

His reasoning only brought on a fresh storm of weeping. Dido didn't think she'd ever cried so much before. Her head hurt with the fury of her tears. She pressed her palms to her eyes, trying to regain control of herself. El Negro continued to rock her. Slowly, slowly, her sobbing subsided.

"Come, my love." He eased her up to a standing position and helped her back into her clothes.

"I'm sorry I..." She avoided looking into his face, not sure what she'd see there. Disappointment she could take, but not distaste or contempt. "Please do not feel I've misled you about my feelings. I haven't. Maybe..." She kept her eyes on the ground. "Maybe if I loved you a bit less, it would be easier for me. Or if I'd had other lovers since...since..." Dido hurried on. "I am sorry."

El Negro didn't answer. Her heart sank. He hated her now. She glanced at him but he was standing with his back to the moon, his expression shadowed.

"I will not bother you, again," she whispered, misery like the weight of a ship on her back, bowing her down.

"You know," he said, his voice gently amused. "When you were Domingo, you did a much better job of listening to me." He grabbed her by the forearms and bent to look into her face. "I love you, Dido/Domingo of Nevis, of Beeston's Estate and, most recently, of the pirate ship, *Fortune's Gift.*"

"But I would not let you frig me and..."

"Quiet," he interrupted, using his captain's voice. "I do not love you because I want your sex, little fool." He gave her a small shake. "I love you. I want you. All of you. Not just what is here." He grabbed between her legs, rubbing his hand flat against the rough cloth of her trousers. The rough gesture shocked her as did the subsequent jolt of pleasure. Alarmed, aroused, and confused, she pushed him away.

"Don't."

He put his hands up, the palms toward her.

"I'll wait. Not forever, but I'll be patient. I won't take you before you tell me I can."

Her heart turned in her chest. "Please. I must be alone. I must speak with the Lady." But she doubted even Oshun could fix what ailed her.

"Stay here, then. I'll go." He spun on his heels and disappeared up the slope. Dido watched him leave. There was nothing she wanted more than to shout 'stop.' To run after him and wrap her arms tight about him but her legs wouldn't move and her mouth was too dry for speech.

Chapter 20

"**W**elcome," said the gray-haired man in the torn trousers. He was a full head shorter than El Negro but his piercing eyes and muscular build said he was not a man to be taken lightly. The people, the *marronas* of whom Dido had so often heard, crowded around behind him, watching the newcomers with frank curiosity. Massa Neville's former slaves peered at the village of thatched huts and small cooking fires with equal interest.

"We come seeking refuge, Jorge," El Negro answered. "These brave people are over sixty strong, not counting the children, and are courageous fighters."

"I know," the man smiled. "We watched your skirmish with the militia. You led them well, my friend, and your people fought like lions."

"Thank you." El Negro inclined his head. "I was well-taught."

At this the man laughed outright. "Yes," he said. "I am a good teacher, am I not?"

"The best."

The two men hugged. Massa Neville's former slaves breathed a collective sigh of relief. They had been unsure of their reception, unsure which of the things the whites said about the *marronas* were true and which were false. Now they could see for themselves that the *marronas* did not eat their children for were there not many peeping out at them from behind their mother's legs? Neither were their necks garlanded with the teeth of humans. No tails hung between their legs. The slaves understood that they had been fed lies to make them afraid and to prevent them from seeking freedom.

"People." El Negro turned to address them. "This is Jorge de Sierras, who welcomes you to his village. Once he was a captain under Juan Bolas but he broke away for form his own community, the community that will be your new home."

The former slaves cheered loudly. They were weary of walking and were glad to have reached their destination at last.

"We have prepared a feast for you and your people, my friend." The chief put an arm around El Negro's shoulders and led him to the center of the village.

Dido, Unmi, and the others ate well that day for the *marronas* stole not only guns from their former owners but also livestock, grains and other foodstuffs. The yam, sweet potatoes, citrus fruits, guavas and suchlike they planted in their valley rounded out their diet. They wanted for nothing and were well-fed.

After the meal, the chief stood up on a chair to talk to them.

"New people, you are all welcome here. I, Chief Jorge de Sierras, welcome you and invite you to make your home among us." The people cheered again. "Here every man and woman is equal and every man and woman is responsible for the well-being of all. We plant together so we may eat together. We do not steal from each other because whatever is needed by another is freely given. Quarrels between neighbors and friends are brought to me for I dispense justice among my people. You will learn more about us as time goes on. I know that my people will benefit from the labor and skill of your hands and also from the courage of your hearts and the knowledge of your minds. We will begin this afternoon to help you with the construction of your new homes. Welcome, again." The cheering and clapping by both his people and the newcomers lasted until the palms of their hands stung and their throats ached.

Afterward, Dido walked around to see if she could find Delia, Pablito, and the other runaways from Beeston's but when she asked for them, nobody had heard their names or knew of anyone who matched their description.

"Perhaps they live in another mountain village," a kind-faced woman suggested. "There are others to the west. They might have made their way there."

Dido hoped so. She hoped that they lived among other people of Guinea and had found safety and shelter and a good life. She supposed she'd never see them again and it was with a heavy heart that she helped her mother with her hut, gathering the sticks for the walls and the roof from the woods roundabout. El Negro had disappeared into the chief's own dwelling and she didn't know if that meant he would be sleeping there or if the two men wanted to talk of the island's doings out of the hearing of others. That night as oil lamps burned in the darkness, he came looking for her as she sat, silent, with her family before their half-constructed hut.

"Good night, mother," he said to Unmi before squatting beside Dido.

"It is good to see you, captain," Unmi responded, giving her oldest daughter an encouraging smile.

"Jorge has offered me a hut in his yard for my use while I stay," El Negro said to Dido, in a low voice. "I was wondering…that is, if you wished you could share it with me."

Dido's heart leapt. She would like nothing more.

"That would please me," she whispered. But what did he mean, while he stayed? Was he planning to return to his ship and, if so, did he mean to take her with him?

They said 'good-night' to her family and he led her to the hut. The first thing Dido noticed was that there was only one pallet. Clean and well-made though it was, it brought her up short in the doorway.

"I will sleep on the hide," El Negro said immediately, reading her mind. A cow hide covered the earthen floor.

Reassured, she walked in. A tin lamp burned in one corner and the hut smelled faintly of lemon grass. Beside the bed, a table, and two chairs, it was empty of other furnishings but in another corner she saw a small collection of cooking pots and calabash gourds.

"Does someone live here?" she asked.

"I think one of the chief's relatives. He did not say."

There was an uncomfortable silence before he let himself down on the hard floor and stretched out.

"I am very tired. You do not mind if I go right to sleep?"

Dido shook her head. Mind? How could she mind? She owed him so much already and now here she was taking his bed.

"I will sleep on the ground," she said, making up her mind. "You take the bed."

He didn't answer. She knew he could not possibly have fallen asleep so quickly but his eyes didn't flicker when she brought her face close up to his and he gave no sign that he was still awake. Dido studied his features by the flickering light of the oil lamp, loving the sweep of his curly eyelashes, the planes of his cheek, even his lined forehead. He looked tired. Little curving lines were etched into the corners of his mouth. Without thinking, she pushed herself forward and lightly brushed her lips against them before springing back up and retreating to the pallet, shocked at herself. For a little while she sat there watching him but he didn't stir. She had gotten away with her stolen kiss. Dido blew out the lamp and settled herself on her bed, listening to the sound of his steady breathing. Outside, the cicadas and other night creatures chittered.

That night she dreamt that all the soldiers of the militia were chasing her across a desert. She had been running for days, weeks, and still they pursued her until, finally, she came to grove where there were many fruit trees. Birds sung happily among the branches and the air was filled with perfume. For the first time since she had begun to run she could not hear the hooves of the militias' horses. Nevertheless, she climbed and climbed until she emerged on top of a huge rock on the edge of a clear and inviting pond. Dido could not tell how deep the water was but she knew it was deep. Without stopping to think, she shed her clothes and dived off the rock into the warm water. But it wasn't water at all. Somehow she was suddenly in El Negro's arms and he was looking at her with such love and tenderness that Dido knew she didn't have to run anymore, she was safe.

Gasping, Dido awoke. It took a minute before she realized where she was. The door and two small windows had been left open and she could see El Negro's dark slumbering form in the light spilling in from the moon.

Driven by a need greater than her fears, she crawled over the floor to him and snuggled into his side. Instantly, and, without speaking, he pulled her to him.

"Have you been awake all night?" she whispered, delighting in the feel of his breath on her skin.

"No but I wake quickly." He brushed her forehead with his lips. "Couldn't you sleep, my love?"

"I wanted to be close to you."

"And now you are, do you want anything else?" His eyes gleamed. Flickers of heat leapt upward from her groin to tighten her breasts.

"No, I…" For a minute she panicked but he kissed her before she could continue.

"Shush." He stroked her hair, calming her. "I said I would wait and I meant it," he murmured. "Never fear me."

So that was how they slept for the rest of that night, face to face, their arms around each other, their legs entwined. When they woke the next day at dawn he did not mention his condition though the bulge in his breeches was plain to see. Dido averted her eyes as he rose to go outside and relieve himself.

After breakfasting with Chief Jorge on roasted yam and salted bonito-fish, Dido and El Negro went to help Unmi with her house. By evening, it was finished.

Chapter 21

On the second night of their stay in the village, Dido and El Negro slept together on the pallet but there was no kissing or touching though Dido was beginning to feel a growing impatience for it. In the morning, when he woke in the same condition as before, she boldly placed her hand on his crotch.

"May I see it?" she asked.

"Of course. None other has a better right." He winked at her and Dido grinned, losing some of her nervousness.

He unbuttoned his breeches and brought his prick out for her to see, pulling back the foreskin to expose the head where a drop of clear moisture glistened. Dido put her finger on it and glanced at El Negro. His face had become tight and drawn as if he was holding his breath.

"Are you alright?"

"Woman, you are torturing me."

Satisfied that he was not in any pain, she went back to her explorations, running a now wetted finger around the cap of his penis before wrapping her hand around the shaft. She had never touched Massa Simon's, had never once even looked at it, but she pushed all thoughts of the slave master away, willing herself to think only about El Negro and what she was doing to him.

The silkiness of his moisture surprised her. She rubbed it between thumb and forefinger and brought it to her nose to smell. The odor was elusive but not unpleasant. Dido rubbed her open palm over the slippery head. El Negro rewarded her with a groan. He clamped his lips, his hands on the ground behind him, his legs open, inviting her journey of discovery.

Dido lowered herself down so his manhood was only inches from her face. She waited to see if the memory of Massa Simon would claim her again. When it didn't, she tentatively bent forward and licked her pirate. El Negro moaned, his face contorting into a mask of mingled emotions. Dido threw herself back.

"I'm sorry, what…"

"Do not stop," he gritted out between clenched teeth. "Do what you want."

So she did. She flicked her tongue over him again and ran her fingers up and down his shaft. He made a panting sound and thrust himself at her. Thus encouraged, she closed her lips around the tip of him, circling it with her tongue as she'd done before. He thrust himself up further but she pushed him back down. She wanted, no, needed total control over what was happening.

Not sure if she was doing the right thing, she inched forward, taking as much of him as she could hold in her mouth, her hands caressing his balls. But El Negro had come to the end of his restraint. Sweat beaded his forehead. With a strangled shout, he punched the ground with his fists. A warm, thick liquid filled her mouth. Dido coughed in surprise and almost gagged. Come dripped down her chin.

"Oh, my love." El Negro pulled her into his arms. He pressed kisses on her nose, her forehead, her chin, licking at the moisture he himself had sprayed there.

"Did you like that?" Dido asked.

"God's blood, light of my heart. I could almost believe in your Oshun, now." Dido laughed and he reared back to look at her.

"Do you know? I think this is the first time I've heard you laugh since I met you."

"It *is* the first time." She felt dizzy with happiness.

"That brings me to something I've been thinking about." His tone turned serious and Dido twisted herself around to look at him. "We are not staying here, Dido. I know we haven't talked about it but this is not for me."

She had known this was coming. He had made no attempt to build himself a hut like the others.

"What is?"

"A life of my own in a place where I am not going to continually be on the run. This is the third village Jorge has created. The other two were burnt to the ground by D'Oyley, Modyford's predecessor. The *marronas* are constantly waging war against the government. We could never be at peace here, not on our own terms. I want to hold you to me at night and watch my children swell in your belly in the day. I want to live to see the hairs of your head turn gray and to watch my grandchildren grow straight and strong through the veil of my old age."

"When do we leave?"

"Ah, Dido." His voice shook. "I was so afraid you'd want to stay, that you'd not want to leave this land."

"Would you have left me here?"

"No. I would have stayed if that was what you wanted but I've not risked my life capturing rich prizes or following Morgan so I might live in a state of constant tension, as the *marronas* do, never knowing when the militia will come after them."

"So," she asked, again. "When do we leave?"

"In another day or so would be a good time. I left Yacahüey in charge of the ship. He must be wondering where I've got to."

"My family…"

"They must come too, of course. That is, if Unmi wishes it."

"I don't think I could bear to be separated from them again."

"They'll come. I'm sure of it."

Later that day Dido and El Negro spoke to Unmi and it was agreed. Unmi and the children would leave the village with them. The family would stay together. El Negro went to thank the Chief for his hospitality and to break the news, leaving Dido behind to answer her family's excited questions.

"Did you like being a pirate?" George asked, his eyes round.

"There were some things I liked," Dido said, choosing her words carefully. "I liked that no man considered himself better than the other because of the color of his skin. I liked that the captain always asked his crew to decide on things together."

"What did you not like?" asked Zaccharias. He was the more thoughtful of the two and Dido found herself drawn to him, his serious, watchful demeanor endearing in one so young.

"Doing my business over the sea."

"Over the sea?" They laughed, demanding an explanation and making faces when she gave it to them.

Blllly the time she'd finished describing the sack of Puerto Bello, they had both decided they would like that life for themselves.

"Yah! Yah!" they exclaimed, slashing at each other with imaginary cutlasses.

"Ho! What's this, do I have new recruits here?" El Negro called out to them, returning from his talk with Chief Jorge.

"They're looking forward to the pirate life," Dido shouted, shaking her head as the boys circled her, shouting. "I told them they'd have to relieve themselves over the sea and eat wormy biscuits as hard as wood but they claim not to care."

"It's a hard life, boys," he said, coming up to them and slipping his arm around Dido's waist, "but a good one too, as long as you do not manage to get caught by either a gale or some overzealous governor wanting to make an example of you. In which case, boys." His voice deepened and his expression became mock-ferocious. "They will hang you and put your body in a cage to swing in the harbor as a message to all poxy dogs who think to follow in your footsteps."

"That is if they catch us." Zaccharias smiled. "They'll not catch me. I'll be too fast for them. I'll have a ship like the *Fortune's Gift* that will fly over the sea like the wind. They'll never catch me."

"So we'll go to the coast and look for these slaves you freed," Unmi broke in. "Suppose they do not wish us to settle with them or what if they've already been re-captured or killed by the Indians?"

"Then we'll look for someplace else," El Negro said, firmly. "Do not worry, Mother. I will find us a home."

Unmi nodded but her eyes showed she was still worried.

"What if Mumma is right?" Dido asked, when she and El Negro were back in their hut.

"Any number of things may happen to us, I'll not deny that, but Jamaica is a small island. The *marronas* cannot make war on the English forever without risking their own destruction. New Spain is big, very big. We can lose ourselves there and live in peace."

"I'd like that. I'd like that so very much."

"Dido, I'll do everything in my power to make it so. I want you to be happy."

He bent down and kissed her. "You are beautiful and good."

"Am I?"

"Like no woman I've ever known."

"And you are just trying to flatter me so I'll do tonight what I did to you this morning."

"If flattery will win me a repeat performance, I won't stop telling you your eyes are like black pools of water into which I should love to dive, your teeth are fairer than pearls, your breasts are sweet melons of desire, your..."

"Melons of desire?" Dido shrieked. "Melons?"

"It's true. I do not lie," he said, his expression changing to mock offence.

Dido doubled over with laughter, imagining ripe melons protruding from her chest.

"And your manhood? What do you call that, a carrot of lechery?"

"It was you I sought to flatter. I have a goal in mind, remember?"

"Oh, yes." Dido's laughter subsided as he began to unbutton her shirt. "Do you wish a bite of melon?"

"Yes." He pretended to nip her breasts but ended up tenderly licking and sucking her nipples.

"Wait." She pushed him down on the pallet and got to her feet. She shrugged the shirt off her shoulders and undid her trousers, pushing them down to her ankles. El Negro watched her closely from the bed, not missing one second of what she was doing.

When she was completely naked, she knelt down on the pallet and began to tug at his buttons. He helped her undo them and remove his breeches. His staff stood at attention. Dido smiled. Holding it firmly but gently in her right hand, she lay down beside her man and slowly began to stroke him up and down as she nibbled on his ear. From his ear, her lips trailed over his skin, tasting the salt of his perspiration, until she reached his mouth which opened to receive her questing tongue. El Negro groaned as she continued to softly stroke him.

"Do you want me to come soon?" he whispered.

"No."

"Squeeze me here then, my love. Yes. Gently. Aaah."

They resumed their explorations of each other's mouths and Dido continued her attentions to his manhood. In minutes, she felt the liquid evidence of his desire once again leaking from his member. This time she rose to her knees and, in one fluid motion, she brought her right leg over and straddled him. She lowered herself down, until the tip of his shaft was at her opening which was already slick with her own juices. She wanted him as much as he wanted her, maybe more. Dido ignored the small tendril of fear curled at the back of her mind and began to lower herself on him. Slowly. Slowly. Her flesh closed around him and he groaned, balling his hands into fist to keep from pulling her down on him all at once.

Dido rocked her hips forward and backward, loving the fullness of him inside of her, loving how the desire shining in his eyes made her feel. His hands roamed over her belly, her breasts. He rocked himself under her, matching his rhythm to hers in a movement as ancient as Guinea itself. Dido closed her eyes, giving herself up to the feelings taking over her body as she crushed herself against him, clamping her thighs tightly to his. El Negro's hands gripped her waist, his face dissolving in pleasure as he neared his peak. Seeing his pleasure added to Dido's. A wave gathered itself in the pit of her womb, pulling her into it like a current draws all in its path.

"Aaaieee," she cried.

The wave swept forward, gathering momentum. Dido's belly rolled and clenched. The wave crashed in an explosion of sensation, surging through her blood, into her bones, shaking her very core.

"Goddess," she moaned. She stayed over him like that for a couple minutes, her chest heaving, her heart racing, before she pushed herself forward to lie on his chest. His arms held her tight even as he slipped out of her.

"Oshun should claim you for her priestess," he murmured, running his fingers up and down her spine.

Dido smiled into his chest. For years, she had ignored the sensuous aspect of Oshun but she would do so no longer. Shifting, she cupped his shrunken shaft in her hand and sucked at his nipple taking deep satisfaction in the low rumbling growl of pleasure her lover made as he gave himself up to her lewd caresses.

Chapter 22

The three women moved through the wooded hillsides of the Blue Mountains as quietly as wraiths. Before they'd left the village, both Dido and El Negro had schooled Unmi and Claribel. "Watch out for dry twigs and fallen leaves," the pirate warned. "They announce your coming as surely as a trumpet."

"Use the shadows," Dido advised. "If we become separated, walk in the streams and rivers to hide your passing but continue on to Port Royal." The plan was for Dido, her mother and her sister to go to Port Royal, posing as market women. Once in the city they would make their way to the *Fortune's Gift* and await the arrival of El Negro and Dido's brothers. Unmi had not wanted to leave her boys behind but they'd had no choice. If they all traveled together they risked drawing the attention of suspicious whites or worse, of the militia. El Negro and the boys would leave the village on the third day after the women's departure. It was a head start that Dido felt would allow her plenty of time to reach the city and help Yacahüey get the ship ready for their departure from Jamaica.

At dusk the women sought what shelter they could and rested until the sky began to lighten again beyond the mountains. El Negro came to Dido in her dreams. In the morning she awoke, quivering with a sharp hunger for the sight of him and for the feel of his body against hers. It took her a few minutes of lying on the hard ground, staring up at the dark tree canopy above her, before she felt completely released from the fury of her fancies.

Once they had eaten, the women walked quickly. By the evening of the third day they could see the lights of the city before them. Unmi and Claribel fell asleep almost immediately that night but Dido stayed awake. She did not know why but she felt faintly uneasy, almost as if an unseen someone was watching her from the forest, someone who meant her no good. Dido shivered in the night air and squinted back the way they'd come but it would be days yet before the new moon would cast much light. She sat down with her back to a rock, her pistol in her hand and her knife in the other but nothing stirred in the forest. Despite herself, she slept.

"Dido. Wake up, daughter."

Dido raised her weapons.

"Mother," she said, relaxing when she saw who it was.

"I did not want to wake you. You slept so deeply but the sun has risen. We must be on our way."

Dido rubbed her eyes. It was true. The gold light of dawn had given way to the pure sunlight of the new day. She rubbed her neck and rose to her feet. The unease she'd felt the night before was still there, like a dull pain behind her eyes, but she could see nothing around them to warrant concern. Small birds flittered about in the branches above the women and leaves murmured against each other in the wind. Dido shook her head to dispel her bad feeling.

"Thank you," she said, taking the journey cake and the *dookenah* of pounded sweet potato that her mother offered. "You ate while I slept?"

Unmi and Claribel nodded.

"Let us go then." She motioned them to move off.

"No. There's nothing to be gained from eating as you walk."

"Mother, I should have been awake long before now. We've lost precious time."

"Eat, my daughter. And then we walk." Unmi sat back down. Claribel followed her lead.

For a minute, Dido toyed with the idea of setting off on her own. They would catch up with her when they saw she meant to leave them behind. Instead, she sank to the ground and took another bite of the journey cake.

"We do not know what we will meet in Port Royal," Unmi said, looking satisfied. "It is better to face the city with a full belly than one which growls with hunger."

Dido frowned but inwardly she acknowledged that her mother was right. Perhaps more right than she knew because Dido could not shake the sense of wrongness that had fallen over her like a cloak since the night before.

"A woman who jumps up after eating risks offending her stomach," Unmi said. It was something Dido had often heard her say as a child. That day it meant the sun was almost directly overhead when the three women finally set off along the road into Port Royal.

It was the first time Claribel had ever been to the city and the first time in many years for Unmi. Dido could tell that the noises and the people made her mother and sister nervous but she did not have the time to soothe their fears. El Negro would have left the village the day before. The *Fortune's Gift* had to be made ready, food bought, water casks stored, any repairs completed; and it all had to be done in a couple days so they could sail the moment the pirate captain arrived.

Dido threaded her way through the people on the streets, glancing back every now and then to make sure Claribel and Unmi followed. At the dock, she hired a black man to row them to the *Fortune's Gift*, anchored in the harbor.

"Please, Oshun," she whispered as they neared the ship. "Let Yacahüey be on board." She would never be able to find the Taino man in Port Royal if she had to look in all the streets and bars for him.

Oshun was on her side. The Taino was sitting on the deck when they climbed aboard. He was alone.

"Yacahüey!" Dido ran up and hugged him. She'd missed the sight of his squat figure.

"Wh…Domingo…I mean…" He held her at arm's length, his expression suspicious. "Is it…?"

"Yes, Yacahüey, it's me Domingo."

"You are wearing women's clothes." The Taino looked her up and down.

"I have no more need for disguise. I have so much to tell you."

"But the captain…you know he's not here…he went to look for you."

"He found me, Yacahüey. It is a long story but he bid me ask you to ready the ship for departure."

"Departure?"

"He comes. He's on his way but we must sail as soon as he arrives. The militia is after him."

"I know."

"He said…what…what did you say?" Dido's voice faltered. The uneasy feeling became a muted roar in her ears.

"There are wanted posters of the captain all over the town. It is said he killed two white men and led a slave insurrection, that he aims to drive the plantation owners into the sea and set himself up as a governor over the freed blacks." Behind Dido, Unmi snorted in disbelief. "Lieutenant Brumant called on all able-bodied men to join the militia. It left for the Blue Mountains today."

Today! El Negro would be halfway to the city by tomorrow. He would walk right into them. She had to do something but she could not think what.

An arm slipped around her waist. "Do not imagine the worst, daughter. Do you not believe he will be able to evade a marching army? They will make so much noise and kick up so much dust he will see them from miles away."

The relief Dido felt at her mother's words did not survive Yacahüey's next pronouncement.

"They sent slave hunters with dogs on ahead. They mean to put a stop to the *marronas* once and for all while they are about it."

"No." Dido wrapped her arms around her stomach. "We saw no slave hunters, no militia," she cried. Perhaps he was wrong or making it all up.

"I do not know why you didn't see them but they left yesterday morning."

The slave hunters would probably have made for Massa Neville's and veered into the Blue Mountains from there, figuring that El Negro and the runaway slaves would have sought the quickest route into the hills. Dido would not necessarily have seen them.

"No."

"I am sorry to cause you pain," the Taino said, his voice low.

"What can I do? I do not know what to do."

"There is nothing for you to do, daughter."

There had to be. She could not just do nothing.

"Where are the men? William and the others. Surely they'll help him."

"They're gone. When word came that Modyford was rounding up men for the militia they left, sailed away on different ships. They didn't want no part of the militia but if they'd stayed it was either join or the gaol for them."

"They've left?" Dido found it hard to take in what he'd said. "Are they…will they come back?"

The Taino shrugged. "I doubt it. Even if they did, what could they do? They love the captain but I don't think there's one among them wants to die for him. I stayed because I promised him and because I do not fear death."

Dido brushed past Yacahüey to lean against the railing. She remembered her unease in the hills. She had thought something was wrong but she had imagined it had something to do with the ship, that they would arrive in Port Royal and find it gone or something like that. It had never occurred to her that Massa Taylor could identify El Negro. She had not imagined the dogs looking for him, him especially. She had thought that when he left the village he would be safe. Even if the militia found the *marronas*, he'd be long gone. Now she wished she had stuck firm to her argument about traveling together. She wondered if they'd already caught him, if he was alive or dead. She had to find help for him but she didn't know where to look. His men had left like the proverbial rats on a sinking ship.

Dido spun around and returned to the small group. She wasn't going to give up, not without a fight. She would save him. She had to.

"We must get the ship ready," she said to Yacahüey.

"But…"

"It is what El Negro wished and I intend to see that his wishes are carried out until he tells me different." It was a bold speech though inside she was cold with fear. He was her life. If they caught him…but no, she would not think about that.

"And if he is not able to tell you different?" Yacahüey's tone was kind though his eyes had clouded with worry.

"Then we must think of what he would want and act accordingly. We shall need a new quartermaster to see to our needs."

"It's not necessary, I have been a quartermaster and know what is entailed, but with what are we to purchase our supplies?"

Dido poured pieces of eight from her box into his outstretched hands.

"If it is not enough, return to me and I will give you what you need."

Yacahüey nodded.

"You know, Dom…I mean Dido, I think I prefer you as a woman." His eyes ran up and down her body appreciatively. "Not just because you're a sweet sight to these tired eyes."

"No?" Dido cocked an eyebrow at him.

"No. You are different, now. As a boy, you were timid. Frightened we would discover your secret, I suppose. Now you are tougher."

Dido did not know what to say to this. Was she tougher? Or was she just determined that the man and the life she wanted would not be taken away from her, not now, not after everything she'd been through.

"You were good to the boy, Domingo, Yacahüey. I haven't forgotten. You'll come with us when we sail, won't you? I do not know where we'll end up but I know El Negro would be glad for your company as would I."

The Taino frowned.

"He is a good captain, better than most. I'll come if he will have me."

"He will." Dido embraced the squat man again. "Wait on me. I must see to my mother and sister before I can go ashore. Then we must hurry."

Once he arrived in Port Royal, El Negro would have to be smuggled aboard the ship and then there would not be one minute to lose. If a wharf-rat or any enemy he had saw him, it would not be long before word of his presence came to the Governor's ears. She didn't think even his friendship with Morgan would save him then.

Morgan. She had forgotten about the commander. He must have heard about El Negro's predicament. Why had he done nothing to come to his friend's aid? Shrugging off the thought, Dido turned to her mother and sister.

"Come," she said, leading them to El Negro's cabin. She opened the door with the key he'd given her and helped them stow away their meager belongings.

"You must stay here," she told them. "I will lock the door after me so no-one may get in but you can leave the port-hole open."

"Where are you going, daughter?"

"Back ashore." She felt too nervous to stay locked in a room while who knows what was happening in the city. "I must go see if I can hear any news of the militia and its doings."

"Will it not be dangerous?" Claribel asked in her soft voice.

Her sister had not spoken much during their journey and now Dido watched her with regret. The girl had grown up during their separation and was practically a stranger to her.

"I'll keep my head down."

"Perhaps you should wear your disguise again," Unmi suggested. "It is easier for a man to go about his business undisturbed than a woman of our color."

It was true. Dido remembered Daniel and his friends with distaste. But she had left Massa Richard's clothes back in the Blue Mountains. No problem. She crossed over to El Negro's closet and threw open the doors. In ten minutes, a dark, slender pirate dressed in rolled-up velvet breeches and a white linen shirt with billowing sleeves emerged from El Negro's cabin. It was the most sober combination Dido could come up with given the armoire's contents but she was glad Yacahüey was the only one around. The Taino's lips twitched when he saw her outfit but he only reported that he'd checked on the ropes and sails and thought he would only have to concentrate on loading food and water on the ship.

Dido nodded. This was good news and meant the money she had given him could go further.

"Are you ready to go ashore now?" she asked.

He nodded and she helped him to lower the rowboat to the water. They parted ways at the dock after agreeing to meet back there in the evening. Dido made the Taino promise he would not leave her behind. Not that she'd mind that so much for herself, Port Royal held no terrors for her in her disguise, but her mother and sister would worry if she did not return.

She made her way straight to the nearest tavern. To her surprise, the place was almost empty. The only customer was an old graybeard who stared at the tankard between his hands as if at a cache of gold. She doubted she would learn anything from him. Dido backed out to try her luck at The Cat and the Fiddle across the street but business there was little better. Her plan had been to sidle up to a group and listen in on their talk. She had been sure she would pick up some news that way but it was beginning to look as if she'd need another plan. Ian would know how to find out what was happening but looking for him would be no easier than looking for a needle at the bottom of Davy Jones' locker.

Dido rubbed her chin as she considered her next move. Port Royal was not the raucous place she knew it to be but while that thought might have cheered her at some other time, it did not have that effect now. All those layabouts and ruffians who could normally be found in the taverns at any time of day had clearly signed up with the militia and were at that very moment hunting her lover. The governor was paying each militia-man a shilling a day and using his share of the loot from the sack of Puerto Bello to do it. The irony of it was like a blade in her stomach. El Negro had fought with valor at Morgan's side to save Jamaica and now the island sought to repay him with the gibbet. She had to find a way to help him but she was just a woman, a former slave. *Morgan is neither*, a voice whispered. *Oshun, of course.* She would find the commander and tell him El Negro was innocent. He had killed those men only in self-defense and in defense of her. Morgan would come to his friend's aid. She was sure of it. She should have asked Yacahüey where she could find him. Her heart lighter than it had been all day, Dido hurried back to the wharf.

Chapter 23

"**M**organ no be here," the tall, leathery-faced man said and pulled on his pipe.

"Not here? What do you mean, 'not here?'" Morgan was here. He had to be here or, at least, if not in the harbor he had to be in Jamaica.

"Just what I said, boy. Word is he's in Tortuga."

"Tortuga!"

"Boy, I'd offer you a shoulder if you wasn't so big."

"Why should I have need of your shoulder?"

"Because you're as good as a parrot, always repeating everything I say." He laughed.

"Will he come here soon?"

"That I could not say but I hear he be planning another expedition. He might never come back till he's good and ready to settle down."

Dido only just managed to bite back the words 'settle down' before they escaped her lips. With Morgan away her hope of finding someone to champion El Negro's cause with the governor was gone as well. But she couldn't give up. A sudden memory of their lovemaking on their last night together, of his lips on hers, and of his hand in her secret places, pulled a wave of fire up from between her legs to her breasts. Dido's nipples hardened even through the band of cloth she had wrapped around her chest. She would not lose him to the gallows. She would not.

Dido glanced up at the sky. From the position of the sun overhead, there were hours yet before her rendezvous with Yacahüey. She ignored her rumbling belly. How could she eat without knowing what was happening with her beloved? She turned and walked away from the harbor, barely noticing where she was going, her mind racing. Her memories of El Negro ran like a song through her blood but beneath the sweet notes echoed a dark lament of anguish and frustration. Had the gods revealed him to her only to snatch him away again? *Oshun, why is this thing happening? Why? He is a good man.*

Maybe it was as El Negro had said, maybe the god of the whites was more powerful than the gods of Guinea. Dido bit her lip. She must have faith in Oshun and Oludumare and the rest. El Negro was not yet in the governor's hands. It could very well be that he would escape capture and bring himself and her brothers to her, unharmed.

Whatever the gods were doing, she wanted to make sure she, herself, had done all she could to make it so. Dido had kept her eyes on the ground as she walked, her mind in a jumble. When she looked up she found herself close to Queen Street. If she turned down the alleyway ahead and then crossed Lime Street she would be only a few doors down from the seamstress's house, the one who'd fixed her clothes the day Dido and El Negro first met.

"Yes, boy, what do you want?" the seamstress asked when Dido came through her door.

"It is me, Anna. Do you remember when El Negro brought me here and you tended my wounds?" Dido extended her arm to show the faint scars of her encounter with Daniel and the others.

"El Negro?" Anna rose from her chair and came to take a closer look at Dido. "Ah, yes. The child-woman. I remember. Where's the captain?"

"Haven't you heard?" Dido sighed. She'd been hoping the woman would have been able to give her some news, any news. "The militia is after him for killing white men."

"That I know. What I asked was, where is he?"

"He's making his way here. My brothers are with him."

"Come. Tell me everything, child." Anna pulled her over to a chair and Dido sat down to relay her story.

"It is clear he killed only in defense of his life," Anna said, nodding when Dido was finished. "But the life of a black man is not considered worth that of a white. Governor Modyford has big dreams for this little island. He wishes to see sugar cane cover the land so that Jamaica's prosperity may surpass that of Barbados."

"What does this have to do with El Negro? He's a pirate, not a planter."

"He is a black man who has killed a white planter, my child. They'll think that if he should suffer no ill consequence for this, other black men will do as he has done. Modyford's dreams of attracting hundreds more English settlers and of presiding over a cane-rich island will come to naught if the planters fear death at the hands of blacks."

"He was killed rescuing me. Had Massa Neville not fired on him, he would be alive today."

"Look, child, the sun that shines in the sky above us is the same sun that shines in Guinea, is it not?" Dido nodded, not sure she saw where the woman was going. "Yet the sights a woman opens her eyes to in Guinea are not the same as those before us. The truth you know about your man is not the same truth Modyford knows. You see an honorable man who risked his life for you. Modyford sees a lawless brigand who does not care for the lives of whites. He fears El Negro for the same reason the whites hate the *marronas* so."

Dido nodded, pondering the seamstress's words.

"Wait," she straightened, blinking. "You said, 'your man.' Why do you say that?"

"It's true, is it not?"

"Yes." El Negro was her man. "But how did you know?"

"I have eyes and I can see that though I call you 'child' you are truly a woman, now. You no longer shrink into yourself as before."

It was true. El Negro had made her a woman. "I have to help him," Dido said, "but I do not know how. Morgan might have interceded on his behalf but he's not come and it's not known when he will return."

Anna nodded. "That one keeps well his own counsel. He may arrive next week or he may not return until next year. You cannot look to him for aid."

Dido's fist clenched in her lap. "I will not see El Negro go to the gallows. I will not."

"A child should know his father."

"What?" Had the old woman lost her mind?

"Your love has seeded your womb."

"What?"

"I have been in this world a long time, child." A fleeting smile gave the old woman a mischievous look. "So long that I can now see things about people as plainly as they themselves can see the marks on my face."

"How? What tells you this about me?" Could Anna be right? Surely it was too early to know. Dido flattened her hands over her stomach. She felt no different. Her belly was as flat as always, perhaps even flatter since she had not eaten since dawn.

"What I'm about to tell you I have told no-one. You must promise me you will keep my secret for there are many who do not understand these things and are fearful."

"You're a witch," Dido breathed. The white holy man who had come to Beeston's Estate every Sunday had often spoken of the evils of witchcraft. *You are the children of Ham who was cursed by God and you've lived long without knowledge of Him so evil takes root in you all the more readily*, he'd told the blacks standing in front of him. *Beware evil-doers and those who, with potions and sorcery, will try to tempt you away from a life of service to the one true God and to your master here on earth.* Only a handful of slaves had given him more than dutiful attention, the rest practiced the art of appearing to listen even as their minds wandered.

"I make no potions to force a man to love a woman and I do not fly through the air at night." Anna looked scornful. "What I can do is look at someone and see things about them in the way they carry themselves or in the way their skin looks or the brightness of their eyes. Other times I see more." She paused. "Other times I see people as they were and as they will be."

"Their past and their future?"

"Not always as simple as that. Do you remember that when I met you I likened you to a cracked vessel?"

Dido nodded.

"When I looked in your face, I actually saw a flagon scored with tiny cracks, no thicker than your hair. I didn't know what it meant until you said you'd never given yourself in love. Then I immediately knew what had happened to you."

"And this time you see a baby," Dido interjected flatly, not sure she believed any of it.

Anna chuckled. "What I see now is that your skin glows, your eyes sparkle as from a hidden fire. I'd also wager that if you were to release your breasts from their confinement, I'd see that they've swelled and are no longer the tiny buds of a child."

"If this is all the evidence you have that I am with child then I fear you may be mistaken. Might not my skin glow because I have just come in from the sun and might my eyes not sparkle because I am near crazed with worry for El Negro?"

"It's possible that I am wrong. I'm not always right but in your case I think I am. We'll say no more on it, however, if it displeases you to think so."

"No, mother. Do not mistake me. I wish to have many babies for my man but I do not want to believe in a thing that is not true."

Anna shrugged but offered no more argument. "Come, child," she said, instead, rising. "You are hungry. Come."

The seamstress led Dido to a back room where she set out a pewter plate filled almost to overflowing with stewed meat, boiled green bananas, and foo-foo, a pudding made of cornmeal and okras. Dido ate while Anna busied herself going back and forth between the room and the yard. From where she sat, Dido could see a small brick oven and the remains of a cookfire. Dido chewed and swallowed hungrily and was soon done. Anna smiled approvingly at her appetite, her expression seeming to say that Dido clearly did not eat for herself alone.

Dido let it pass. If the old woman wanted to believe she was pregnant, well, where was the harm in that.

"I must go now. Yacahüey will be waiting for me at the wharf."

"The Taino."

"You know him?"

"He's a good man." She frowned. "Do you hear that?"

"What? I don't…" Then she did. Hoofbeats and muffled shouts.

"It is the militia-men. They have returned."

Dido's throat dried. An icy wind roared in her ears, chilling her to the bone.

"They've caught him, mother."

"Come." Anna grabbed Dido's hand in hers and the two women half-walked, half-ran toward the commotion. "The sound comes from Fort Carlisle."

"What's happened? What's happened?" they asked the people they met who were running in the same direction. Nobody knew.

The crowds thickened the closer they got to the fort, horses and people swirling around before the huge, open doors. Dido let go of Anna's hand and pushed her way to the front just in time to see a line of men, each tied to the other at the wrists, being pulled into the fort.

"Are they *marronas*?" she asked a turbaned black woman beside her.

"Yes," the woman replied, her eyes on the closing fort doors. "They are Chief Jorge's men but it's said the Chief, himself, escaped with many of his people. They've fled deeper into the mountains where the whites fear to go."

"What of El Negro? Was he caught as well?"

"What is left of him." The woman glanced at her and began to walk away.

"What do you mean? Is he…is he dead?"

"Not dead but close."

"At least he walked on his own two feet," a nearby man chimed in.

"You mean, they beat him?"

The woman kept walking but the man answered her.

"His face was bloody and one arm hung at his side as if he does not have the use of it. You could see the pain it cost him to walk but he's not a man to suffer himself to be dragged."

"Was he…did he seem to look for anyone?" Had he sought her face in the shouting crowd?

"No. I think it must have taken him every ounce of his strength not to fall on his face. He had none left for more." The man shot her a keen glance clearly wondering why this should interest her.

"And were there two small children with him? Two boys?"

"I saw no children but mayhap I did not see everything."

Despair encircled her heart like a vise.

"Child, what?" Anna had found her. "Did you see him? Why do you look so?"

Dido grabbed the older woman's hands. "They have beaten him, mother, beaten him badly, this man said." She looked around for her informer but he had disappeared. "I do not know if George and Zacchariah are with him or no. The man didn't see them. Oh, mother." Hot tears stung her eyes.

"Hush. Hush now." Anna stroked her back with her free hand. "Because one man did not see them does not mean they weren't there. Everyone is talking of El Negro's capture. That is what excites them. They would not notice two small boys."

"Yes. Yes, that's true." Dido wiped her eyes. If she was going to dress like a man, she should at least try to act like one and not give way to tears like some little girl. "How can we find out what they intend? I need to know more. I need to get to him if he's hurt."

"I know a woman who works in the fort. Tonight, when you have returned to the ship I will go to her home and see what she can tell me."

Dido had forgotten all about going back to the *Fortune's Gift*. Pain wrenched her heart at the idea of leaving El Negro in the fort with no way of knowing she had been there, no way of knowing she had no intention of leaving him to his fate.

"There is nothing more to be done here," Anna said, her eyes kind. "You…"

Dido did not let her finish. "You say you can see the future, mother." She clutched the older woman's hands. "What do you see for him? Will he escape the gibbet? Tell me."

"I'm sorry, child. He is one of those around whom there is such a brightness and a swirling of color that I could never tell his past from his future."

"But did you ever see the gallows?"

"No, child. Never."

"Did you see him being captured?"

Anna didn't answer.

"Tell me. You must tell me." Dido loosed the other woman's hands to grasp her shoulders and give them a little shake. "Did you see this fort? Or the militia? Did you see them beating him like a dog?"

"No." Anna pushed Dido away. "I saw none of these things. I saw only you."

"Me?"

"A week maybe a month before he brought you to me, I saw your face like an image in steam when I looked at him."

Dido's throat dried.

"I said nothing to him or to you when you came in that day looking more like a suspicious street urchin than a woman but I knew that the gods of Guinea had given you each to the other. Men take wives and women take husbands but this does not often affect what I see. Few men and few women will have a love so strong that such as I will see the image of their beloved when we look at them."

"Do you see his face when you look at me?"

"Yes, child. It has been there from the time you first showed up at my shop."

A thought like sunshine in her heart brought a smile to Dido's lips. "Those whom the gods of Guinea mean for each other, surely they cannot be separated by man." What sense would it make for them to bring her and El Negro together only for her to witness his execution? None, that was the answer. Still, her doubts persisted. Why had they allowed his capture?

"Perhaps the old gods are at war with the white man's God," Anna suggested as if reading her thoughts. "Perhaps El Negro's capture is the white God's doing."

"Perhaps." Dido had no time to ponder this intricate puzzle. Darkness had closed in fast around them. Yacahüey might not wait much longer for her. She must hurry if she wanted to return to her mother and sister to inform them of what had happened.

"Anna, I will come to you tomorrow to learn what you've discovered about the captives. If there's any way you can send word to him or to my brothers, let them know I'm here and that I'll do all in my power to free them."

The two women embraced and Dido set off for the wharf, half-walking, half-running.

She need not have worried. When she arrived, breathless, Yacahüey was sitting cross-legged on an old crate, looking like a man with all the time in the world.

As they rowed back to the *Fortune's Gift*, they compared the stories they'd heard. Yacahüey's mouth tightened when Dido told him of the reports that his captain had been beaten.

"The Governor means to start the case on Friday," he said.

"Friday! But that's only four days away!"

Yacahüey nodded somberly as he pulled on the oars. "Modyford knows the captain is well-respected among the Brethren and by Morgan. He fears that when Morgan and the rest hear of El Negro's capture they will return before he can close the gibbet on him and hang him from the fort walls."

"Would they try to free him?"

"To a man."

But it was no use getting her hopes up, the harbor was almost empty and, if what Yacahüey had said about the trial starting on Friday was true, everything could be over by Monday.

"Do you think they will let me see him tomorrow? I need to see him and to know what has happened to George and Zacchariah." She would take her herbs and liniments with her and attend to his wounds.

The Taino looked her up and down. "Perhaps if you dress as a woman. If you go as you are now, they might think you one of his crew and not let you in. Take some pieces of eight to persuade any as seem obstructive."

Dido nodded. She would rain coins down on the guards like a shower if that would gain her entrance.

Chapter 24

"**I** want to come with you. I must know about my sons. How can I stay here in comfort not knowing if they are dead or alive?" Unmi grabbed Dido's arm, tears running down her face. "You cannot ask such a thing of me. I must come with you."

All night her mother had turned and twisted while Dido lay listening, barely breathing, wanting to comfort but needing it herself. The pain in her heart swelled and swelled until, by morning, she thought her chest would explode. She had risen from the bed, her bedclothes damp with sweat. She didn't think her mother had slept at all.

"Mother, you are safer here."

"I do not want to be safe. I want to know if my sons still breathe."

Dido glanced at Claribel who had shrunk back against the wall to watch them with frightened eyes.

"What of her? Do you not care what might happen to her if you do not return?"

Unmi spun around. With a horrified gasp, she hurried to her younger daughter and threw her arms around her.

"I do not know what I'll find at the fort. I do not know what this day will bring or the next, Mother. All I know is that I must find some way to free El Negro and my brothers too, if they are with him. I need to be able to do that without having to worry about you or about her."

Unmi nodded, making a visible effort to calm herself. "I understand. I'll stay but, please, try to send word as soon as you can."

"That I will." Dido crossed the floor to what remained of her little family. The three women hugged, their arms tight about each other.

"Walk well, daughter."

Dido picked up the satchel with her herbal powders and liniments and opened the door.

Yacahüey waited for her on deck with two other crewmen. If the others were surprised to see a woman come out from their absent captain's cabin their faces did not betray it.

"Today I continue to provision the ship," Yacahüey said to her, as they rowed ashore. "But I must do it with greater discretion than before lest anyone ask why

El Negro's ship is preparing for departure even as he languishes in the gaol. I trust these men to keep their mouths shut as they help me. They have no love for Modyford." He nodded at their backs. "Should you need me for anything, come to the wharf. If I'm not there, they will know where to find me."

Dido nodded. Her eyes had not left the fort since she had gotten into the small boat. *Where was he*, she wondered. *Was he thinking of her or was he in too much pain to think of anyone or anything*? She drew her skirts in around her and clasped her hands in her lap. *Please, Oshun, keep him safe*. An answering breeze cooled her face. Dido's spirit lifted as if the goddess had laid her hand on her in comfort.

"Anna," Dido said, barely waiting to pass through the seamstress's open doors before she began speaking. "Did you talk to the woman? What did she say?"

Anna's eyes gleamed as she motioned Dido to a chair.

"Your brothers are captives, too. They're well. She has seen them and says they've suffered no hurt. The younger one is frightened but the other one keeps his hopes up by telling him stories and singing songs."

Dido beamed with pride, remembering the instant bond she had felt with Zaccharias. No doubt he was just as frightened as George but he would not show it. He was being strong for his little brother.

"What of El Negro?"

"Ah, child, the news there is not as good."

Dido's hands clenched and she pushed her back against the chair, preparing for the worst.

"The militia set upon the village before he had time to leave. Modyford sent orders on ahead to San Jago to the other contingent to advance by night thus tricking Chief Jorge's look-outs for it's well-known that the whites prefer to fight by day and sleep at night."

"Mother, tell me, please, how is he?"

"His right arm is broken and he's in great pain. The other men say he brought down many of the militia and was the last to surrender. They say he fought until he could no longer stand though it took more than five men to drop him. Even when he was down they would not stop kicking and hitting him. T'was the governor who called them off though he were in no rush about it." She paused. "She says he be in a bad way."

"I must go to him." Dido rose to her feet, her satchel in hand.

"Ask for Ernestina. She'll take you to Massa Leacock, that be the name of the gaoler. It is his permission you'll need if you want to see your loved ones."

Dido nodded but she was thinking that come hell or high water she intended to see El Negro and her brothers, permission or not.

"Return to me if there is aught you need," Anna called after her as Dido spun away, retracing the steps she'd taken the previous evening.

There were hardly any people around outside the fort's doors which were shut tight. Dido had stepped back in frustration, wondering how to gain entrance, when she saw a small window cut in the wall off to the side.

"Inside!" she called. "Hoy!"

A grizzled white man appeared before her.

"What d'ye want?"

"I've come to see Ernestina."

He disappeared without another word. Dido hefted her satchel over her shoulder and peeped through the opening, trying to see if she could catch a glimpse of the captives but there were few people about and all looked as if they had business in the place. Had the man gone to fetch Anna's friend? Dido was just about to call out again when a round-faced woman emerged at the other side of the courtyard, hurrying in her direction.

"Are you Dido?"

Dido nodded.

"Walk straight down along the wall until you reach the corner. Turn left. There is a small door there that I will open for you."

The woman was waiting for Dido when she arrived.

"I told Massa Leacock you are come," she said, motioning Dido to follow her. "He wants to see you."

"Can I not go to El Negro and my brothers first?" Dido glanced around, hoping for the sight of them but the fort was a confusing maze of small buildings. Even if she refused to follow Ernestina, she would have no idea how to find her way. She stifled a small groan of frustration.

"If I do not take you to him, it will go ill with me," Ernestina said, her expression sympathetic as if she knew something of what Dido was feeling.

"I understand. Please lead the way."

The gaoler's office was up a flight of steps in a building almost right in the middle of the yard. A man stood at one end looking out the window. He did not turn around when they entered.

"I have brought the woman who wishes to see the pirate and the little boys, sir," Ernestina said, clearing her throat.

It was as if the man had not heard.

"Sir, I…"

"I am not deaf, Ernestina."

He turned around.

Dido breathed sharply, trying to mask her recoil. His face was covered in boils. No, not boils. In huge warts, some as big as her thumb. She looked at him in disbelief and saw that the eruptions of flesh were on his neck, his arms, they even pushed up through what remained of the hair on his head.

"Does my appearance frighten you, girl?"

How could she hide it? Dido nodded rapidly, not trusting herself to speak. What had happened to this man?

"Be comforted in knowing you are not alone." He picked up a glass on the table before him and downed its contents in one gulp. Dido noticed that beneath the warts he had the appearance of a man who drank—his wrists and hands were puffy and his eyes, what she could see of them beneath the warts on his eyelids, were bloodshot.

"So you are El Negro's woman?" He came closer and she could smell the rum on his breath. The scent seemed to rise from his very clothes.

"Yes."

He laughed.

"Only the prettiest for our most famous Afric pirate, eh?" His expression turned fierce. "Well, go on then. Do not let me keep you." He made sweeping gestures with his hands. "Once the trial starts he'll have no visitors and it will be the gallows for him, don't you know?"

Dido started to tell him he was wrong, El Negro was innocent, but Ernestina grabbed her arm. She allowed the woman to pull her away.

"There's no profit in arguing with such as him," the woman said.

"I'm looking for justice, not profit," Dido snapped, following her down the steps and around the corner.

"And is this where you hope to find it? Look, there is your man. In there." Ernestina pointed to a low square building which at first seemed windowless until Dido looked closer and saw the slits in the wall. A man armed with a musket stood in front of the door. Ernestina marched up to him with Dido right behind.

"Massa Leacock's says she's to be let in," Ernestina said.

"Did he now?" The man scowled at Dido.

"He did." Ernestina squared her arms and glared back at him.

"Who is she?"

"Massa Leacock knows who she is and he said she is to be let in." Ernestina spoke firmly in a tone that brooked no further argument. The man grimaced. He fished at his waist for the keys to the thick wooden door and fumbled with the keyhole, taking his sweet time.

The smell of human waste, blood and perspiration billowed out from the room. Dido gagged, her eyes widening in horror. She remembered the Dutch slaver and closed her eyes in a quick and silent prayer to Oshun. There was nothing she wanted to do more than turn and run away from what she might see inside but she forced herself to cross the threshold.

Dido blinked a couple of times to accustom herself to the lack of light.

"Dido! Dido!" A small body detached itself from the darkness and threw itself at her.

"Zaccharias?"

"No, it's me, George."

"And me." Another small body launched itself at her.

Dido hugged them, crying.

"How did you find us? What will happen to us? Where's Mumma?"

"She's here in the town," Dido replied, not knowing how well the watchman outside listened but sensing the presence and alertness of the other captives. "I came as soon as I could. Are you hurt?" Her hands ran over them, checking for broken bones, torn skin.

"We are well but we're hungry. We've had nothing to eat since yesterday morning."

Dido dug into her bag and pulled out the six bread loaves she'd bought on her way to the fort.

"Please share it among all," she said, as bodies stirred around her.

Low murmurs of thanks rose as the boys did her bidding.

"Where…" She was going to ask for El Negro but it was then that she saw him. He sat propped against a wall, his legs straight out in front of him as if he had not the strength to draw them in. She could not tell from where she stood if his eyes were open or closed, if he slept or was awake.

"Come," Zaccharias whispered. "I'll take you to him." His hand slipped into his sister's and he gently pulled her toward the still form.

"Is he…?" She could not finish the question or take her eyes away from him.

"He breathes but he has said nothing since we were captured."

The people made way for Dido to pass but she was not aware of them. She invoked Oshun with every step she took, pleading for strength to help the pirate.

"El Negro, my captain," she cried, reaching him at last. She fell to her knees beside him.

He didn't move. His eyes remained closed.

A savage fear fountained in her heart but she fought it down. Her fingers gently grazed his cheek. Though she wanted to throw her arms around him, to squeeze him to her breast, she knew she could not. She didn't know where he was hurt or how badly and could not risk aggravating some injury by her embrace.

"Ernestina," she called.

"I am here," the woman answered from the doorway.

"May I have a basin of cool, fresh water and as many clean cloths as you can spare." She looked at his swollen legs, his tattered shirt. "Also, he'll need clothes. Please go to Anna and tell her to send what she thinks will fit him. Bring the water first."

The people beside them cleared a space for her as she began to dig into her satchel. She laid out on the ground the things she had brought, the phials, the leaves of the aloe vera and the leaf-of-life, the ship surgeon's tools. She would not know what she'd need until she cleaned away the blood and filth all over him.

Ernestina returned quickly with the basin and the cloths which the captives passed from hand to hand until they came to rest by Dido's side. Dido broke a piece of the aloe vera leaf open and dropped it in the water before soaking one of the cloths in it. She wrung it dry and began to wipe El Negro's face. A shudder passed through him as the cool, damp cloth touched him but then he relaxed, turning his head so slowly toward her that the movement was almost imperceptible.

His lips parted but the sound that came out was more a moan than a word.

"Hush, don't talk," Dido whispered, her heart breaking. His face was a mass of scars, the skin lumpy and broken with the blows they had given him. Thankfully, none of the bones appeared damaged.

Dido rinsed the cloth in the basin turning the water red with El Negro's blood. Tenderly, she dabbed his eyes. They were puffy and choked with pus.

He moaned again.

"I'm here, beloved. Do not try to talk for you need your strength." She leaned forward and brushed his battered forehead with a kiss as light as the mists that sometimes fell on the Blue Mountains.

Six times she had to send Zaccharias for fresh water before she was satisfied she had done the best she could. Anna arrived before she began to bandage his arm, it was the right that was broken and not the left as the man had told her.

The older woman stood quietly at her side as she worked but Dido could sense her rage at what had happened to him.

"You must hurry, Dido," Ernestina said from the door. "Massa Leacock has sent to say you have only another hour."

Dido nodded. With Anna's help, she applied the various poultices and liniments to El Negro's wounds, glad to see that for all the harm the militiamen had done, the only stitches he needed were on his upper left arm where he'd received a finger-long gash. A couple of the other male captives helped the women get him into the clothes Anna had brought. They spread a cloth below him and lowered him gently back down.

"Is there any other who needs my help?" Dido asked when she was satisfied she had done her best for her pirate.

A few of the others had suffered wounds though none were as badly off as El Negro. Dido saw to them quickly before returning to her lover's side.

"I must go now, my heart, but I will return," she whispered in his ear. "I'll not let them have you. I will not."

His good hand sought hers and held it weakly.

"Massa Leacock coming," Ernestina called, her voice panicky. "You have to go now, Dido."

El Negro moaned low in his throat.

"I will be back," Dido murmured. She brought his hand to her face and pressed his palm to her cheek. There was a fierce heat in her heart as she picked her way back out to the sunlight and the fresh air that suddenly felt like a special blessing from Oshun. She strode after Ernestina without once looking in the gaoler's direction. Her beautiful pirate with the skin of velvet and the bearing of a prince lay broken in a room half the size of his own cabin. She walked along the wall, thumping it with her fist, imagining it was Modyford's face she pummeled.

El Negro would not heal, could not heal in such circumstances. She feared that despite her ministrations, corruption would set in and fever would rob him of consciousness. If that happened, there was nothing she could do to help him. Sickness would take him before the gibbet could.

At the door to the fort, she thanked Ernestina and pressed a piece of eight into her hand.

"I'll come again tomorrow. You will let me in?"

Ernestina nodded.

"Walk well, daughter. These are hard times."

Dido grimaced. "For some more than others."

The woman closed the door. Anna and Dido looked at each other, their faces tight with anger and worry.

"What will you do, child?" the seamstress asked.

"I will get him out. Him and my brothers."

Anna nodded slowly but her eyes revealed her doubt.

"Have you need of me?"

"Not now, mother. Return to your house. I'll call you when I am ready."

The two women embraced.

"I will help you in any way I can," Anna said, before walking off.

Dido watched her go, her mind a tangle of thoughts. The only clear thing she knew was that death would not claim El Negro, not while blood coursed through her veins. Shango would have to take her first. Tossing her near-empty satchel over her shoulder she headed to the wharf.

Chapter 25

"**I**t will not work, Dido. We be too few in number."

Dido rounded on the Taino. "It must work. It has to work."

They were all in El Negro's cabin, Dido, her mother, Claribel, and Yacahüey. Dido had spoken little since rejoining El Negro's skeletal crew at the wharf and she had kept to herself after she returned to the ship. The plan forming in her mind required all her attention. It had to be flawless before she presented it to Yacahüey and the others. Dido had gone over it again and again until her thoughts dizzied her.

"After Ernestina lets me in with the guns, you and the men use a grappling hook to climb over the walls," she repeated, speaking slowly and carefully so there could be no misunderstanding. Yacahüey shook his head but he heard her out. "You overpower any who seek to oppose you while I release the captives. Once I hand them their weapons, they will assist you. Many of them are able-bodied. What could be easier? It will be child's play for us to return to the ship and sail out of the harbor."

"You said, El Negro was badly injured," Unmi objected. "Whoever carries him will not be able to run fast."

That was the part she had fretted about the most but she thought she had the answer.

"We can make a carrier for him, Mumma. If we stretch some sailcloth over a wooden frame as long as he is tall, four men will be able to carry him easily and with speed."

Unmi turned to Yacahüey. "Why do you say this plan will not work?"

"Three of the crewmen who were on the ship this morning have signed on with the *Swallow* which sails tomorrow with the dawn. Only two men remain. Three are not enough to take a fort."

"Four!"

Yacahüey smiled at her. "Even with you, we are not enough, brave Dido. And even had we more men, the fort is near the Governor's house. Do you think he will not hear what is happening and send to rouse the militiamen?"

Dido took a breath, about to interrupt him but he held up his hand. "I heard you out," he said, frowning. Dido shrugged. Her eyes narrowed. "We would never get out of the fort," Yacahüey continued. "If, by some miracle we did, and we made it back to the ship, the fort's guns are trained upon the harbor. By the time we readied our sails, the gunners would be at their stations. We'd have little hope of evading whatever they fire at us."

"We can get more men. We can go into the taverns and…"

"Dido, any men as would come with us, would want to be paid and what have we to offer them?"

"There is gold. There is El Negro's share of the prize from Puerto Bello." Dido looked around the room as if expecting the treasure chest to suddenly reveal itself.

"Even if we could find where he has hidden it, I doubt we'd be able to purchase more than ten men's loyalty with it. Men fear the gallows too much to fight against the Crown."

"You don't want to help him escape," Dido said, almost whispering. "That's the truth, isn't it? You want to see him hang so you can lay claim to his ship and find his treasure."

"You are angry and overwrought or you'd never say such a thing." He crossed the room and gripped her by the shoulders. "I've known El Negro longer than you. He is like a brother to me but what's the use in risking my life in a fool's cause? Do you think I've not thought on how to free him? Thought and thought. Few have ever escaped from that prison. I can think on no way of saving him." He shook her. "How can you think I do not want to?"

Dido saw the pain in his eyes and knew she'd been unjust. "I'm sorry, Yacahüey. I had no right. Forgive me."

"Can you not offer the gaoler a bribe?" Unmi asked, suddenly.

Yacahüey and Dido spun around to her.

"A bribe?" It was so simple, so glaringly simple she'd never thought of it.

"Yacahüey says El Negro's treasure would not be enough to buy ten men but it need only buy one if that one is the gaoler."

"We don't know where he has hidden it," Dido objected.

"We have two nights and two days to look," Yacahüey pointed out.

"Yes," Dido breathed, her eyes shining. "Yes." Surely that was more than enough time, the ship was only so big.

But though they searched all that night and the next morning, they still hadn't found the pirate captain's treasure by the time Dido left at noon to return to the prison.

"He had a fever during the night but it broke this morning," Zaccharias murmured, crouching beside her.

Dido unstoppered the flask of bush tea she had brought and laid it gently to El Negro's lips. He took a sip and turned his face away.

"What is that?" George asked through a mouthful of one of the meat patties she had dispensed to all the captives.

"It's a drink made with the leaf-of-life and other herbs. It will give him the strength to get better."

"He doesn't like it."

"It's as bitter as young lime but you must try. Please, my love." She would not speak about him as if he were not in the room before her. She offered the flask to him again and was encouraged when he took another sip, then another. A little of the tea ran down his chin. She wiped it off, looking closely at his face all the while.

The cuts and bruises looked no better, perhaps a little worse but she had expected that. From her experience at Beeston's she knew that some wounds got worse-looking before they began to heal. She checked all the dressings and replaced those that required it.

"Will they hang us, Dido?" Zaccharias asked.

Her brother looked old, like a wizened version of the boy he'd been only a week ago. He had traveled a lifetime since leaving the plantation.

"Not if I can help it," she responded, reaching out to caress his face. How like their mother he looked. Wordless, she opened her arms to her brothers and hugged them tight. They had to find El Negro's treasure and, when they did, Massa Leacock had to take it. She would not even allow herself to imagine any other outcome.

"Could it be he took it to shore?" Unmi asked, later.

"Those times he went, I was either with him or saw him go," Yacahüey said. "He carried nothing."

Night had fallen and they were gathered in El Negro' cabin.

"Could…" Claribel began tentatively. "Could one of the men have stolen it?"

"He kept the cabin door locked most times. He gave me the key just before he went haring off to free Dido."

Unmi glanced at her daughter, a question in her eyes. Dido grimaced and gave the smallest shake of her head. No, she believed in the Taino and his loyalty to El Negro. Whoever had taken it, if it had been taken, it was not Yacahüey. Had he wanted to, he could have taken the ship itself after its captain disappeared. The very fact that El Negro had given him the key and none other spoke of the trust he placed in the man. She would not dishonor that with further suspicions.

"We must renew our search. We can leave no barrel unexamined, no rope unturned. Please." She looked at each in turn. "El Negro's life and those of the boys depends on us."

They searched the whole ship, turning everything upside down, but it was no use. They still came up empty-handed.

Exhausted, Dido retired to El Negro's cabin with her mother and sister. She had meant only to take a short rest before resuming the search but, in minutes, she was asleep.

When she awoke, it was to an almost completely dark cabin. Dido lay still, listening to the sounds Unmi and Claribel made as they slept on. A shaft of moonlight through the open porthole illuminated El Negro's armoire and her gaze wandered over the intricate carvings thrown into relief. She shifted her head to get a better look. There was something funny about the armoire. In the moonlight, it seemed somehow bigger. Dido smiled at herself and her imaginings. She was letting her experiences of the past couple weeks affect her thinking. *Oshun, do not let me lose my wits now*, she whispered. She had not prayed, really prayed to the in a long time but now she closed her eyes and opened her heart to the goddess. *Most gracious mother, do not let them take what is mine*, she whispered in her heart, *you who are full of understanding and know my spirit well. Mother of abundance, keep my brothers safe from harm. Return them to their mother's care. Mother of pleasure, return my lover to me.*

Oshun's love washed over her like water from a cool, mountain spring. Dido opened her eyes feeling renewed. Whatever her own failures, Oshun had not deserted her. She was sure of it. Her gaze fell on the armoire again. There really was something strange about it. It…it was almost…Dido sprang up from the bed. A shaft of light pointed to it like the finger of Oshun, goddess of the moon.

Dido's hands flew over the armoire. What was Oshun trying to tell her? Dido stepped back to take another look and saw it. The armoire appeared much deeper than she knew it to be, as if it could hold another row of clothes behind the first. Dido threw open the doors and shoved the clothes aside. She flattened her palms against the back, feeling the rough surface, so different from the smoothness of the rest of the carefully-made piece. Had it always been so? El Negro had said he'd had it taken off a merchant ship. Either El Negro or its previous owners would have seen the value of creating a hidden compartment at the back. Big enough even to hold a man, if needs be.

"Dido…what?" Her mother had woken.

"Mumma, light a candle," Dido said, her voice high with excitement. "Light as many as you can. Bring them here."

As her mother rushed to do her bidding, Dido threw the clothes out, flinging them to the floor in her haste. When El Negro was free, he could buy himself a hundred more silk shirts, a hundred more velvet breeches. Dido knocked on the back of the wall and rejoiced at the hollowness of the sound. She was right, she knew she was right. But how was she to remove the clever contrivance? The candlelight Unmi raised behind her showed her the answer. Small holes were carved into both the right and left-hand corners. Holes big enough for a man's index finger. Dido slipped her fingers in and pulled. The false back gave way easily and Claribel jumped forward from the bed to help her and Unmi pull it out. Once it was out of the way, the women crowded around the open doors of the armoire. A leather chest lay revealed in the cavity the panel had hidden. The women pulled it out into the middle of the cabin floor.

El Negro was so confident about the hidden compartment he'd not bothered to lock the chest. Dido threw it open and fell to the floor in relief.

Gold necklaces, jeweled rings and brooches, gold coins and gleaming daggers winked up at her. The captain's share of the booty from many prizes. It was enough, she felt sure, to ransom even the king of the white people. Tears of gratitude coursed down her cheeks as her mother and sister hugged her.

"He cannot refuse these riches," her mother said. "With such wealth this gaoler can leave Jamaica with no fear of being held accountable for the escape of the captives. He need not fear Modyford."

"Yes, Mumma. Yes." To Dido, it was almost as if El Negro and her brothers were already free. She could see them in her mind's eyes. The boys laughing and dancing, Zaccharias once again the cheerful boy she'd known, and El Negro, healed and strong, so strong. How she longed to feel his arms around her once again.

Chapter 26

"**I** want no gold."

Dido stared at the gaoler. She could not have heard him aright.

"This that I've brought you." She shoved the diamond and emerald necklace across the table to him. "It is only one of scores like it. As I've told you, there be rings and coins and other things besides."

"I want none of it."

Did he think the jewels were fake, worthless? Without a word, she picked up his silver snuffbox and brought it down on the diamond. The stone glittered, unchanged, in the sunlight when she removed her hand but the base of the snuffbox now had a dent.

"Look at me," the gaoler snarled. Dido glanced at him and looked away. His face was red with the strength of his emotions, the boils fat and hideous with fury. "There will be no gem among your treasure that will improve my looks. Wherever I go, I will still be shunned and thought fit for little more than I do now in this pile of stone."

"You could buy yourself anything you want. I don't understand." She could have wept with frustration. El Negro's trial would start tomorrow. The gaoler *had* to take the bribe. He just had to. "These things are of high value among your people."

"I do not dispute that but there's something I value more." A fleck of spittle appeared at the corner of his mouth and his eyes acquired a faraway glaze.

Dido frowned. If he started speaking of honor, she would fly across the table and strangle him with her bare hands. She had not searched the *Fortune's Gift* all day and all night for most of the past two days, to hear such as him prattle of honor.

"I have not had a woman in many months. Not since the only doxie who would have me died. My cock is all but withered." His hands went to his groin and he cupped himself there, stroking himself with his thumb. "Let me lie with you and you shall have what you want."

"What?" There was such a roaring in her ears, she knew she could not have heard correctly.

But when he repeated himself, the tumescence in his pants now noticeable, she knew there was no mistake.

"You are quite beautiful for your kind," he said, his eyes never leaving her face. "I've thought on you often when I'm in my bed." His smile left her in no doubt as to the direction his mind had turned.

"No, it is impossible." How could he ask that of her? "With all the gold I can bring you, you could buy any woman you want."

"I take your friend Ernestina when I wants her."

"So why do you need me?" she asked. "And why do you say, you've not had a woman in years?"

"Ernestina belongs to me. I own her. She cannot refuse me though she tried to at first. I soon broke her of that. But with her it is like mating with a mule more than a woman." Did Ernestina know that was how he thought of her? Dido felt a fresh stab of grief for the woman who had befriended her. "I wants a woman like you, with fire in her belly. I want El Negro's woman. Do you not think I haven't seen him come swaggering into Port Royal, time and again?" He laughed scornfully. "Acting as if he's some great hero, hobnobbing with the likes of Morgan. I always knew his true nature would be revealed one day and now, by the grace of God, it has. For all his velvet and silks, all his fine airs, he's nothing but a savage blackie."

"That's the truth, then, isn't it?" Dido shook her head, looking him full in the face for the first time since she'd arrived in his office that morning. "You do not want me for my looks, you want me because of El Negro's love for me."

"Why should I not have what I'm sure he values more than all his treasure, for he'd never have left it otherwise." The gaoler smiled, showing the stumps of his rotten front teeth.

She could not, she could not. The very thought of lying with him turned her stomach.

"I...I will consider what you've said."

"Come to the door at eight tonight. I'll have Ernestina bring you to me."

Dido turned at the door.

"What guarantee do I have that if I do this...this thing, you will let El Negro and my brothers go free?"

"Whenever El Negro looks at you, he'll remember that I had you for I'll make sure to tell him and I know that, whatever his health, he will understand. I'll get greater pleasure from knowing that he lives, every day, with this knowledge than from seeing him swing from the gallows. I'll not go back on my word."

Though Dido tried to mask her feelings so her brothers would sense nothing amiss, it was more than she could do to conjure a smile as she entered their cell. She distributed the food she had brought and made her way to El Negro who moaned as she laid her hand across his forehead. He was burning up.

"How long has he been like this?" she asked her brothers.

"Since last night," George said, his expression fearful. "Zaccharias tried to give him the tea but he would not take it. Is he going to die, Dido? I liked him."

"No," Dido said fiercely, dropping to her knees to gather El Negro's hands in hers and bringing her face close to his. "He will not die." Could he hear her? He had to hear her. "He must live for me and for his child."

"Are you...are you pregnant, Dido?" Zaccharias looked at her with awe.

"A wise friend says I am." She kept her doubts to herself, hoping against hope that El Negro had heard and understood.

She spent the rest of her visit sponging her lover's body. By the time she had to leave, his fever was gone but she feared it would soon return. He needed to be in his own comfortable bed where she could look after him around the clock and where he could smell the fresh salt air. He would never recover if he remained in the cell. Then again, that was not the Governor's intention.

"There is something you're not saying." Yacahüey's eyes searched her face.

"You imagine things." Dido summoned a smile but could not keep it. "You must be ready," she said, hurrying on, hoping he wouldn't notice. The Taino was just too observant.

"Do not worry. It will all be done as you say. But I do not understand…if he doesn't want the gold, what else can you poss…" His eyes widened and he hissed sharply. "It is you. He wants you."

Dido nodded, concentrating on the view of the harbor visible over his shoulder. They were returning to the wharf. Dido had joined her mother and sister for dinner on the *Fortune's Gift* but had, herself, been unable to eat. Not even for the sake of the child she might be carrying could she force food between her teeth

"You cannot do this thing. I cannot let you. El Negro would never forgive me. We must find another way.

She shook her head, grimacing.

"There's no other way, we've thought and thought and now time has run out."

"This…The man is a fiend."

Dido gave a half-strangled laugh. Yes, Massa Leacock was a fiend but what did you call a woman who would contemplate sleeping with such a creature, whatever her reason?

"I must go."

"Dido!"

"Do as I have said." She placed a hand on his forearm. "Let my mother know her sons will be restored to her tonight but do not tell her the price. Do not betray my secret to any." It was her turn now to search his face.

"I'll not fail you." His hand covered hers. "Love comes not cheap in this world."

"But it comes and that is what I must remember tonight." What she didn't tell him was that she planned to exact an even higher price for her body than El Negro's freedom alone.

From the wharf, she hurried to Anna's house.

"Ah, child, what will you do?" Anna asked, her eyes brimming with concern when Dido outlined the gaoler's demand.

"I have no choice. I must submit." Dido massaged her temples. Her head hurt. "We are too few to take the fort by force and, even if we did, Yacahüey has pointed out we'd not escape into the open sea before the alarm would be raised."

The old seamstress nodded but remained silent. There was a distant look in her eyes.

"Did you hear me, Mother?"

Anna did not answer.

"Mother?" What was wrong with her?

"Yes, child. What is it?" The vagueness had not completely left her face.

"I was speaking to you but it did not seem you heard."

"It matters not. What time is your meeting with Massa Leacock?"

"Eight."

The seamstress rose to her feet, looking suddenly purposeful.

"Rest then, child. Go." She made a shooing motion into the interior of the small house. "Take my bed. You will need your strength this night. Have you eaten?"

"No, mother, but I cannot."

Anna looked at her with sad understanding. "Then rest for there is nothing more for you to do."

It was true. There was nothing now but to wait.

"Do you still have the necklace you offered him?"

"Yes." Dido had forgotten to leave it behind on the ship.

"Give it me."

Dido retrieved it from the pouch in her bosom and dropped it into the older woman's outstretched hand.

"Do you have a debt? If you need more, I can…"

"No," Anna interrupted her. "This should be more than sufficient for my needs. Rest now. I will return before you must leave." She ducked through the door and walked away down the street, a curious figure with her quick, mincing steps, the corners of her shawl fluttering behind her.

Dido pushed aside the curtain separating the sewing area from the rest of the house proper. There were only two rooms beyond, the smallest contained a rocking chair, a large round table and some high-backed chairs, while off to the side, a door led to a bigger room in which Dido was surprised to find a large, well-constructed four-poster bed, sumptuously made with coverings of creamy linen, lace-trimmed silks and a bounty of large pillows. So this was where Anna's earnings went, Dido thought, smiling. Many a plantation Missus would covet such a bed.

Dido climbed into it, thinking she wouldn't be able to sleep, her thoughts raced so, but, in minutes, she had drifted off. When Anna shook her, hours later, she could not remember her dreams.

The room was lit by oil lamps and candles.

"What time is it?" she asked groggily.

"After seven. Drink this."

Dido frowned at the cup.

"What is it?"

"Nothing but water, child. Come, it will refresh you."

Dido drank thirstily. Anna poured her another cupful when she was done and, this too, Dido drank quickly.

"It is time," she said, dully.

"Yes, but here. Take this. I've brought a sleeping draught for you to give him." She held out a leather pouch containing a small vial. "It is known that he likes his drink and it's probable he'll have some on hand when you go to him. Do your best to empty this in whatever he drinks from. If his cup is empty wait until he has filled it to use the powder."

"A sleeping draught?"

"It will drop him like a stone after only one swallow."

"You mean, I should get him to drink it before...before...."

Anna nodded vigorously.

"Did you buy it with the necklace?"

"Yes, child. The plant from which the draught is made is rare so the powder is costly. I believe you'll think it money well spent when the draught does what it's supposed to do. Do not let him see that you have it. Go with the gods."

Dido slipped out of the house. Anna's powder gave her new hope and she walked quickly. She wanted this night to be over as fast as possible. She wanted to watch the rising sun from the deck of the *Fortune's Gift* as it sliced through the waves, El Negro and her family on board with her.

Ernestina let her in almost as soon as she knocked. Without speaking, she led Dido to the gaoler's house in a corner of the fort and closed the door after her.

"You are early, my lovely," the gaoler said, coming forward to meet her. "Good evening."

Dido glared at him. Not even Massa Simon had been as loathsome.

"Nothing to say?" He grimaced. "Come then. Let us be about our business."

Smiling widely, he gestured to another room. Dido strode past him, shrinking away so they would not touch. His bed was as different from Anna's as light from day, being made of iron, the mattress covered only with a thin, dirty, cotton sheet. Dido's gaze swept the room. It was plain and contained only a couple chairs, a rude armoire half the size of El Negro's, and a small sideboard on which rested two oil lamps. The carafe and the cups between the lamps drew her attention. The carafe contained a honey-colored rum. But the gaoler watched her like a hungry chicken hawk. She would have to find some way of getting him out of the room. If he stayed, she doubted she could distract him long enough to remove the pouch from her bosom and empty it into the carafe.

The gaoler's hands at her shoulders startled her.

Without thinking, she twisted nimbly away from him, only just managing to repress a shudder of disgust.

"Why do you hesitate? Do not play with me."

"There is nothing further from my mind." She forced a smile to her lips, praying he would not notice it did not reach her eyes.

"It is only that I...that my modesty compels me to ask that you step outside while I undress." She dipped her chin and looked up at him through her eyelashes. "I have not lain with many men...please indulge me."

He threw back his head and laughed. "Well, girl, I have nothing to lose, so why not? It shall be as you wish." He was almost through the door when he stopped and turned back, crossing over the sideboard.

Dido froze. It could not be but it was. He poured himself a drink, lifted the cup to her, smirking, and walked out. Dido fought the urge to let loose a string of curses. What were the chances that he'd want another cupful before bedding her? She didn't know but she had to try. She would not give in now. She poured the contents of the vial into the carafe and swirled it around until the liquid was again as clear as before. *Oshun*, she whispered, and felt an answering warmth of encouragement. The goddess was with her. Dido quickly shucked off her clothes and jumped into the bed, drawing up her knees under her chin. This was different from what she had experienced as a child, she told herself. She had gained nothing from what Massa Simon did to her but she had everything to gain from whatever happened with Massa Leacock. If he drank the draught, all well and good, but, if he did not, she was prepared to do whatever he wanted.

"I'm ready," she called.

He was instantly back, his eyes darkening at the sight of her.

His hands fumbled at his shirt laces and then at his breeches, his face red with excitement. The dim light was forgiving of his warts but Dido was hard put to stifle a gasp of surprise when she saw how they covered every inch of his skin. Only his flaccid cock was free of them.

"Come," he said, roughly, pushing her backward onto the bed.

"Do you not want another drink?"

"I want you."

His mouth sought her nipples.

Dido fought the rising tide of nausea that threatened to overwhelm her, her gaze fixed on the ceiling as she tried to pretend nothing was happening to her.

The gaoler rose above her. Dido closed her eyes tight. But something was wrong. Instead of a hard cock, she felt only a swinging fleshy softness. She risked a peek. He had not hardened. Was this the work of Oshun? The goddess could withhold pleasure as surely as she could grant it.

His face was a mask of dismay, embarrassment and shame.

"Maybe if you have some more rum," she said gently. "I've heard men say it enhances their performance."

"Bring it to me," he ordered.

Dido bounded off the bed to search the other room for his cup but he forestalled her.

"Just bring me the carafe itself."

Dido bit her bottom lip to hide her smile as she returned to the bed and handed the carafe over.

The gaoler put it up to his mouth and drank greedily, spilling rum down his chin in his haste, before handing it back to her. Dido replaced it on the sideboard. By the time she turned around she could see the effect the draught was having on him. He was having trouble keeping his eyes open.

"I..." He tried to rise from the bed. "What..."

He keeled over on his face.

Without looking at him again, Dido gathered up her clothes and dressed. She ran to the outer chamber, grabbed the keys, flung open the door and almost received the surprise of her life as Ernestina stepped from the shadows.

"You have the keys?" the other woman asked.

Dido held them up.

"You...Anna told you?"

"Yes. She thought you might need my help. If the draught had not worked,

I was to hit him with this." She held up a wooden club. "Before he could violate you."

"Thank you."

"I did nothing. Come now, we must hurry."

The women ran, keeping to the shadows, but the fort was quiet and no-one saw them.

At the door to the captives' cell, Ernestina took the keys from her and quickly unlocked the door.

"Quick," Dido whispered into the darkness. "Come."

She had spoken only of El Negro to Massa Leacock but the minute he'd demanded to lie with her she knew she would free everyone for it, not just her pirate captain.

Dido's brothers were the first out of the door and she had to shush their cries of surprise and delight. The other captives poured out behind them until finally two men emerged shouldering El Negro between them. Dido led the group outside the fort. The carrier she had asked Yacahüey to make was beside the wall. She showed four of the men how to hold it before allowing El Negro to be laid gently into it.

"Ernestina." She turned to thank her but the woman brushed away her gratitude.

"I'm coming with you."

Dido nodded. She should have suggested it herself. Who knew what the gaoler would do to the woman if she stayed?

"We must split up," she said, speaking in a low voice. "Take seven of them. Go to the wharf. Seek out the Taino and have him row all of you to the ship and then return for the rest. Let no-one see you if you can help it."

Ernestina nodded and beckoned to those who would go with her. They ran down a nearby alley and disappeared.

Dido glanced again at El Negro. He had not stirred since they'd put him in the carrier. Did he know what was happening?

"Follow me," she said to the remaining people. With her brothers beside her, Dido set off at a half-run, half-walk, taking another direction from the one Ernestina had chosen. Every now and then she glanced back but the men holding the carrier had no difficulty keeping up. Behind them, the fort remained dark and quiet but they were not safe yet. There was still the chance that the breakout could be detected before Yacahüey returned from the ship. Yet Dido already felt freer than she ever had in her life. As she ran, freedom was something she could taste in the salt air, giving her wings.

Two Years Later

A lusty scream ripped the morning air and Dido smiled to herself. Assou was awake and ready for his mid-morning meal. She stirred the arrowroot pap she had just finished preparing and hurried inside. In Anna's arms, Assou kicked and bellowed even louder at the sight of his mother. Dido deposited the bowl of pap on a nearby table and reached for her son.

"He likes to eat," the older woman said as Dido took the child from her.

"He'll be a giant," Dido responded, spooning the creamy mixture into his mouth. Assou settled down, a look of deep concentration on his face. "A giant," Dido repeated, staring at him, amazed all over again at how he filled her heart.

At Beeston's Estate, when her dreams turned to the life she would live in freedom, she'd never imagined herself a mother. Then again she had never envisioned all of this. She looked through the open doorway to the hills in the distance and then dropped her gaze to the houses of the other villagers. Yacahüey had brought them safely to the place where the *Fortune's Gift* had left the Africans rescued from the Dutch slaver. Their community had thrived in the intervening months. They had built homes for themselves and cleared a large area in which they planted such crops as they were able, having discovered many useful plants growing wild. And they had named the place Liberty. It was that more than anything else that made Dido feel she was finally where she belonged.

Beside her, Anna picked up the sewing she had abandoned when Assou began to cry. She was now like a second mother to Dido, a grandmother to Assou. It was she who looked after him while Dido was out in the fields with Unmi and the others. When Dido saw her on the wharf the night they ran through Port Royal a keen rush of joy had carried her straight into the woman's arms. In a sense, Dido thought, she had never let go.

"What, Assou? Eating again?"

Dido turned to smile at her husband who had entered by the back door.

"He has your appetite," she said, mischievously.

"If that's so, then we can only pray to Oshun that his sister has yours or there will be no food left in Liberty for anyone else."

Dido and Anna laughed and Assou paused to look questioningly at his father before returning to the more important business at hand.

"El Negro, how often have I told you she carries another boy?" Anna asked. "Look how he rides high in her belly."

"Yes, yes." El Negro bent over to brush his lips against his wife's forehead. "I know what you've said, you've repeated it often enough, but a man can dream, can he not?" He passed his hand lightly over Dido's swollen belly. "I want a little girl who looks exactly like my love. I'll carry her everywhere on my shoulders and tell her stories about her brave mother."

Though this man, her husband, had never appeared in those long-ago dreams, he was the sweetest of all to Dido. Her eyes roamed over him greedily, drinking in the sight of him, fully restored to health. She would have gone on without him if he'd died as they sailed over the sea but by the third day of their escape she had known she would not have to. They had married as soon as they landed, letting Yacahüey do the honors. Dido had worn the white dress Anna had given her so long ago and El Negro was resplendent in his velvets. But the ceremony wasn't necessary. They were tied to each other in a way that was much deeper and stronger than the words of any ceremony could convey. Oshun had created him for her and her for him, their life together, a truer treasure than any pirate's prize.

Biography

Eugenia O'Neal's first novel, *Just an Affair*, was selected as one of the best African-American romances of 2003 by the readers of Affaire du Coeur Magazine. Her other full-length work is the non-fiction, *From the Field to the Legislature: A History of Women in the Virgin Islands*. You can visit her at http://eugeniaoneal.com/.

2/09 - 0
4/09